Nether Regions

A Beforelife Story

Nether Regions

A Beforelife Story

Randal Graham

Published by ECW Press
665 Gerrard Street East
Toronto, Ontario, Canada M4M 1Y2
416-694-3348 / info@ecwpress.com

Editor for the Press: David Caron
Cover design: David A. Gee
Author photo: © Anna Toth

LIBRARY AND ARCHIVES CANADA CATALOGUING
IN PUBLICATION

Title: Nether regions / Randal Graham.

Names: Graham, Randy N., author.

Identifiers: Canadiana (print) 20220209499 |
Canadiana (ebook) 20220209529

ISBN 978-1-77041-471-6 (softcover)
ISBN 978-1-77305-987-7 (ePub)
ISBN 978-1-77305-988-4 (PDF)
ISBN 978-1-77305-989-1 (Kindle)

Classification: LCC PS8613.R3465 N48 2022 | DDC
C813/.6—dc23

This book is funded in part by the Government of Canada. *Ce livre est financé en partie par le gouvernement du Canada.* We acknowledge the support of the Canada Council for the Arts. *Nous remercions le Conseil des arts du Canada de son soutien.* We acknowledge the support of the Ontario Arts Council (OAC), an agency of the Government of Ontario, which last year funded 1,965 individual artists and 1,152 organizations in 197 communities across Ontario for a total of $51.9 million. We acknowledge the support of the Government of Ontario through Ontario Creates.

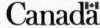

PRINTED AND BOUND IN CANADA   PRINTING: MARQUIS   5 4 3 2 1

For S. & P.

Chapter 1

He thinks, therefore I am.

Narrative convention dictates that any human-shaped shadow gliding along a moonlit rooftop is proceeding with malice aforethought and up to no good. When the edges of that shadow hint at pointy bits resembling rifle barrels, grappling hooks, and blades that stubbornly fail to glint in the moonlight, the suggestion of sinister intent is thrown into what you might call sharp relief. When you see the shadowy figure vault across an alley and settle into what could only be described as "a tactical position," it's best to ditch your assessment of this figure's state of mind and focus instead on putting as much geography as you can between yourself and ground zero.

He thinks, therefore I am.

The shadowy figure of present interest did have something on its mind, but you couldn't call it malice aforethought. As for whether the shadowy figure was up to no good — he'd be the silhouette most likely to insist that good and evil are contestable, ideologically informed notions that inescapably depend on one's current frame of reference, prevailing social mores, and assorted contextual factors he'd explore through numerous questions that were as pointed as the knives on his bandolier.

That's just the shadowy figure's way.

He thinks. Therefore I am.

That was the thought that presently burrowed into the shadowy figure's brain. It was one of the worst thoughts he'd ever had; one of those pesky neural spasms that turn up at four a.m. and jackhammer their way to the forefront of your mind, like a repeating scrap of melody that you can't entirely place and, after it replays in your head about 230 times, makes you wish you'd never heard of music at all. It was grating in the way that chewing aluminum foil is grating, as ignorable as a kidney stone, and precisely as much fun as spotty wifi.

Not to put too fine a point on it: it wasn't a thought the shadowy figure liked, the figure in question being the "I" in the phrase "He thinks, therefore I am."

The thought did have the virtue of being true, inasmuch as the shadowy figure would admit that truth existed. But it was dangerous. It was a wound. It ignited a mental brushfire that threatened to burn this shadowy figure's thread from the tapestry of Detroit.

That's "Detroit" as in the place you go when you die, by the way — an afterlife where the locals don't believe in death before life, and where any suggestion of a pre-mortem world is written off as the sort of bunk you get from the basement-dwelling conspiracy-mongers for whom the collective noun is "subreddit."

At least, that's how things *used to be* in Detroit. The idea of a beforelife *had been* written off as bunk — by practically everyone in Detroit — until fairly recent events had snatched the blinders from the bulk of the Church of O and blown the doors off any notion that the mortal world was a myth. This had filled the minds of a Chosen Few with a host of dizzyingly uncomfortable ideas. And for the shadowy figure we've been watching for the last page and a half, the chief uncomfortable idea was "He thinks, therefore I am."

He'd been *willed* into existence. He was another man's idea; thought into being by a City Solicitor with the power to bend reality into whatever shape he liked. The shadow was just another one of the City Solicitor's machinations — an idea set into motion and brought to life by a passing thought. And he'd sprung into existence with a name that had been dredged out of a mortal life that even the City Solicitor couldn't recall.

That name, in case you hadn't already guessed, was "Socrates."

Socrates, the immortal philosopher-cum-assassin who'd been thought up out of nothing, brought into being by an unconscious spasm of the City Solicitor's will.

He thinks, therefore I am. And if he can think me *into* existence . . .

Socrates shuddered. He knew the final station of that particular train of thought. That knowledge had — against all expectation — turned him into the sort of person who shuddered. But tonight, on the moonlit rooftop, he was doing something about it.

Socrates slid into position and crouched against a crumbling chimney, where he scrutinized the drizzle-obscured tableau of the streets below. He heard the hum of the xenon lights. He watched petty criminals perpetrating their petty crimes. He saw beggars begging, muggers mugging, hustlers hustling, and assorted dregs of Detroit damply dregging their way through the dark, empuddled streets.

His current vantage point was found in one of the grubbiest corners of the Eternal City, if you can have a corner anywhere in a city that has no edge. It was a neighbourhood called the Wallows, the drainage ditch where the detritus of Detroit settled out of the view of citizens who'd prefer not to acknowledge that places like the Wallows exist — the sort of place where even Detroit's most wanted criminals would feel safer being escorted by police.

An especially grubby denizen of the night shuffled along the rain-soaked street and stopped in front of a door that was, by all appearances, kept in better repair than any architectural feature

3

in the Wallows had any right to expect. The figure stopped, wiped his nose on a drenched sleeve, and knocked three times.

Socrates pressed assorted intracranial implants into service, enabling him to eavesdrop on the dialogue below.

"Password?" said a voice.

"Don't be an arse!" said the knocker.

"Who's an arse?"

"You're an arse! Askin' me for the password right up front, like that. You should start with 'who's there' or something similar."

"But I know who's there. There's a peephole."

"Could be a disguise, couldn't it? Or a kind of look-alike thingy. Doppelgänger, right? And if one of them comes to the door and you go callin' for passwords right off the get-go, they'll know this is the type of joint that needs a password, right? They might just be at the wrong door askin' for a cup of sugar, and then you go tippin' 'em off to the fact that we've got what you might call one o' them secret societies. So before all that, you ask who's at the door all nonchalant like, and if they say 'Franky Whoozit' or 'Kelly Wossname' you just tell 'em to hit the road!"

"Fine," said the man inside.

"Let's try it again."

This was followed by several seconds of relative silence that persisted until the rain-soaked caller cursed under his breath, wiped his nose a second time, and knocked again.

"HALT! WHO GOES THERE?" bellowed the man behind the door.

"You're not an old-timey guard!"

"Fine!" said the man inside. "So, what's your name, then?"

"You know who it is by now, Nick."

"Don't call me Nick," said Nick. "You're supposed to call me 'Elder Wall.'"

"It's pissin' rain out here, Elder Wall," said the drenched knocker.

4

"I can see that," yawned Elder Wall, dryly.

"Just lemme in. It's Barry."

"*Elder* Barry," corrected Elder Wall.

"C'mon, man. Just lemme in!"

"Password first."

Elder Barry hitched up his collar against the damp, leaned into the door, and whispered the password: "*Nine alphanumeric characters and at least two special symbols, case sensitive.*"

The door creaked open. Elder Barry shook himself like a Shar-Pei climbing out of a bath and shuffled in.

Socrates fixed his gaze on Elder Barry, twitched his left eyelid in an anatomically unlikely manner, and whispered the words "hitchhike, ocular, lock target," and "execute."

A tinny and officious-sounding voice inside the assassin's head replied.

"Kindly restate command," it said.

Socrates cursed.

"Syntax error, restate command," said the voice.

Socrates pinched the bridge of his nose and cursed again.

One of the more annoying things that Isaac Newton had done before his mysterious disappearance was to reprogram Socrates' intracranial implants to include a new, top-of-the-line, interactive heuristic neural interface, which the scientist had designated the Intracranial Socratic Autonomous Augmentation Cybernet, or ISAAC for short. He hadn't just named it after himself; he'd also programmed it to speak in his own voice. His school-mastery, self-important, assassin-bothering voice. Hearing that voice reminded Socrates of the *most* annoying thing that Isaac had done.

Somehow, so far as Socrates could tell, the little weirdo had managed to fill the assassin's head with memories of two distinct timelines — two timelines in which Isaac himself had two conflicting lives. In one of these timelines, Isaac had been on call 24/7 as the City Solicitor's personal secretary, and in that capacity had been responsible for supplying and maintaining Socrates' cybernetic enhancements. In the other timeline he'd been Detroit University's Lucasian Chair of Math. Socrates could distinctly remember both timelines. From his perspective they overlapped and blended together and contradicted and existed alongside each other in ways that even the assassin — who was known for being clever — couldn't grasp. They couldn't both be real. They were mutually exclusive, frequently requiring the scientist-slash-secretary to have been in two different places at the same time. But there *were* portraits of Isaac hanging in old DU commemorating his service as the school's Lucasian Chair. There were also employment records indicating that Isaac worked full time at City Hall. They covered the same time period — the assassin had double-checked. There were patents issued to Isaac in his capacity as a university chair, and also tangible artifacts — like Socrates' neural implants — that made sense only as gizmos Isaac had made during his role as the City Solicitor's aide.

Isaac appeared to be Schrödinger's Nerd, both a math professor and a personal secretary, and Socrates couldn't seem to open the box.

It wasn't simply that Isaac was good at managing time, holding down two jobs at once. There were manifest contradictions. In one timeline Isaac invented the Instantaneous Personal Transport system — teleportation stations that could whisk Detroit's travellers from spot to spot in the blink of an eye. In the other timeline Isaac had shown conclusively that teleportation was impossible. Yet teleportation was real: Socrates had his own personal IPT system built into his intracranial systems, and it still worked like a charm. There were IPT stations for public use. Yet Socrates had a vivid memory of papers Isaac had published showing that teleportation never had been, and never would be, possible. As much as Socrates liked a puzzle, this specific paradox was a pain in the assassin.

He'd tentatively concluded that this parallel-time paradox was Isaac's revenge for all the arguments he'd lost. The plan must have looked like this: introduce into the assassin's intra-cranial system some sort of parallel-world perception device allowing Socrates to track two distinct quantum realities and perceive events that took place in each one, but never explain how the system worked. Don't leave clues as to which time-line, if any, counts as the "real" or "base" reality. Don't leave behind a handbook, a guide, or a set of built-in instructions — just disappear into the ether leaving Socrates with an apparently malfunctioning set of cybernetic enhancements that the assassin couldn't repair, turn off, or remove.

"Awaiting command," said ISAAC.

Socrates tapped his right temple three times and tried again. "Hitchhike—"

"Syntax error," chirruped ISAAC. "Please restate command."

"Why do you do that?" said the assassin.

"Restate query."

"Why must everything be a 'syntax error' or an 'input error,' or a 'pebkac fatal crash' with you. I know you understand me. You've been programmed to—"

"Kindly rephrase query."

To the extent that Socrates would admit to being sure of any-thing, he was sure that ISAAC understood him perfectly. Prior to his disappearance, every version of the flesh-and-blood Isaac had been widely acknowledged as Detroit's foremost inventor, computer programmer, and all-around science twerp. He could design an adaptive heuristic AI system just as easily as the assassin could subdue a coma patient. And yet the ISAAC system seemed resolved to respond to every Socratic command with a storm of queries, follow-up questions, calls for amplification, or requests to repeat the command in plainer terms.

Socrates ignored the irony in this arrangement. Instead, he pinched the bridge of his nose a second time and tried again, this time pausing between words and enunciating his commands as clearly as any self-respecting set of vocal cords would allow.

"Hitchhike. Ocular. Lock target. Execute."

"Command accepted," chirped ISAAC. "Executing rider within."

And with that, the assassin found himself sharing the visual experience of Elder Barry.

Seeing the world through someone else's eyes has a tendency to overwhelm the senses — the sort of feeling you might expect from eating a sketchy mushroom. It takes some getting used to, and typically leaves the subject feeling as though they're midway through an adventure in which the words "tequila" and "roller coaster" play starring roles.

It didn't faze Socrates at all. To him, looking at things from someone else's point of view was second nature.

Through his borrowed vantage Socrates watched as Elders Barry and Wall made their way into the sort of foyer that you wouldn't expect to find in this neck of the woods. For one thing, it was an honest-to-goodness foyer. Most doorways in the Wallows led directly into a more or less "open-concept" crack den, or hideout, or bawdy house, as the case may be, without bothering with all the fuss of setting space aside for a lobby. The entrance hall was all the more surprising because it was populated by curio cabinets — and it's a well-accepted principle of economic and geographical distribution that anything you might call a "curio" has no business being anywhere within several miles of a region like the Wallows.

Within the cabinets was an eye-catching assortment of half-built clocks, electronic doodads, and other mechanical contrivances with their innards exposed for all to see — "all," in this context, referring to that small class of persons who might be allowed past Elder Wall. The fact that every gizmo on display appeared to be both portable and valuable attested to hidden security measures that went beyond a single password-checking guard. The fact that every gizmo on display couldn't be found anywhere else in the known universe attested to the fact that this was the home of the man the locals called "The Tinker."

The Tinker, who Socrates currently thought of as "Tonight's Main Course," swam into Socrates' borrowed field of view as Elders Barry and Wall rounded a corner, passed through a set of double doors, and entered a study.

The Tinker was seated at a large, fussily carved mahogany desk festooned with wires and bits of metal that gave the impression that a large mechanical clock had run out of time and gone to pieces. He presently eyed a complicated-looking circuit board through what appeared to be some species of futuristic magnifying glass.

"I still say you're blowing this out of proportion," grumbled the Tinker, not bothering to look up.

"We've been over this, Ben," said Elder Barry.

"And please don't call me Ben," sighed the Tinker.

"Sorry — er, Elder Tinker?" hazarded Elder Barry.

"No," said Elder Wall, "that was last week. He changed it back to Elder Richard. Before that it was Elder Statesman."

"I thought it was 'Elder Barry.'"

"You're Elder Barry."

"I know, but I thought Ben said that he—"

"Silence, please," sighed the Tinker. He set down his magnifying glass and massaged his temple — a habit shared by anyone who'd spent any amount of time close to Elders Barry and Wall.

Barry and Wall bowed their heads and folded their hands in solemn silence.

The Tinker sighed and rolled his eyes.

"What I mean," said the Tinker, taking care to speak in the slow, deliberate manner of a headmaster in an underperforming school, "is that I want you to call me 'Elder Silence' from this point on."

This drew a chuckle from Elder Wall.

"Is something amusing?" inquired the Tinker.

"Sorry, boss. It's just that when you said 'Silence,' right, what Barry and I thought you meant was that you were tellin' us to shut up."

"I gathered the gist," said the Tinker.

"It is kind of a dumb name, gov," offered Elder Barry. "Elder Silence, I mean. Ripe for misunderstanding is all I'm saying."

"No one solicited your opinion, Elder Barry," said the Tinker.

"I'm just sayin'—"

"Kindly stop."

"It's not like you really need a code name, anyways," said Elder Wall, "let alone changing it up all the time. I mean, we meet in your house."

"But we won't always be meeting in my house," said the Tinker. "It's important to cultivate good habits. An ounce of prevention is worth a pound of cure."

"Speakin' of which," said Elder Barry, "it's about time we hit the road."

"I don't accept that we have to leave at all," said the Tinker. "You're too risk-averse. Jumping at squeaks and shadows. Who's to say we're in real danger?"

"There was another disappearance last night," said Elder Wall.

"That's six this week," said Elder Barry. "They're happening closer together now."

"You're both missing the larger picture," said the Tinker. "You're asking too much. I have more to leave behind than both of you put together," he added, with the air of one who felt that, whenever anything of a disastrous nature hits the fan, it's the wealthy who suffer most. "You're asking me to give up my life and home to abate an imagined danger. They who can give up essential liberty to obtain a little temporary safety—"

"'—deserve neither liberty nor safety,'" chorused Elders Barry and Wall, who'd heard this speech before.

"I've been thinking about that one, gov," added Elder Barry, screwing up his mouth in what he must have felt was an expression of sagacity. "I'm not sure it makes any sense."

"Yeah," said Elder Wall. "You're always saying stuff like that. Like 'a penny saved is a penny earned,' or 'never leave that till tomorrow which you can do today,' or 'lost time is never found again.'"

"Or 'haste makes waste!'" said Elder Barry.

"Right," said Elder Wall. "All those little sayings. They sound all right at first, but when you think about them for a minute—"

"That 'liberty' one's the worst," said Elder Barry. "I mean, you're sayin' that giving up freedom in exchange for a bit of safety is dumb, right? But say there's a hurricane, or a tornado, or one of them tsunamis or similar, right? And to avoid gettin' swept up in the thing you stay home and locked inna basement for a few days, forgoin' a bit of what you might call liberty, if you follow, so you stay safe and sound while the thing blows over."

"Or, like, wearin' one of them protective devices when you visit Madame Bazaang's House of Carnality!" offered Elder Wall, waggling his eyebrows suggestively. "You can't tell me that that ounce of liberty isn't worth a pound or two of safety there — or do I mean the other way 'round? — anyway, I just don't think you've thought these sayings through."

"You're missing the point," said the Tinker. "It seems to me you're suggesting I disappear in order to forestall my own potential disappearance."

"Yeah, but we'd be disappearin' on our own terms," said Elder Barry. "If it's us doin' the disappearing, voluntary-like, see, we decide where we end up. We get to our contact at the hospice, she tells us where to go, and then poof, we're safe and sound."

"But who's to say the eventualities you fear will even come to pass?"

"Look, gov," said Elder Barry. "We've been over this. There's a pattern. They're comin' for everyone who saw."

"How would anyone know what I saw?" snapped the Tinker. "Perhaps I didn't see anything. They can't know. It's not as though one can see through another's eyes."

"You were there, Ben—"

"Silence!"

"You were there, Elder Silence. You saw it. You were in the cavern with us."

"I was in the back of the chorus," protested the Tinker. "Up on a stage. Wearing a robe with a deep hood. Even I couldn't be sure of what I saw—"

"Holes openin' in the air? Stars and galaxies poppin' up out of nowhere? Ring any bells?" said Elder Barry. "The anomaly and the City Solicitor tearin' up the *walls of reality*?"

"Earthquakes and lightning!" said Elder Wall. "Volcanoes sprouting up, right there in the cavern floor!"

"Mere illusion!" scoffed the Tinker. "One can't always trust one's senses."

"You were sure enough back then," said Elder Barry. "Couldn't stop yakkin' about it! Just like the rest of us. An' then you started with the anonymous letters to the papers, tryin' to tell 'em what we saw."

"Thank Abe they didn't print them," said Elder Wall.

Elder Barry grunted agreement. "Everyone who saw what we saw," he said, "everyone who knows what we know, they're disappearing!" he said. "The rest of the chorus," he added, snapping his fingers, "gone, just like that. The other acolytes on the stage," he snapped again, "poof, and no hint where they've gone. There's only a handful left."

"Coincidence!" said the Tinker, rising from his desk. "Or maybe they've gone into hiding somewhere because they're as paranoid as you. I still say it was all a mass hallucination. A shared psychosis. A delusion brought about by hidden forces we don't fathom. Much remains undiscovered. Beyond our senses. Why, before my early experiments with electricity—"

"We've heard the kite story before, gov," said Elder Barry.

"I'm simply saying we can't be sure about what we saw," said the Tinker. "My line of sight was obscured. At the height of the event my vision was blocked by—"

He cut himself off, apparently seeing a landmine buried at the end of that sentence.

"Blocked out by the amber cocoon?" said Elder Barry. "Is that what you were about to say? You were standin' on the stage, watching the City Solicitor and the anomaly shreddin' the scenery, when POOF, you and the rest of us were sealed in some kinda amber cocoons and could barely see or hear what happened next?"

"So where'd the cocoons come from?" pressed Elder Wall. "Seeing dozens of amber cocoons suddenly pop up out of nothing wasn't any hallucination. I still had bits of amber stuck in my robe when the thing was over!"

"And how 'bout the City Solicitor — freezin' people, movin' stuff with his mind, and teleportin' around the cavern. Regular lawyers can't do that," said Elder Barry, who'd met several.

"And what if we did see all of it?" cried the Tinker. "Why should anyone want to come for us? Why would anyone seek to make us disappear?"

"On account of what it means!" said Elder Wall.

"You're proposing to tell me what it means?" said the Tinker, rounding on Elder Wall and poking him squarely in the ribs. "It's been six years since the grotto! Six years! And I've thought about practically nothing else since that day. I dream about it at night. And I haven't the faintest notion of what it means."

"It's what Norm Stradamus said," said Elder Barry, reverently.

"It's what the Church knew all along!" said Elder Wall.

Elder Barry approached the Tinker and squeezed his shoulder. "Think about it, Ben. The City Solicitor, the anomaly, they could do all that stuff because this world ain't what it seems. They proved it. We're in the afterlife! So the beforelife's really real. Not *real* like the other stuff we used to say we believed in — but really, really real, if you take my meanin'. We all came from it. We were all in the beforelife, we died, and then some, some . . . what did you call it, Elder Wall?"

"Some immortal and incorporeal spark!"

"Some in-cor-po-real spark inside us left the beforelife and turned up here, washing out of the Styx with an unkillable shell that looks like whatever husk you had in the mortal world. It all adds up, like Norm said. Detroit ain't a physical place. It's all made out of whatdoyoucallit."

"Primordial ether!" suggested Elder Wall.

"Primordial ether! Stuff that bends to the will of those who know the truth!" said Elder Barry.

It would be wrong to say that Elder Barry's last remark had captured Socrates' attention, as the assassin had already been hanging on every word of the recent slice of repartee. But this last bit of dialogue had caused Socrates to further corrugate an already furrowed brow.

"It's the Secret," said Elder Wall, reverently pronouncing the capital S. "If you believe it, you shall receive it. We can manifest our desires, just like Norm and the hospice contact said. With enough practice, every one of us can do it! We can all—"

"Bend reality," or words to that effect, would have marked the conclusion of that sentence had Elder Wall's remarks been allowed to come to fruition. Unfortunately for Elder Wall, they hadn't. The reason was that, on the cue "We can all," the custom-made electric lights in the Tinker's home had all switched off, bathing those present in what seemed, given the current mood, to be a particularly terrifying shade of impenetrable black.

There was a sudden retina-searing flash of light followed by the crackling sound of too much electricity filling too little space. The immediate sequel was an eye-watering, brain-squeezing change in pressure that cracked ceiling tiles, caused numerous complicated gadgets to rattle on their shelves, and provided a fair approximation of the feeling you'd get if your submarine suddenly dropped from sea level to the bottom of the Mariana Trench. Reality seemed to flex its muscles, expanding and contracting as though the world was being reflected in a funhouse mirror, or some cosmic force was fiddling with the controls that govern reality's aspect ratio.

There was the sound of a fuse being ignited and a second flash of light that burned its way through the Tinker's optic nerves and imprinted an image of itself inside his skull. The light resolved into a sliver of blue incandescence that arced and danced its way through the darkness, moving like a more terrifying version of those ribbons twirled by gymnasts. The movements of this ribbon of light were accompanied by the sort of low, tooth-shattering buzz that might emanate from a digitized cicada, and the slightly acrid smell of complex mole-cules being sliced into their constituent atoms.

Somewhere in the back of the Tinker's terrified brain, the filing system that attaches words to phenomena fished out a folder labelled Whip-comma-Boson — a weapon adopted by that narrow class of person who combines a ballerina's grace with a sociopath's views on vivisection.

There was a series of truncated screams followed by the meaty sounds of prime cuts of Elder hitting the floor.

The Tinker became keenly aware that he was standing perfectly still at a moment when this was a bad idea. He did his best to correct this problem. He spun on his heel and contrived to run into the darkness, managing two strides before something gripped the back of his head and redirected him face-first into a wall.

The Tinker had no way of knowing whether he remained conscious for the next few ticks of the clock. When he had enough composure to be aware of anything, he was aware of the echoes of the blue light of the boson whip fading from his view. After a couple of eternities, the lights flickered on and normal vision was restored.

Well, "normal" for a highly specific value of normal. Where Elders Barry and Wall had stood there were now two pairs of legs, still upright, but now cauterized at the thighs and lacking any sort of close association with other parts of the Elders, which were scattered around the room in sizzling chunks of various sizes. The field of view also featured a larger-than-usual number of assassins.

Socrates squatted down and brought his face within inches of the Tinker's. He looked at him like a cat might look at a catnip-coated mouse. And then the assassin finally spoke.

"Pleased to meet you, Benjamin Franklin," he said.

Chapter 2

"S-S-Socrates!" sputtered the Tinker, also known as Benjamin Franklin.

"Nice place you have here," said Socrates, who reached into the recesses of his cloak and extracted something resembling a complicated dentist's drill.[1]

"W-w-what?" sputtered Franklin.

"I said you've got a nice place. Well appointed. Sturdy walls. Solid construction."

"I-I'm a mason," stammered Ben.

"Not much in the way of security, though," said the assassin. "One guard, a few old-style mechanical locks, a pair of motion detectors, a couple of—"

Here the assassin broke off — not so much because he'd finished what he had to say, but because he was interrupted by the "click" of a wall panel dropping away to reveal what would appear, on subsequent forensic examination, to be seven small gun barrels mounted on a rotating head; a sort of miniature, high-tech Gatling gun that could unleash a sudden hellfire of trespasser-piercing rounds. This it proceeded to do, either because the gods of irony had been listening to the

---

1   Editor's note: The phrase "complicated dentist's drill" isn't meant to refer to an ordinary drill for a complicated dentist, but rather to a complicated version of a drill that might belong to any dentist, complicated or otherwise.

assassin's comment about the lack of security, or because Ben had managed to press a panic button on his watch.

The roar of gunfire filled the air and wobbled every available eardrum, and was followed by the percussive rattle of bullets putting masonry to the test. The bullets struck the opposite wall with such force that they left three square metres of plaster looking like an especially crater-laden moon. A few of the rounds managed to penetrate the wall and escape into the Wallows: the one place in Detroit that never featured innocent bystanders, and where a few stray bullets would probably feel right at home.

Ben stared through his bifocals in disbelief. This wasn't because he'd been surprised by the sudden burst of gunfire, but because, given the placement of his little security measure, and the placement of the perforations in the opposing wall, the ammunition had to have passed right through the space that was currently filled by the assassin.

The assassin appeared to be less bullet-riddled than Ben had hoped.

Socrates didn't seem to have moved. And he seemed to have no more holes in him than he'd had when he arrived. Nor did he seem fazed by the sudden passage of dozens of masonry-piercing rounds. This came as a bit of a disappointment to Ben. While Detroit is the one place where the phrase "guns don't kill people" is both true and apolitical, he'd been counting on his Gatling gun to cause Socrates at least a moment or two of inconvenience.

The assassin merely grunted an impressed sort of grunt, raised a censorious eyebrow at his prey, and carried on fiddling with his drill.

"That's no way to greet a guest," he said.

"Th-th-the way to secure peace is to be prepared for war,"

sputtered Franklin. "They that are on their guard, and appear ready to receive their adversaries, are in much less danger of being attacked than the supine, secure, and negligent."

"That doesn't really jibe with what you said about giving up liberty for safety," said the assassin.

This seemed to catch Ben off guard, as if he hadn't been expecting a rhetorical critique at this specific point in his affairs. He did his best to rally.

"H-h-he that would live at peace and ease must not speak all he knows, or judge all he sees," he managed.

The assassin cocked his head and raised an eyebrow.

"You're serious, aren't you?" he said.

"W-well . . . y-y-yes," the Tinker managed. "Why shouldn't I be?"

"I mean you really talk like that," said the assassin. "You say those things out loud? Your little fortune-cookie observations."

Ben sputtered like a soda siphon before the assassin charged ahead.

"I mean, I have read some of your work," said the assassin. "It's always a good idea to research a target before you turn up for a job. Prudence, professional courtesy, that sort of thing. So I knew you were fond of churning out these little punchlines. But I honestly thought it was just a brand."

"A brand?"

"A way to get suckers to buy into your schtick," said the assassin, twisting a knob on the base of his fiendish drill. "All of that half-baked parlour wisdom. I know your readers file that bilge away and trot it out at dinner parties when they can't think of anything clever to fill dead air. It never occurred to me that you'd speak like that in person."

"Well, I . . . I —"

"I mean, come on. 'A penny saved is twopence dear'? 'He that lies down with dogs will rise up with fleas'? That sort of thing. They might look all right on a quilt. But in conversation?" The assassin paused here and attached an especially diabolical-looking bit to the end of his drill.

Ben propped himself up on the study floor, sweating and puffing like he'd run a couple of marathons fuelled by donuts. He stared at the drill, then at the assassin's face, and then at the drill again, looking a good deal like a spectator at Wimbledon who knew he'd be ripped to shreds when the match was over. It was a complicated moment. On the one hand, Ben was faced with an assassin who, if the rumours could be trusted, could end his target's life by erasing the victim's memory. It's probably best to give someone like that a bit of leeway. On the other hand, the assassin had been more than a little rude about the helpful, homey sayings that had been Ben's conversational bread and butter.

He did his best to muster a tone that passed for defiance, failed to come within several miles of it, and managed to whimper "F-f-force shites upon reason's back!"

"Exactly!" said the assassin, grinning. "That sort of thing. Those little asinine quips. Nonsensical garbage."

The Tinker blinked at the assassin like a chimp watching a round of three-card monte.

"You ought to keep that habit in check," said the assassin. "To express oneself badly is not only bad so far as the language goes, but it does some harm to the soul."

He punctuated that sentence by pressing a button on his drill, which proceeded to issue a whirring-mechanical-scream that the Tinker felt in his molars.

"Then again," said the assassin, putting a stop to the racket, "maybe the fault's all mine. I know only that I know nothing. But as long as I have you with me, maybe you could shed a bit of light on something you said."

"S-s-something I said?" said the Tinker.

"When I first arrived," said the assassin. "When you first laid eyes on me, you said the word 'Socrates.' I'm wondering why." This might seem like an unexpected turn in the conversation. If you'd walked a mile or two in Socrates' shoes, you'd understand.

Before the revelatory events in the Church's grotto, the inevitable shriek that Socrates heard whenever making his presence known was almost always punctuated by something along the lines of "you're real?" or "it's really you?" or "aren't you just one of those stories people tell kids to scare them straight?" Note the punctuation lurking at the end of each of those phrases: they're all questions. Every version carried a hint of disbelief.

This disbelief grew from the fact that, before the grotto, the assassin was generally thought of as a myth. He was just one of those stories that criminals tell each other to pass the time while casing a joint or picking up a ransom; one of the yarns conspiracy buffs invent to explain things that require more than a fourth-grade reading level to grasp; a fever dream of anti-vaxxers and flat-earthers. People didn't really believe there was a living, breathing killer more graceful than a gazelle, more agile than a cat trained by a ninja, and more ferocious than a former spouse who learns you've come in to a pile of cash. They didn't honestly believe that, in a world where human beings were immortal, the job of "assassin" was one that attracted a qualified applicant. And they especially didn't believe that the mythical Socrates had the honest-to-goodness power to wipe your mind — to destroy your memory, your personality, everything that made you you, through a process that was called the "Socratic Method."

That had changed after the grotto. The people who'd been there — those adherents of the Church of O who'd seen the battle between Penelope and Detroit's City Solicitor — they knew Socrates was real. They'd heard about his incursion at Detroit University just before the Intercessor had entered the grotto. They'd learned that his open arrival at DU had set the prophecies in motion, shoving the Church of O toward the revelation that the beforelife was *real*. Not "real" in the way that word applies to things like "the fortitude of the human spirit," "the power of positive thinking," or "untapped human potential," but "real" in the way of a concrete block, or a property tax bill, or a cold bath. Manifestly, undeniably, bone-chillingly real. If Socrates hadn't attacked the people at Conron Hall — if he hadn't helped the City Solicitor track down Ian and Rhinnick and Norm Stradamus and the rest of those who'd met up in the grotto — then the Church would still be operating on faith instead something that was, it turned out, much more frightening, namely, *evidence*.

And so now — the Tinker's objections notwithstanding — they believed. They really believed in what they'd only *felt inclined* to believe before: in the beforelife, in resurrection through the Styx, in the Great Omega who lived in the mortal world and bestowed gifts on her people, and in Socrates himself — the afterlife's only assassin — the closest thing to a mortal peril you could have in a world where the phrase "eternal life" is considered redundant.

Some members of the Church had had the privilege of seeing Socrates just before the final battle. They'd watched him go toe-to-toe with that other perfect warrior — the one called Tonto — in a display of fight choreography that would have broken most special effects budgets had it not actually happened in real life. They'd fought each other in an eye-watering exhibition of martial perfection until they'd come to a literal standstill — a standstill imposed when the City Solicitor had burst into Conron Hall and frozen the two combatants with a thought, uttering something ominous about having the power to think them out of existence, and something even stranger about having dreamt up Socrates in the first place.

Thus it was that, when Socrates had encountered the last few targets on his list — those members of the Church of O who'd borne witness to these events — they hadn't met him with expressions of disbelief. Now they didn't merely believe; they no longer relied on faith; they simply *knew*.

So they'd called him by his name.

"It's-it's your name," said Benjamin Franklin, who seemed to have developed a stutter.

"What makes you say that?" said Socrates, cocking his head to one side.

"Well, I mean . . . umm . . . the outfit? The, er, boson whip? The state of my colleagues?"

"Former colleagues."

"F-f-former colleagues?"

"Mindwiped, I'm afraid," said the assassin. "Or rather, they're being mindwiped now, if you want to be picky about it. It's a process. I've injected them with something that I call Stygian toxin. You'd probably find it interesting. Once it works its magic they won't remember anything. Let's call it a vaccine against dangerous truths. The people you knew as Elders Barry and Wall have ceased to be. Clean slates, if you catch my meaning. They'll leave their former troubles behind them, if that's any consolation."

It wasn't.

Franklin took a moment to gaze around his study, drinking in the various bits and pieces of Elders Barry and Wall that were strewn around the room. On the one hand, he was pleased to see that the boson whip had cauterized the wounds, preventing what might have been a bloodbath in a study where Franklin liked to keep things tidy. On the other hand . . . well, an assortment of *other hands* were scattered around the room, as well as other feet, other elbows, and a host of unidentifiable bits that comprised the jigsaw puzzle that remained of the rest of his gang.

The assassin followed Franklin's gaze.

"I'll admit that these are striking pieces of evidence, apt to cause anyone to reach for a conclusion. Let's stipulate that there's been a boson whip attack, and that your comrades are a little worse for wear, and that I'm the cause. But — forgive me for being obtuse — why does this make you think I'm someone to whom the name 'Socrates' applies?"

"Well . . . who else has Stygian toxin?" asked the Tinker.

"How should I know?" said the assassin, who would have shrugged a shoulder had he not been in the midst of delicate surgery on his drill. "Possibly lots of people. Yet you just heard me say I've applied some of it to these fellows who were your colleagues — and you decide that, along with a boson whip, an outfit, and little else, this makes me someone you might call 'Socrates.' Explain."

"I've heard the rumours," said the Tinker. "I've heard the stories. About you — Socrates, I mean — stepping out of shadows, stealing memories, wiping minds. They make an impression. And you look just as you've been described. The black body armour. The shimmering cloak. Even the beard. The scars. The . . . the—"

"The head that looks like a pumpkin?" said the assassin. "Don't spare my feelings. I've looked in mirrors. But please, bear with me. Had anyone who told you those stories ever seen this Socrates person before?"

"I don't suppose so," said the Tinker.

"And have *you* ever seen Socrates?"

"N-no . . ."

"And you've never met me?"

"Well . . . no—"

24

"But you've decided, based largely on hearsay and rumours, that I might be a mythical being to whom the name 'Socrates' applies."

"I-I suppose so," said Ben. And it was at this moment that Ben, who was known for being struck by bolts of one kind or another, was struck by a bolt of inspiration. What it led him to say was this:

"How did you know I was Benjamin Franklin?"

"I did research," said the assassin. "It's taken years. I tracked down members of the Church of O. I asked them questions. I asked about their fellow members. I searched through city records for the names they told me. Contact tracing, I like to call it. I found the address for Benjamin Franklin, whom I'd been told was singing in the chorus when an event of particular interest took place in a sacred grotto. I read everything I could about this Benjamin Franklin person, reasoning that the unexamined life is not worth taking. I waited outside your home, listened to your conversations, and I heard you confirm much of what I'd heard. I heard you say you were in the grotto. And I heard the men who used to call themselves Barry and Wall call you Ben."

"Oh," said Ben, flatly. And then he added, "B-b-but you are Socrates, aren't you?" hoping against hope that the answer might be "no."

"As far as I know," said the assassin, offhandedly. "One can't be sure of anything, though. I have answered to that name in the past. As for who Socrates truly is," he added, philosophically, "who can say?"

"Three things are extremely hard," said Ben, sweating profusely. "Steel, a diamond, and to know oneself."

"Not half bad," said the assassin. "Plenty of things harder than steel, though."

This carried on for quite some time: the assassin breezing along with his cross-examination and Ben stammering out a hodgepodge of homespun wisdom and answers to Socrates' questions. Socrates kept at it until he was sure he'd learned everything that he couldn't simply steal from Franklin's soon-to-be-hacked digital archives — a process to which ISAAC attended presently.

The process bore a good deal of fruit. For starters, Socrates learned of a person called "the Regent," and he learned that Norm Stradamus had led his flock to the Regent's lair. Once Socrates gathered all that he could, he called the proceedings to an end.

We now return to the Socratic dialogue in progress.

"I-I don't think there's anything else I can tell you," said the Tinker.

"And yet I'm still sure I know nothing," said the assassin.

"You know," hazarded Ben, "I think you might be a good deal happier if you let me go."

"Really?" said the assassin, who seemed intrigued.

"I do," said Ben. "Hear me out. You see, the noblest question in the world is 'what good may I do in it?' And you'd do some good in the world by setting me free. It's better to take many injuries than it is to give even one. So, if you'd just let me go, you may find yourself a good deal better off. As you might've read in my almanac, 'you may be more happy than princes if you were more virtuous.'"

He contrived to beam at Socrates, doing his best to waft pheromones of sincerity in the assassin's general direction.

"You may be right," said the assassin, thoughtfully. "But I can't help thinking of something else you wrote."

"Oh?" said Ben.

"It was something along the lines of 'three people can keep a secret, if two of them have had their memories erased.'"

"Th-th-that doesn't sound like one of mi—"

There was a "thunk," followed by the sound of something boring. It wasn't boring to Benjamin Franklin; it was boring *into* Benjamin Franklin. There was an ear-splitting whir of a micro-surgical drill as the assassin removed a bit of the Tinker's brain known as "the paleomammalian cortex," which he then popped into a vial and placed in a pocket.

One of the *less* annoying things Isaac had done before his departure was to identify the part of the brain that he called "The Seat of Regeneration." It had long been understood that, all things being equal, the body of a dismembered Detroitian tended to regenerate from whatever hunk of the putative corpse contained the head. Through a series of grisly tasks carried out in the name of science, Isaac had ascertained that, if the head itself is carved up into its constituent chunks, the bit containing the limbic system, also known as the paleomammalian cortex, is the seed from which the reconstituted Detroitian will sprout. This was a boon to Socrates, in particular, as it saved a good deal on transport costs and let him know which anatomical bit to seal in concrete, freeze in nitrogen, or otherwise set aside for safe-keeping in a manner designed to delay regeneration as long as possible. The Stygian toxin would be enough to remove every trace of the subject's memory. But Socrates was thorough. He knew that having a host of loosely affiliated amnesiacs turn up in rapid succession might cause eyebrows to rise and questions to be posed. If you sealed them off in various places, preventing regeneration for a century or three — well, these things tended to blow over, even among a populace that lived forever, kept good records, and had that extra dose of patience that comes along with eternal life.

This procedure, as grisly as it was, was equally useful when applied to those victims whom the assassin decided not to subject to his mindwiping Socratic Method. Sometimes it was useful to keep a chunk of brain from which you might regrow a past victim — say, a Benjamin Franklin, for example — who'd re-spawn with his or her memories still intact. Freeze the seat of regeneration, and keep it around until you needed to renew your interrogation or consult a former founding father.

The assassin palmed the extracted bit of Benjamin Franklin — the essence of Ben, if you like — and decided whether or not to wipe all traces of "Benjamin Franklin-ness" from the neurons that might, if permitted, regenerate the Tinker.

The assassin brushed a bit of skull-dust from his gauntlet, reflecting on what he'd learned from tonight's soiree. Regrettably, there were questions even Franklin couldn't answer. Who was this "Regent" person of whom he'd spoken? Where exactly was her lair? What was her relationship to the Intercessor? Where had she taken the High Prelate? And how had they managed to hide the lion's share of the scattered Church of O for the past six years?

There was another name that Franklin had mentioned. The name of a person the assassin had seen before, and one who was now, according to Franklin, working to help newly manifested princks find their way to the tatters of the Church of O's congregation. The person Elder Barry had called "the hospice contact." The person who'd led an underground railway into the Wild — a hidden part of the Wild where members of the Church of O discussed what they had learned in the sacred grotto; where they'd do their best to spread the virus of hidden "truths" that they'd observed when the City Solicitor fought Penelope.

These were the truths that Socrates feared, the infection that could burn his threads from the tapestry of Detroit.

"ISAAC," said the assassin. "Search all records for references to an adherent of the Church of the Great Omega. Name: J-O-A-N. The J is silent and invisible."

Chapter 3

It's been said that if you want to make a cake from scratch you must first invent the universe. Opinions differ on whether or not that's true. But if it is, Abe the First — mayor of Detroit and supremely powerful ruler of what some would call "the afterlife" — was a better baker than most.

He'd been the first to make the journey across the Styx — or rather, the first person to exit the beforelife and check in to the hereafter. The jury was still out on the question of whether there'd even been a Styx when Abe had first turned up. Based on the few stories shared by the ancient cognoscenti — those who'd shown up shortly after Abe's arrival — Abe awoke in apparent nothingness.

The phrase "apparent nothingness" is a weird one, but it works. There was, in point of fact, nothing apparent to Abe on his arrival. But it was a nothing that must have been made of . . . well, *something*. It was something that responded to Abe's will. Something Abe could shape and twist and sculpt to manifest his wishes. Something that, he'd eventually learn, everyone could bend to their will once they'd arrived in wherever it was that this apparent nothingness called home. These arrivals — those who'd shown up on the heels of Abe's awakening in this plane of apparent nothing — could force the place to do their bidding, reshaping assorted bits of the all-encompassing-nothing to produce whatever they liked.

It turns out this isn't as nice as you'd imagine.

Oh, sure, it's fun to fill the skies with dragons and gold and superheroes and damsels in distress and starships and galaxies made of cheese. But the novelty soon wears thin. For one thing, you have to budget for other people — the sort whose imagination leads them to fill the world with filing cabinets, cubicles, bus delays, and lawyers.

There are other problems too.

Imagine you love being a teacher. Now put yourself in an afterlife where no one needs to "learn" because they can manifest whatever knowledge or qualifications they want without ever having to hit the books or attend a class. Or imagine your true calling is to heal the sick and injured — but you're stuck in a world where perfect health is only a wish away. Perhaps you're the altruistic sort whose own idea of "personal pleasure" involves lending a hand to anyone who needs it — but you find yourself in an afterlife where no one needs you at all because they can have whatever they want by wishing for it.

An obvious loophole comes to mind. You could just dream up a crowd of people who need your help — a bunch of mentally constructed pseudo-people you could wish into existence; people who you could teach or heal or help in any number of ways you'd find rewarding. On reflection, you'd quickly realize that you'd also have to be the one who created their need in the first place. You're the one who made the peril. You're the one who made them sick, you monster. More to the point, you'd know that the people you were saving had never needed saving at all — they were just a "make-work" project that you'd wished into existence so that you could fill your idle hours. You'd made them all from scratch and deprived them of what "real" people had: the power to make their own wishes come true.

You might be okay with that. Maybe you think that a dash of unfulfilled altruism is a fair price to pay for eternal Utopia.

Think again.

One of the weirder features of eternity is that it provides plenty of scope for unlikely things to happen. So as improbable as it seems, someone's going to turn up feeling that the afterlife would be a whole lot better if every inch of available space was filled with clowns.

Someone else will fill the air with country music.

Someone's going to want clouds that smell like gorgonzola and rivers that run with gravy.

If the beforelife is any guide, a lot of someones are going to turn up wanting to run the place and boss everyone around. Someone's picture of paradise is going to involve crushing his enemies, seeing them driven before him, and hearing the lamentation of their women. If you're not a fan of universal clowns, twangy-guitars, high-fat water features, or tinpot rulers, you might balk at some of the changes manifested by your fellow dearly departed.

You could always take a stab at changing things back. Or maybe you'll dream up a slice of Utopia that excludes those other people, a discrete little dimensional subdivision of the afterlife where you can be alone and free of other people's crazy ideas. Maybe someone else will try to overrule your little expansion. Or maybe it'll work out fine and you'll secure a private Utopia by hermitting yourself off in another world no one can reach.

You might get lonely.

In the real-life Utopia — the infinite plane of wish fulfillment Abe discovered — things got messy shortly after other people started arriving. Picture a big house where every resident takes a stab at renovations. The whole place slid into chaos — a constant to and fro of conflicting wishes redesigning the shape and smell and sound of the world hereafter. Nothing was permanent. Nothing was predictable. There was no scope to plan your day based on rules you knew in advance, just the conflicting and convulsing will of individual members of the herd, and the heaving, erupting will-born manifestations of the "apparent nothingness" swirling all around you.

That's how it was until Abe, Firstborn of the River, took it upon himself to quell the storm. He convinced his fellow ancients that the chaos couldn't last. He showed them that, by dedicating themselves to directing their wills in concert — by having a large number of First Ones bend their wills in one direction — they could generate something that, if you squinted a little bit and looked at it in the proper light and at just the right angle, looked a little bit like order.

It was in the same zip code as order, at least.

So Abe and his fellow First Ones, in open defiance of what you might think of as the laws of thermodynamics, quelled the chaos and tamed the wild. They settled the nature of nature. They placed boundaries on the scope of their own power to manifest wishes and limited the extent of others' power. They established "rules" for the afterlife — something you might think of as Detroit's constitution. The most important of these rules was given physical form and named the Styx: a river that more or less completely suppressed the pre-mortem memories of new arrivals.

Why would that help? We're glad you asked.

Newcomers would cross that river without remembering that they'd ever had a beforelife. They'd still have all the usual wiring that makes you human — the capacity to learn, think, and feel; all the instinctual bits of coding that inhabit the human brain; even the seeds of a personality — but they wouldn't have any honest-to-goodness memories of their lives. They wouldn't know they'd died elsewhere. They wouldn't cotton on to the fact that they'd shown up, free of injury and cured of all disease, perfectly reconstituted in some post-physical realm. They had no reason to question how their body had moved, perfectly healed, to a spot that was somewhere other than the realm where their spark of life had found its origin and where it had, albeit briefly, been snuffed out.

They came as blank slates, ready for Abe and the other ancients to fill in the blanks with whatever information they liked.

New arrivals had no reason to think that the fabric of Detroit could be rewoven to accord with their expectations. That's the genius bit, really. Detroit *still did* respond to their expectations. It's just that, given the coding at the core of human minds, everybody turned up expecting the world to act in conventional ways. Abe curated those expectations. He reinforced that deep coding; expectations like "tomorrow is probably going to look like today," "what goes up will generally come down," "the strong have a marked tendency to prey upon the weak," and — this one was crucial — "most dreams go unfulfilled."

Abe fuelled that expectation. With the help of the other early arrivals, Abe wove together the built-in expectations of everyone else who came to Detroit, knitting them into a comfortable, humdrum pattern — a pattern that was, when push came to shove, what everyone hoped for and expected. And that isn't Utopia. Humans weren't wired to live in Utopia. They're wired to complain. They're wired to adapt. They're wired to scrounge for their survival in a world of scarce resources and skinned knees and predators lurking on the horizon, whether those predators come in the form of giant quadrupeds with sharp teeth or international corporations. People need threats, worries, and scarcity to survive. Abe gave it to them. He gave them a world filled with Mondays, rain delays, income taxes, rejection letters, and underpants with itchy tags. It was a world with competition, self-improvement, trials, and triumphs. A world that allowed the human brain to flex the neurons at its

33

disposal, to use its potential, rather than wallowing around in its own unbridled and easily fulfilled imagination.

It was a world that *didn't* allow imagination to run wild; a world that didn't run the risk of turning into something right out of M.C. Escher's sketchbook.

All of which brings us back to Abe himself. Take a moment to imagine the inner workings of his mind. Imagine the self-control; the discipline that it takes to corral the thoughts of others, to rein in their base desires, to convince your fellow ancients that what they really wanted wasn't a world of whimsy and granted wishes, but a world of order, rules, bad first dates, and disappointment. To pluck the threads of communal hopes and dreams and direct them into a world of static rules, knowable laws, and carefully managed expectations.

Imagine the mind of Abe the First. And now imagine what it takes to give that mind a case of the jibblies.

Abe had a case of the jibblies now.

This is because he was about to do something he'd never done — which is saying something, since Abe had been around for at least eleven millennia, and in that time had done almost everything that was doable. But here he was, staring squarely down the barrel of something he never thought he'd face. Something that up until five years ago he wouldn't have thought possible. It certainly flew in the face of everything Abe knew about the Rules that governed Detroit, about the biology of immortals, and even about the limits of taste.

Abe suppressed a shudder and steeled himself for the coming storm — a storm that, by all rights, ought to have been called "the precipice of doom," or "the harbinger of end times," or possibly "the cataclysm that made all other cataclysms look like seaside picnics." The actual name of the dreadful event utterly failed to strike the appropriate note of doom, and was a phrase that Abe never thought he'd have to hear.

It was called a "birthday party." An honest-to-goodness birthday party. Celebrating the only child ever born to human parents in Detroit.

Chapter 4

"But why mark this day, in particular, O Gobbler of Diced Melon?" bellowed Hammurabi, Giver of Law, Ancient King of Babylon, and Abe's "plus one" for the birthday party. Because he'd spoken at his usual eardrum-bursting volume, he'd sent several birds rocketing out of treetops and a handful of small children running for cover.

Ham's question had been shouted at Abe the First, who stood next to Ham at a long outdoor buffet on the stately grounds of Stafford Manor, home to a couple known by the Church of O as "the Intercessor and the Anomaly" but to everyone else as Ian and Pen. The home stood on one of those gloriously huge country estates you sometimes get when one half of a married couple is borderline omnipotent and can rearrange the landscape however she pleases. It featured not only the manor itself, but also a couple of private forests, enough gardens to keep a herd of botanists busy for an infinite stretch of time, and an entire postal district of guest houses — any one of which might have been given its own special volume of *Better Homes and Gardens*. The homeowners weren't within earshot now — which is saying something when it's Hammurabi doing the shooting.

The estate was decked out for a luau-themed party, featuring brightly coloured garlands, music scored for the steel guitar, and about an ocean's worth of fruity drinks with tiny paper umbrellas. There were also more bouncy castles than you usually see, face-painting kiosks, pineapple-shaped piñatas, and a whole platoon of buffets groaning under the weight of island-themed foods, including the one where Abe now stood with Hammurabi.

Abe tried his best to down a mouthful of melon before answering Ham's question. Or rather he tried his best using conventional means, Abe thinking it would count as showing off if he were to use world-bending powers instead of chewing.

Ham poked Abe in the ribs and asked again.

The Supremely Powerful Ruler of the Afterlife held a luau-themed napkin over his mouth and managed to sputter out the words "What are you talking about?"

"Why celebrate this day as an anniversary?" said Ham. "The very passage of time itself is subject to Penelope's whims! All days are as one to her. Seasons pass as she desires! Who's to say that today, as it is reckoned by any standard calendar, coincides with the date of this young man's manifestation?"

"He didn't manifest," said Abe. "He was born."

"Pah!" spat Hammurabi, aerosolizing several grams of poi. "Do not remind me of this, O Speaker of Profane Things! Your uncouthness offends me! The very idea—"

"It does take some getting used to," said Abe.

And it did, even for Abe. He'd been hanging around Detroit for more than eleven thousand years, and before Pen and Ian had rolled the dice on their little procreative experiment, the afterlife had always had a stable birthrate of exactly zero kids per millennium, together with the commensurate lack of OB/GYNs, pregnancy tests, birthday parties, and workouts designed for pregnant mums. All of that had quietly changed around six years ago, right about the time that Pen decided to have a baby. When Pen decided something, it tended to happen. And so it was that, six years later, Abe and Ham found themselves shuffling around in the uncomfortable way of adults at a child's birthday party.

Ham, whose complexion generally fell toward the beetroot end of the spectrum, blanched at the whole idea.

"Babies are not born here!" he protested.

"The evidence suggests otherwise," said Abe.

"Not among humans, O Pedantic Splitter of Hairs!" boomed Ham. "Animal babies? Yes. A new generation of plants? No question! But human beings are born of the river! Thus it has always been, and thus it shall ever be! Newly manifested humans are carried to Detroit through the currents of the Styx. They wash ashore, they are greeted by their guides, and they get on with their immortal lives!"

"Usually," said Abe. "I'll grant you that. But—"

"The very idea! Live birth from a human mare!"

"A human mother," corrected Abe.

"From a human mother, then!" boomed Ham. "It is the stuff of science fiction! And not even the proper sort of science fiction one can speak about in public! This is the stuff you find in the shop's back shelf, behind a curtain, beyond a sign marked 'literature suitable only for the deranged!'"

"Don't make it weird, Ham," said Abe. "There are plenty of kids in Detroit. Just think of Evan as one of them."

This was, of course, entirely true. There were babies in Detroit. Millions of them. Life in the mortal world can be horrifically short and tragic, and babies' souls cross the Styx in greater numbers than most people would like to admit. But up until now these babies had turned up in Detroit like everyone else — they washed up on the shores of the Styx and were carried off to appropriate homes where some stayed infants forever and others, for unknown reasons, matured into various stages of adulthood. But conception and live birth? They were found in most branches of the animal kingdom, to be sure, but while Detroitians might be comfy with the idea of cats and grasshoppers gestating all over the countryside, the idea of an organic, non-river-based human birth was almost unthinkable. It had always been assumed that one of the biological truths of immortality — a trait shared only by humans and certain species of squid — was that it precluded the messy business of procreation.

"It turns the stomach!" boomed Ham. "It freezes the gizzard! How one so wise and radiant as Penelope, Breaker of Worlds and Revealer of Hidden Secrets, could lower herself to . . . to . . . ooh! Yes please, O Kindly Bringer of Spanakopita!" he added, suddenly pirouetting in the direction of Albert Einstein, who joined Ham and Abe at the buffet.

Yes, it was *that* Albert Einstein.

One of the nicer things about living in the hereafter is that you can rub shoulders with a lot of interesting people. This is especially true if, like Ian and Pen, you were among those few residents of Detroit who could remember what people had done before they died. A lot of noteworthy historical types had turned up for the birthday party. These ranged from Pen and Ian's favourite entries in the history books — the likes of Abraham Lincoln, Elizabeth Cady Stanton, Sun Tzu, and Harriet Tubman — to other people who Pen and Ian hadn't heard about before they'd shuffled off the mortal coil, like Detroit's city councillors and the powerful decamillennials who helped Abe and Pen shore up the walls of reality.

Albert Einstein had been at the top of the list of party invitees. It didn't matter that he — like practically everyone else in the afterlife — had forgotten everything he'd ever known of the mortal world. Great minds from the beforelife tended to remain pretty great in the hereafter, and conversations with the likes of Albert Einstein, Marie Curie, and Edgar Cayce were every bit as captivating as you might guess, even if they had no notion that a mortal world existed, let alone who they'd been when they'd lived in it.

With all these now-immortal luminaries crowding around the landscape, it takes an especially bright light to stand out on Detroit's marquee. Einstein managed. He'd even attracted Abe's attention. Even robbed of his mortal memories, Albert had somehow pieced together most of the truths about Detroit. He'd been roughing out a paper about price fixing in oil futures and had, just to make the economic curves fit the assembled data, come uncomfortably close to blowing the lid off every secret that Abe had kept hidden from the public. To prove one of his assumptions about free markets, Albert had ended up showing that Detroit had to be a non-physical realm where there resided a few ultra-powerful entities who could weave primordial ether to suit their whims. He'd figured out that there *really was* an MC in charge of $E = MC^2$. Abe had found himself with no choice but to block the printing of Einstein's paper. And then Abe had connected the last few remaining dots for the professor, explaining in no uncertain terms that Albert had to keep a lid on what he'd discovered. The professor was surprisingly fine with that. He took it in stride and took up a middling career as an improvisational jazz musician, there being no "real" physical laws left to explore.

"I could not help but overhear ze conversation," said Albert, passing Ham a tray of treats. "Und I must say, vis great respect, zat Ham's point about ze timing of zis party eez corrrrect. Penelope could make zis day or any day ze anniversary of ze young man's arrival. Vere Penelope und Abe are concerned, all time is relative."

"You're right in theory, Albert," said Abe — something he'd said to Professor Einstein several dozen times since Albert's manifestation. "But Pen doesn't do that sort of thing. She doesn't mess with time. Neither do I. We don't change anything without a good reason."

"Of course you do, O Cosmic Fibber!" protested Ham.

"We keep our powers in check," said Abe. "That's part of the deal. If an emergency comes up, sure, we'll do what needs to be done. But most of the time we just help keep things running smoothly."

"I've seen you turn a cup into a bird," objected Ham.

"Those were weird circumstances."

"And freeze a cavern full of acolytes!"

"That was an emergency."

"You've conjured beer and sandwiches out of nothingness!" said Ham.

"But only when it's just you and me around," explained an increasingly exasperated Abe. "And only when it can't affect anything else. Look—"

"I saw you perform miraculous feats zis very morning!" said Einstein.

"That was a card trick," said Abe, pinching the bridge of his nose. "Performing straight-up miracles goes against everything we're trying to do. If Pen started slowing down and speeding up time, or if I made a cloud that rained elephants, or turned the rivers to bubble gum, people would notice."

"It vould cerrrtainly leave un imprrrression!" admitted Albert.

"And if people started noticing," said Abe, "they might figure out the truth. We'd have an even harder time keeping everybody in line. So no, we don't just run around the place doing 'magic.' We don't—"

"Vish human children into being?" said Albert, raising an eyebrow.

Abe was spared the fuss of responding by a voice calling from somewhere south-southwest of the buffet. It was shouting the words "Hey guys!" in a cheerful sort of way. And while it's possible that there shouldn't be one voice that you could mathematically prove was perfectly average, this one might be a contender.

The voice belonged to Ian Brown, who was spending the day putting cracks in his "average man" reputation by co-hosting a birthday party for the first child ever born in the hereafter.

The fact that the birthday boy was Ian and Pen's five-year-old son, little Evan Stafford Brown, cast further doubt on Ian's status as the most humdrum man in the world. Ian still had his aura of mediocrity, to be sure. He was wearing a Hawaiian shirt and baggy cargo shorts with oversized pockets sewn in the legs, which helped.

He bumbled along the grass toward the buffet, beaming hugely.

"Ian Brown!" shouted Ham, saluting his host with a bucket-sized drink topped by seven paper umbrellas. "This glorious libation you are serving, O Gracious Host: what is it called?"

"It's a mai tai," said Ian, still beaming. "I invented it!"

"Vell done!" said Einstein, who recognized true genius when he bumped into it.

It's a widely known fact that, if you turn up in Detroit with any memories of the beforelife, you'll soon find yourself locked in a mental institution where you'll be treated for Beforelife Delusion. There are silver linings, though. One of these is the fact that, provided your memories include a few lucky details, you can take the credit for inventing a lot of things — basically anything you remember from the beforelife that hasn't already been discovered in Detroit. But while this is a notable perk of being an especially gifted princk, or preincarnator — someone who remembers the beforelife — it doesn't present as many advantages as you'd think. You can't invent something if you don't know how it works. Most people who've ridden bicycles all their lives couldn't make one. For most microwave users, the process by which the device works is indistinguishable from magic. The same goes for an internal combustion engine, a telephone, a radio, and anything more complicated than bows and arrows. Most simple machines have already been discovered in the hereafter, leaving little scope for scientifically minded princks to flex their inventive muscles.

Detroit was, technologically speaking, way ahead of the mortal world. Isaac Newton had done his part for technical advancement, hanging around Detroit for centuries and inventing everything he could imagine. Galileo, Leonardo da Vinci, Pythagoras, and Euclid weren't princks, but like most people they'd hitched up in Detroit with their mortal habits and inclinations intact, and they'd spent the years since their manifestations doing what they did best. They'd been pushing the boundaries of science since swimming out of the Styx, and would go on pushing those boundaries *ad infinitum*. Detroit's scientific geniuses don't have to stand on the shoulders of giants: the giants are still around, and they aren't leaving. The point, though, is that with all these scientific heavyweights cluttering up the patent office, Ian had quickly learned that he would never find a place as one of Detroit's foremost inventors. One thing that he did know how to "invent," though, was a cocktail.

It'll come as no surprise that Ian's alcohol intake was about average. He liked cocktails, and mixing them was a hobby. And despite the many scientific advances he'd observed here in Detroit, he'd been surprised to learn that there was no trace of the mai tai, the piña colada, the margarita, the Sazerac, or the Bloody Mary. So, Ian had introduced these recipes to an eternally thirsty public, and was now regarded as a minor celebrity.

He'd even invented a pan-galactic gargle blaster, showing off.

Ham drained the last few dregs of his bucket-sized mai tai and pulled its creator into a boozy hug. "It is good to see you, O Glorious Barkeep!" he said. "Let us leave Abe and Albert to the buffet, and speak of secret things!"

"Secret things?" said Ian, shooting Abe a look of terror.

"Yes, yes!" boomed Ham. "Drink recipes, the mysteries of birthday parties, notes on how this little spawn of yours was conceived!"

Ian made the choking, sputtering sounds of a drowning man who's slipping under the waves for the third time. Ham didn't appear to notice, and steered Ian away from the buffet and across the lawn. Abe and Albert didn't raise a finger to stop the abduction, both of them presumably looking forward to the aural relief that follows Ham's departure.

It's important to note that Ian liked Hammurabi. He really did. The two were natural allies. One was a venerated ruler and codifier of laws, and the other was a regulatory compliance officer — an enforcer of city ordinances, local bylaws, and little low-level orders that keep the streets clean, gutters cleared, and library books in circulation. They ought to have gotten along like a house on fire — which they did, in a manner of speaking, provided that the house is filled with kerosene and gunpowder and explodes at random intervals in a way that would threaten to put Ian on the hunt for a change of pants. It was Ham's explosive way of asking absolutely every question that showed up in his famously curious mind — without any notion of a "conversational filter" or a thought that some questions are best left unshouted — that made Ian cringe and sometimes run for cover.

Ham was remarkably quiet, on the Hammurabic scale, as he steered Ian out of the buffet zone, down a yew alley, and then through a gap in a hedgerow that led to a little garden nook — a well-manicured alcove featuring benches, flowered hedges, and all the fixings. Ham made a show of peering around the landscape to make sure the coast was clear.

Ham leaned into Ian, bathing him in the combined scents of poi, mai tais, and patchouli.

"This is all very exciting, O Tender of Bars!" he said. "The young man's fifth manifestival!"

"Birthday," said Ian.

"Birth . . . day," said Ham, rolling the word around his mouth and testing its flavour.

"Yeah," said Ian. "It's Evan's birthday."

"Which is . . . *not* a manifestival," said Ham, doubtfully.

"I thought Abe explained this to you."

"I didn't believe him."

"You didn't believe him?"

"I couldn't believe him. Pah! That old trickster speaks in riddles. And the word portrait he painted of this . . . this . . . *birth* notion . . . I tell you it is the stuff of nightmares!"

"You don't know the half of it," said Ian, who'd been there, up close and in person.

"And conception!" added Ham.

"That part was okay," said Ian, blushing.

"Now Ian," said Ham, rubbing his hands together, "you must give me all the details."

"The . . . details?" gulped Ian.

"Every bit! Spare no particulars!"

"Well. I mean—"

"Which of you conceived the child?"

"Well, we both . . . I mean . . . what?"

"Whose idea was he?"

"Oh! Well, Pen's, I suppose. I came around right away, though. We both wanted him—"

"So, Penelope conceives of the child and then what? You drew him out of the river, yes?"

"Well, no," said Ian. "That's the whole point. Penelope wanted to have a child in the normal way."

"The normal way. Yes. So, you acquired him from someone who drew him out of the river?"

"No!"

"You found the child lying beside the river—"

"The river wasn't involved. He—"

"A small tributary, then? Some type of 'conception estuary'? Or perhaps a child puddle? A birth canal?"

Ian suffered a mild convulsion. He'd have spat out a drink if he'd had one.

"No, Ham!" he said. "The river had nothing to do with it. That's why Evan's special. He's the first baby born in Detroit. Like, actually physically born here."

"But we are all physically born, O Falsifier of Data. I was born of the river. You were born of the river. That is the way of things! We are all born of the Styx!"

"Okay, fine. But Evan's the first baby born from human parents. Biologically, I mean."

Ham made the face displayed by every tasteful person when someone describes their significant other as a "lover." After a few facial spasms he managed to stifle his revulsion and forge ahead.

"The spark of life, though, it comes from the river," he said. "It forms there, and human beings emerge from the river's depths."

"You know that isn't true, Ham," said Ian. "I know you've heard all this before. Everyone you meet in Detroit was born in the beforelife first. As mortals. They lived out their mortal lives and then they died. And when we die, we cross over. The river . . . it's just a mentally constructed representational thing. A sort of metaphorical boundary between worlds."

"You've been speaking with Abe again."

"Well, it's true! But in the beforelife, live birth is just how it works. It happens to everybody."

"In the manner of base creatures, you mean!"

"Sure. But even you had to be born that way, in the beforelife. Centuries ago, your mother and father, Mr. and Mrs. Hammurabi, they must have—"

"Disgusting!" shouted Ham, causing a couple of nearby acorns to slip their moorings. "So, Abe wasn't lying?"

"Does he ever?"

"All the time, O Naive Ass."

On the cue "O Naive Ass," a slight rustling at the edge of the garden marked the arrival of Ian's favourite person; the one responsible for safeguarding his memories of the beforelife and making sure that his own life in the hereafter didn't feature the useful ignorance that Abe and the other ancients tried to force on everyone else.

"There you are!" called Penelope. Her voice carried a hint of chuckle, as though she was in on a joke she didn't have time to explain. She stepped through a gap in the hedges and entered the little garden nook.

"You're missing the party!" said Pen. "Let me guess: Ham cornered you and wanted to know how babies are made?" she added, arching an eyebrow at Hammurabi.

"It is true!" said Ham. "I humbly seek your forgiveness, O Divine Hostess! I beg of you, do not turn me into an intestinal worm!" he added, feigning terror.

"Not this time," she laughed. "Why don't you follow me back to the pool and meet Evan? He says it's almost time for the cake!"

Ham shifted in the twitchy way of a cornered uncle who's been invited to a ballet recital and can't think of a good excuse.

"You *do* want to meet him, don't you?" said Ian.

"Of course I do, O Detector of Slight Discomfort."

"Don't be weird, Ham," said Penelope. "You'll like Evan. I promise!"

"Liking him is not the issue! I'm sure I will love the boy as if he were my own . . . my own . . . what is the word? Puppy? Spawn?"

"Son, Ham. Son," said Ian.

"I will love him as if he were my own son! But he is yours, and that's what troubles me. This child comes from you!

Penelope! The world-weaving anomaly — and one who has not yet plumbed the full extent of her powers. One who rivals even Abe! This child sprang from you, and this terrifies me!"

"He's Ian's son, too," said Penelope.

"But more importantly, he is yours!"

"Hey!" said Ian.

"Evan is the spawn of a being with almost unmatched powers. The child of a goddess! And what is he made of, I ask? Part of Penelope? Parts of the primordial dark that constitutes Detroit itself? What if the boy has even a tithe of his mare's abilities?"

"His mother's abilities," whispered Ian.

"His mother's abilities, then!" boomed Ham. "What if he, a stripling with the mind of a mere infant, what if he can bend the world? What if he can weave the threads that form the cosmos itself, shake Detroit to its foundations, or change the world to match his whims?"

Ian and Pen exchanged uncomfortable glances while Penelope stammered something along the lines of "well, I mean, we'll just have to make sure we raise him right."

"Aha!" boomed Ham.

"Aha what?" said Penelope.

"I saw the looks you exchanged!"

"What looks?" said Ian.

"You exchanged uncomfortable glances!"

"No we didn't," said Pen.

"You did! They confirm what I suspected!" shouted Ham.

"What are you talking about?" said Ian, miming the universal signs for "keep your voice down" — hand gestures Ham had come to view as a ritualistic part of every single conversation.

Ham rounded on Pen theatrically, like one of those badly written district attorneys who tricks witnesses into giving up the goods. "A-HA!" boomed Ham.

"A-ha what?" said Penelope, stepping back.

"You did not say, 'I'm certain that Evan has no powers,' or 'I ensured he'd have no power when I created him'—"

"I didn't create him! Well, not in the—"

"I understand, O Pedantic Goddess! But you suspect he has your power, or at least some measure of it! You would have denounced the very idea if you did not. I can see it in Ian's eyes, even now!"

"Nice poker face," said Pen, swatting her husband.

"And this is why I maintain that this child is a bad idea, Oh Breaker of Worlds! An abomination!"

"Shush, Ham. Someone might hear you," said Penelope.

"Not if you don't want them to hear me. You can block their ears if you want. Whoosh them elsewhere. Reverse time so that I haven't made my observation!"

"Don't be a jackass," said Pen, still peering around uncomfortably. "You know I don't do that sort of thing."

"Ah, but you can, O Radiant One. You can—"

"Call me Pen."

"But you can, O Radiant Pen. You can do whatever you want. And if you hear sense, you will *wish* this ill-considered abomination you've created back into the oblivion from whence he emerged!"

If you'd been eavesdropping on the present conversation and you didn't know Ham and Pen, you might have chosen this specific moment to put on a helmet and run for cover. Ham had, after all, just referred to Penelope's child as an "ill-considered abomination." And he might have called her uterus "oblivion." You can't go around saying things like that without budgeting for a certain amount of offence. Weirdly enough, Pen didn't flinch. Whether this was because she saw Ham as a favourite uncle, or because she understood that he'd never met a human mother, who could say? Whatever the reason, she refrained from tossing Ham into a nightmarish sub-dimension or turning him into a sumo wrestler's pants. Instead, she smiled tolerantly and adopted the tone of a schoolteacher dealing with a duller-than-average child.

"I can't just wish him away, Ham. And I wouldn't do it if I could. I didn't just 'think' him into being. Evan was *born*, like babies in the beforelife."

"But you *did* think him into being," said Ham. "Billions of people have done the . . . well . . . the same unspeakable acts that you and Ian must have performed to bring this little one into being, and what has the harvest been? Countless eons of human coupling, and no younglings! No spawn! It was only *your power* that made you able to have this pet."

"Child!" said Ian.

"Let us address the thing directly, O Skilful Dissemblers!" boomed Ham. "Does this child take after his mother? Does he have powers?"

Ian and Pen exchanged a second set of worried glances, using that semi-telepathic communication that spouses use when they aren't sure how much private intel they can spill in mixed company.

"Well . . . I mean . . ." stammered Pen.

Ian appeared to inspect his shoes. When he finally spoke, he used the soft, confessional voice you'd expect to hear from a kindergartner who's been caught eating a classmate's crayon.

"Only a little," he squeaked.

"ONLY A LITTLE?" boomed Ham, in all caps.

"Just small-time stuff," said Ian. "And only around Pen."

"What has he done? How long have you known?" pressed Ham.

"Not long!" said Ian.

"He stopped a thunderstorm, once," said Pen, picking at her skirt. "When he was a baby. That's when I knew. I watched him do it. He was lying in his crib, I was singing a lullaby, a storm rolled in, and, well, it's hard to describe—"

"The infant snuffed out the storm?"

"Well, yeah. He did. And I know he did it, because I could see him doing it . . . I could see him — I don't know how to put it other than saying I saw him tugging at the threads of reality, if that makes any sense to you. He twisted reality at the margins, rearranging the world in a way that just didn't include the storm."

"The boy has the power to change the world!" boomed Ham.

"Not exactly," said Pen, her voice faltering. "It was as if . . . well, it was like the power didn't come from him. The threads he wove, I could almost see them — see him twisting them in his little brain. They sort of . . . well, I mean . . . they came from *me*."

Ham probably would have asked the obvious questions, say, "What do you mean they came from you?" or "What does this portend, O Cryptic Hinter?" but he was stopped in his tracks by the sudden arrival of Abe, Mayor of Detroit, Firstborn of the River, and Ruler of All He Surveyed — who had a tendency to pull focus in any garden spot that he chanced to enter.

"Where's the birthday boy?" said Abe, clapping his hands. "I'm itching to see him! I haven't seen the little guy in—"

Here he paused, seeming to note the cloud of gloom encircling the party.

"Did you know, O Keeper of Secrets?" asked Ham, gravely.

"Did I know what?"

"Did you know the boy has powers?"

"Oh. That," said Abe, flatly.

"You *did* know!" bellowed Ham.

"Maybe a little," said Abe. "But I think we'll be okay."

"Maybe he'll grow out of it," said Ian.

51

"GROW OUT OF IT?" boomed Ham.

"We're hoping it's just a phase," said Abe. "Evan's a kid. He's still connected to his mother. Like there's a thread running between them. He can tug on that, somehow. He seems to siphon off a bit of her power when he needs something. Like a para—"

"Please don't call my son a parasite," said Penelope, dully.

"So the boy can draw upon his nearly omnipotent mother's power?" said Ham, aghast.

"That's how it looks," said Pen. "On his own, or around Ian, he's just a regular little boy. But when he's with me he just sort of pulls at me. At my powers. I feel it flowing from me to him. He makes little changes to the world. Just marginal things. It's definitely not me directing what happens — it's my power, but Evan weaves it."

"The child can bend the will of one whose power rivals yours!" boomed Ham, rounding on Abe and prodding his shoulder. "How can you allow this? How can you stand idly by while others wantonly create omnipotent infants—"

"He's not omnipotent!" said Ian.

"Near enough!" shouted Ham.

"It's not like I had much choice," said Abe. "And all we can do now is watch the boy. See what happens. Do our best to keep a lid on things and keep his meddling local."

"Keep it local?" asked Ham, doing an excellent job of standing in for the reader by openly asking what the hell was going on.

"We call it the Patch," said Penelope.

"A bubble of self-contained reality," said Abe. "It was Pen's idea. Pen and Ian's estate exists in its own little zone of reality, one that we've hived off from the rest of Detroit. Evan can't leave it. People can only come and go if Pen lets them. Things that happen here can't affect the outside world."

"Whatever happens in the Patch stays in the Patch!" said Ian, helpfully.

"Einstein calls it a field of impermeable causality," said Abe.

"EINSTEIN KNOWS?!" boomed Ham.

"What matters," said Pen, "is that nothing inside the Patch can influence anything outside it. You and the other guests could enter because I invited you. I allowed it. If I hadn't, you wouldn't have been able to reach the Patch, find the house, or even think about where we were."

"It's pretty neat," said Ian.

Ham crossed his arms and tapped his foot with the overblown theatricality of a background performer in a high school play. "I thought you said you didn't warp reality, O Dissimulator of Truths!" he said.

"Sometimes we have to make exceptions," said Abe, "and this was important."

"But how does this protect the boy?" asked Ham, still thirsty for information.

"You know that thing Pen and I do, with the ancients?" said Abe. "Shoring up the walls of reality and all that? We do that here. Think of the Patch as invisible walls that keep everyone safe. It lets Penelope and Ian have some time to themselves, and it lets us see what Evan can do without putting anyone else at risk."

Ham made the puzzled face of an art history major taking a calculus exam. "So," he said, "if the boy decides to, say, turn himself into a dragon, and tries to fly into Detroit—"

"I don't think he can be a dragon," said Ian.

"But if he could—" pressed Ham.

"He'd be a dragon inside the Patch," said Penelope, "but he couldn't get outside. If I let him out of the Patch, he might make more changes there. But only when I'm nearby. He needs me as a source of power."

"The Patch works perfectly," said Abe. "And it's probably more precaution than we needed. It's starting to look like Evan can't do anything big. He might adjust the weather a bit, or wish for an extra plate of dessert, but nothing fit for a headline."

Penelope picked at her skirt again while Ian appeared to take an interest in his shoes.

"You're making those looks again!" boomed Ham.

"What's he done?" said Abe, intrigued. "I didn't feel him making changes,"

Ian and Pen exchanged a round of pregnant looks.

"It's . . . it's . . . just—" stammered Penelope.

"Well—" began Ian.

"Spit it out, O Radiant One," cried Ham, "You can snuff out stars and change the spin of planets — surely you can tell us about your child!"

Penelope's face settled into the resolved expression of someone about to rip off a bandage.

"We're going to need more candles on the cake," she said.

"What do you mean, O Cryptic Riddler?"

"Evan's eleven," said Ian, still staring at his shoes.

"He's five," said Ham. "I know this. I have done the math."

"He *should* be five," said Ian, putting a weird amount of topspin on the word 'should.' "But . . . I mean . . . last week we got talking about birthdays, growing up, that sort of thing, and Evan asked when he'd be big. He wants to ride a mini-bike, have a datapad of his own, and he wants to go downtown by himself. Anyway, I mumbled something about waiting until he's eleven before he's allowed to do those things and then—"

"He decided he was eleven," said Pen. "And then he was."

If synchronized eyebrow furrowing had been an officially sanctioned sport, Abe and Ham would have scored a perfect 10.

"But it was more than that," said Pen. "I knew he'd been on the brink of turning five, but then I . . . I . . . I could remember his tenth birthday. And his ninth. As if I'd really been there for them."

"I remembered them too," said Ian. "It took Pen at least an hour to convince me that there'd been any kind of change. I could have sworn that we'd lived here in Detroit for about twelve years and that we'd had Evan for eleven of them. When Pen got me to really think about it, though, I couldn't remember much beyond his first five years and then an extra helping of birthdays . . . but it still seemed real. Like I'd lived through all that time, but not fully. Does that make sense?"

"Not in the least!" boomed Ham.

"Evan changed history in our bubble," said Pen.

"You've only been in the Patch six years," said Abe.

"I know!" said Pen. "But it's like he's . . . well . . . he's compressed time in here, or something."

"But not entirely," said Ian. "The trees didn't suddenly get any bigger or anything. The calendars didn't change. It's still the same year. It's just that I can remember extra birthdays. And Evan is turning eleven. He really is. He's five feet tall!"

"But does the boy understand?" said Ham. "Does he do these things on purpose? Does he understand his powers?"

"I think he does," said Ian. "I mean, he definitely knows he's special. We explained that he was the only person really born in Detroit."

"Why would you tell him this?" said Ham, aghast.

"All kids want to know where babies come from!" said Ian. "Besides, he's Detroit's first native son. He deserves to know that he's special!"

"But he understands his powers?" pressed Abe.

"He did use them on purpose," said Pen. "We talked about it afterward. He wanted to be eleven. He said he saw those threads that I described, the ones that flow through me to him, and he . . . well he sort of grabbed them. Intentionally. He made himself eleven."

"I told him he shouldn't do that," said Ian. "Not without his mom's permission. I gave him the whole 'great power and great responsibility' speech. He wasn't happy."

"He hasn't done it again," said Pen. "Not since changing his age."

There's an expression people make when they realize, too late, that they've swiped right on their own first cousin. Ham made that face now.

"And can he do this with other ancients?" asked Ham.

"Change their age?" asked Ian.

"No, no! Can he steal their powers, in the way that he steals his mother's?"

"Well, no," said Ian. "I mean he . . . wait, what?"

"I presume, O Incautious Testers of Hypotheses, that this party is a test," said Ham. "A party attended by both Penelope and Abe. And other ancients. Others who strengthen Abe's grip on the walls of reality. All gathered in the same place at the same time. You wish to see if the boy can grasp hold of their wills too, yes? An experiment you're conducting within the safety of the Patch?"

Penelope looked at Abe. Abe looked at Penelope. Eyebrows were raised, and lower lips were chewed.

"I hadn't thought of that," said Abe.

"Think of it now!" boomed Ham.

"What if he can?" said Ian, now doing the little dance you see people doing in queues for public toilets. "What if Evan can . . . I dunno . . . grab the threads of power, or whatever you call them, that flow through Abe and the others — what could he do?"

"He might do anything!" said Ham.

What Evan *did* was shout "Mom," while his apparently eleven-year-old legs carried him through the gap in the hedge and into the little garden nook. He had bright red hair and a smile that could coax a refund out of a pawnbroker, but otherwise looked like a perfectly average kid. He was followed by Albert Einstein and a troop of assorted children with painted faces, balloon animals, and other evidence of a party.

"It's time for cake!" said Evan, pointing at the mathematically inclined jazz musician who he'd come to call "Uncle Albert."

Einstein carried a two-tiered cake. It was topped by eleven candles.

The shorter members of the herd called out variations on the theme of "we want cake." Einstein joined in, pronouncing the double-yous as vees. Evan trotted up to his mother and grabbed the hand that wasn't presently holding Ian's.

"Cake!" he shouted, in the charismatic way of a five-year-old inhabiting an eleven-year-old frame.

Penelope's brow remained furrowed as she turned to Evan and spoke. "Just wait for a minute, Evan. We're talking about grown-up things," she said.

"What kind of things?" asked Evan.

"Nothing you need to worry about," she said, patting his head and looking away, "you'll understand when you're older."

The little mother-and-son vignette was closely followed by one of those overlapping conversations that call to mind the penultimate act in musicals, the bit where the themes of prior acts merge into a medley — a medley that cleverly blends songs you wouldn't have thought to put together. This particular score included the following noteworthy numbers:

Ian, speaking to Abe: "Maybe you ought to get out of the Patch. What if Ham's right? With you and Pen together, and so many other ancients around—"

Evan, speaking to Pen: "What's Dad talking about, Mom?"

Assorted kids, to no one in particular: "Cake! Cake! Cake!"

Einstein, speaking to Ham: "I still don't see vy ze boy is eleven!"

Ham, speaking to Abe: "—some new and dangerous power! A special connection to Detroit!"

Evan, soliloquizing: "—and why does Uncle Abe have lines that look like the ones that flow through Mom?"

These overlapping elements carried the medley to a crescendo that featured Ham shouting "We must make haste!"; Penelope turning to Abe and saying, "We have to reinforce the Patch!"; Abe turning to Evan and saying, "What do you mean, lines?"; and Evan falling silent and starting to frown.

You couldn't blame the boy for what happened next. You really couldn't. He was a five-year-old child housed in an almost-teenaged body. He'd been sidelined at his own birthday party. He'd been shushed and ignored and told that he'd understand things when he was older, that there were important grown-up things he couldn't be told. He knew that a lot of important-seeming adults were saying a lot of things about him without giving any hint of an explanation. He knew that they were delaying cake.

He had all the impotent fury of an impatient, frustrated five-year-old boy bathed in hormones that emerge when you're eleven.

Evan looked at his birthday cake. He looked from the cake to the assembly of nattering grown-ups, back to the cake, and then back to the grown-ups again. He looked at lines that flowed through Pen and Abe — all the shimmering lines of power that only Evan could fully perceive.

He reached out for them with his mind.

One by one, the birthday candles lit themselves.

Evan had already had ten birthdays — including a few that had been crowbarred into the timeline through the boy's knack of stealing his mother's power. He knew the secrets of birthday lore. He knew that when you blow out candles, you make a wish.

Evan reached out, once again, to the little sparkling threads that flowed around him. He could see them everywhere, now — not just passing through Abe and Pen. There were little shiny ones that flowed through the children. There were spiralling, sparkling ones that seemed to flow through Uncle Albert and touch the sky. There was a dull thread dangling from Ian. There were thick, sparkling, colourful ones that flowed through and around Penelope, as well as the brightest lines of power he'd ever seen, lines vibrating through Abe the First and connecting him to the ground.

Evan noticed that he had no threads of his own.

Evan reached out once again. He gripped the threads — every thread that he could see.

He yanked as hard as he could.

He blew out his candles and made a wish.

Reality lurched three steps to the left.

Ian woke up in the hospice.

Chapter 5

If you've ever been wrenched from sleep by an assassin straddling your chest and flicking your nose, you'll know exactly how Ian felt.

No? Well, it wasn't good. It was better than waking up in the River Styx after being killed by a train, but still: not good.

The last thing Ian remembered was his son's fifth birthday party — or possibly his eleventh — where he'd been surrounded by a crowd of kids and ancients and spousal anomalies all talking over each other in what a thesaurus aficionado might have described as a cacophonous hullabaloo. He'd been dimly aware of Evan spewing germs all over a plate of communal food — a practice commonly known as "blowing out birthday candles." This had been followed by a lot of eyes widening in horror, a moment of general confusion, and then suddenly "flick," right on the nose, jerking Ian out of a sleep that he couldn't remember starting.

"Mr. Brown!" hissed a voice.

Against his better judgment, Ian opened his eyes. The room was drenched in shadow. He could tell he was in the hospice, what with the memorable bouquet of floor polish and disinfectants, the tangle of polyester sheets, and the moonlight glinting on laminated posters that said things like "Hang in there, Baby" and "It's darkest before the dawn." Ian paid almost no attention to these details, though, as most of his sensory resources were focused on the assassin perched on his chest.

"Mr. Brown!" hissed the assassin.

"Wh-wh-where's Penelope?" cried Ian. "Where's Evan? How . . . where . . . what—"

"You're needed, Mr. Brown!"

"I'm . . . I'm what?" said Ian, still struggling to dislodge cobwebs from the interior of his skull. He contrived to sit up, which was more than he could manage with about 250 pounds of assassin pinning him down, not to mention the thirty or forty pounds of body armour and gear that passed for Socrates' attire. The assassin's knees held Ian's arms to the bed, telegraphing the phrase "resistance is futile" directly into Ian's brain.

Ian managed to burn about sixteen calories wriggling under the weight of the assassin before admitting defeat and sinking back into the bed that, whatever else you might say about hospice furnishings, was cozy.

"You must find the Sword of Shmunganuu!" whispered the assassin.

"S-s-sword?" said Ian, in the broken croak of someone who's several espressos shy of sentience. He topped this off with an impressively quick rush of vocalizations that the assassin heard as "ohmygodyouresocrates!"

"I am," growled the assassin. "But what matters is the sword, Mr. Brown. The sword! You'll need it to stop Abe!"

"Abe?" said Ian, achieving about ten blinks per second. "Why would I want to stop Abe?"

"You must stab him, straight through the heart, on the twelfth of Abeuary. The future of all Detroit depends on this!"

"Stab Abe?" said Ian.

"You'll retrieve the sword from the Oracle!"

"Who?"

"The Oracle of Detroit! She will ask three questions!"

"What?! What questions? I . . . hold on," said Ian, whose adrenal glands were doing their level best to shift their host from a quasi-vegetative state and into the realm of the merely groggy. "I'm . . . I'm not just going to go and stab Abe! I mean, why should I? Because you told me to? Or because some wizard gave me a sword or—"

"Not a wizard, Brown, the Oracle!"

"And why would anyone want to stop Abe? What's he done now?"

The assassin's grin pierced the shadows. He looked like a bearded jack-o'-lantern.

"You really don't know anything, do you?" he said.

"Anything about what?" said Ian.

"Anything about anything."

"I never said I did!" said Ian. "I don't know how I got here, I don't know about any swords, I don't know how to answer an oracle's questions, and I don't . . . what are you smiling at?"

If there's ever going to be an emoji meant to convey the phrase "amused, but tinged with hints of psychopathy," it could be modelled after the face that Socrates made at Ian now.

"There is no oracle," he said. "There is no sword. What there is, Mr. Brown, is a plot to subvert Abe; a plan to remove him from office. When I found you here in the hospice, I wondered whether your presence here was a corner piece of the anti-Abe puzzle, so to speak. Possibly some elaborate plot involving you and your highly unusual wife. But judging by your reactions—"

"A plot against Abe?" said Ian.

"That's what I said. Try to keep up," said Socrates.

"And you're here to stop it."

"No."

"You're here . . . for me?" said Ian, cringing.

"No."

"Then what are you doing here?" said Ian, tilting his head sideways on the pillow like a recumbent golden retriever.

"None of your business," said the assassin.

"Have it your way," said Ian, approximating a shrug with those bits of his limbs that still had scope to move. "Any chance you might just leave?" he added, hopefully.

"Not just yet," said Socrates, who suddenly dismounted Ian and scooched his way to the foot of the bed. He sat in a cross-legged pose that gave the impression he was settling in for a slumber party. "There's much to discuss," he added, gravely.

Ian struggled his way into a seated position and flicked on a bedside lamp.

"So why am I here? And where's Penelope?" he asked.

"Penelope's gone," said the assassin. "So is Abe. There's no sign of either of them."

"What do you mean Penelope's gone?" said Ian, perking up. "And what about Evan?"

"Who's Evan?"

"He's my son. We were at his birthday party."

Socrates' face slipped into a puzzled expression indicating that the concepts of "son" and "birthday party" might require a little unpacking. He pressed for footnotes in his customary way, dragging Ian through a messy slab of Socratic dialogue that took about ten minutes and is best left unrecorded.

"Sounds ghastly," said the assassin, at length.

"You don't know the half of it," said Ian. And then in a plaintive voice he added, "Look, Penelope can't be gone. That doesn't make sense. Where could she be?"

"She has to be somewhere," said Socrates, philosophically. "Abe too. But I can't find either of them." Catching a glimpse of Ian's suddenly furrowed brow, the assassin tapped behind his own left ear and said, "Tracking software. On-board I-Ware. I should be able to track your wife wherever she goes."

"You track my wife?"

"What matters is that I can't track her now. That should be impossible. Isaac outdid himself."

"Isaac Newton?"

"A helpful twerp," said Socrates. "And now he's gone missing too; that's another matter entirely. But as for Abe and your wife, I haven't had so much as a ping from them in seventy-two hours. It's as though they've ceased to exist."

Ian made all the usual preparatory gestures that one makes to start an objection: he raised a finger, opened his mouth, and raised himself to his full height — at least as far as he could manage while still wrapped in a duvet and seated in bed. The assassin waved him off.

"I know, I know," said Socrates, brusquely, "that's unlikely. They must be somewhere, but I can't find them. And then yesterday I got wind of this new plot to unseat Abe. I doubt that's a coincidence. Mark my words, Brown. Something's afoot. Something dangerous — something new."

The normal thing for a man in Ian's position would be to probe a bit more deeply into his wife's disappearance, his son's whereabouts, the plot to unseat Abe, and whatever mysterious series of events had led him to wake up in Detroit Mercy Hospice without remembering how he'd arrived. Ian didn't. One of the side effects of hitching one's wagon to a nigh-omnipotent spouse is that you learn to take a lot of things in stride. It wasn't so long ago that Penelope had accidentally hidden herself as a thought inside Ian's head, emerging only after Ian had been shot at point-blank range by the City Solicitor and dumped in the River Styx. That had worked out all right in the end. Then Penelope had gone toe-to-toe with Plato in the Church of O's cavern and twisted the universe into several unnatural shapes that ought to have permanently dissipated every soul in the hereafter, and even that had turned out fine. Wherever Pen might be, Ian was sure that she'd be safe. And it seemed more likely than not that she'd be flexing her omnipotence to keep Evan safe, as well.

As for Ian's own well-being . . . well, it had taken about six years, but he'd gotten used to the ins and outs of immortality. When push came to shove, however stressful and oppressive things might seem, they'd eventually come to an end. Ian would survive — an outcome that's practically built into the definition of "immortal." Ian would *que sera sera* his way through whatever might be coming, and then he'd be reunited with Pen. He was sure of it; he could feel it in his bones. There are upsides to the knowledge that you're never going to die and that your wife can rewrite the cosmos faster than you can change your pants.

Ian's state of relative calm lasted for precisely thirteen-point-seven seconds, which was the amount of time it took him to remember what Socrates could do.

Ian pulled the duvet up to his neck and pressed his back into the headboard.

"You're . . . you're not going to wipe me, are you?" he whimpered — a sentence that sounded a good deal weirder than he'd planned. "That memory-erasing thing you do? The Socratic Method?"

"Wipe you?" said the assassin, tilting his head to one side. "On the whole, I think not. I think I've found you for a reason, Mr. Brown. I'm not a great believer in happenstance."

"I . . . I am," said Ian, cringing. "That's why there's a word for it."

"I find myself in this hospice," said the assassin, "on an errand that has nothing to do with you, and here I find you — the man who, despite having absolutely no discernable merits—"

"Hey!" said Ian.

"—despite being the most flavourless, milquetoast, inoffensive gnat to ever flit across anyone's path, has shown an unmatched capacity to get in my way and thwart my plans."

Ian's face slid into a mask of surprised innocence that had the words "who me" tattooed all over it.

"Three times, Mr. Brown. Three times I've been tasked with removing you from the field of play. And three times I've failed. You'll recall, I trust, the time I was inconvenienced by your comrade, Vera Lantz?"

"Oh, sure," said Ian.

"Or the times I found myself entangled with your mysterious guide?"

"Tonto!" said Ian, brightening.

There aren't many names that have the power to cause an ice cream headache, but for Socrates, it seemed that the name "Tonto" could do the trick.

"Do you know where she is now?" said Ian.

"I don't," said the assassin, with the air of someone who was content for that state of affairs to persist. "But what interests me, Mr. Brown, is how events spiral around you. How I, with a reputation for being something of an unstoppable force, keep ending up in the ditch because of a simpering fool like you."

Ian peeped out from behind the duvet and squeaked the words "Bad luck?"

"And now I find you here, once again popping up in my path while I'm on a critical mission, appearing precisely where you're least expected."

"So you really weren't looking for me?" said Ian.

"Why would anyone look for you?"

"You just said that you went looking for me three times!"

"But not this time, Mr. Brown. Tonight I'm here for someone else. Someone named Oan."

Imagine the face you'd make if your waiter brought you a plate of deep-fried lint. That's the face that Ian made now.

"Oan?" he said, agog.

66

"That's right," said the assassin. "It's spelled 'Joan,' but the J is—"

"Silent and invisible, yeah, I know her," said Ian. "She's the sharing room director. But what could you possibly want with her?"

Socrates stared at Ian like a pawn-shop dealer appraising a sex toy made of gold — a stare that telegraphed the message "I'd rather not be seen in public with this thing, but it might be worth a fortune." That's a highly specific message for a facial expression to convey, but Socrates managed. And eventually he spoke.

"I'm here to interrogate her," he said. "She's the key to the next step on my quest."

"What kind of a quest?"

Here the assassin paused again and stroked his chin.

"A quest to . . . stabilize certain elements of reality," he said. "Once I get what I need from Oan, I'll be on my way."

"I think you've got the wrong person," said Ian, doubtfully. "Oan's the sharing room director. She doesn't know anything. She just teaches useless stuff about vision boards and the healing power of crystals and patchouli candles and—"

"She knows where to find the Church of O," said the assassin.

"What do you want with the Church of O?"

"We have dealings."

"Have you tried the grotto?" said Ian, helpfully.

"I've tried the grotto," said the assassin.

"The last time I checked they were in the grotto," said Ian.

"They aren't there now."

"But what do you want with them, really?" said Ian. "They're just a bunch of harmless weirdos. They worship a talk-show host."

"The Church is the key," said the assassin.

"You said Oan was the key."

"There are two keys!" barked the assassin. "The Church is the final goal. Oan is how I'll find them. I need to stop the Church from carrying out its plans."

"They're the ones plotting against Abe?" said Ian, wriggling out of the duvet.

"No. Or rather, I don't think so."

"So why do you want to stop the Church?"

"I was about to tell you that, Mr. Brown. Stop interrupting."

"Sorry," said Ian.

"It's getting annoying."

Ian made the apologetic facial shrug that's part of the core curriculum in Canadian kindergarten.

"The Church is going to ruin everything," said the assassin. "I mean that quite literally. I take it, Mr. Brown, that you know how Detroit really works?"

Ian blinked.

"You're allowed to answer questions," said the assassin. "Do you know how Detroit works?"

"More or less," said Ian, shifting. "Penelope and Abe talked about it after she fought the City Solicitor. How Detroit isn't really a physical place. She called it a mental construct. Something made up of the thoughts of everybody who's in it. Is that what you mean?"

"It is," said Socrates. "And the Church wants to reveal that truth to others."

"That's bad!" said Ian.

"It's very bad," said the assassin.

"Pen said that if people knew what Detroit really was, if they remembered the beforelife and figured out that they were in a non-physical afterlife that responded to their wishes—"

"They'd ruin everything," said Socrates. "That's what I said."

"That's why Penelope helps Abe," said Ian, who suddenly seemed keen to brag about his wife's career. "They keep everyone in check. They call it 'shoring up the walls of reality,' keeping people from remembering the beforelife, or doing anything else that might let them realize what Detroit really is. If they didn't, people's random thoughts might tear the place apart."

Here Ian broke off and mused for the space of several breaths. "It's kind of funny, when you think of it," he said, picking at the duvet, "it's almost as though Oan's right. I mean, all that stuff she says in the sharing room — "if you believe it, you'll receive it" — it's kind of true. If people really believed they could shape the world however they liked, then they really could!"

"Indeed," said Socrates.

"That's ironic!" said Ian.

"What's ironic?"

"Oan being right all this time. With all that sharing room stuff. Manifesting your desires; the universe listening to your wishes."

"That isn't ironic at all. It's simply the case that Oan is fundamentally correct in her assessment of the nature of Detroit. Irony doesn't enter into it."

"Well it seemed ironic to me," muttered Ian.

"The problem is that the adherents of the Church don't merely believe her, Mr. Brown. They have evidence that she's right. They observed the malleability of Detroit with their own eyes, down in the cavern. This is knowledge, Mr. Brown. Actual first-hand knowledge — much more powerful, much more dangerous than faith. They can see that their teachings about the beforelife are true. They understand that Detroit is merely a concrete manifestation of their wills and expectations. They do not, so far as I know, suspect Abe's role in reining in those expectations and shaping the world that they perceive. But they do understand that they have a part in constituting the world. They wish to spread that knowledge, Brown, to share their message. If they do, if they convince enough souls that this world is not what it seems, teach them that they can change Detroit to suit their whims—"

"All hell breaks loose!" said Ian.

"All what breaks loose?" said Socrates.

"Never mind," said Ian. "I just mean things'll be bad. Abe explained the chaos he tamed when he made Detroit. I don't think he could do it again with so many people already here, working against him. Not even with Pen!"

"That's why we have to stop the Church."

It took Ian the better part of three seconds to process the pronoun in that sentence.

"Wait . . . we?!" he said.

"That's right, Mr. Brown. You're going to help me."

"But why me?"

"You're an important part of the plan."

"I'm not part of anyone's plan! You said you didn't expect to find me!"

"But now I have," said the assassin. "And you'll recall that I don't believe in happenstance."

"Yeah, you said. But—"

"I take it you know the one about gift horses and mouths?" Ian made the puzzled expression of one who had heard all there is to hear about gift horses and mouths and yet couldn't imagine how the allusion fit his current situation.

"You have a knack for interfering with my objectives, Mr. Brown. Changing my plans. Redirecting outcomes. Whether this is because of some trait that your wife has bestowed upon you, some powerful 'blessing' she has imprinted on you to keep you safe, who can say? But now that I have you here, I find myself thinking that it might be an error to waste such a resource."

Ian had never thought of himself as a resource, and in his wildest dreams would never have pictured himself as a candidate to be sidekick to an assassin. He would have said so, too, but for the fact that getting a word in edgewise can be a problem when Socrates wants to hold the floor.

"As you point out, Mr. Brown, your sharing room director is quite correct. She's right about how things work in Detroit. And I can't help but think that you've manifested in my path for a reason. That reason is to assist me."

"But I don't want to assist you!" said Ian.

"You don't have a choice."

"Look, Mr. Socrates—"

"Just Socrates."

"Look, Socrates, it's like you said. I'm nothing special. All those times I got in your way — that was Pen. You know that. You know what she's capable of. She's the powerful one. I'm just along for the ride."

"Are you quite finished, Mr. Brown?"

"I'm just saying that I don't think I'll be useful," said Ian. "I'm just a normal, average guy. I can't go off on some cloak-and-dagger mission — I'd get in your way."

"You're forgetting your singular gift, Mr. Brown."

If Ian's "singular gift" was staring blankly at netherworldly assassins while wearing a terry cloth robe and sitting in bed, he displayed that gift now.

"You have information," said the assassin. "Information unavailable to anyone else in Detroit — with the possible exception of your wife. And I don't think she's in any position to help."

"Neither am I!" said Ian.

"My point, Mr. Brown, is that you remember the before-life."

"Plenty of princks do!" Ian protested. "The hospice is full of them."

"Not like you, Mr. Brown," said the assassin, who now stood and started pacing around the room. "Most princks remember nothing more than a few scraps of their lives. Scattered images.

A general sense of some key aspects of their life in the mortal world. Being a teacher, or a soldier. Living through a traumatic event. A couple of life-defining moments. But not you, Brown. I've read your file. You didn't turn up in Detroit holding a few scattered snippets of your life; you retained full-blown memories of everyday, mundane events, just as vividly as the rest of us remember life in Detroit."

"So?"

"That sort of information carries power, Mr. Brown. Rattling around in that head of yours is a treasure trove of knowledge about people's pre-mortem lives. Biographical information. Hidden facts about my prey — their aptitudes and inclinations, knowledge culled from their history in the mortal world."

Ian sputtered like a lawn mower that wasn't inclined to start. He managed something along the lines of "but, but" before the assassin cut him off.

"You won't deny that you have this sort of information."

"I mean, a little," said Ian. "I remember who some people were. But it's not like I carry a copy of *Who's Who* with me. I only know about people I knew in person. Or famous people. Actors, politicians. Historical figures. Like you."

"Like me?"

"Sure. I know you're Socrates. You were an ancient Greek philosopher. Or at least you're a version of him, I guess. I missed most of the details, but Pen and Abe said that you might not be the real Socrates. The one who taught—"

"I'm real enough," said the assassin, bristling at the suggestion that his reality was in doubt. "Do you know about Plato?" he asked.

"Sure."

"You know he's now the City Solicitor."

"I know he used to be," said Ian. "Penelope said he disappeared. And I didn't realize he was Plato until Pen told me. It's not like I could spot him on sight. Pen told me that he's barely even a princk. I'm not sure how much he knows about his life in the real world."

"The mortal world, Mr. Brown."

"You know what I mean," said Ian.

"It's not as if Detroit isn't real."

"It's sort of real," began Ian, "but Pen says—"

"What matters is that you have information about my prey. Things that they might not know about themselves. You know more about Plato's history than he does. Somewhere in your synapses you hold details about his life that are hidden, even to him. That sort of secret holds power."

"You're going after the City Solicitor?" asked Ian.

The assassin waved him off.

"Tell me what you know about Oan," he said.

"Nothing from the beforelife," said Ian. "I mean, she must have had a beforelife. I'm pretty sure everyone does. Well, everyone except Evan. But no, nothing about Oan before Detroit."

"Isaac Newton?"

"Everybody knows about Isaac Newton."

"But you remember his beforelife?"

"Parts of it," said Ian. "It's not like I ever met him — he lived before my time. I couldn't tell you what he liked for breakfast or what his favourite sports teams were. But I've read a little about him. I've watched a few documentaries. Read some books."

"And what do you know of his preferences? His abilities? His history?"

"Well . . . kind of a lot, I guess!" said Ian, brightening. He wasn't used to entrancing an audience, heavily armed or otherwise, with his passing knowledge of history. He dropped the duvet altogether and sat up like a cocker spaniel who's been told that he's a good boy.

"There was the whole story with the apple hitting his head," said Ian. "That one's probably fake. And he thought up gravity. He wrote *Principia Mathematica*, and invented calculus just to solve some glitch in his work. That's stuff anybody would know — in the beforelife, I mean. And I think he might have been gay. He was a member of the House of Lords, he was obsessed with alchemy, and he had a dog named Diamond who burned down his house. Isaac's house, I mean, not Diamond's. Although they probably lived together, now that I—"

"And Abe?" said Socrates.

"What about him?"

"What do you know of Abe's beforelife?"

"Not much," said Ian. "I didn't know who he was at first. Pen explained that he's probably Abel, from the Bible."

"What's the Bible?"

"Right. Long story."

This wore on for quite some time. Socrates rhymed off a hit parade of more or less recognizable lights from history's marquee, running the gamut from Marie Antoinette to Elvis Presley. Ian responded with as much beforelife trivia as he could muster. Somewhere along the way Ian seemed to forget that Socrates hoped to use this information for purposes that would set any functional moral compass spinning. It was just after Ian had given up the goods on Mata Hari that the assassin's demeanour suddenly shifted, moving from "partly sunny with a chance of mindwipes" to "heavily clouded with a significant risk of torture."

Ian noticed right away. The look on Socrates' face was enough to set Ian reaching for whatever protection was offered by a feather duvet.

When the assassin spoke, his voice carried so much gravity that it might have led Isaac Newton to revamp his calculations. What he said was this:

"And what of the prophet, Norm Stradamus? What do you know of him?"

"Why so interested in Norm?" said Ian.

"I'm asking the questions."

"It's just that you seem worried about him."

"No, I don't."

"Sure, you do. You got all weird when you brought him up. Like you were suddenly on edge."

"Do you know about Norm Stradamus or not?"

"I think I do," said Ian. "But what's the deal with—"

"What do you know?" insisted Socrates.

"There it is again," said Ian. "You're being weird about Norm Stradamus. If I didn't know any better, I'd say you're nervous."

"Answer the question, Mr. Brown!" growled the assassin.

The growl had a marked effect. It was the same effect that an unsheathed sword, a cocked pistol, or a primed syringe of Stygian toxin might have had.

"There isn't much to tell," said Ian, nervously. "I mean, I'm pretty sure that Norm is Nostradamus. A French prophet. I think he lived in the 1500s."

"The what?"

"The 1500s. B-Y," said Ian. "Beforelife years, I mean. It's the way we reckoned time in the mortal world. Nostradamus lived in the fifteenth century. Or the sixteenth century, I suppose. They started counting at zero, see, and—"

"But you know details about his life? His abilities? The extent of his powers of prophecy?"

"A little, I guess," said Ian, who wasn't giving himself nearly enough credit. Ian had grown up with more than a passing interest in games of the swords, dragons, and elves variety, and you can't spend your teenaged years playing Swords & Sorcery without accruing a treasure trove of knowledge about anyone halfway famous who ever dabbled in the occult. The upshot was that he knew a fair amount about the life of Nostradamus. He even knew some of the prophet's quatrains by heart.

"What do you know of the prophet's powers?" pressed the assassin.

A lightbulb switched on in Ian's head. It registered at least three hundred watts and shed a good deal of light on the assassin's twitchy mood.

"This is about Vera, isn't it?" said Ian. "She's a prophet too! One of the times you came for me she knew you were coming. She prepared for you. Helped us escape. She set a trap that blew you to bits!"

"I got better," said the assassin.

"But you're worried about Norm's powers! You're afraid he can do the same thing: look at the future, see you coming, make some sort of preparation! And you think that, I don't know, knowing all about the ins and outs of his powers, or something about his past predictions, will give you an edge. Offset his powers. Like maybe your knowledge of his past might make up for his knowledge of the future!"

The assassin's face betrayed impatience.

"We can discuss this on the road, Mr. Brown," he said.

"On the road?"

"You're coming with me."

"No, I'm not!"

"You don't have a choice."

"I think I do."

"You have to do this for your wife."

"My wife?"

"Tall girl. Dark hair."

"I know who she is!"

"You said it yourself, Mr. Brown. Penelope helps the mayor shore up the walls of reality. And you know why. She works to prevent the chaos that would erupt if people knew the truth of

76

Detroit. That's what I'm trying to do. Penelope's missing. Abe is missing. And there's a growing threat of people spreading the truth. I'm doing my part to end that threat. Tracking the knowledge. Contact tracing. Preserving the secrets of Detroit. You can either come with me and play a role in helping achieve your wife's goals, or you can stay here on your own without any prospect of finding Penelope anytime soon. Make your choice."

Ian had read Socratic dialogues in school. He hadn't liked them. He'd hated Socrates' feigned ignorance. He'd hated the way Socratic questioning left its victims backed into corners, feeling battered and abused. That's how Ian was feeling now. And now that he had a chance to offer a face-to-face rebuke to the interlocutor-in-chief — or at least some version of him — he couldn't manage to hold his tongue.

"I hate Socratic dialogues," he said, and meant it to sting.

"I'm rather enjoying Ianic ones," said the assassin. "So, are you coming with me, or not?"

"Can you at least tell me the plan?" said Ian, defeated.

"Sure thing," said the assassin. "We'll start out with you telling me everything you can about Norm Stradamus."

"Nostradamus."

"Or Nostradamus, if you prefer. I'll make any adjustments necessary to account for his prophetic abilities. After that, I'll get the Church's coordinates from Oan and deal with her. You and I will pop over to wherever the Church is hiding, stake out the joint, share any notes you might have about the pre-mortem lives of anyone present, and deal with them. Then poof, reality's saved."

Ian raised an inquiring finger.

"The whole thing will probably be over by noon tomorrow," said the assassin, brightening. "We'll just get the show on the road and—"

"Ahem," said Ian.

"Ahem?" said the assassin.

"What do you mean by 'deal'?"

"Deal?"

"*Deal* with Oan. *Deal* with the Church. That's what you said."

"Oh. Mindwiping them, of course," said the assassin. "Oblivion's kiss. The Socratic Method. The only way to secure the future. The problem we're facing, as I see it, is the impending spread of knowledge. Wipe out the knowledge, wipe out the threat."

"But you can't go around wiping people!" said Ian.

"Of course I can," said Socrates, taken aback. "It's sort of my brand."

"But—"

"Don't get squeamish on me now, Mr. Brown. We have to eradicate this cancer of knowledge that you've unleashed."

"That I've unleashed?"

"Of course," said the assassin. "If it weren't for that little display that you and your wife unleashed in the grotto, we'd be fine. But now that genie's out of the bottle. What's done is done. The knowledge is spreading. We have to stop it."

"But I can't help you if you're going to go around mindwiping people!"

"It's the only way."

"But . . . but what if it isn't? What if there's something else we can do?"

"I'm nothing if not open-minded, Mr. Brown. You have a suggestion?"

Ian instituted a brief stage wait while rummaging through his mental filing cabinets in search of a plan that didn't involve murder — or the closest thing to murder that you could manage in the hereafter. He blurted out the first passable thing that came to mind.

"We could explain things to them. Explain the danger they're creating."

"It wouldn't work."

"It'd work with Oan!" said Ian, struck by a bolt of inspiration. "She thinks I'm a big deal! She called me the Intercessor! She thinks I'm a link to the Great Omega — a person they worship in the beforelife. I could tell her that it's the Great Omega's will that Oan should keep the secret — that she help us . . . I dunno . . . stand as a bulwark against the forces of anarchy and chaos. Keep pandemonium at bay. She'd eat that up."

The assassin stroked his beard.

"No," he said. "Not good enough. There's still a risk she'd spill the beans."

"But I could convince the rest of the Church too!" said Ian, desperately. "I'll get Oan to take us to them, make them . . . uh . . . adopt secrecy as doctrine. They think I'm some kind of religious icon. Maybe as big a deal as Norm. They'll listen to me. They might even help suppress the truth if I say they have to! You don't have to wipe them."

"My plan's safer," said the assassin.

"Not for them!" Ian protested. "And besides, I'm not helping you if you wipe them. Pen wouldn't want that. You say you can't track her — that doesn't mean that she can't still . . . *do things*. Or maybe she can still change things through me like she did before. How did you put it earlier? Changing plans? Redirecting outcomes? Maybe Pen's still doing that, wherever she is. And you can bet that any plan that involves wiping everybody is going to fail if she has anything to say about it," he added, crossing his arms. "So if you want my help, we'll do it my way or not at all!"

The assassin stroked his beard again. It's one thing to press a helpful chump into service by making him tell you what he knows about your prey. It's quite another when that chump has a nearly omnipotent wife who might show up at any time and blink you out of existence. Socrates had never read about Scylla and Charybdis — they being among those elements of ancient Greek culture that hadn't made their way to Detroit. But he understood being trapped between a rock and a hard place. Or stuck directly between Penelope and a princk.

"All right," he said, at length. "We'll try it your way for now. I'll give you a week. Get the information from Oan, determine where we find the rest of the Church, and convince her to keep quiet about the nature of Detroit. You think you can handle that, Mr. Brown?"

"I do!" said Ian, who seemed to be warming up to the idea. "We're going to be like Butch and Sundance!"

"Who and what?" said the assassin.

"Never mind," said Ian.

And thus it was that Ian Brown, who'd previously done everything that he could to escape the hospice, now resolved to stay put and endure whatever treatments awaited, all in an effort to save the memories of a church full of people who'd tried to throw him into the Styx last time they'd met. These are the sacrifices one sometimes has to make for a spouse's job — especially when that job involves preventing the netherverse from soiling its trousers and spiralling into a gumbo of unrestrained expectations, uncontrolled thoughts, and distastefully mixed metaphors.

Somewhere, tucked away in a hived-off corner of the netherverse that wasn't quite Detroit, in a hidden patch of reality that was shielded from the thoughts and expectations that gave the afterlife its form, Penelope screamed.

Chapter 6

Ian's first day in the hospice didn't turn out as you'd expect. He'd spent it unconscious. His little midnight chat with Socrates had happened during Ian's *third* night at the hospice, which was the first night Ian had been sufficiently *compos mentis* to have a chat of any kind. The first morning to greet a fully aware Ian — the morning after Socrates disappeared through a window and left our hero to deal with Oan — started out with a wrestling match.

At least that's how it seemed to Ian. He was still in bed, and was suddenly jerked from sleep by being folded into a shape that seemed to combine the worst traits of a camel clutch, a half nelson, and the dreaded rear admiral. And if Ian was any judge, his wrestling opponent was a twelve-foot giantess from the super-colossal heavyweight division of the Netherworldly Wrestling Federation.

"Abe's drawers!" bellowed the giantess, whose voice brought to mind the roar that would herald the dawn of Armageddon, before flipping Ian flat onto his back.

Ian made the sort of noises that haunt the guards of Guantanamo Bay.

"Oh, so you're awake now, are you?" boomed the wrestler, revealing herself not to be a giantess at all, but rather a normal-sized and much-more-frightening Matron Bikerack, Boss Nurse of Detroit Mercy and purveyor of every uncomfortable remedy in the book. She grabbed one of Ian's legs and contorted it in a way that Mother Nature never intended.

"Gah!" Ian explained, eloquently.

"We've got to keep you limber!" cried the matron, using the sergeant-majorish voice that always left ceiling tiles raining down to the hospice floor. "Sleeping for days, living in the streets for who-knows-how-long! It's a wonder you're not in worse shape than you are!"

It's widely known that nurses are, on the whole, made of sterner stuff than ordinary people. Where your average person cringes at the thought of certain bodily excrescences getting anywhere in what you might call "sniffing distance," a nurse can wade through rivers of biological muck while preparing medical ointments, reading a hieroglyphic chart, and smiling kindly at someone shouting at them for Jell-O. This was certainly true of the matron. She was the nurse to end all nurses. Ian had no idea who she'd been in the beforelife, though he assumed she must have had one. He expected she might have been one of those west country veterinarians who can openly talk about their next meal while elbow deep in the business end of a plough horse. Or maybe one of those butchers who can stand up to their hips in entrails while straining out any bits unfit for haggis. Or possibly she'd been Vlad the Impaler. Whoever she'd been, she now seemed to occupy the office of the patron saint of nurses, reeking of competence, professionalism, and patients.

The matron flipped Ian again and jabbed him square in the back with what he judged to be a steel-tipped elbow. Ian made another series of inhuman noises, these ones reminiscent of bagpipes, which his current configuration quite resembled.

"It's not so much that I blame you, Brown," boomed the matron, picking up the threads of a conversation Ian must have missed, "and I'm not angry, no, not angry at all. I'm just disappointed."

Ian cried out again, perceiving that a mustard plaster or similar implement of torture had been affixed to a sensitive part of his person. This was probably a foul.

"It's just that you seemed so normal! I mean, apart from your delusions. You just believe you had a life before the river," she soliloquized. "A simple, straightforward case of BD. No unnatural ideas about 'reincarnation,' no belief you'd been a dog or a sea horse or some such creature, no hint of *ego fabularis* — just a nice, placid chap who always did what he was told, kept his head down, accepted his treatment, and minded his p's and q's. A perfectly normal patient." She twisted Ian's lower body into a knot that would have made a sailor proud. "Nothing to make a mark in a medical journal, no hint of causing trouble, just a perfectly average, garden-variety princk."

Ian could tell the matron meant this as a compliment. He really could — even as he was being bent into pretzel form. But he'd spent so much of his time — spread across two different worlds — hearing variations on the theme of how unexceptional he was that he'd finally had enough. He wasn't average at all! He was married to a cosmically powerful entity, for starters. Nothing average about that. He was the father of the first child born in the afterlife. He was the Intercessor, for Abe's sake — a church icon revered by several dozen certifiable zealots who'd happily give their lives for Ian — if giving your life was something you could do in Detroit. If that didn't add up to "exceptional," then Ian didn't know what did. And so it was at this moment, covered in ointment and contorted into an unintentional upward dog, that Ian decided to deal pretty harshly with the matron's suggestion that he was some kind of humdrum sheep without a glimmer of *je ne sais quoi* to set him apart from the rest of the herd.

He was on the point of unleashing something fairly venomous when it occurred to him that he might hurt the matron's feelings, so he kept the remark to himself.

"I won't bother asking why you escaped," said the matron, pausing to "tut-tut" with the force of a jackhammer. "It's plain as day. You fell in with the wrong crowd! A whole gaggle of Napoleons! Not to mention Mr. Zeus. And Rhinnick Feynman himself, worst of the lot!"

"I haven't seen them in ages!" Ian grunted. He would have said that in a nostalgic sort of way had it been possible to be wistful with a brawny health-care thug twisting him into balloon animals.

"I wish I could say the same!" she said, grunting with the effort of treating Ian like Plasticine. "Feynman came back not long after you'd all escaped. It was the strangest thing too," she added, pausing to hold Ian in a pose that would have had Special Forces veterans giving up whatever they knew about troop deployments. She stared off into the middle distance, reminiscing. "I'll be jacked if every last one of us in the hospice didn't forget who Rhinnick was! No clue he'd been a patient! Like a fog fell over all of us, hiding every memory of Rhinnick Feynman. We gave him the run of the place, too, having him help out Dr. Peericks with a case!"

"Rhinnick worked with Dr. Peericks?!" gasped Ian, interrobanging like nobody's business.

"I know!" exclaimed the matron. "It's as bizarre a thing as I've ever seen. We didn't recognize him at all! He was right here, plain as day, no disguise or assumed name, and we let him come and go as he pleased! An escaped patient!"

She twisted Ian again, prompting a noise that might have summoned a caribou if any had been nearby.

"And then a few days later," she added, "POOF!"

"Poof?" groaned Ian, into a pillow.

"Poof!" said the matron. "We all remembered. It was too late to do anything about it then — Feynman had disappeared again. We haven't heard from him since! Dr. Peericks wrote a paper about it!"

"Really?" said Ian.

"He did!" said the matron. "I think it was called—"

"'Subject Specific Instance of Mass Amnesia in a Convalescent Health-care Setting: Reflections of a Patient/Psychiatrist,'" said Dr. Peericks, breezing into the room and closing the door behind him.

"Catchy," said Ian, still speaking into the pillow.

"And how are you doing, Mr. Brown?" said the doctor, taking a seat in the bedside chair. "It's good to see you awake."

"Grrnk," said Ian, as the matron twisted him into another pose.

"I'll tell you my theory," she said, answering a question no one had asked. "All of that mass-amnesia stuff was Feynman's doing. Some trick he played on all of us. It's his way! Sowing trouble wherever he goes. Causing confusion. Unleashing hamsters. He did the same with Mr. Brown!"

"He did?" said Ian.

"He did!" said the matron. "Feynman stoked your delusions! Made you think there was some hope of finding clues about the beforelife. I've seen that sort of thing before. But I must say, Mr. Brown, that in your case I expected better!"

"Perhaps, if you've almost finished, Matron Bikerack—" began the doctor.

"I won't be another moment," said the matron, releasing her victim, who collapsed like a bad soufflé. She affixed some form of medical contrivance to Ian's scalp. It beeped twice, which she appeared to take as good news.

"If that'll be all, Matron?" said Dr. Peericks.

"Of course, Doctor," she said, pausing to pat Ian's hand. He hadn't imagined that she'd be capable of anything hailing from the same solar system as "gentle," but this was certainly from the same galactic cluster. Her task completed, the matron weighed anchor and tugboated a cart of medical accessories out of the room.

"Now Ian," said Dr. Peericks as the door clicked shut, "I can't tell you how glad I am that we found you. Tell me how you've been."

"Oh, fine," said Ian, scooching into a seated position against the pillows. "How are you?"

"Perhaps I should have been more specific," said Peericks. "What I really want to know is how you're doing, what your mental state is. Whether you're still suffering from BD, or if your delusions have dissipated while you've been out of our care."

"Oh, that's not a problem anymore, Doc," said Ian, doing his best to radiate mental health in every direction. "No more delusions, no more wondering about the beforelife being real, everything's all squared away. But, can I ask you a question?"

"Of course."

"You said you were glad you found me. I'm still not sure how I got here."

"You were unconscious," said the doctor, "lying in a gutter somewhere in the Wallows. Rough neighbourhood. The police picked you up for vagrancy. They ran a scan of your DNA, saw you listed as an escaped hospice patient, and brought you here right away."

"Oh," said Ian, sliding deeper into the bed. "That makes sense."

"So how did you wind up in the Wallows?"

"No idea," said Ian, truthfully.

"Where have you been since leaving us?"

"Oh, here and there," said Ian. "You know, minding my own business, not causing trouble, that sort of thing."

"And no more delusions?"

"None," said Ian.

"That's where we run into problems," said Peericks, leaning in. "You see, you've been talking in your sleep."

"I have?"

"You have. And you kept saying 'Penelope.'"

"You shouldn't be listening while I sleep," said Ian.

"Your fixation on this Penelope person troubles me," said Peericks.

"Sorry about that," said Ian.

"The last time you were here you kept insisting that Penelope was your wife. In the beforelife. And that you'd left her there when you crossed over, and that all you wanted to do was get back to her. Sound familiar?"

Ian nodded and pulled the covers up to his chin, as though they might shield him from a barrage of psychoanalysis.

"And you're still dreaming about this Penelope person?"

Ian paused and appeared to make the face of a person doing long division before he settled on his response.

"I . . . guess so," he said. "But that doesn't mean I have delusions, does it? I mean, it's all right for people to have dreams about past delusions, right? Like, say I used to have visions about a purple hippopotamus, and you cured me, but I still remember having the visions about the purple hippo so he sometimes turns up in my dreams? That's not delusional. That's just memory. That'd be no reason to keep me locked in a hospice, right?"

"Maybe," said Dr. Peericks, doubtfully. "But it also brings to mind another theory I was working on when you escaped. I thought you might have been mindwiped."

"Mindwiped!" said Ian.

"That's right. A barbaric procedure. They used to do it to princks in the olden days, to reboot their personalities by erasing memory engrams and putting their brains back to square one. I've been wondering whether someone might have tried something similar with you and botched the procedure, leaving some of your old memories still intact. Memories from here, in Detroit, from some time before you were first checked in to the hospice. That'd explain some things — like why the apparent memories you retained were so specific — not like regular BD patients at all. And it'd explain why they didn't fade over time. But I'm still not convinced," he added, rising from the chair and starting to pace. "The mindwipe theory can't account for some of the other things you said while you were sleeping."

"What other things?" said Ian.

"You kept talking about family. You said the words 'my son,' which didn't make any sense at all. You talked about mothers and children. You seemed tormented."

This seemed fair enough to Ian. He was worried about his son. He'd been fretting about Evan's biology-defying growth spurt, about his trick of drawing on Pen's power. And he'd been fretting about other family members too. Ever since Pen had first suggested having Evan, she'd been trying to find her parents, hoping to track them down and supply her son with the full-blown grandparent experience. There'd been no sign of them at all. No hint of where they might be in Detroit. That had been bothering Pen a lot, especially in the days leading up to Evan's party. It had been bothering Ian too. It was no wonder that he'd been dreaming about the family.

Ian resurfaced to find that Peericks was still speaking.

". . . so I've brought in a specialist," said the doctor. "You aren't the first patient to have delusions about a family. Plenty of princks have them — false memories of biological offspring, brothers and sisters, that sort of thing. I have a colleague who's devoted his career to studying these types of cases. So I've invited him to see you. He's an expert in HPV."

"HPV?" said Ian, perplexed.

"Human Procreative Visions," said Dr. Peericks. "The delusion that humans are capable of producing children. His specialty is princks who think they remember human mothers. Hold on, I'll bring him in."

The thing about narrative convention is this: it allows you to make predictions. If the author sticks a gun on a nightstand, you know it's going to be used by chapter's end. If there's an orphan running loose in an ancient kingdom that's fallen to ruin, you know the orphan is going to be the missing heir. And if a psychiatrist in the afterlife introduces you to a specialist who's interested in talking about your mother, you can bet your share of the royalties that it's going to be —

"Sigmund Freud!" said Ian, goggling as Dr. Peericks ushered the man himself into the room. Ian shouldn't have been surprised. He'd been in Detroit long enough to know how the place basically worked, and he'd been around Rhinnick long enough to acknowledge that stuff you read a moment ago about the force of narrative convention. But it was still a bit alarming to think that Dr. Freud himself was about to take a peek under the hood to see what made Ian tick.

"You've heard of me!" said Freud, smiling.

"Y-y-yes," stammered Ian, backing as far into the pillows as they let him.

"Very interesting!" said Freud. "Und I'm most interested in your case presentation!" he added, pulling a small datapad out of his pocket and tapping the screen. "It says here zat you — you believe zat your past life ended by . . . Abe's drawers! . . . *a train going through a tunnel*! Ve vill have to explore ze psychological underpeenings of zese metaphorical constructs!"

89

He set his datapad aside, rubbed his hands together, and sat on the foot of Ian's bed. "Let's get to vork!" he said, beaming.

Ian didn't know a lot about Sigmund Freud. He'd skipped those documentaries. He was pretty sure that Freud had invented psychotherapy. And Ian knew a penis or two about Freudian slips. He vaguely remembered something creepy about Oedipus and Electra, and something about cigars just being cigars. All the little things he knew made him expect that there was virtually no chance of him getting through his upcoming treatment with his ego fully intact — let alone his superego and his id.

It was at this precise moment that Ian found himself thinking the unthinkable.

He wished that Matron Bikerack would come back.

* * *

He definitely had freckles. That much was certain. And he had red hair — everybody agreed on that. It was also generally agreed that he stood about six feet tall. But apart from that, opinions varied. It was like no one had ever gotten a clear look at him. No one had ever snapped a picture and given his face a thorough inspection. No one had made a careful study. He had a face that struck a blow against eyewitness identification. But whatever the cause, whenever people described the mysterious red-haired stranger who was now surrounded by neck-craning onlookers on the campus of Detroit University, they tended to be vague about the details, as though this stranger's face was somehow wrapped up in a macroscopic version of Heisenberg's uncertainty principle. It's possible that you could tell where he was going or even the speed at which he moved, but you couldn't really describe how the fellow looked.

Perhaps the word we're looking for here is "inscrutable."

The crowd had gathered in one of Detroit University's residential quadrangles — the one that was called the "concrete beach," situated between Founder's Residence and the Rosa Parks Observatory. They'd been drawn to the spot by word of mouth — which is an odd phrase when you think about it. They'd come to hear from the unnamed, mysterious, hard-to-describe stranger who made confusing, rambling promises about a golden age of Detroit.

He stood in the centre of a roughly circular crowd, standing on a bench artfully made from steel girders, shouting something or other about making Detroit great again. The people were confused.

A voice from the crowd called out. It said, "Erm . . . sir?"

"And we'll begin our march to greatness!" said the red-haired stranger, ignoring the interruption. "We'll take back everything that's been lost! We'll—"

"Sir?" cried the voice again.

"What? What is it?" barked the stranger.

"When was Detroit ever great?"

"What do you mean 'when was Detroit ever great?'"

"It's just that you want to make it great again, right?" said the voice, which seemed to belong to a rumpled little man in a corduroy jacket that was at least one size too big. "Well, I'll be 847 years old next Tuesday—"

"Merry manifestival!" cried a chorus of friendly voices.

The little man smiled and waved. "And like I was saying, I'm almost 847, and things weren't any better or worse 847 years ago, so far as I can recall. They've pretty much stayed the same ever since. Sure, there've been some ups and downs and bumps in the road and—"

"But with me, you'll get back everything that's been lost!" said the stranger, trying to rally.

"But what's been lost?"

"Everything!" said the stranger, oozing genuine emotion. His whole way of presenting himself might have brought to mind one of those street preachers you sometimes get in public spaces, except he wasn't especially beardy or dressed in sackcloth, and there wasn't a doomsaying sandwich board in sight. Another thing people agreed on when they were asked about the stranger was that he was clean-shaven and well-dressed, wearing a suit with all the trimmings. But had the suit been blue or grey? Was his tie solid or striped? What about his shoes? Here again, opinions varied. They could agree on the word "dapper," though, a word that rarely comes within several miles of your garden-variety prophet of doom. Even so — there was a hint of a street-preacherish air about him.

"I'm not talking about a few centuries ago!" continued the hard-to-describe, red-headed, somewhat dapper yet street-preacherish stranger. "I'm talking about the olden days! Before you manifested! A time when everything was—"

"I'm 3,726!" cried another voice from the crowd. "So far as I know, Detroit just keeps getting better. Telephones, for example."

There was a murmur of appreciation for telephonic communication.

"Telephones don't matter!" said the stranger.

"And beer!" shouted Umtag the Befouled, who'd manifested eight thousand years ago, in the dark days before the process of fermentation had been discovered.

There was a loud and heartfelt round of applause for beer.

"You don't think things were better before beer, do you?" said Umtag.

"You don't understand!" said the stranger. "You won't lose any of those things if you join with me. You'll have that and so much more! Nothing's going to be lost in the Restoration!"

The crowd, with one voice, murmured the word "*Restoration?*" in italics with a question mark or two.

"Everything you want, you'll have," said the stranger. "Stop letting yourselves be fooled! These things that you think you need — beer and phones, new technology, other distractions, all the passing fads, and . . . and *things* you expect to make you happy — they're just tricks! Just smoke and mirrors. They're not even real! They only keep you in the dark. They blind you to the world you refuse to see!"

"Ummm . . . telephones are real," said a nearby observer, holding one in her hand.

"Technology isn't smoke and mirrors," croaked a beleaguered student wearing a gold-trimmed jacket bearing the words "DU Engineering." She looked about as worn down as a fourth-hand bathmat and smelled vaguely of Umtag the Befouled's favourite invention — all of the diagnostic criteria required to confirm she'd earned the jacket. "It's science," she said. "Science is real. I should know. I pay tuition for it."

There was a flutter of half-hearted, debt-ridden laughter.

"Don't believe what experts tell you!" cried the stranger. "They'll tell you the world is round. It isn't! They'll tell you vaccines work. They don't! They'll tell you the climate is changing. But it can't! Because they won't let it!" He ignored the skeptical susurrations and reached into a pocket, pulling out a ten-dollar bill.

"The world works just like money!" he cried, brandishing the bill. "Look. Money exists because you believe in it! That's the only reason! Money isn't *really* real. It isn't anything! It has value because . . . because the elites who block your power have told you it matters — they've told you that money *means something*. But it's just paper! Or little bits of information stored in a database somewhere in City Hall. And you work, day and night, so that some . . . some *bureaucrat* will press a couple of buttons, or some computer will move some numbers from an employer's account to yours!

I'm telling you: it's all an illusion. Nothing you think you see is real!"

He could sense that he'd lost the crowd. Nothing alienates an audience of exam-ready students like the idea that the cash they're hoping to earn in future careers doesn't exist. A few people started to boo.

"What?" the stranger shouted, with a voice that seemed unnaturally loud, somehow drowning out the jeers. "Who do you trust, then? Scientists? You listen to their ideas? What do they tell you? They mess with numbers. They spin theories. And what are theories? They're just guesses! Made-up arguments to distract you from what's real!"

He paused here for dramatic effect. The pause was filled in short order with the voice of one of those tiresome, pedantic weasel-types who major in pre-law and start at least two-thirds of their sentences with "well, actually."

"Well, actually," said the voice, "that's not what the word 'theory' means. Not in science, anyway. It means more than just an idea. It's a thoroughly supported explanation of phenomena tying together the bulk of explanatory evidence, observations, and hypotheses. Like the theory of gravity. You wouldn't say gravity's 'just a theory,'" he added, with an air of self-satisfaction.

The crowd grew quiet. So did the stranger. What he said next was barely a whisper, yet it was easily heard in every corner of the quad. What he said was this:

"You think gravity's real?"

The pre-law student locked eyes with the stranger, lifted a textbook to shoulder height, and dropped it. It the ground with a thud. If a thud could sound smug, this one did. There was a smattering of applause.

As inscrutable as the stranger's appearance was, everyone looking at him could tell he was starting to seethe.

"All that proves is that you don't have imagination," said the stranger, through clenched teeth. "The book drops because it does what you expect. You've been fooled. You've been trapped by the Big Lie — a lie that gives you limitations. It limits your expectations, it limits what you can get. You dial down what you expect the world to give you. I can free you from those limits."

If a crowd could agree on anything, this one appeared to agree that this was the time for derisive laughter.

The laughter dropped off just as suddenly as the textbook had dropped from the pre-law student's hand.

What didn't drop was the stranger.

He rose.

He rose about nine feet into the air, levitating above the crowd with his arms spread wide.

"Do you still believe in gravity?" he said.

The scene shifted. The mocking crowd stopped mocking. A lot of them left, shaking their heads and muttering things along the lines of "some kinda trick" or "street magician." The ones who stayed behind, though — the handful of care-worn, soul-crushed, debt-burdened students who searched for answers that they couldn't seem to find in class, those students who couldn't get ahead however they tried, those students who found themselves beaten down by "the Man" without any notion of who "the Man" was or why he had it in for them — they fell silent. They stood in something approaching awe, reaching up toward the hovering man of mystery, straining to touch him, reaching out to grasp some piece of his . . . his radiance? His glory? His growing, charismatic aura that reached into the depth of your soul, *pulled* something from within you, and made you want to cry out his name?

What was his name?

He rose farther above those who remained, stretching his hands out broadly as though embracing the people below, his indescribable face looking benevolently upon them and drawing them in.

His gaze shifted. So did his face. You'd still be hard-pressed to find two eyewitnesses whose testimony would get the same picture out of a competent sketch artist, but at least they'd have agreed that there'd been a sudden and unexpected change in the stranger's expression.

He suddenly looked perplexed. His indescribable features took on the look of someone who's just removed the foil from a chocolate truffle and found a Brussels sprout inside, or someone who dug into a serving of fruit cocktail and found an eye.

He stared into a distant hedge. He stared at something no one else saw. It was something that, by all rights, he shouldn't have been able to see, either. Not if Isaac Newton had anything to say about it. The cloaking device was perfect. The only thing that ought to have been able to penetrate its light-scattering imperceptibility field was one of Isaac's own ocular scanners.

The stranger's puzzlement disappeared. He looked right through the imperceptibility field and . . . well . . . *he perceived.* Then he smiled a crooked smile.

Socrates met his gaze and gulped.

On the wings of a command whispered to the ISAAC system, the assassin disappeared.

Chapter 7

"I'm sorry, but Mistress Oan is still unavailable. I'll be sure to let her know you called as soon as I perceive her."

Ian hadn't heard any of that — not in the usual way, at least. The words hadn't been said out loud. They'd been *thought* at Ian by Peericks's office assistant, Mr. Searle, who for reasons lost in history had washed up from the River Styx as a brain in a vat.

Well, just a brain, really. The vat was added sometime later, once two things had been discovered; namely that Searle was a fully conscious adult human brain with his own set of dreams, beliefs, and aspirations, and that letting him move about the place without a vat tended to leave a gooey trail on the carpet.

One of the more surprising things about being a brain in a vat is that you have to cope with your own special varieties of stress. You do get to float around all day without having to worry about exercise, think about your posture, or fret about wrinkles — which, if you know anything about brain anatomy, are a positively useful thing to have — but you still have a lot on your mind; or rather, you still have a lot *on you*, a mind being pretty much all there is of you.

There's the pH of the tank, for starters. An unduly alkaline bath can give you a migraine. There's water temperature, too, a self-respecting brain in the vat being more than a little concerned with shrinkage. There's also the constant worry of having your vat's built-in thought-projection matrix fall into a state of disrepair, particularly in the wake of the disappearance of Isaac Newton, who'd invented it in the first place. No one knew how the system worked. It had something to do with preganglionic fibres, synaptic potentials, and teensy pieces of duct tape floating around in Isaac's brine. This gumbo somehow turned Searle's brainwaves into speech whenever he wanted his thoughts to be heard. Not proper speech as in the sort that arrives as words through the ear canals of nearby observers. More like the memory of words you'd heard a few seconds earlier, without all the bother of actually engaging tympanic membranes first.

Ian had once tried thinking back at Searle, giving telepathy a whirl and hoping for the best. It hadn't worked. You had to speak to him out loud. How your speech made its way into whatever passed for his speech processing centre was more than Ian had ever felt comfortable asking. Probably something to do with the vibrations your voice made in the brine. And Searle wasn't silent, either. Far from it. When he pressed his vat's telepathic gizmo into service, the brine would bubble and burble in a pleasant, percussive way, creating a rhumba-esque accompaniment that played gently in the background whenever Mr. Searle projected his thoughts at people around him.

Ian found it restful. So did Searle, come to think of it. There was a part of him that loved bobbing around in a liquid suspension. Possibly the hippocampus. But whatever the cause, Searle's vat did quite a lot to ease the stresses that came with the status of being a disembodied brain.

The vat couldn't touch Searle's biggest fear, of course. It was the universal fear shared by all brains in vats: that you might actually be an undergraduate student enrolled in an introductory philosophy seminar.

Mr. Searle, the brain in the vat found in Dr. Peericks's office, had largely dealt with that last problem. Dr. Peericks had helped. He'd helped Searle realize that, if he really were a philosophy student coping with the delusion that he was a brain in a vat — rather than the other way around — there'd be clues. He'd have pants, for one thing. And a bus pass. And rather than being an intake supervisor and administrative assistant in Peericks's office, he'd probably be a barista.

He still worried about other things too — all of the everyday stresses that arise for brains in vats. *Will I ever meet another brain in a vat with whom I can form a meaningful neural connection? Or I know I'm 60 per cent fat, but how do I look in this suspension?* But today the worry centres of Searle's brain — or rather the worry centres of Searle — were focused entirely on one question, which was this: Was Ian going to be okay?

He'd been talking in his sleep all week. Dr Peericks had been obsessing about what he'd said. Things about having a wife. And having a son — a child that proceeded from his wife's body, of all the Abe-forsaken ideas. Solid evidence that Ian was still convinced that he'd lived a life before Detroit. That wouldn't do. And a day or two after awakening he'd started turning up at the doctor's office looking for Oan. Looking for *Oan*, of all people. Any patient who deliberately sought a chat with Oan was a patient who made Searle's own disembodied concerns seem like a walk in the park. Or a bob in a pond. Yet here was Ian, turning up three days in a row and growing increasingly desperate to meet with the hospice's sharing room director.

It wasn't natural.

So — just to drive home the point around which we've been circling for several paragraphs — Mr. Searle was downright vexed.

"It's just that I really need to see her," said Ian. "It's very important."

"I understand," burbled Searle. "But there's nothing I can do. She's on vacation. We aren't expecting her back for at least a week."

"But I have to see her!" said Ian, wringing his hands.

"You're not going to bring up that Socrates person again," said Searle, whose brainwaves registered notes of genuine concern.

Ian had tried everything to convince Searle of the importance of seeing Oan. He'd finally been so desperate that he'd resorted to the truth. Or at least large chunks of it. He'd tried to explain that Oan was in danger, that Socrates the assassin had placed a metaphorical target on Oan's back, and that if Ian didn't warn her, she faced the prospect of losing her mind — one prospect that really ought to draw sympathy from someone like Searle, whose mind was all he had.

It hadn't worked. On the upside it hadn't gotten Ian into trouble. It didn't come close to the strangest claim Searle had heard while working in Dr. Peericks's office; it wasn't even the strangest one he'd heard that day. Searle had received the story with the sort of detached professional interest you show when people tell you that they're gluten intolerant, or that they don't vote because they can't trust the deep state.

"Perhaps we should talk about something else, Mr. Brown," said Searle, patiently, as his brine burbled a soothing island rhythm. "How are your sessions with Dr. Freud?"

Ian cringed.

"They can't be that bad," said Searle.

"He kept showing me Rorschach tests."

"What's a Rorschach test?"

"Oh, right," said Ian. "You don't call them that in Detroit. Dr. Freud kept calling them Holtzmans."

Searle tut-tutted in his tank. It made a pleasant gurgle. "You can see why we're worried about you, Ian," he said. "You keep hinting at your belief in another world — your delusion that there's a world before Detroit."

"It just doesn't seem fair," said Ian, musing. "I mean, Rorschach invents these inkblot tests, right, which probably took a lot of effort. And then someone else who learned about them in the beforelife dies before Rorschach does, or just turns up in Detroit as a princk with the memory of Rorschach tests intact, and then he takes all the credit. So the things are called 'Holtzmans' here, forever. It doesn't seem right. Holtzman probably doesn't even realize that it's plagiarism. Is it called plagiarism when it isn't in writing? Patent infringement? Anyway, I did the same thing with drinks, but I don't think that's as bad."

"And how did the Holtzman tests go?" pressed Searle, who would have furrowed his brow if he had one.

"Not well. I thought the first one looked like spaghetti. The second one was a donut and the third one was poutine."

"Poutine?"

"French fries with curds and gravy."

"Ah. So you were hungry."

"That's what Dr. Freud said!"

"He's very good."

"He didn't believe me about Socrates, either."

"Oh Ian," burbled Searle, "it's no wonder Peericks and Freud are worried. You can't go around the hospice spreading these conspiracy theories—"

"It's not a conspiracy theory!" said Ian. "I was there. I saw it first-hand. Socrates came to my room and threatened Oan, right out in the open. The only way I can save her is—"

"You need to listen to me, Ian," said Searle. "Socrates isn't real."

"But he is—" said Ian.

"You're suggesting that Abe has assassins in his employ?"

"Well, not really—"

"You say he worked with Isaac Newton, yes? And the two of them, in turn, worked for the City Solicitor? And the City Solicitor works directly for Abe. Ergo," burbled Searle, winding up for the *coup de grace,* "Socrates, according to your little conspiracy theory, works indirectly for Abe."

"Not necessarily—" began Ian.

"Does Abe strike you as a man who doesn't know what's going on in City Hall? Does he strike you as a man who's uninformed about what's happening under his nose?"

"Well, no," admitted Ian.

"And you avow that he has assassins on his staff."

"One assassin."

"An assassin who has the power to wipe the memories of his foes, all done in the service of a City Solicitor who you now assert is a famed philosopher from the mortal world, one who formerly went by the name Pluto."

"Plato," said Ian.

"And all of this somehow relates to the fact that the beforelife is real, that real human memories of the beforelife are disrupted by the river, and that people can't handle knowing the truth about Detroit."

"Okay, when you put it like that it *does* sound crazy," Ian admitted. "But it's all true."

"I'm sure it's very real to you," said Searle, "but you've admitted it sounds strange. That's a healthy place to start. I'm sure Drs. Peericks and Freud will have you sorted out in no time."

"But—"

"If you don't mind, Ian, it's time for my break," burbled Searle. "Be a lamb and wheel me into the hobby room."

Ian did as he was asked. And when he arrived at the hobby room he was met by the usual assortment of boosters and well-wishers who greeted Searle practically every time he entered a crowded space. Searle was one of the most popular people in the hospice. For one thing, he was always willing to lend an understanding ear — or at least an understanding parietal lobe, which is the bit that really matters — and for another, he never stole your lunch.

Ian hadn't taken more than a few steps away from Searle and his pals when he spotted someone familiar sitting by herself in the hobby room's far corner, at a table that was covered in pipe cleaners, rubber bands, jars of paint, pots of glue, bits of construction paper, plastic cutlery, and more scissors and wires than you'd ordinarily see in a home for the psychically unbound.

Ian recognized her on sight.

"Vera!" he said.

"Ian!" said Vera, turning around.

"You remember me?" said Ian, taken aback. "I heard you'd been mindwiped!"

"I was," said Vera. "I got better."

"But that's not possible!"

"I know!" said Vera. "I got lucky. Television," she added, tapping the side of her head. "It sort of replayed a lot of my memories as dreams and visions. I call them reruns."

"Gosh," said Ian. "So what are you doing here?"

"Building something," said Vera. "Hand me a wrench."

"They don't have wrenches here."

"Oh, right. That's a difficulty."

"But I mean, what are you doing in the hospice?"

"Oh!" said Vera. "I got myself checked in!" she added, rather deftly twisting a bit of cardboard into a makeshift wrench.

"But you don't have BD," said Ian.

"Nobody does. It isn't real."

"*They* think it is," said Ian, italicizing the "they."

"But the beforelife's real. You can't have 'beforelife delusion' if the beforelife really exists. It stands to reason. And I've seen solid evidence of the beforelife. I had a vision of Isaac Newton being reborn as some kid named Stephen Hawking."

Ian's jaw didn't actually drop to the floor, as that almost never happens. But it did droop on its hinge while Ian struggled to form a response.

"Whatever," said Vera, waving him off. "The point is that I got myself checked in so that I could get in touch with you."

"With me?"

"Yeah," said Vera. "I knew you'd be here." She tapped the side of her head again.

"Right. Television."

"It comes in handy," said Vera, matter-of-factly. "I had a vision of you in the hospice, but couldn't for the life of me figure out what in Abe's name would make you come back. Spoon, please."

"I didn't come back!" said Ian, passing Vera a spoon. "Not on purpose. I passed out at a birthday party. Next thing I knew I was in the hospice with an assassin on my chest."

"Oh. Well, that does make a lot more sense."

"You've got a funny idea of what makes sense," said Ian.

"Glue," said Vera.

Ian retrieved a bottle of mucilage — the sort with the squashy rubber tip with the little anatomical slit that always ends up looking like a congested toddler's nose.

"So what are *you* doing here?" said Vera, affixing various bits and bobs to whatever it was that she was building. It seemed to involve lots of colourful cardboard cut-outs, strings, wires, and crayons.

"I didn't mean to be here at all," said Ian. "Like I said, I passed out at a birthday party and woke up in the hospice. Socrates was sitting on me."

"That can't have been fun," said Vera.

"He said he was here to wipe Oan. To stop her from spreading word of the Church of O, and explaining how Detroit is a—"

"A mental construct, sure, I get it."

Ian squinted at her sideways. "You get it?"

"Of course I get it. Socrates is probably worried that people could think him out of existence. You know, since he isn't real."

"Socrates isn't real," said Ian. He'd meant it as a question, but it sounded a good deal more like a statement of facts he didn't believe, like "sandwiches are racehorses," "my shoe is an interdimensional portal," or "the election has been stolen."

"Not real in the way that we're real," said Vera. "He's not from the beforelife."

"I haven't quite gotten my head around that," said Ian, who hadn't.

"Right. Well, you know how you met Tonto when you first came out of the river, and she seemed too good to be true, and it turned out that your wife had just manifested Tonto out of her wish to have some sort of street-savvy protector who'd keep you safe from any danger, right? Well, the same thing happened with Socrates. The City Solicitor — his real name is Plato, right? — well he manifested Socrates in the same way. Unconsciously, just like Penelope did with Tonto. And Socrates must be thinking that, if he can be thought into existence, he can be thought right out of it too. If people learn they can bend Detroit to their will — if they figure out how to pull at the threads of whatever Detroit's made of — then someone's likely as not to come along and wish Socrates right back out of existence. Poof!"

"Poof."

"Poof! I'd be scared if I were him too. Hand me the scissors."

Ian handed Vera the scissors.

There was a chorus of mingled huzzahs and hear-hears accompanied by a round of applause from the gang at the other end of the room, probably resulting from something clever

Searle had thought at those in attendance. Whatever it was, it hadn't reached as far as Ian, who paused to inspect whatever it was that Vera was making.

"What is it?" said Ian.

Vera scratched her head with a spork. "No idea," she said. "I expect I'll know when it's done."

"Fair enough," said Ian. He knew it'd probably be impressive. Vera's weird ability to see the future, the past, and far-off places had two surprising side effects: she could determine the purpose of any constructed object on sight, and she had a preternatural grasp of engineering. She could build practically anything. And if she wanted to spend her time in the hospice making something out of construction paper and glue and what appeared to be a bucket of dried macaroni, Ian wouldn't get in her way.

"It doesn't add up," he said.

"What doesn't add up?"

"What you said about Socrates, and his worry that he could be thought out of existence. I mean, I know how Detroit works. You know how Detroit works. But I can't change the place. You don't see me making Socrates disappear, or moving mountains, or filling the place with Tontos."

"Yeah," said Vera, tying a bit of yarn around a three-dimensional cardboard figure of a golf cart. "That part's complicated. I suppose it has something to do with critical mass."

A look of understanding failed to wash across Ian's face.

"Critical mass," Vera repeated. "Picture a river. Didn't you say that Abe and Penelope and the ancients sort of direct the wills of others, like a series of dams directing the flow of a river? The dams are strong; they make the river hold its course. But if you get enough water pushing at them in just the right direction — then blammo!"

"Blammo?"

"A dam can hold only so much water. It's a function of the strength of the dam and the force the water exerts against it. That force is a function of mass and velocity. But in our case the water is made up of all the individual drips who live in Detroit. Regular people like you and me, with normal amounts of willpower, amount to no more than a drop compared to people like Abe and Pen. So they can guide our expectations, keep us from manifesting anything that goes against the current. But if enough of us knew the truth, if enough of us knew that somewhere hidden within us was the power to weave the fabric of Detroit, and if we could use that power in concert, all pushing against the dams put up by the ancients, well, we'd bust the dams, jump the banks, and do whatever else it is that water does when you can't keep it all dammed up."

"Blammo," said Ian, dully.

"Blammo," said Vera.

"That's why Socrates came to the hospice. The dams will break if we don't stop Oan."

"But why Oan?" said Vera. "She's harmless!"

"No, she isn't," said Ian, gravely. "She could ruin everything!"

Vera made the puzzled and disapproving look of a child who's mistaken lard for ice cream. "You can't mean Oan."

"I do mean Oan!"

"Droopy lady, wears a lot of sweaters, smells like patchouli?"

"I know who Oan is," said Ian.

"I mean, I know she's a pain in the neck," said Vera, "and Rhinnick always thought she was an absolute terror — especially when they came within an inch of getting married—"

"Excuse me?" said Ian.

"Excuse me what?" said Vera, who seemed to be making a cardboard snowflake.

"Who got married?"

"Nobody!" said Vera. "Or rather, probably lots of people. But Rhinnick and Oan didn't. I mean, they almost did, which is what I suppose you're driving at. Anyway," she added, threading a piece of yarn through a needle she'd made of construction paper, "it's a long story and I won't bore you with it now, but Rhinnick got it into his head that Dr. Peericks loved Oan — he was totally wrong about that, of course, but that's what he thought. And he thought it might be a good idea to woo Oan on Peericks's behalf, and when he did he must have left the doctor's name out of it, because Oan left the conversation with the idea that Rhinnick was wooing her himself! One thing led to another and—"

"Rhinnick almost married Oan!" said Ian, amazed.

"He wriggled out of it in the end, like he always does. I've never seen him so relieved. Except perhaps if you count the time he thought he was marrying me."

"What?" said Ian.

"Never mind," said Vera, waving a dismissive pipe cleaner. "You were telling me about Oan."

"Right," said Ian. "She's still involved with the Church of O. The people who worship the Great Omega. A lot of them were in the cavern when—"

"—when your wife fought the City Solicitor, sure. Rhinnick told me about it."

"Well, it's made them understand that they were right all along — that the beforelife is real. That Detroit is the after-life — and that it's a sort of non-physical place made up of the thoughts and expectations of everybody who lives there. They've seen how it can be changed by acts of will: Penelope demolishing the landscape, the City Solicitor throwing planets at her, that sort of thing."

"Gosh," said Vera.

"And Oan's one of the Church's biggest boosters. She's probably doing her best to drum up members. The more the Church grows and spreads the word of what they saw in the cavern — sort of, I don't know, emboldening people with eyewitness accounts of all kinds of crazy apocalyptic magic that can be unleashed with willpower and whatnot—"

"I see your point! So how do we stop her?"

"I'm not sure," said Ian. "Socrates wants to wipe her."

"That'd do it."

"Of course it would do it. But we can't let him."

"I suppose not. It would make things easier, though."

"I want to persuade her to stop helping the Church."

"What, just be straight with her? That'd be nice, for a change. Just tell the other side what you want and why you want it, and cross your fingers they do what's right. Hand me a straw."

"We can't give Oan the whole truth, though," he said. "Just a version that she can swallow. Something that reinforces things she wants to believe."

"Like what?"

"What if I tell her that it's the Great Omega's will that she keep the beforelife secret? Like — I dunno — some sort of sacred truth that the Church isn't supposed to reveal? They can welcome people to worship the Great Omega if they like, but they can't reveal where she lives. That sort of thing."

"Sounds pretty flimsy."

"It's religion," said Ian, shrugging.

"And I don't see why she'll take your word for it."

"I'm the Intercessor!" said Ian, seeming more than a little pleased with himself.

"Abe's drawers! You are!" said Vera. "At least they think you are. Most of Rhinnick's troubles got started because the Church kept thinking of him as the Intercessor's right-hand man! It was pretty funny, actually — church officials bowing and scraping as if Rhinnick was something special. I mean he is, of course, but—"

"If they put that much faith in Rhinnick for being my room-mate—"

"—just imagine what they'd be willing to do for you!" said Vera, clapping her hands. "All right, it's a plan. We'll get you close to Oan, you drum up as much religious authority as you can muster, and tell her to cheese the proselytizing and put the lid on any truth about the beforelife being real."

"Right," said Ian.

"Right! If she can convince the Church to accept these new teachings, and get 'em to stop spreading the word about the beforelife—"

"The dams hold, the river stays its course, we never hit crit-ical mass, and Detroit is saved!"

"It still doesn't help us find Penelope," said Vera.

"How'd you know I was looking for Penelope?"

"Aren't you always?"

"She'll be okay," said Ian. "She always is. And I imagine she'll find me, sooner or later."

Vera looked down at the table and grabbed the edges of whatever she'd been making. She pulled on its northeast and northwest corners and then stood up, drawing it up from the table and giving the thing — whatever it was — a series of shakes, like someone trying to joggle the feathers out of a pillow. Her little assemblage seemed to be on the point of falling to pieces when assorted bits of it slipped their moorings and disentangled from their neighbours.

The entire thing *unfurled*. It unfurled into a sort of three-dimensional hanging cardboard-and-construction-paper tap-estry, or a vertically oriented diorama featuring tiny, lifelike figures made of craft-room tidbits, so realistically made that Ian could identify some of its principal subjects on sight. There were Socrates and Oan, Ian and Vera, and a mysterious-looking figure with a face that seemed familiar but also difficult to pin down. There were at least a dozen Napoleons. There was a figure of Rhinnick Feynman on a golf cart and an unmistakable Tonto dangling from a bit of string and spinning like a top as she made her way through a group of robe-wearing figures. They all had the look of highly detailed Christmas ornaments, dangling over some sort of battlefield or staging area formed of construction paper, yarn, and other hobby-room materials.

Ian squinted and took a second look. No Penelope.

"It's beautiful," said Ian. "But . . . what's it for?"

"I'm not sure," said Vera, who looked as puzzled as Ian felt. "I think it's important. But I don't think it *does* anything. I think I could tell."

"So why'd you make it?"

"No idea. I just cut and pasted and twisted and connected whatever came to mind, and this all just . . . happened."

"And you've no clue what it is?"

"I think," said Vera, cocking her head and squinting a bit while giving her hanging diorama a gentle shake, "it's a prediction. From television, I mean."

"You make predictions through construction paper now?"

"Why not?" said Vera. "Sometimes it's poetry, sometimes it's prose, why not wall art, dioramas, haikus, or interpretive dance? I don't make the rules. I just convey the predictions. And whatever this thing is, I think that's why I made it. It shows what's going to happen."

"When?" said Ian.

"There you have me," said Vera. "Sometime in the future, I suppose. But I have a feeling that it's not just what's going to happen. It's . . . well, I think it's what we have to *make* happen. It's the endgame. Our goal, I mean. I think we're looking at the plan. The plan to keep Detroit from falling apart. If we make this happen," she added, nodding toward the diorama, "everything keeps hanging together. If we don't, everything falls apart."

"Gosh," said Ian. "It's a shame we don't know what it means."

"I was thinking the same thing. But at least we know the players who need to be put together before everything comes to an end."

"So, we need to get Oan and me and you and Socrates and Rhinnick all together in one spot before everything gets sorted out?"

"It looks that way," said Vera.

"Well, that's more than we knew when I showed up," said Ian, keen to pick out silver linings.

The two of them stared at the diorama for several minutes, sometimes squinting as though it might resolve itself into a more instructive form, sometimes tilting their heads from side to side. They gave the overall impression of a pair of curious pigeons faced with a schematic of the Large Hadron Collider, or a couple of baffled primates inspecting a 3-D diorama that held secrets of the future — which is precisely what they were.

Ian left for his next appointment while Vera stuck around and put her "vision" away for safekeeping, a process that also involved tossing away those extra bits of materials she had used during its construction. If you happened to occupy the position of an omniscient narrator, it was at this point that you'd have noticed something troubling — something that might, if we've learned anything from Chekhov's gun, the pricking of thumbs, or little kids who tell Bruce Willis that they see ghosts, have given you pause to think "good gracious, that's going to matter down the road." And perhaps you'd do your best to shout at Vera and ensure that she noticed it, too, just in case her failure to do so threw a wrench into the midst of a future chapter.

The thing you noticed in your capacity as an omniscient narrator, the thing that Vera had missed entirely, was this: a small, built-to-scale cut-out of a character that was meant to be part of the "endgame diorama." A figure Vera had made subconsciously, and that she'd unconsciously dislodged from the edifice when she'd shaken it to allow it to take shape.

You couldn't blame her. The figure was tiny — maybe 1 or 2 per cent of the size of the other figures included in the work. It was fairly cute. And if the previously mentioned examples of foreshadowing are to be trusted, Vera's failure to notice its presence in her art was what you might have called "foreboding."

It was a tiny, perfectly rendered, three-dimensional cardboard hamster.

* * *

Night fell on Detroit Mercy, sustaining only minor contusions. Ian made his way to his room and quickly became aware of the feeling that you get when you're certain that you're alone but also sure that someone's watching. It feels like a breeze tickling your neck, or a whole platoon of spiders dancing a paso doble along your spine.

Ian tucked himself into bed.

The feeling persisted.

He put a pillow over his head.

The feeling persisted.

Ian sat up and opened his eyes. They adjusted to the dark.

He didn't believe them. He blinked twice, gave them a rub, and looked again.

What he said sounded a good deal like "Whattafuh?"

What he saw was Oan. She was about eight inches tall, shimmering with a pale blue light, and standing on his bedside table. But it was definitely Oan. A teensy Oan-shaped apparition.

For a moment Ian wondered if he'd been haunted by Oan's ghost, which seemed impracticable given its size and also the fact that they were already in the afterlife.

The tiny apparition spoke. What it said was this:

"Help me, Intercessor. You're my only hope!"

Chapter 8

"Just plain old paranoia, I imagine," said Joel, stamping his feet against the cold. "Not that I'm complaining."

"Tell me about it," said Leila, fiddling with her bandolier. "Lepton-primed tri-modal Gatling lasers, though? Auto-responsive shield-nets? Full sensor array?"

"Best kit I've ever had," said Joel. "I always knew Luther was way over-the-top about security, but I never thought I'd lay eyes on one of these babies," he added, caressing the tachyon burster hanging from his belt.

"Shame we won't get to use them," said Leila, accurately.

"Yup. Looks like another quiet night."

"Still. Nice to see this stuff up close."

"Did you hear that?" said Joel, suddenly giving the impression that distant branches of his family tree included hypervigilant rabbits.

"Hear what?" whispered Leila.

"A sort of whooshing sound," said Joel.

"Whooshing?"

"Yeah. Like a gust of wind through a tunnel."

"That'd be more of a whistle," opined Leila.

"Nah, this was a whoosh." Joel took a half step backward and lowered his targeting reticule into position.

"I didn't hear anything," said Leila. "Probably just your imagination."

"Could be," said Joel, scanning the horizon. "You can't blame me, though. This whole thing has me spooked."

Leila hoisted her rifle and trained her targeting sensors on a suspicious-looking hedge. "You're spooked by a few religious nuts having a meeting?"

"You're not a believer?" asked Joel.

Leila made one of those distinctive little "chuckle-snorts" that people sometimes make instead of going to all the trouble of working through the syllables of "preposterous." She followed this with "A princk? No way. You?"

"They're not just princks," said Joel, still staring into the middle distance while turning a dial on his targeting system. "It's more than that. They wanna go back."

"To the beforelife. I know. Luther hates the idea. But are you a believer?"

"What do you think?" said Joel.

"You don't seem like the type."

"I'll tell you what I think," said Joel, who dropped his gun to his side and raised his targeting reticule, apparently convinced that the coast was clear. "It doesn't matter whether the before-life's real or not. It's all beside the point. Gimme a good blaster at my side, a set of ablative armour, and a gig with full dental. That's religion enough for me."

"Still, you can't explain some of the stuff they've seen."

"Some of the stuff *they say* they've seen," corrected Joel, deftly bridging the gap between hearsay and heresy.

"There must be something to it," said Leila, leaning back against the wall and producing a pack of gum from a jacket pocket. "Or at least enough to rattle some cages. Luther said there've been disappearances."

"Luther says a lot of things."

"He said that the Tinker's missing. Gum?"

"Nah," said Joel, waving her off. "And the Tinker's gone missing before."

"I heard Luther say a whole chapter disappeared a couple of nights ago. Five or six members. Gone without a trace. You've got to admit that's weird."

"Probably off on some kinda pilgrimage. You know how obsessive these guys get."

"That's more than a dozen members in two weeks."

Joel tilted his head slightly and lifted his shoulders, making the disinterested little shrug that's common among people who yawn in the face of mysteries — the pragmatic sort of people who'd skip to the last page of whodunnits if they ever bothered to read.

"At least they pay well," said Leila, philosophically. "And we get to handle this gear. Still, I'm not sure why they think we need it."

"Why's not in our pay grade," said Joel. "They point, we go. They order, we execute."

"Buncha weirdos, if you ask me."

"Now Leila—"

There was a whoosh. This one wasn't confined to a guard's imagination, and it definitely wouldn't have been confused for a whistle or a gust of wind passing through a tunnel. It was more like the sound you get when someone darts from shadow to shadow with such grace and impossible speed that nearby molecules of air let out little objections as they try to get out of the way; or a barely detectable susurration of a funeral congregation whispering at the edge of earshot.

Speaking of earshot: Joel's was. He was shot, right through his ear — the one on the left side of his head, if that makes a difference — without any more warning than that which was supplied by the little funerary whoosh. The bullet's impact — if the projectile under advisement *was* a bullet — had made no sound other than the barely audible "thwapp" you hear when a bug connects with your windshield at high speed.

The effect was similar.

It probably sounded a good deal louder to Joel. Sadly, we'll never know. Several intersecting rivulets of blood combined in a fair approximation of the Nile River delta as they trickled down Joel's neck. Leila mightn't have noticed at all if Joel hadn't dropped to his knees, grinning a goofy sort of grin as reason abdicated her throne.

Any outside observer could tell this wasn't Leila's first rodeo. It wasn't a rodeo at all, come to think of it, but it also wasn't Leila's first stint as a highly paid, highly trained, and even highlier armed guardsperson. Her reflexes — which you probably wouldn't call catlike, as she didn't let them sleep upwards of twenty-two hours per day — pressed themselves into service automatically, more readily than any self-respecting cat could have responded to the whir of an electric can opener.

She dove headfirst to the sou'sou'west and connected with the ground in an acrobatic roll that would have made an Olympic champion proud, especially if they'd had the observational power to notice that Leila had activated at least three different switches on her gear before somersaulting back to her feet with a pair of laser rifles trained on the shadows behind Joel.

The high-pitched whine of the auto-responsive shield-net cut the silence of the night. Barely visible lines of iridescent light criss-crossed the ground around Leila's position, providing the only clue that something high-tech and unfriendly was bound to happen to any interlopers silly enough to approach.

Joel was gone. Not in a metaphorical way. Not even in a way that was like a simile. He just wasn't there. There was a dark scuff on the pavement where Joel had crumpled, but whether it had been made by Joel or someone else was the sort of question best left to a team of forensic investigators who weren't distracted by other concerns, such as the question of whether the person or persons responsible might still be somewhere in the shadows.

"Who—" Leila began.

Given the chance, she probably would have gone the whole route and said "who's there?" or something equally appropriate and clichéd, but she was unconscious before the instructions made the journey from brain to mouth.

Rest assured that Leila's going to be all right. But what she'll also be is saddened by the disappearance of several pieces of swanky gear. This included a small electronic pad containing orders, encrypted instructions, secret phrases, and every other bit of digital information a guard needs when standing post for a group of zealots whose highly touted paranoia, as so often happens, turned out to be thoroughly justified.

Socrates strolled through the lobby of Nakatomi Tower at precisely half past ten, waving appropriate pass cards and credentials as he proceeded to Mr. Luther's personal elevator bay — the one that held an assortment of lifts, including one ready to head straight to the penthouse while pointedly ignoring lesser floors for lesser residents on the way.

Socrates pressed the call button. The doors slid open. He stepped in. And then, thanks to various implants that were designed by Isaac Newton and installed before his mysterious disappearance, Socrates spoke in a voice that wasn't his.

"Luther, ninety-eight-august-thesis-dissent. Mark," intoned the assassin.

"Welcome home, Mr. Luther," said the elevator, cordially.

* * *

"Most excellent friends," intoned Martin, signalling everyone to take their seats. He was always doing that. *Intoning.* It wasn't enough to just *say* something. You didn't hear people reporting that Martin had "uttered," "observed," or "stated" something. It was always on the heavier end of the spectrum; always "intoned," "dictated," "testified," or "proclaimed." It was rumoured that there'd been at least one instance when, apparently struck by a fit of whimsy, he'd merely "pronounced."

Tonight, he wasn't whimsical at all. Not by a long shot. He'd assembled every member of what he'd come to call his "cabal": a handful of members of the Church of O who didn't like how Norm Stradamus ran things. Norm spent far too much time focusing on making his way back to the beforelife rather than changing things for the better, here in Detroit. The cabal thought the Church was ripe for change. It needed a good housecleaning. The cabal was comprised of rabble-rousers. Naysayers. The ones who felt the Church was an itch that was in desperate need of scratching. They were reformers who pictured themselves, perhaps not without some justification, as *visionaries*.

Martin had spent several years putting his little group together. Years searching for just the right sort of "great souls" — like-minded members of the Great Omega's flock; those who were faithful up to a point, but never blinded by belief; those who saw how various heresies had been woven into the doctrines of the Church; and those who had the force of personality required to put things right.

And now he'd called them to assemble once again, gathering 'round the gaudily carved table in Martin's penthouse, to discuss what was to be done about recent events.

"I don't see why we need a meeting," said Elizabeth.

"We could have dealt with this in a text," said Sid, fiddling with a handheld screen.

Martin ignored them both.

"Mo," he intoned, gravely.

"What?" said three men, all at once.

One of the downsides of Martin's cabal was the inclusion of three members who all went by the same name — three impressively credentialed and long-standing acolytes of the Church of O who referred to themselves as "three guys named Mo." They liked to sit together, which only made things worse. They always wore togas, saris, robes, or other garments drawn from the drapery end of the menswear spectrum as though they'd settled on these as a kind of "Team Mo" uniform. Martin was sure they did this just to get under his skin.

"Mohandas," sighed Martin, massaging his forehead — something he frequently found himself doing when confronted with multiple Moes. "Have all of the necessary precautions been taken? Are the guards in place? Are the doors secured? Have the alarms been activated, the sensors engaged, the cameras switched on?"

"I have seen to it myself!" said Mohandas.

"And you're sure the measures are adequate?"

"It would take an army to breach them, Elder Luther!" said the Mo of current interest, bowing his head. Had he bothered to read earlier portions of this chapter, or either of the present volume's highly regarded prequels, he would have known that you can't go around saying things like that without expecting Socrates to show up at any minute. But this particular Mo hadn't kept up with his reading, and so he said his piece with the air of confidence that makes Socrates' sudden appearance all the more satisfying for those observers who are safely out of harm's way.

"And has our guest been made aware of the need for secrecy?" intoned Martin. "He's been instructed that nothing heard in this room is for interlopers? Nothing is to be shared with heretics, the uninitiated, or knowlessmen?"

"He has, Elder Luther," replied a Mo.

"Then what are we waiting for?" said Sid. "Let's get this show on the road!"

"Well said," said Elizabeth. "No more delays. We've taken all the steps you asked, Martin, just as we always do. What happens here won't be known to the outside world; at least not until the time is right for our plans to be set in motion."

Martin gazed around the room like a field marshal assessing the troops. He respected every member of the cabal. He really did. Liz was a tad imperious; Siddhartha got a bit preachy about fad diets and exercises; and Mo, Mo, and Mo were a trifle trying, it was true; but every one of them came to the table with good ideas. So, when Mohandas had brought news of a strange, charismatic, hard-to-describe street preacher who'd been moving about Detroit and amassing followers by the dozens — a man Mohandas insisted shared the cabal's objectives — Martin had been more than a little intrigued. He'd tried to arrange a meeting right away.

The preacher wasn't available. But he did agree to send an envoy — one of a dozen or so close advisers who'd been charged with carrying word of the preacher's "movement" to every corner of Detroit. That envoy — one who claimed to be the preacher's right-hand man — was here, tonight.

"Show him in," intoned Martin.

Mohandas hitched up his robe or sari or sarong or whatever he called the bright, floral fabric presently swathed about his person and left the room. When he returned, he was followed by a pointy little olive-skinned man dressed in a black, belted cassock.

The first thing you'd probably notice about the new arrival — apart from the fact that he was pointy, little, olive-skinned and dressed in a black, belted cassock — was his gaze. It was the intense sort of penetrating stare that could shuck an oyster at fifty paces. It tracked around the assembled faces before settling on Martin, who rose from his seat and gestured toward an empty chair.

"Welcome to my home, Mr. Yavelli," intoned Martin.

"Mack, please," said the guest, taking a seat.

"I'm given to understand that you've come to propose an alliance."

"I have," said Mack, steepling his hands in front of his face.

"Well spit it out, man!" said Sid, a little testily. "Give us the goods. We've heard of this new prophet of yours and his plans to improve the Church and—"

"He's no prophet," said Mack, his eyes narrowing. "Not in the strictest sense. He doesn't hide behind vague forecasts or predictions, scrying the landscape of the future and searching the mists for signs of change; he brings about the change himself. He does not merely look to the future; he forges it, with our help."

"I'm sure that's all very important," said Elizabeth, "but what we want to know is if this change-bringer person of yours is willing to work with us. To work with those who feel the Church has to refocus its efforts on—"

"He is," said Mack. "Rest assured, he will reunite the factions — bring together all of the splinter groups that have formed from the greater whole of the Church of O. Those who wish to return to the beforelife? My liege will speed their passage. Those who wish to improve the here and now, to bring about the paradise that Detroit is meant to be? He is the answer to their prayers. His objectives match your own. His greatest hope, his singular promise to the people of Detroit? To make Detroit great again."

"When was Detroit ever great?" asked one of the Moes.

"Are you all right?" asked Sid.

The others seated around the table exchanged a series of puzzled glances.

"Are you all right, Mo?" Sid repeated. "Your voice is strange. Muffled." And you had to hand it to Sid for being observant. As annoying as he might be when chatting about the latest vegan recipes or the newest stretching regime, he was always keenly mindful of his surroundings.

"It's just a cold," said the strangely muffled Mo, waving him off.

"Ask yourself this," said Mack, ignoring the interruption, "what is Detroit's most pressing problem? What is it that keeps our world from achieving true greatness?"

Several members of the cabal spoke at once, making it hard to tell who blamed the ills of Detroit on social media, who suggested that most problems were caused by politicians, and who listed a confluence of factors ranging from gluten to standardized spelling. Mack ignored them and carried on.

"It's *the lie*," he said, in a low, serpentine voice. "The lie perpetrated by Abe the First, and others like him. The lie that we are limited by that which we observe."

This caught the cabal's attention, and a mumble of agreement made its way around the room. Only a few of those assembled — Liz, Martin, and one of the Moes — had been present when the City Solicitor had struggled against the anomaly in the Church's sacred grotto, but they'd told the others everything they'd seen. Everything about the two combatants punching holes in the walls of reality — messing about with the background whatever-you-call-it that made up the raw materials forming space and time and mass and thought and energy — they knew that somehow, in some way, what had happened in the grotto signified some-thing. Something about the rules that held the world in place, and the fact that it was possible to break them — to go well offside the boundaries of reality without receiving a penalty, and to break the laws of physics without even having to pay a fine.

"But what can we do about the lie?" pressed Sid.

"Can you think of nothing?" asked Yavelli.

"We could try frogs," ventured the middle Mo. "A plague of frogs? Nothing beats a plague of frogs."

Mohandas pinched the bridge of his nose. "That's your answer to everything."

"It's worth trying, s'all I'm sayin'," said Mo. "It doesn't have to be frogs, though. Could be locusts. Probably easier to get. Less slimy too. I'm just sayin' it's worth a go."

"And why not elephants?" sneered Sid.

"Logistical problems," mused Mo. "Hard to get 'em all in one place."

"Thank you, Moses," sighed Martin, making a placating gesture, "but perhaps we might return to the matter at hand?"

"Just an idea," mumbled Moses.

"You were saying?" said Liz, nodding Mackward.

"The only way to defeat a lie," said Yavelli, somehow managing to hiss his way through words that didn't have esses, "is through the power of greater truths!"

This generated a general mutter of approval, as slogans do.

"And the first truth we wield," said Mack, "is that Abe is not, as he would have you believe, the first-born of Detroit."

The mutters suddenly switched gears and became gasps.

"But — I mean — he *is* the first-born of Detroit," suggested Moses. "The clue's right in his title. Abe the First."

"Who is to say he was the first?" asked Mack.

"Well, Abe, I guess," said Sid. "And whoever showed up next. I mean, he would have shown up right after Abe and seen that no one else was around, right? And he'd say something like 'oh, I guess you were first,' and then the idea just sort of caught on. But everyone knows it. It's just how it is."

"Abe is nothing more than an immigrant," sneered Mack.

There was another exchange of puzzled glances — the sort you'd see if someone suggested socks should be made of cheese, or that Gregorian chants had too much cowbell, or that a subject-matter expert could be outvoted by a pair of dunces who did their "research" online.

"But surely, Mr. Yavelli," began Liz, "all are immigrants in Detroit. This is a truth known to the Church. We are born in the beforelife. We migrate here on death."

"That's right!" said one of the Moes. "We all remember!"

"*Most* of us do," corrected Liz. "But not Sid, the poor dear. He isn't a princk, you see."

"I am!" objected Sid. "I remember the beforelife, same as you!"

"No you don't. But there's no shame in that—"

"I remember plenty of things!"

"Name three."

"My friends," intoned Martin, "it is a well-established doctrine that one needn't be a princk to join our cabal, nor to join the Church of O at large — one need only accept the truth of the beforelife, whether or not one can recall it."

"As I was saying," said Yavelli, coming to realize that steering a conversation with the cabal was a bit like riding a ginned-up bull, "there's nothing special about Abe."

Two of the Moes gasped out loud. Liz clutched her pearls. Martin raised his left eyebrow half an inch — the farthest he ever went in the way of showing emotion.

"He's an immigrant," said Yavelli, not hiding his disdain. "No different from any other specimen drawn from Detroit's unwashed masses — the common rabble and detritus of our great city. Indeed, Abe is far worse, for he sets himself above his fellows. But the master I serve — the one who has come to free us from the lie — has promised a winnowing, separating wheat from chaff. He will remove the blindfolds of Detroit's misguided masses, cull the herd of those who blindly follow Abe's illegitimate rule. He is the one who should truly lead us. For unlike Abe, he is entirely *of* Detroit. He is Detroit's only true, native son, one never touched or tainted by the soul-staining curse of human mortality."

Every member of the cabal leaned forward at this juncture, indicating rapt attention — but whether this was because they were drawn in by Yavelli's message or because they couldn't believe the extent to which their guest was fully out to lunch, no one could say. He'd certainly grabbed their attention. The faces made by every member of the cabal could be plotted along a spectrum featuring points corresponding to words like "taken aback," "gobsmacked," and "flabbergasted."

Or rather, those words described the reaction of every cabalist save one. It was one of the guys named Mo. Not Mohandas, who'd invited the guest in the first place and whose gaster was thoroughly flabbered. And not Moses, who was merely taken aback, possibly because his mind was still lingering wistfully on the plague of frogs. The Mo who failed to seem the least bit astonished was the strangely muffled Mo who apparently had a cold. The one who'd been unusually quiet tonight. The one who loved the heat, refused booze, and never, ever showed up for group photos. It was, perhaps, this Mo's penchant for staying out of the spotlight that led his fellows to miss a number of recent changes to his appearance — say, the unusual lumps beneath his garment, suggesting an arsenal of items hidden from view; or that his beard wasn't quite as long as usual; or that his head was shaped like a pumpkin; or that his posture was unusually suggestive of a cleverly disguised assassin ready to pounce.

He was presently perched on the edge of his chair and raising his index finger politely.

"A point of order," he said.

"What is it?" demanded Martin, suddenly yanked from his gobsmacked state.

"It's just, our guest is making a lot of grand claims," said the mysterious Mo. "Claims about this leader he wants to rule us. He's asking us to forge an alliance with a man we haven't met. Someone who can't even bring himself to meet with us in person."

"He has sent me in his stead," said Yavelli. "One of his chief confidants and advisors, among the most fervent of those who've been called to serve the master in recent days. I am ordained to speak in his name—"

"You haven't told us his name," said Mo, placing his hands on the table and leaning in.

"Ah," said Mack Yavelli, rising. "Then perhaps the time has come; there are no secrets among friends. Our master's name is the name that we call ourselves; our organization. The name adopted by his disciples. All of those who've heard his calling; those who share his path. We call ourselves—"

* * *

"Evangelists?" said Vera. "As in, *followers of Evan?*"

Ian and Vera were sitting cross-legged in a little pillow-and-linen fort that they'd erected on Ian's bed. They were hiding under a sheet and illuminating their faces with a flashlight, campfire story–style. The rest of Ian's room, and most of the hospice, was cloaked in darkness.

"That's right!" said Ian. "Evangelists! Oan's little hologram said that some mysterious prophet and his gang of followers were joining up with the Church, and that the prophet's name is Evan."

"I'm sure there are loads of guys named Evan."

"It's too strange to be a coincidence," said Ian.

"Have you been paying attention? Detroit is practically one big, strange coincidence."

"I know. But I'm sure it's him."

"How can you be?" said Vera. "You said your son was a little boy."

Ian chewed his lower lip. "That's where things get messy," he whispered. "He might be older now."

"Like a week older," said Vera, who was good with figures.

"No. He changed his age. Right before his fifth birthday he decided to be eleven. And then he was."

"Oh. Well, that's a difficulty," said Vera. "And now you think he's a grown-up."

"Oh, god," said Ian, palming his forehead — an act that temporarily messed up the bed-linen fort and sent the flashlight tumbling to the mattress.

"What now?" said Vera.

Ian rearranged the fort and put the flashlight back in position. "It's just . . . he really wanted to be a grown-up. Pen and I were always telling Evan that some things would have to wait until he was older. Things like leaving the Patch, riding a motorbike, visiting City Hall—"

"So this whole thing is the fallout of bad parenting," said Vera, diplomatically.

"That's not fair!" Ian protested.

"I didn't say it was fair. I'm just glad I didn't have parents. At least none that I can remember."

"The point," said Ian, steering the conversation toward less turbulent waters, "is that I think Evan decided to be an adult, and now he's running around Detroit and causing trouble. Oan says he's gathering followers. Loads of 'em. Mostly men, she says. Disaffected, loner types who aren't happy with Detroit but don't think they can make a difference. That's how she described them."

"Why would they follow a kid?"

"They don't know that he's a kid."

"Yeah, but he is one," said Vera. "On the inside."

"Maybe not," said Ian. "I mean, when he decided to be eleven, Pen and I could remember birthday parties. He sort of . . . I dunno . . . shifted reality, somehow, using Penelope's powers, so that he'd actually lived eleven years. Or at least he'd inserted them into his past. I'm not sure how it works. He kind of messed with his own history."

Vera looked at Ian with the mildly perplexed but open-minded face of a mathematical genius who's perfectly comfortable with imaginary numbers, but not quite sold on the notion of using them to count up anniversaries.

Ian took about five minutes to explain Evan's knack of stealing his mother's powers, of making changes in Detroit that were somehow, but not quite entirely, similar to the changes Abe and Pen could make. Once he'd finished bringing Vera up to speed with the reading public, he added, "From what Oan said, he seems to have an adult appearance now. And it sounds like he isn't behaving like a kid, either. Maybe he's . . . I don't know . . . inserted grown-up memories? Do you think that's possible?"

"Who knows?" said Vera. "But maybe none of a grown-up's real experience. And all of the emotional range and self-control of a five-year-old kid."

Ian rearranged the fort so he could sit with a pillow tucked up under his chin — an act that any of the professionals in the hospice might have written off as a symbolic-but-largely-impotent form of self-soothing behaviour, psychologists and psychiatrists being strangely uninformed when it comes to the widely known protective power of pillows.

"So what does Oan want?" asked Vera.

"She said she's been working with the Church, recruiting princks from the hospice. She's been finding likely candidates in the sharing room and then sending them to her contacts in the Church. Like some kind of underground-railroad operation."

"Makes sense," said Vera. "The hospice is full of princks. But why does the Church want 'em?"

"Building up their numbers, I guess," said Ian. "More people who believe in the beforelife. More people who'll be open to believing what the Church learned in the grotto."

"Critical mass," said Vera.

"That's right!" said Ian. "But Oan says the Church has started focusing all of its efforts on building a bridge to the beforelife. The Church leaders seem to think that they can do it if they have enough believers."

"So what does she need from you?"

"It's Evan," said Ian. "Oan didn't know it, but the last few groups of princks she shipped to the Church ended up in Evan's gang. She said he converted one of her contacts, and that contact started redirecting most of the new recruits to Evan's people. Now they've started following Evan. The Church leaders freaked out and now they've locked Oan away in some place she called 'the Regent's chateau.'"

"Oh, crap," said Vera, who probably would have smacked her forehead if the pillow fort had afforded her the scope to make the gesture.

"What?"

"The Regent. She's a really powerful princk — not like Abe or Penelope powerful, but really strong. She was the one behind the torture of the Napoleons."

"The what?!" said Ian, a good deal louder than he'd intended.

"Long story," said Vera, "but I wouldn't want to be on the Regent's shit list. And I wouldn't want to be Oan right now, either. What are you going to do?"

"She wants me to throw my weight around as Intercessor. Bring Evan's converts back to the Church and show them the truth of the Great Omega, that sort of thing. The Regent and Norm are worried about Evan's message."

"What message?"

Ian shifted around uncomfortably. "I . . . well I don't know where he got these kinds of ideas," he began.

"What ideas?"

"Hateful things. Stuff about immigrants, for starters."

"Immigrants?" said Vera.

"Yeah. People from the beforelife."

"That's crazy," said Vera. "We're all people from the beforelife."

"Evan isn't," said Ian. "He was born here. Pen and I told him that he's special. That he's the first native Detroitian. There's no one else like him."

"Abe's drawers, Ian, it's like you were *trying* to screw the kid up."

"Parenting's hard!"

"But why would people follow a guy who hates immigrants? I mean, the followers know they're immigrants, too, right? Everyone in Detroit's an immigrant."

"Not me," said a gravelly voice beyond the sheet, causing Ian and Vera to establish joint world records in the seated high-jump, which also had the effect of causing pillows and bed linens to cascade around the room. Ian dropped the flashlight, too, which landed in such a way that it illuminated a pumpkin-shaped face that was now grinning at Ian and Vera.

"Abe's drawers!" cried Vera.

"S-Socrates!" cried Ian.

"At your service," said the assassin, switching on a bedside lamp as though he wasn't the least bit worried about being

caught roaming the hospice after visiting hours were over —
which, to be fair, he probably wasn't.

"And who do we have here?" he added, smiling at Vera.

Vera crossed her arms and arched an eyebrow at the assassin.
"What do you mean by that?" she said.

"I mean *who are you*," said the assassin. "Who might you
be? What do you call yourself?"

"Those are all different questions," said Vera, peevishly. "I
mean, *who I am* is a philosophical question, right? *Who might
I be* is probabilistic. *What do I call myself* depends on a lot of
things; for example, right now I'd call myself a little pissed off."

"What's your name, girl?" asked Socrates, testily.

"That's better!" said Vera. "Precision empowers! You should
always ask for the information you want. And 'Vera Lantz' is the
answer. My name, I mean. You're going to have to express yourself more clearly if you're going to go around pestering people
with stupid questions."

The assassin stood there tapping his foot at the medium,
who blinked back at him and smiled. Ian leaned on his headboard and settled back to enjoy the show.

"And do you know who I am?" asked Socrates.

"Of course I do, ass," said Vera. "We've met before, and
it wasn't a meeting I'd care to repeat. You invaded my shop,
scared off my friends, and wiped my memory with that horrible
serum of yours. I suppose you're back to finish the job?"

"I shouldn't have to finish the job," said the assassin, clearly
intrigued. "I watched my serum take effect. I watched your memories slipping away. You lost your mind as the serum overtook
you. And I would have stayed longer but for the fact that you —"

"Blew up my shop."

"You blew up your shop with a Class-Twelve explosive
device that also wiped out about three city blocks," said the
assassin. "You blew your own neighbours to bits."

"They'll get better," said Vera, coolly.

"But *you* shouldn't have," said Socrates. "Recovered your memory, I mean. That's what I'm driving at."

"Television," said Vera.

Socrates took perhaps four seconds to process what this meant. "So . . . your powers are still intact," he said. "You're still a medium?"

"A petite, thanks very much."

The assassin stared blankly.

"It's the best joke wee mediums have," she said, smiling around the room to see if anyone had noticed the extra *e*.

"So psychic powers gave you a path to retrieve your memory," Socrates mused, showing that, whatever his faults, he was swifter on the uptake than most people in Detroit. "A useful power," he added. "It's quite a troupe we've assembled here. I come with my own set of skills, Ian has insights into other people's pasts, Vera can see the future—"

"I'm sure that's all very interesting to you," said Vera, "But what I want to know is what you're doing here now, and what that . . . that *thing* is on your thigh?" she added, wincing.

Socrates looked down at his leg — the one that featured an unexpected glob of wet, pinkish goo.

"ISAAC system, initiate scan," said the assassin, which he followed a moment later with "Ah, it's a bit of Gandhi. He was scrappier than you'd expect."

Ian opened and closed his mouth like a beached trout before managing to whisper the word "Gandhi," followed by an exclamation point and a pair of question marks.

"Mohandas Gandhi," said Socrates. "One of those zealots from the Church of O. I infiltrated a secret meeting at Martin Luther's place and—"

"Martin Luther King!" exclaimed Ian.

"No, nobody named King," corrected Socrates, "First name Martin, last name Luther. A little religious twerp. Portly chap. I wiped him," he added, breezily, "him and the rest of his little cabal. Not that I had much choice. I mean, I suppose I could have let Moses off with a warning, but—"

Ian gripped a handful of bedding and wrung it for all that he was worth. "You . . . you *mindwiped* Martin Luther, Gandhi, and Moses, all in one night—"

"Some fellow named Sid, too — travels under the name 'Buddha.' Plus there was Liz, and also—"

"Jesus!" cried Ian.

"Could be," said the assassin, "I didn't catch all the names."

A world of increasingly worrisome possibilities blossomed in Ian's brain.

"I did let Mack Yavelli go," said the assassin, shrugging his shoulders in a conciliatory way.

It was at this point that Ian actually smote his own brow — something you don't often see outside the script of old-time musical comedies.

"Mack was useful," explained the assassin. "I put a tracker in him. He has no idea, of course. But he works for some religious leader named Evan, and I thought I'd trace—"

"Evan?" cried Ian, who seemed to have stopped worrying about being overheard.

"That struck me as odd, too," said Socrates, "this prophet having the same name as your son."

"He *is* Ian's son," explained Vera, "He's set himself up as a cult leader. He's messing around with the Church of O."

"He's doing a lot more than that," said Socrates. "He's trying to unseat Abe. But at least you've solved one mystery."

"One mystery?" said Vera.

"The time-dilation field."

"The whatnow?" said Ian.

"Time-dilation field. Time flows strangely around Evan. It's changing his rate of aging, altering how he perceives time, even the pace of events unfolding around him. That could explain how he's done so much in the space of only a couple of weeks. My sensors picked up the field when I first saw him."

"You've seen Evan?" cried Ian.

"Sure. At the university. I didn't know it was him. I was tracking more church members and found Evan recruiting followers of his own. Strange guy. I can't really describe him. Even ISAAC's imaging processors couldn't hold a stable image. And he has some of the City Solicitor's power. Or some of his mother's power, I suppose, now that I realize who he is."

Ian sat in his bed, quietly staving off madness while Socrates and Vera descended into a two-person symposium on the technical ins and outs of time dilation. Ian emerged when Vera poked him in the ribs and asked a question.

"I asked you what happens next," she said.

"Me?" said Ian. "You're the medium."

"And you're the Intercessor who speaks for the Great Omega. At least the Church says you are. Oan must think you'd be able to help or she wouldn't have—"

"Oan!" exclaimed Ian, smiting his brow a second time. He turned on his heel, opened the drawer of his bedside table, and fished around for the little holographic projector he'd found earlier.

"This is how Oan sent her message," he said, handing the small metallic circle over to Vera. It was covered in a thin web of interconnecting filaments that glowed with a pale blue light.

"Oh, wow!" said Vera, who had knack with anything that your average layperson might describe as a high-tech thingummy. She turned it over in her hands. "This isn't just a holographic projector. It's a personal IP—"

Before she could say the letter *t*, completing her diagnosis that this was, in fact, an Instantaneous Personal Transport device, Vera was interrupted by the device itself. It throbbed loudly and emitted a pulse of light that enveloped Vera and Ian. In less than half a tick of the clock, they were elsewhere.

One of the many noteworthy things about Socrates is that he's fast. Like, really fast. Picture a fast thing that you know about, and he's probably faster than that. Take a cheetah, for example. There's no contest. Socrates could take down a gazelle before the cheetah knew it was hungry. A hummingbird? Socrates wins hands down. Socrates could beat a roomful of victims faster than any hummingbird could beat its wings. Perhaps a ray of light in a vacuum? Now we're talking. But even in the face of Professor Einstein's theory of special relativity, Socrates' speed was relatively special. And thus it was that, when the IPT in Vera's hands started to throb — when it shed the aura of light that enveloped Vera and Ian in less than half a tick of the clock — Socrates acted.

What he did was dive. Straight at Ian. It was a full Socratic tackle, something experienced by few people in Detroit, and only a few others in the beforelife, where Socrates 1.0 was known for getting a bit physical when debates didn't go his way.

The growing globe of light had initially enveloped just two targets, as intended by its creator. It now enveloped a third — the assassin — and teleported him right along with Ian and Vera.

The other thing about Socrates is that he doesn't like surprises, and he has an on-board teleportation system of his own. Having diagnosed the purpose of the teleportation trap almost as quickly as Vera, Socrates activated his own on-board IPT in the nanosecond between the time that he tackled Ian and the moment that Oan's teleportation trap had rematerialized them elsewhere.

Vera, Ian, and Socrates shimmered into view at their destination. Ian and Socrates shimmered away, to somewhere else, less than a microsecond later, leaving Vera alone wherever the IPT trap had taken her.

Time has a funny way of bending, stretching, expanding, and contracting when you find yourself disassembling in one spot and reappearing in another. And in the microsecond before Ian and Socrates redirected themselves away from wherever it was the teleport-trap had tried to take them, they both managed to catch a glimpse or two of the place where they'd left Vera.

"What the hell?" said Ian, squinting and rubbing his temples.

"Gah!" exclaimed Socrates, extracting himself from Ian and clawing at the side of his own head.

"What's wrong?" said Ian, rising. The answer came in the form of a small shower of sparks bursting from the assassin's ear. They left little scorch marks on his earlobe and singed his hair.

"What the hell!" Ian shouted, again.

"Fzzbzz-tk-whaoh-bzzz-Uuungk!" cried the assassin, or words to that effect. He slumped to his knees and clutched his head with both hands as sparks continued sputtering from his ear.

"It's . . . it's the implants," he managed, at length. "Something . . . something went wrong in the transport!"

It was at this point that the assassin collapsed entirely and writhed around on the floor, doing a passable impression of a severed live wire carrying several million volts.

Ian wasn't entirely sure how to respond. You can understand the dilemma. On the one hand, Ian was faced with a fellow human in pain. On the other hand, the human in question was Socrates, and Ian supposed that Socrates might deserve it.

Ian watched the writhing assassin for the space of several heartbeats — punctuated by buzzes and sparks shooting from the assassin's ear — until the assassin, whose recuperative powers were almost as legendary as the Socratic Method, finally struggled to his knees and caught his breath.

"Are you . . . all right?" ventured Ian.

"I will be," said the assassin, grimly. "It's the implants."

"Yeah, you said," said Ian.

"Something's shorting them out."

"Too bad," said Ian.

"And Isaac's not around to repair them."

"That's a shame," said Ian, showing genuine interest. "I'll bet Vera could do it."

Socrates looked up at Ian with a look that registered equal parts exasperation and contempt.

"Did you see what I saw, Brown?" said Socrates, unsteadily rising to his feet and adjusting his bandolier.

"Did I see what?"

"Where we transported. Into a room full of people. All standing in a circle. Presumably waiting for you and Vera to teleport into their midst."

"We were teleported?" said Ian.

"You don't understand anything, do you?" said the assassin, pausing to deal with a final sputter of sparks from his left ear. Once they stopped, he spent about twenty seconds bringing Ian up to speed on the ins and outs of teleportation.

"So who were they?" said Ian. "And where did they take us?"

"I've no idea where they were," said the assassin, massaging his temple. "The ISAAC system failed. It didn't record the destination. The whole sensory array has gone haywire; self-repair protocols won't engage. But wherever we were," he continued, wincing, "it was the Church that brought us there."

"That'd explain all of the robes," said Ian.

"I recognized Norm Stradamus in the circle," said Socrates. "Oan was there too."

"And Cleopatra!" said Ian, remembering. "At least, I think it was Cleopatra. Some Egyptian-looking lady draped in gold. She had a dog. One of those jackal-looking types."

"Sounds like the Regent," said the assassin. "And did you see who was standing next to her?"

"No."

Socrates paced around the room. If you were to look at him at this moment and draw a comparison with a caged tiger, your analogy teacher would probably give you a gold star.

"Things just got complicated," he said.

"What do you mean?"

"Tell me, Brown," said the assassin, turning to Ian and gripping him by his shoulders, "why in Abe's name would Tonto be working with the Church of O?"

Chapter 9

"The matrix won't hold him! He's too strong!"

"What's she saying?"

"Search me. He just disappeared!"

"Don't let her go!"

"Where's the hamster?"

"Grab hold of her!"

"We're heading across the river!"

"Hold her in place!"

"Who's Karen Zobol?"

Don't be embarrassed if you're confused. Those in attendance were too. Oan, for example, hadn't a clue what Vera had meant by "the matrix won't hold him," nor did the Regent have any notion of why Vera might want a hamster. All they knew was that Vera was charging around the room, shouting italicized bits of dialogue and rebounding off the keeners in the front row of the mob of white-robed acolytes surrounding her.

One thing Vera had shouted — the phrase "we're heading across the river" — really grabbed the mob's attention. It landed especially hard on Norm Stradamus, who shoulder-checked his way to the front of the circle surrounding Vera, shouted for silence, and made a series of shushing gestures at the crowd.

"She's prophesying!" he cried, gesticulating wildly in an attempt to calm the mob. "Hold her in place!"

A gaggle of sturdy acolytes clad in XXL robes grabbed hold of Vera and wrestled her into a more or less stationary position, pinning her arms to her sides and holding her in an uncomfort-able group hug. The resulting tableau looked like a gaggle of spa patrons re-enacting Iwo Jima with Vera standing in as the flag, or a collection of berobed Twister players surprised when caught in the act.

The acolytes blinked at Norm in unison. Vera stared directly at him, or perhaps directly through him, showing no signs of concern. The surrounding mob carried on whooping it up with all the enthusiasm you'd expect from a gang that had captured a valuable medium and small appliance repair person.

Norm stepped forward, as wary as a bomb defuser during his first day on the job, adopting a posture you might describe as a full-body cringe. He wrung his hands, came within arm's reach of Vera, and stared into the medium's eyes.

He hadn't foreseen what happened next. The medium shouted "Don't call me child!" at the top of her lungs about three-quarters of a second before the words "Be calm, child," made their way across Norm's lips. He made an undignified little "yip" and jumped about three centimetres straight up, which is a quite a leap for a man who's almost entirely com-prised of gristle and beard.

"Leave him alone!" shouted Vera, though who she meant and why she wanted him left alone had to be shelved as unsolved mysteries.

It was at this point in the proceedings that the crowd parted like that famous sea you've probably read about, allowing the Regent to emerge front and centre with her pharaoh hound, Memphis, trotting along behind. A couple of stately steps brought her alongside Norm.

"How do you know?" she asked. She'd spoken in barely more than a whisper, but such was the magic of her personality that she brought the flock to silence.

"How — how do I know?" asked Norm, bowing slightly.

"You said the girl was prophesying."

"Ah," said Norm, smoothing his robes. "Well . . . uh . . . Madame Regent, Your Grace," he stammered, toadying like nobody's business, "I do recognize the symptoms. Of prophecy, that is. I am the Church's first prelate. Its chief prophet, after all. My power of foresight is well known. And I've seen this woman prophesy before. We know the signs. Witness the vacancy of her eyes," he added, gesturing toward the medium's face. "The frenzied manner with which she ran headlong into our adherents."

"She was trying to escape," said the Regent, flatly, "her mind unhinged by fear."

"No, no, Your Grace!" said Norm. "I sense no fear in her! She answers questions not yet asked! She's picking up threads of conversations from another time and place. She spoke of the river!"

"We're heading across the river!" cried Vera, her face suddenly shining with exultation.

"That's it!" said Norm, placing his hands on Vera's shoulders. "Steel yourself, Ms. Lantz! You're speaking in riddles. Focus your efforts. Set your mind upon the river!"

"If you believe it, you will receive it!" cried Oan from somewhere deep in the mob, apparently feeling that a dose of sharing room philosophy was just what the doctor ordered.

"I won't help you!" Vera announced to no one in particular.

"You see!" cried Norm, "she understands that we need her help!"

"This would have been obvious," said the Regent, waving a hand dismissively. "We clearly went to great pains to acquire Ms. Lantz. And the Intercessor too. But why has he vanished? Where's Ian Brown?"

"Search me. He just disappeared!" said Vera, staring off into space.

That particular slice of text might seem familiar. That's almost certainly because, only a few short pages ago, three lines down from the heading of Chapter 9, the same words were typed out in italics, indicating that Vera had shouted them while charging around the room and rebounding off the mob. The words struck Norm as familiar, too.

"You see!" he cried, excitedly, "she repeats an earlier answer! She answered Your Grace's query about the Intercessor before it had been asked. Her mind is racing through time. She is accessing television!"

There was a collective *ooh*, followed by a slightly louder collective *ahh*.

"Vera!" said Norm, his voice husky with emotion, "you *must* help us. You must help us cross the river. You said we're heading across it! You must tell us what you've seen!"

Vera closed her eyes in apparent concentration. "I don't know how," she said. "I . . . I can't see how they're supposed to work. I . . . I . . ."

"How what are supposed to work?" demanded Norm, now shaking Vera by her shoulders.

Vera gasped like a pearl diver finally coming up for air. She opened her eyes and shook her head in a way that seemed to dislodge whatever cobwebs had been draped across her mind. Her eyes cleared. She drew in another deep breath and appeared to absorb her surroundings.

It's hard to know how to react to a flock of people dressed in robes. They might be nothing more worrisome than an academic procession or a roaming gang of lawyers looking for victims of personal injuries. They could be a crowd of hospice patients or a collection of people waiting for a massage. On the somewhat more dangerous end of the spectrum is the mob of religious devotees — but here again, these things are graded on a curve. In Detroit, where no one had ever felt the fear of death and there had never been a whiff of racism — people of all shapes and sizes and hues having come from the same River — a crowd of white-robed religious fanatics was a million times less frightening than it could be in other places.

Vera's reaction to this particular gang revealed a certain amount of pique. She struggled against the hands that gripped her and unleashed an array of imaginative curses that telegraphed an impressive command of Detroit's obscene vernacular.

"Let her go!" cried Norm. "She has rejoined us in the present!"

Grips loosened and hands retreated into billowing white sleeves as Vera swatted them away.

"Why am I here?" Vera demanded.

"You can help us!" said Norm.

"Help you how?"

"You can help us cross the river! You spoke of it in your visions!"

"Fat chance!" said Vera, registering defiance. "You can't go around kidnapping helpless mediums and then expect them to lend you a hand!"

"But I've foreseen it!" protested Norm.

"That's right!" said Oan, emerging from the crowd like a rabbit popping out of a hedge. "The prophet's quatrains make this clear!"

"They herald your coming!" said Norm. "They foretell of a day when you will guide our Church's passage to the beforelife."

"You're making that up," said Vera.

This appeared to shake Norm to his core.

"I'd never!" he protested. "That's sacrilege! That's highly unethical! You are a seer, too, Ms. Lantz. Surely you know that it's the highest form of heresy to misstate the contents of prophesy!"

"I suppose so," said Vera, who didn't. But then because she was never one to let opportunity's knocks go unheeded, she took a stab at improvisation.

"Since we're all being truthful and sharing prophecies," she said, "I suppose I should tell you what I've seen."

"You've had a vision!" said Norm, as the crowd leaned in.

"I have," said Vera. "It's about you. And the Church. And all of you trying to cross the river."

There was a collective intake of breath.

"That's right!" said Vera, gaining steam. "It showed me that none of you will ever see the beforelife unless you let me go."

"Ms. Lantz!" said Norm, aghast.

"What?"

"Shame on you!"

"I'm serious!" protested Vera. "There was a verse in there about kidnapping me! You know that my visions sometimes come in poems, right? Well this one went 'There once was a prophet named Norm, whose prophecies weren't even warm—'"

"I must insist that you put an end to this charade!" said Norm.

"There was a haiku too!" Vera continued, shouting over Norm's protests and counting out syllables on her fingers:

Norm Stradamus. Ass.

He thinks he sees the future.

Let Vera go. Dick.

This drew an assortment of giggles from the crowd. The Regent snorted and covered her mouth with her hands.

"Cease this folly!" cried Norm. "This shameful display is most unseemly, and I—"

"I'm just getting started!" cried Vera. "Just wait'll you hear my prophetic rap!"

Adopting her best b-boy pose, Vera managed to get through about three bars of beatboxing and appeared to be on the point of spitting some rhymes when she took the unusual step of rolling her eyes all the way backward, craning her neck to stare directly at the ceiling, and reciting a free verse in a voice that you would probably call "sepulchral" if you hail from a world that features nods to human mortality. It went like this:

In his house at R'lyeh, the first one, dreaming, lies. Surrounded by all and none; both real and not; removed from those who traverse the river. Charon's Obol must be paid . . .

"Who's Karen Zobol?" asked Oan, with genuine interest. The interruption drew an immediate "shush" from Norm, but not before the question had snapped Vera out of her trance.

She awoke to the mob crowding around her and staring into her eyes.

"Umm, uh, what just happened?" said Vera.

"Television!" cried Norm, as the crowd issued another set of synchronized oohs and ahhs.

"Oh," said Vera, flatly. "Anything good? Like maybe a sign that you ought to let me go home?"

"You don't remember what you saw? What you said?" pressed the Regent.

"It happens that way, sometimes," said Vera, shrugging. "I don't make the rules. So what did I say?"

"You spoke of the river!" said Norm.

"And Karen Zobol!" said Oan.

"Who's Karen Zobol?" asked Vera.

"But the river," pressed Norm, "we must know what you saw of the river!"

"Sorry. No idea."

"You said something about a payment. And the first one, dreaming," prompted the Regent.

"Surrounded by all and none; both real and not; removed from those who traverse the river. Karen Zobol must be paid!" supplied Oan, helpfully.

"Doesn't ring any bells," said Vera, shrugging again. "But if I had to hazard a guess, I'd say it means that unless the Church lets me go they won't have a prayer of—"

"Ms. Lantz!" cried Norm.

"What now?"

"I must insist that you be truthful! These blasphemous efforts to bend prophecies to your advantage is frankly appalling! I never thought one blessed with foresight could stoop so low!"

"Oh, put a sock in it!" said Vera, crossing her arms. "It was worth a shot. Besides, you're the one who's going around kidnapping people. Teleporting people here against their will. Forcing people to help you cross rivers—"

"We're ever so sorry," said Oan. "We had no choice. Prophet Stradamus's quatrains made it clear that—"

"Norm's quatrains?" scoffed Vera. "You're going to tell me this old dustrag wrote a scrap of verse about some medium who helps you cross a river? And maybe her name sounds a bit like Vera? Or something else that you can crowbar into the current situation and make it mean whatever you like—"

"Now, Ms. Lantz!" Norm protested.

"There is justice in her remarks," observed the Regent.

"And I suppose your little verse told you to kidnap Ian too?" said Vera. "It looks like you're about an Intercessor short! I'll bet you didn't see that coming! What did you want with Ian, anyway?"

"I need him!" said Oan. "He's going to help me with—"

The Regent silenced Oan with a gesture. "Mistress Oan," she said, arching an eyebrow, "there's no need to share all of our plans with this one. And we can explore the ins and outs of prophecy later. For now, it is enough that Vera finishes Isaac's work."

"Isaac's work?" said Vera, taken aback.

"Yes," said the Regent. "You shall finish what Isaac started."

"So you don't need me to see the future?"

"I have that covered," said Norm, inclining his head. "We know of your other gifts, Ms. Lantz. Your insights into techno-logical devices."

"So?" said Vera.

"So we need you to finish Isaac Newton's work on the sarcophagus! The device he built to send the Regent to the beforelife!"

"Pah!" said Vera, or words to that effect. "I wouldn't know where to begin!"

"We have the prototype!" said Norm. "And with your spe-cial skills—"

"Isaac Newton's one in a billion," Vera protested. "Maybe one in ten billion. I can't—"

"But you must!" insisted the Regent. "You must take us across the river!"

"And you'll have help!" said Norm. "Elder Marie has already embarked on the process of re-creating the—"

"Isaac's work was too advanced!" Vera protested. "It was so far ahead of anything else I've ever seen that it's basically magic."

"But you said it yourself!" cried Norm. "In the snippets of prophecy you uttered when you arrived! You said we were heading across the river!"

This seemed to catch the medium off guard. Her pos-ture straightened and she stroked her chin in something approaching a thoughtful manner. "I did, didn't I?" she said.

"Yes!" said Oan, "when you first appeared!"

"It's coming back to me, now," said Vera. "They get a bit jumbled sometimes — my visions, I mean — especially when a pack of raging arseholes teleports me against my will and circles around me like a—"

"Yes, yes," said Norm, interrupting, "I must apologize, but our need is most dire. We needed you with us. But please, focus! You said you saw us heading across the river!"

"No," said Vera, concentrating, "I didn't say that *I saw* anything. I said *the words* 'we're heading across the river.' That's what I saw. The words themselves. Not a picture of us heading across the river. Just words, written out. Like I was reading them from a page. And . . . and there was more to it. The words said, 'We're going to the promised land. We're headin' 'cross the river' . . . and then something about peace on the other side."

All eyes seemed to swivel and focus intently on Norm Stradamus. That is, all eyes except for Norm's, as that would have given him a headache. The prophet did seem to be looking inward, though.

It was the Regent who broke the silence.

"She knows, Prophet Stradamus. Prophetess Vera knows *The Song*."

You could practically hear the capital letters and italics.

"So it would seem," said Norm, agog.

"Whatever in Abe's name could this mean?" asked Oan, clasping her hands over her heart.

There was a collective pause, as though everyone in the room was suddenly stuck on an especially fiendish sudoku — one that included algebra, irrational numbers, and similar betrayals of proper math. Norm suddenly seemed to rally.

"It is a sign!" he cried, his eyes darting around the room as he smoothed some wrinkles in his robes. "A sign of the future. She . . . she confirms that which I have already foretold!"

There was a sudden outbreak of murmuring in the crowd.

"We shall cross the river together!" Norm shouted, raising a hand. "We shall once again assemble together in the before-life — in the promised land itself! The day I've always foretold approaches, fellow believers," he continued, gathering steam and seeming increasingly convinced of what he was saying. "The judgment day is upon us!"

The murmur grew and metastasized into a full-blown hubbub that travelled around the crowd. It blossomed into whistles, hoots, and applause.

The Regent smiled. Even her dog, Memphis, howled.

Vera crossed her arms and scowled.

Behind the crowd, unobserved by the cheering mob, Tonto slid her hand away from the holster under her robe, bit her lip, and left the room.

Chapter 10

"We have to rescue her!" said Ian.

"Why would Tonto need to be rescued?" said Socrates.

"Not Tonto! Vera! We have to rescue Vera!"

Ian and Socrates were standing vis-à-vis in the assassin's vast study, which Ian found surprising. Some of this was explained by the method of their arrival, unexpected teleportation often giving rise to mild to moderate episodes of discombobulation. But the bulk of Ian's surprise came from the fact that Socrates had a study at all. He didn't seem like a "study" person. A lair? Sure. A secret hideout? Absolutely. Even an underground philosopher's cave would have fit the bill. But a heavily bookshelved room that featured a museum's share of art, antique furniture, an enormous granite hearth, and floor-to-ceiling windows that showed a panoramic view of the River Styx — it didn't exactly scream "abandon hope all ye who enter here, for an assassin dwells within." More like "use a coaster and keep your feet off the furniture."

"I'm not sure I agree," said Socrates.

"You don't?"

"We don't have to rescue Vera. Rescuing Vera strikes me as optional, at best."

"But we have to help her!"

"She'll be fine."

"She won't be fine!"

"Of course she'll be fine. It's not as though they can kill her," Socrates added, in case Ian was still struggling with the finer points of immortality. "They can't even wipe her memory. She's perfectly safe."

"They could hurt her!" cried Ian, doing an urgent little dance. "Vera said that the Regent's people tortured Napoleons! Who knows what they'll do to her? We have to help her!"

"Calm yourself, Brown!" urged the assassin. "She'll be fine, whether we rescue her or not. Vera's problems will practically take care of themselves."

Ian ditched his little dance and cocked his head to one side like a baffled spaniel. Socrates noticed.

"She'll be fine as soon as we deal with the Church," said the assassin.

Ian made a face suggesting a need for further annotations. Socrates answered with a stare — the sort of exasperated stare you get from cat owners when litter training isn't going so frightfully well.

"Our whole plan, Brown?" he said, austerely. "Saving Detroit? Keeping the afterlife from slipping off its axis? Any of this seeming familiar? Option A: you do your bit as the Intercessor and convince the Church's leaders to keep a lid on the nature of Detroit. Option B: I wipe everyone who saw your wife's display in the grotto — everyone who knows that—"

"Okay, okay," said Ian, "I get it. I still know the plan. But we need Vera! And we need to get her diorama!"

"We need her whatnow?" said the assassin.

"Sort of a 3-D model thing. It tells the future."

"Vera has a diorama that tells the future?" said Socrates, dully.

"Well, no. I mean yes. I mean, Vera tells the future, right, and she made a diorama of one of her visions. It shows where we all have to be to save Detroit."

"And she has this with her?"

"No, she left it in her room. But we—"

"So we go to the hospice, get this fortune-telling knick-knack, and we'll have all the intel we'll need."

"No! We still need Vera! She can interpret it. Explain all the little bits. We need her to—"

"Maybe so," said the assassin, "but by the time we've found Vera all of our problems will be solved. We'll have found the Church of O and taken care of them. Vera will no longer be needed to interpret dioramas or make predictions, nor will she be in need of rescue. As for where the Church is hiding—"

"The Regent's chateau!" cried Ian, and you could practically see the lightbulb pop into view above his head. "It's what Oan said, in her message. She's being held at the Regent's chateau!"

"That makes sense. That woman you saw with the pointy dog — the regal-looking woman who seemed to radiate raw power—"

"Cleopatra!" said Ian.

"Could be," said the assassin, "I've never heard her called that name. But the woman we saw fits the Regent's description. If she's there, and Oan's there, it's a good bet that we were in that very chateau before the ISAAC system returned us to my study."

"But why would it do that?" whinged Ian. "We were where we needed to be!"

Socrates' eyes narrowed. "We weren't prepared, Brown," he said. "What if Tonto had taken up arms? What if the Regent, someone rumoured to be an ancient, has even a fraction of your wife's power? What if Norm had foreseen our arrival, and made preparations? You can't wander into a battleground like that without—"

"But we were right there!"

"And so were they. Expecting you. Expecting Vera, too, I'd wager. As for whether or not they anticipated me — who can say? Norm sees the future. If he can match Vera's power, it's likely that he foresaw my coming. His people may have prepared. Perhaps that's why my ISAAC system shorted out — some countermeasure deployed at the Regent's home. We need to prepare before we attempt a further incursion."

"I see what you mean," said Ian, who'd never gotten around to reading *The Art of War*. "I guess it's lucky we got away."

"You can thank Newton for that," said Socrates. "The ISAAC system is set to transport me to safety if certain . . . contingencies are met," he added, warily. "A partial system failure, for example. And as you've seen, the system is—"

It's been said that the universe has perfect timing, although many people disagree. The person who said this first probably had a taste for irony or a better run of luck than most observers. In the present instance, the universe's sense of timing manifested itself through a sudden buzzing and crackling from Socrates' left parietal lobe, which, judging from the sudden look of shock on Socrates' face, heralded something unexpected and unpleasant.

This was followed by the disappearance of almost exactly half the assassin. The left half, from his perspective. Where Socrates' leftward bits ought to have been there was nothing but the space that they'd been taking up a moment before. Socrates' right half stayed put, apparently unperturbed. If you're wondering how the assassin looked side-on — what you'd see if you looked at the bit where the two Socratic halves ought to have joined — rest assured it wasn't as ghastly as you'd imagine. It was just a sort of wavy bit of light, like those heat mirages you get wafting up from highways in the middle of summer.

Ian had seen a lot of weirdness since his arrival in Detroit, and things had gotten weirder still since Pen had joined him. But when you think of it, the sight of your philosopher-cum-assassin-slash-captor-cum-partner half disappearing in his study is near the top of whatever Buzzfeed list ranks weird (number seven will *blow your mind*).

Socrates blinked. Apparently just his right eye, but one couldn't really be sure.

"Umm," said Ian, raising an index finger.

"I know!" snapped the assassin. "Plato's beard!" he added, apropos of nothing obvious.

"Plato's beard?" said Ian, with genuine interest.

"Or Abe's drawers!"

"So you were cursing."

"Yes I'm cursing!" said the assassin, or at least half of him. "You may not have noticed, but my cloaking system is — gah!" he added, in response to another round of sparks and shorting circuits.

"I thought Plato was the City Solicitor?" said Ian.

"He is!" said Socrates, whose right arm seemed to be reaching for gadgets found on his left side, which was still undetectable. The parts of him you could see gyrated strangely, and looked a good deal like one-quarter of an Argentinian tango.

"He was clean-shaven," observed Ian.

"What?" shouted Socrates.

"The City Solicitor. No beard. Your curse doesn't make any—"

"Would you stop gabbling and make yourself useful!" said the assassin, who now fell to the floor with all the agility and grace you'd expect of a highly trained acrobat who's lost control of several parts of his body and can't locate the remainder.

"What can I do?" asked Ian, patiently.

"Third bookshelf from the left. Second shelf from the bottom. Blue book. Pull it out."

Ian complied, partly for what you might consider humanitarian reasons, but also because he was genuinely fascinated with what was going on and rather keen on seeing what might start happening next.

What happened next, after Ian had pulled the book, was the appearance of a sleek, black touchscreen in the middle of the wall across from the hearth.

"Touch the panel!" barked the writhing half-assassin, who gave the impression that he was having a bad day.

Ian complied again.

"It wants a password," said Ian, reviewing the screen.

"Gardenia 4 gateaux Pi Alpha Magnesite Wattle 437 dash Sigma Sigma Backslash-slashback Sigma Sigma Sigma eleven mark case sensitive user error we owe a cock to Asclepius!" cried the assassin, if that's the sort of thing that can count as a cry.

Ian moved to the screen and started hunting-and-pecking on its shimmering, virtual keyboard, an effort that was hampered by the fact that the QWERTY system had never made its way across the Styx.

"Gar . . . den . . . ia . . ." said Ian, rather slowly, followed by "and then was that the *word* four or is it the *number* 4, like the numeral?"

"Password accepted," said the voice of Isaac Newton, coming from nowhere in particular.

There was a click, a pop, and a buzz, and the assassin appeared whole, lying on his back and gasping for air.

"Ah," said Ian, stepping toward the assassin and staring down at him. "I guess the spoken password works."

"It does," gasped the assassin.

"Are you all right?"

"I'll be fine. It's the ISAAC system."

"I gathered."

"I suspect . . . that was a system check," said Socrates, still catching his breath. "It's cycling through a number of my augmentations, assessing their functionality."

"Neat," said Ian.

"It activated my cloaking system."

"I think it's broken," Ian suggested.

Socrates struggled to his feet and dusted himself off, checking to see that all of his various parts were attached and more or less up to factory specs.

Ian twiddled his thumbs and rocked on his soles for a space, unsure of the etiquette involved in changing the subject in the wake of an uncomfortable-looking cloaking system failure. Socrates noticed.

"Something on your mind?" said the assassin, wearily.

"What happens next?" said Ian.

"We figure out the terrain. We start by collecting Vera's diorama, then we try to zero in on the chateau. To do that, we start with Tonto."

"Tonto?"

"Tonto. She's at the chateau. I saw her clearly. And she's connected to you. Your wife dreamed her up to help protect you."

"Okay," said Ian, doing his best to string along.

"Can you locate her? Make contact?"

"No. We sort of lost touch after the grotto."

"You lost touch?" said the assassin, radiating disbelief. "With a perfect being designed to protect you? How do you just lose touch with—"

"She said she lost her purpose," said Ian, shrugging. "I didn't need her anymore. Not once Pen was here. Having Pen around made Tonto's job redundant. So, she left. She said she needed a reason to live."

"You just go on living," said the assassin, speaking with a severe tone suggesting Ian had touched a nerve. "That's how it works," he added. "So what's she doing with the Church?"

"No idea. But I'm sure she's all right. Maybe she's being some kind of mole."

"A mole," said Socrates, flatly.

"A spy. Working against the Church from the inside!"

"I know what a mole is," said the assassin, "and the important part of being a mole is reporting back to the side you're really on. And Tonto isn't."

"So what's she doing there?"

"I asked you first," said the assassin. "But it seems that this is a mystery we'll have to address later."

"But we have to go back there, now!" protested Ian. "We can't leave Vera and Tonto with them. We can't just—"

"I suppose I could defrost Ben Franklin's brain," suggested Socrates.

"You could what?" cried Ian, making the shocked and dismayed expression that was becoming second nature ever since he'd signed up to work with the assassin.

"Ben Franklin," said Socrates, nonchalantly. "Religious chap. I have his brain in cold storage. It'd take him at least a week or two to regenerate to the point that he could tell us anything useful, but then I imagine he'd be able to — what is it, Brown? Why do you look like a surprised fish?"

Ian stared at the assassin, opening and closing his mouth like a Pez dispenser set to "rapid fire."

"Mr. Brown?"

"You — you have Ben Franklin's brain?" Ian managed.

"Yes. What's the problem? I suppose you're going to tell me he was a big deal in the beforelife."

"He *was* a big deal in the beforelife!"

"Mayor of the mortal world or something?"

"He's a founding father! He invented electricity!"

"You can't invent electricity," observed the assassin. "It comes pre-invented."

"You know what I mean."

"I assure you I don't, Mr. Brown. But the point is that here in Detroit, Franklin's a bigwig in the Church. Biggish-wiggish, at any rate. And he knows about the Regent. He had a number of files about her, and her chateau, but nothing establishing its location. He may have its coordinates locked away in his memory. But as I said, it'll take time to retrieve them, and time is of the essence."

"So what do we do?" said Ian.

Socrates weighed this for a space. Rather than answering, he took the less conventional step of drawing a pistol from his holster with lightning speed and instantly firing off five rounds.

He fired them at Ian. Two of them grazed the target's shoulder, a third nicked Ian's neck, and the last two parted Ian's hair without making contact with his skull. They left five impact craters in the masonry behind Ian.

The effect on Ian was about what you might expect. He performed the sort of improvised jig you might get from a dancer on an electrified floor, shouted words that don't bear repeating, and came close to losing control of at least two sphincters.

Socrates kept his pistol drawn and slowly pivoted on the spot, surveying the room.

"What the hell was that?" cried Ian, once he'd regained enough composure to cry anything at all.

"Testing a theory," said the assassin, warily.

Ian patted various bits of himself and tried to catch his breath. A tiny trickle of blood discoloured the arm of his hospice robe.

"Hmm," said the assassin.

"Hmm?!" shouted Ian — discovering, in that emotionally fraught moment, that it was possible to shout a word like "Hmm."

"No sign of Tonto. No sign of Penelope," said the assassin.

"What?"

"I put you in peril, Brown."

"What?" said Ian again, his conversational skills having waned a trifle in the current circumstances.

"By firing at you. I put you in danger. Tonto's back in the field of play. I wondered if we might use that; use the connection you have with her. Or your connection to your wife. I wondered whether one of them might show up if you were in danger."

"But you shot me!" cried Ian, cradling his arm.

"You'll get better. Don't be a baby."

"I could have been—"

"What? Killed?" said the assassin. "You're forgetting where we are."

"I could have been hurt!" cried Ian. "Badly!"

"You weren't in any real danger. Unless you moved, I suppose."

"And what? You just expected Tonto or Pen to—"

"I expected nothing, Brown. As I said, I was testing a theory. I can't be sure what your wife perceives, wherever she is. Can she tell if you're in danger? Who knows? If you're in *apparent* danger, might that be enough? I pushed the boundaries of your safety as much as I thought you'd be able to bear. Two of those rounds carried Stygian toxin — my mindwiping serum. Perhaps your wife might have sensed the potential loss of your mind."

Ian clutched the top of his head and shouted several anatomically unlikely things that he hoped would happen to Socrates soon, all of which were deleted by prudish copy editors. The assassin put an end to this display by grabbing Ian's unshot arm.

"Listen, Brown," he hissed, "the stakes are higher now. The Church has gathered in the chateau. They've captured Vera, suggesting something is in the works. All the while, your son Evan amasses followers, plotting to team up with the Church to push his agenda of revealing Abe's Great Lie. And *you know* what that lie is, Brown. You know what it is this *son* of yours plans to reveal."

"I think—"

"He wants to expose the truth of Detroit!" barked the assassin. "The existence of the beforelife. The knowledge that people can shape Detroit and overturn the laws of physics through acts of will. He threatens my own continuity, Brown — my very existence. I do not take that lightly. He threatens to break the order imposed by Abe and the other ancients. If your son and the Church succeed, the entire world slips into chaos."

"But why would he want that?" said Ian, backing away. "Why would Evan—"

"Who can say?" said the assassin. "The Church has its own reasons. As for Evan, I'm at a loss. His agent merely spoke of his plan to spread the truth. To put an end to the lies spread by Abe and the ancients. It seems he wants to supplant Abe and rule Detroit in the mayor's stead; but why he'd want to rule what would remain of Detroit once the truth was made known . . . again, I'm at a loss."

Socrates stepped away from Ian and touched the spines of several books, causing a panel to slide away and reveal a secret room, one that Ian might have described as a robot's change room. It was lit by a harsh blue light and featured enough high-tech weapons, gadgets, and gizmos to outfit a small platoon of technically minded commandos. Socrates stepped in and helped himself to several items, stashing them on various parts of his person before turning back to Ian.

"We're leaving," he said. "We'll start by collecting Vera's diorama. Then we'll follow the tracker I placed on Mack Yavelli. He's been meeting with church officials on Evan's behalf. It's a good bet that he'll lead us to the chateau, or someone who knows something about it. We can make plans on the way."

Ian made a face that telegraphed an objection. Socrates noticed.

"Is that a problem for you, Brown?"

"Well, not a problem as such," Ian began, picking at a piece of imaginary lint on his robe. "It's just—"

"Spit it out."

"It's just . . . well, I can't see why you need me with you."

"But I need—"

"I know, I know," said Ian, "you need me to give you 'beforelife intel' about targets you find along the way. Norm Stradamus and Mack Yavelli, for a start. And I'm happy to help. I really am. But why can't I do that from here?"

Socrates weighed this. He went as far as stroking his chin.

"No," the assassin said, at length. "On the whole, I think it's best to take you along."

"But—"

"I've made a decision, Brown, and I'm through explaining myself to you."

"But I can't see why you—"

"I think we'll make quite the dynamic duo," said the assassin, airily. "Let me get you something to wear besides those robes, possibly something in red and yellow. If you can't help out in a fight, at least you'll draw the enemy's fire."

* * *

"My name's Larry," said Larry. "I used to be a princk."

"Welcome, Larry!" said a chorus of earnest voices.

Larry and a gaggle of like-minded former residents of Detroit Mercy Hospice were in the basement of the North-by-Northeast-Detroit Community Centre, enduring the monthly meeting of "prehab": a support group for reformed princks coping with life after BD. They were seated in a circle of folding chairs not far from a table of donuts and tea.

"It's been six years since my last episode," Larry added, drawing a smattering of applause.

"Congratulations!" said Eleanor, who'd been leading prehab groups for sixty years. "Please share with the group; tell us how your life has changed since your recovery."

"Well, it's gotten better, that's for sure," said Larry, smiling a smile that failed to reach his eyes. "When I thought the before-life was real . . . well, I felt trapped."

"You *were* trapped," said Sarai, sitting in the chair to Larry's left. "You were trapped in the hospice."

"It's more than that," said Larry, shifting in his seat with the discomfort common to salt-of-the-earth types who aren't fans of giving speeches involving things like "personal growth" and "coping strategies." "It's like . . . I was trapped by an idea," he added. "The idea that I was missin' something. Like, I dunno, friends from the beforelife. I . . . I wanted to know who they were. I wanted to know if they missed me. If they'd be princks, too, when they crossed over. I wondered if I'd been a good guy in the beforelife, and maybe if that's why I was a princk."

"That's always the way," said Maurice, perched in the chair at three o'clock. "I always wondered whether I'd been someone important. Like an actor."

"I used to think I'd been a mayor!" said Constantine, garnering sympathetic noises from the circle.

This was typical of princks. Hardly anyone turned up in Detroit recalling life as an assembly-line worker, a day labourer, a chicken catcher, or any clock-punching specimen who — while every bit as important to the machinery of life as anyone else — isn't the sort whose workday generates many memories you'd want to carry beyond the grave. The most noteworthy exception was probably Ian. He'd retained a lifetime's worth of mortal drudgery: a life he'd spent in the headline-grabbing world of regulatory compliance. He could still quote his five favourite bylaws down to the sub-sub-paragraph level.

"It wasn't 'til I let go of the past," said Larry, staring at his own gnarled hands, "the beforelife, I mean — that I could move on and . . . and get on with what matters. The here and now. Real life. I was so . . . so stuck on the beforelife that I forgot to live in the now."

"You've got to be mindful of the present!" said Maurice, calling up a bit of sharing room wisdom he'd learned from Oan.

"You'll never reach your potential if you're reaching back to the past," said Horst, gesturing with a donut.

"Especially to a past that doesn't exist," said Sarai.

"Once I let go," Larry continued, "I felt . . . I dunno . . . sorta free, like. Like I could finally stand tall. Spread my wings kinda thing."

"And where has that freedom taken you?" prompted Eleanor, leaning in.

"Slaughterhouse," said Larry, a revelation that always drew the sort of reactions you'd expect. Sarai and Horst made a pair of faces that hinted at ethical veganism.

"No, no, it's not so bad," said Larry. "Good honest work. All the livestock and blood and — well, you know," he added, skipping over the sorts of details that might put people off their donuts. "I mean, it isn't great. Not the job of my dreams, right? But when I was a princk it was worse. I figured I'd ended up at the slaughterhouse because I'd been . . . I dunno . . . a jerk or something. In the beforelife. Or maybe a bully. Or cheated at cards. But now I know the beforelife ain't real, I know I'm not payin' for something I done wrong. It's just dumb luck. It's just society. It's all unfair, I mean. The shit hits the fan and it ain't divided evenly."

"That's right!" said Jacob, chiming in for the first time. "I'm not single and livin' on my own in the Wallows 'cuz of karma, or 'cuz it's the afterlife I earned. It's just 'cuz of other people. Keepin' me down, like. Takin' up all the available wives."

Grunts of agreement circled the room.

"I'm right there with you," said Wide Mike, an impressively massive member who'd spent the last meeting complaining that Big Tech was keeping him down by censoring what he could say online. "It's not past lives what's keepin' us down. It's what Ken was talkin' about last month. That unequal distribution thing."

"Here, here!" said Ken, who probably meant to say "hear, hear" but didn't read enough to have seen the expression in print.

"We're all oppressed, every one of us!" said Simon. "Desperate, lonely, and celibate, like Jacob—"

"Hey!" said Jacob.

"Or broke, like Larry," Simon continued, "or shut out of the world, like Wide Mike. We're not reaping what we've sown in some life before Detroit. We're just taking it on the chin because the Man is keeping us down."

"It's like my wife!" said Earl, a veteran member.

"What about her?" said Simon.

"She has this friend. A friend from work. His name's Stephon. He wears tight suits."

The group shared a moment of tilted heads and synchronized blinking.

"Well, why's he always look so nice in them tight suits?" said Earl, through gritted teeth.

Eleanor straightened up and reached for the metaphorical reins she used to keep the group in check. "Thank you, Earl, but I'm not sure that you—"

"It isn't right," said Earl, ignoring her. "Like, I could look nice in tight suits, right? There's no reason I couldn't."

"No," said Eleanor, drawing the word out for a couple of extra syllables. "I don't suppose there is. With enough diet and exercise I'm sure you—"

"It's just why should he look so good in 'em? That's all I'm askin'. Those little tapered legs."

"No reason at all," said Ken.

"He's oppressin' me!" said Earl. "With them sleek lines. All that tailoring. And the cute little bum—"

"All right then," said Eleanor, folding her hands, "I think perhaps we ought to return to—"

"I'm bein' oppressed too!" said Ken.

"Might we just—" began Eleanor, still failing in the role of ringmaster.

"It's my old roommate," said Ken, rising. "From the hospice, I mean. He has a new SUV."

"A new SUV?"

"That's right!" said Ken. "And I don't have one, is what I'm sayin'. And now my Pat's always askin' me why we can't have one."

"Oppression!" cried Earl.

"And what about all them guys with pretty wives!" said Jacob.

"Or husbands," said Horst.

"Sure, or husbands!" Jacob allowed. "It isn't right!"

"It's all the elites!" said Wide Mike, his eyes now burning with the passion of a man who isn't sure who the elites are, but is 100 per cent convinced that they aren't him, and should be.

"That's right!" said Earl. "Lawyers, and actors, and scientists—"

"And Stephon!"

"And old roommates with SUVs!"

"It's like it says in the *Twelve-and-a-Half Precepts*!" Jacob said, slamming a fist into his open hand.

"Now, Jacob," said Eleanor, "I don't think this is the right time for—"

"No, no, hear me out!" said Jacob. "It's the best book ever.

Peter Jordanson. The first precept, right, is to look at the job in front of you. That means not looking back. Like, not even back to the beforelife. We can all agree that's good sense, right?"

Various noises of approval rose from the rabble. Even Eleanor seemed to agree.

"And Jordanson's second precept, right?" Jacob continued, gaining steam. "Say what you mean and mean what you say!"

"Ignorance is a choice!" cried Ken, who'd read Jordanson's book too.

"That's true, that's true!" said Maurice, steamrolling right over Eleanor, who was trying to say something or other about all choices being valid.

The group had descended into a lively discussion about precepts four through twelve when Sarai, who was fairly new to the genre of pseudo-philosophical-self-help literature, piped in with a question.

"What's the half-precept?" she asked with genuine interest.

"Subscribe to my channel for more content!" chorused Jacob, Ken, and Earl.

"I think we may have gone off the rails," said Eleanor. "Larry was sharing with us, sharing the meaning he's found by leaving BD behind him."

"I think what Jacob's saying makes sense, though," said Larry, now that the floor was once again his. "I done some of my own research, right? About economics and politics and psychology. On social media last Sunday. And the Jordanson stuff all fits!"

This carried on for quite some time.

They say that a lie can travel around the world before truth puts on its trousers, and that no known cancer metastasizes as fast as a petty grievance. They're right about those things. What's less well publicized is the result you get when anti-social envy steeps in misconstrued half-truths backed up by hours of self-directed research at Social Media U. Any smallish mind caught in the grip of this world of petty grievances can compress to such density that it generates a whole array of physical forces — magnetism that attracts the downtrodden, for starters, gravity that pulls conspiracy-seekers into orbit, and a philosophical vacuum that instantaneously hoovers up anything that resembles clear-headed thinking or common sense. In all of these senses, and probably several more, it sucks.

One critical aspect of the vacuum spawned by petty malevolence is that it creates a void of leadership that practically begs to be filled. Thus it was that, just as Eleanor had fully lost control and Larry, Jacob, Ken, and Earl had turned the meeting into a symposium on the theme of how the Man was keeping them down, a resonant voice made itself known in the doorway.

"I can tell you who that *man* is," said the voice.

The voice was followed by the entry of a figure the prehabbers had never seen — one they couldn't really describe by the time he left. They all agreed that he had red hair, and that his clothes were perfectly tailored — though not oppressively, like Stephon's. Apart from that, opinions varied. Some thought he was clean-shaven, others remembered him having a beard. Horst thought he remembered mutton-chop sideburns and a handlebar moustache. This was despite the fact that the figure had held everyone's rapt attention from the moment he strode in like he owned the place — or, more accurately, like he owned the whole of Detroit.

"The man who keeps you down," said the mysterious figure, "is Abe."

Confused muttering filled the air. It was one thing to be sure that you were a victim of the Man. It was another to suggest that he was . . . well . . . an actual honest-to-goodness man. This was particularly true when it was suggested that this "Man" was Abe the First, the universally beloved Mayor of Detroit.

"That doesn't sound right to me," said Sarai, frowning.

"Abe is . . . well, he's great!" said Maurice.

"Best mayor we've ever had!" said Earl, garnering grunts of approval.

"*Only* mayor we've ever had," observed Ken.

"And who in Abe's name are you?" asked Eleanor, rising to greet the mysterious figure.

"My name's Evan," he replied, shaking Eleanor's hand. He continued holding her hand as he spoke.

"I'm here to show you the truth," he said. "To tell you that you can have more. You can have what you deserve; have a world that will serve up whatever you need."

It takes a lot of chutzpah to pull off a paragraph like that, but Evan managed. There was something about his way. All eyes were glued on his indescribable face, all ears tuned in to a voice that seemed to skip right through any part of the brain that handled things like "reason" or "judgment" to take up residence in the bits that just liked to do what they were told.

"The beforelife is real," he said, something that flew in the face of months of hospice treatment and several years of prehab. "Follow me, and I'll show it to you. Follow me, and I can prove that you've been kept from what you deserve. Kept down by Abe, who hides the truth for his own purposes, who keeps power out of the hands of everyone else. You've always known the truth. Your lot in life — your circumstances — these aren't things that you deserve."

"That's what I've been sayin'!" cried Larry.

"It's forced on you!" said Evan. "Forced on you by people who stand to lose their own power if you rise above the lives they've picked for you. The people who push the Big Lie."

It was at this point in the night's proceedings that every single observer agreed that Evan glowed. Literally, that is. With a white, radiant light that drew tears from watching eyes.

Evan's eyes saw something different. They saw that the glow didn't come from him. It was reflected. It was reflected from the tiny threads of multi-hued, glowing light that only Evan could perceive, threads of light that flowed from the tiny sparks of will in the peevish little minds of those around him. The barely consequential threads that each individual member of tonight's prehab meeting contributed to Detroit's existence.

They were threads laden with envy and petty grievances. Threads twisted by injustice, real or imagined, and small complaints about all the little things that made life turn into a stream of disappointments. These were the threads of discontent, threads willingly given over to anyone who could offer hope.

Evan reached for the threads, grasped them, and pulled.

Chapter 11

"No! This one goes here, that one goes there!" barked Vera, gesturing with a hydro-spanner as she directed a team of oil-stained acolytes hard at work on the sarcophagus.

That sentence bears some explanation.

The sarcophagus, you'll recall, isn't what we might think of as an ordinary, run-of-the-mill sarcophagus in the beforelife, Detroit lacking the need for vessels designed to house human remains. This sarcophagus was an over-engineered piece of machinery that more or less resembled the traditional shuffling-off-the-mortal-coil variety in shape and size, but was originally designed, here in Detroit, as a resting place for ancients who were taking their final nap — sliding into a torpor after hanging around Detroit for at least ten thousand years. These ancients, having put in their fair share of time bustling about the land-scape, now put their bodies to rest in these high-tech sarcophagi and let their unconscious minds help Abe shore up the walls of reality that kept things running smoothly in Detroit.

The weirdest thing about these sarcophagi is that they probably don't exist. Not really; not in the way that, say, a cheese sandwich exists in the beforelife, or a Zythroformin exists in the mortal dimension of Ammon-Ra, a dark and twisty realm that will be mentioned only one additional time in the present work. Back in Detroit, these sarcophagi, like pretty much everything else, existed only as mental projections — things dreamed up by the thoughts and expectations of souls

172

who dwelt in the sweet hereafter — insofar as a place like Detroit is allowed to be described as sweet. But like most of the mental projections in Detroit, which included everything from cheese sandwiches to trombones (trombones being the closest equivalent to the Ammon-Ra–based Zythroformin), the projections that took the shape of this sarcophagus served a purpose. They were quasi-physical, mentally conjured totems that focused the thoughts and expectations of those who perceived them, and they shaped those expectations to work out in ways that could, more or less at least, be explained by physical laws as they were understood to operate. The same principle explains why anything in Detroit works as you might expect. A humble prism based in Detroit is spun of the same ephemeral threads of thought as everything else that "exists" in Detroit, and it refracts light — or rather the threads of thought that pass for light in Detroit — because it has the physical make-up that splits what passes for light into its constituent frequencies, just as anyone who understood the working of prisms might expect. A Detroit-based rubber ball, again a projection of thoughts and expectations, falls down in response to gravity and bounces off hard surfaces because (a) those who perceive it expect it to behave that way, and (b) those who understand the beforelife-based physics that underlie gravity, rubber, and bouncing fully expect the constituent parts of the rubber ball (and the world around it) to be put together in a way that yields the results.

The sum of this navel-gazing is the fact that science and engineering really do matter in Detroit. A sufficiently high-tech gizmo — one that doesn't have an intuitive explanation or function based on principles that are readily understood — works only because (1) those with highly specialized training perceive and expect the constituent parts to work in ways that are predicted by that highly specialized training, and (2) these well-trained scientists and engineers convince enough slightly less–trained people that the gizmo in question works in particular ways. These slightly less–trained people, in turn, convince even-less-trained observers that (for example) the teleporter designed by Isaac Newton actually does cause matter to fade out of existence in Spot A only to reappear in Spot B: and so it does. The rest of the public — meaning, almost everybody else — can't distinguish the working of a toaster oven from voodoo and just believes what they're told. In short, everything operates a good deal like it does in the mortal world, with the extra confusing added layer of complexity that nothing in the afterlife is actually real apart from the thoughts and expectations of the observers. In short, not to put too fine a point on it, the whole place is just a big Platonic cave, and this is why the City Solicitor finally went a bit off the rails.

Now, where were we? Vera! Right. She was directing a bunch of acolytes in the repair of a sarcophagus — one that Isaac Newton modified to suit the Regent's purposes. While an ordinary Detroit-based sarcophagus merely holds an ancient at rest while also directing and amplifying that ancient's thoughts and expectations in a way that helps Abe shore up the fabric of reality, this sarcophagus was designed to direct and amplify the very specific thoughts and expectations of the Regent — in other words, those thoughts and expectations that are directed at punching a hole through Detroit's metaphysical boundaries and allowing the body locked inside the sarcophagus to return to the mortal world. Think of it as an Instantaneous Personal Transport that whooshes the subject not from Spot A to Spot B, but right out of the afterlife — right out of the pages of this book — and into the living room beside you.

So why in the name of Abe's sixth leg[2] would Vera be helping

---

2   Readers who've come to this point in the narrative may object to plenty of things, and in particular they might object that Abe, who we've seen on many occasions, has two legs. These readers are wrong. In fact he has fifteen. Like anyone who leads a sufficiently adventurous life for

the Regent's people fix the thing? You'll recall that Norm and the Regent indicated that their whole purpose in kidnapping Vera was to have her "carry on Isaac's work" and replicate the various feats of engineering it took to make the sarcophagus send its occupant out of Detroit and into the mortal world. If you've been paying close attention, you might have expected Vera to balk — she's certainly no fan of the Regent, she doesn't share her goals, and given her status as a recently kidnapped captive being held in the Regent's chateau she might be expected to be uncooperative. And you'd be entirely right. But recall that the Regent is very powerful indeed, and has a fair-sized helping of the power exhibited by Penelope, Abe, and the City Solicitor — the power to weave the threads of others' thoughts and expectations and shift reality in ways that suit her will. Thus it was that, when Vera balked, the Regent grasped a small pyramidical structure, looked Vera in the eyes, waved a hand in a way that practically screamed "these aren't the droids you're looking for," and Vera — suddenly seeming even chirpier and more enthusiastic than usual — said, "All right, let's get to work!"

She was assigned a team of technically minded acolytes who could assist. And thus it was that she'd been working with them for a little over a week, doing her best to get this show on the road and pop the Regent into a techno-coffin en route to the mortal world. In the moment of going to press she was standing with her team of assistants and barking out a lot of commands and technobabble.

---

many thousands of years, Abe has had his share of accidents. Several of these have resulted in some form of dismemberment. This world being Detroit, Abe's legs grew back — that is, a new leg formed where the old one had been attached. And Abe being Abe, the public wanted to save any dismembered bits of the beloved Mayor as important relics. Eight of Abe's former legs are stored in formaldehyde in Detroit-based museums, as are four of his former hands, an old hip, and a bit of tummy fat he had removed a few years back.

We now rejoin the unfolding narrative.

"Just get out of the way," said Vera, shooing away a handful of acolytes who were clustered around the machinery. She lay down on one of those little rolling devices mechanics use to get under cars, trucks, or high-tech sarcophagi, as the case may be, so that they can fiddle with transmissions, undercarriages, and other hidden technical bits that make things go.[3]

She pulled a bundle of tools in with her. Once she was tucked away in the space beneath the machinery Vera started tearing into the gizmo's innards, evidenced by the sort of racket you get when you drop a satellite on a casino. "You still there, Norm?" she called, her legs still poking out from below.

"Erm, um, y-y-yes?" stammered the prophet, appearing front and centre and crouching down near Vera's feet. He seemed a touch out of his element, Norm having been drawn from the "scrolls and melting candles" end of the fortune-teller spectrum, rather than the more rarified bit that was comfortable when surrounded by pneumatic lifts, hydraulic wrenches, bundles of live neural cabling, and banks of diagnostic computers fit for launching missions to Mars.

"Tell me more about this prophecy of yours," called Vera, her voice resonating out from under the sarcophagus.

"Erm, my prophecy?" said Norm, crouching even farther down and ending up in the sort of crooked posture that makes chiropractors grin and arrange to finance second yachts.

"Yeah. The song you mentioned. You said it's a good one."

"Yes, yes it is," said Norm, "but, ah, I'd imagine you'll want to concentrate on the matter at hand. The, erm, the sarcophagus, I mean."

---

3 In the mortal world, these devices — things that allow you to roll under other things while gazing upward — are known as "creepers." Look it up. The people of Detroit instead settled on "one of those little rolling devices mechanics use to get under cars."

"I'm a multitasker," said Vera, punctuating her remark with a vague wave of her left foot. This was followed by the sound of a socket wrench pounding metal into submission. "I work best when I'm distracted," Vera added. "So this prophecy. It's not a quatrain, then?"

"N-n-no," the prophet stammered, twisting the hem of his robe through gnarled fingers. "As I said, it takes the form of a song. A new prophetic form I've recently been exploring. Erm, inspired by you, in fact."

"Thank Abe for that," said Vera, laughing. "The last thing Detroit needs is another quatrain from Norm Stradamus."

"My latest vision is — I beg your pardon, madam?" said the prophet, taken aback.

"C'mon, Norm. Name one quatrain that made a single, solid prediction. One that actually came true."

"I prophesied that you'd help us!" said Norm, defensively.

"That doesn't count. You made that happen."

"There are my Napoleonic verses!"

"Yeah, but there's probably thousands of Napoleons," called Vera, her voice still sounding like she was shouting from the bottom of a well. "Predict whatever you like about Napoleons," she added, "it's probably true of at least one of 'em!"

Norm tugged at his collar and kept his gaze directed squarely at Vera's feet, carefully avoiding the glances of nearby acolytes who were busy pretending not to be listening in. "I . . . I mean . . . well, I picked the winner of last year's regeneration regatta," he said, eventually.

"You probably foretold it would snow in Abeuary, too," said Vera, dismissively. "I'm not saying you aren't doing your best," she added. "I'm just saying I wouldn't rely on The Collected Quatrains of Norm Stradamus when making investments or placing bets. I read a few of your more famous ones last night."

"Y-you did?"

"Not very helpful," observed the medium.

"T-to which quatrains are you—"

"There was one about the treacherous man. How'd it go? The treacherous man who rose to rule Detroit for a short time? It could mean anything. I mean 'a man quickly raised from low to high estate'? That could be practically anybody. And saying he turned 'disloyal and volatile' before governing Detroit — that's meaningless, right? If anyone other than Abe took over Detroit, then that person has, by definition, turned disloyal. It stands to reason. And if this man goes from not being the mayor to suddenly being in charge of everything, then he's automatically raised from low to high estate."

"Yes, well, that's one way of viewing the—"

"I mean, let's say it's about the City Solicitor," Vera mused. "He used to work as a lawyer, then he was in charge for a bit, had a short rebellion against Abe's rule, challenged the safeguards that keep Detroit in check—"

"Very possibly!" said Norm, brightening. "You see, the prophecy fits the facts perfectly. It reveals events that took place long after I wrote the—"

"On the other hand," said Vera, "it could mean Isaac."

"Erm, Isaac?" asked Norm, whistling slightly on the "s."

"Isaac Newton, sure. He started out as the City Solicitor's personal secretary, right, then he mucked around with history and gave himself the power to overturn the laws of physics. If that's not 'ruling Detroit' then I don't know what is. And he seemed pretty disloyal and volatile to me — he turned against Abe's rules, he—"

"Well, yes," Norm admitted, speaking over a new and especially piercing mechanical whir that came from the spot where he imagined Vera's head to be. "This, too, could be a valid interpretation—"

"Or it could mean Abe himself!"

This one seemed to catch the prophet off guard. He just stood there, looking like a seer caught in the headlights, before gaining enough composure to make an interrogative noise that even those observers who weren't gifted with second sight could interpret as meaning "what do you mean, Abe himself?"

"If you wanted to play Abe's advocate, you could say Abe has only ruled Detroit for a short time, right? I know it's been eleven thousand years, but that's a drop in an infinite bucket. And he rose from low to high estate — in the beforelife he was just some nondescript, run-of-the-mill guy, and now he's here, ruling as mayor."

"But disloyal and volatile?" ventured Norm in defence of his quatrain's honour.

"That's just perspective," said Vera, brushing off these pesky details with a second wave of her left shoe. "And what about the next verse, the one about the enslaved populace?"

Norm managed to bend his spine into something resembling a posture of reverence while adopting a voice that was the auditory equivalent of calligraphy, something he'd probably have described as either "eldritch" or "arcane." The verse he recited went like this:

> From the enslaved populace, songs, chants, and
>   demands,
>
> while Princes and Lords are held captive in prisons.
>
> These will in the future by headless idiots
>
> be received as divine prayers.

"Could mean anything," said Vera. This was followed by a sound that was either someone under the sarcophagus blowing

179

a raspberry or an unseen fuel-line releasing pressurized contents, either one of which would be crude.

"While it's true that facts have not yet revealed the prophecy's meaning," Norm began, before the medium slid out from her little cubbyhole, stared up at the rambling prophet, and interrupted.

"But that's the problem, isn't it?" she said, wiping a smudge of oil from her nose. "You write these verses that could mean whatever you like and wait for facts that fit them. Some of your poems are, what, four or five hundred years old? You've had centuries to take whatever facts you happen to find and then crowbar them into submission to make them fit whatever you wrote."

The nearby acolytes muttered among themselves and shuffled their feet as Norm just stood there, looking wounded.

"I mean, it's all right for what it is," said Vera, pulling a rat's nest of neural cabling out from the bowels of the machine, "it probably makes for diverting parlour conversation, but when it comes to letting people make plans for the future, you have to admit it kinda stinks. Hand me the plasma drill," she added.

Norm made a pained expression as several acolytes turned away in the hope of letting the prophet preserve a shred or two of dignity. One of them passed a plasma drill to Vera, who rolled back into the sub-sarcophagal zone.

"So tell me more about this new song," she said, calling out from her little workspace.

Norm did his best to rally.

"Yes, well, it's been said that this is the most important of my visions," he said, brightening.

"Pretty low bar," Vera shouted over the screech of her drill.

"Now, Ms. Lantz!"

"Sorry, sorry, that was rude," shouted Vera, who then did something that caused the innards of the sarcophagus to pulse with a pale blue light. "You said I inspired it?"

"Yes! You inspired its form! It isn't a quatrain. When last you . . . well . . . erm, *visited* the chateau, your revelations took the form of a lengthy poem."

"Two chairs. Yeah, I remember."

"And you mentioned that it was the first of your visions to take a poetic form."

"That's right," called Vera, a phrase she punctuated by banging something hard on the underside of the sarcophagus at least seven or eight times — it was hard to get an accurate count on account of the echoes.

"Well," said Norm, "your willingness to adopt a new prophetic form struck me as inspiring. Why not revisit my own habits, I said to myself, abandon quatrains for now and see what visions may come? And that's when I started to write the song. The song you partially foresaw when you first arrived!"

"The bit about headin' 'cross the river," said Vera.

"Exactly right!"

"So what's the rest of it?"

"It isn't finished. Each line coalesces in my mind only after hours and hours of deep meditation and inner searching."

"Just tell me the bit you have."

"Oh, very well," said Norm, straightening. "So, the part you already know says that we're going to the promised land, we're headin' 'cross the river — note the vernacular — that you can wash your sins away in the tide, and that everything will be peaceful on the other side, meaning the other side of the river."

"Right," said Vera.

"The remaining lyrics suggest that we'll find a world that's free of care, a place where the sun shines brightly and all troubles can be forgotten."

"Doesn't sound very catchy."

"You can rush neither art nor prophecy!" said Norm, harrumphing. "Besides, you have to hear it set to music."

"Sing a few bars!" said Vera.

"It isn't ready!"

"C'mon! Give it a whirl!" said Vera, sliding out from her crawlspace and giving the prophet an encouraging thumbs-up.

"Patience, Vera, patience. My meditations must continue."

"So what's the big deal with the song, anyway?" said Vera, sitting up and wiping another smudge of oil from underneath her left eye. "Why all the meditation and stuff?"

"Can't you see?" said Norm, adopting a rapturous air. "The song predicts the Church's exodus from Detroit! Our excursion across the Styx to the mortal world! The goal we've always sought: to commune with the Great Omega in her realm! You see, our trip across the Styx is the event that is signified by the line 'we're headin' 'cross the river.'"

"Pfft. That could be any river!"

"It's obviously the Styx!" said Norm. "And the previous line specifically mentions the promised land!"

"Probably just some real estate deal."

"You're being difficult and obstructionist!" said Norm, who wasn't wrong. He also wasn't used to having his prophecies challenged out in the open by competing fortune tellers, particularly ones whose services as a medium and small appliance repair person were required to make Norm's own predictions — if you could call them predictions — come to pass.

Vera cleaned a socket wrench on her trousers while locking eyes with Norm. "Look," she said, "I'm just being honest. You're making all of this up as you go along, and then making your song appear to predict things that you want to happen. It's like me making up a limerick about winning the Detroit sweepstakes just because I'd like to win. Say, *There once was a seer named Lantz; who saw lotteries called in advance; she won ten zillion bucks, and gave zero—*"

The climax of Vera's limerick was to be lost in the mists of time, for rather than finishing off her poem, such as it was, Vera rolled her eyes back in her head, lay back on her little rolling platform, and started flopping around like a landed herring.

After the moment of inaction you'd expect as onlookers tried their best to digest this sudden turn of events, Norm dropped to his knees at Vera's side. The nearby acolytes clustered around the central action — an act that was mostly symbolic, given that no one had a clue what they should do once they'd arrived at ground zero. Norm, for his part, moved his hands toward Vera and then suddenly withdrew them without ever making physical contact. He repeated this procedure at least three times, reaching forward and then withdrawing, like a dieter hovering over a slice of cake, or a squeamish dog owner trying to bring herself to pluck an intestinal worm from the business end of her pet.

This state of affairs persisted for a solid seven seconds, until Vera sat up suddenly, stared at the ceiling with rolling eyes that would have made ophthalmologists wince, and recited the verse she'd first unleashed on her arrival at the chateau, this time sounding even more sepulchral than she had the first time 'round:

> In his house at R'lyeh, the first one, dreaming, lies. Surrounded by all and none; both real and not; removed from those who traverse the river. Charon's Obol must be paid ...

You can't go around saying things like that without budgeting for a broad range of reactions. In this instance they ranged from foot shuffling and throat clearing all the way to outright flight, as two of the acolytes hitched up their robes and exited stage left.

Norm just stood there gaping, while Vera returned to normal and said, "Could somebody pass the pliers?"

"Erm, your pliers, Ms. Lantz?" said Norm, still gaping.

"A little hand tool," said Vera. "Sorta like tongs."

"Erm, Ms. Lantz—" began Norm.

"What?" said Vera.

"It's just that—"

"Spit it out!"

"It seems your television was on. Just now, I mean."

"Oh. Anything good?"

Norm blinked at Vera as though she'd sprouted a second head. "You . . . I mean . . . that is to say . . . you repeated the same phrases you recited on your arrival. The lines about the first one, dreaming, and a payment being made to Karen Zobol."

"Weird," said Vera.

"Profoundly so!" said Norm. "But what does it mean?"

"Search me," said Vera, shrugging. "But now that you mention it . . . I do feel . . . well . . . something," she added, folding her arms in the little self-embrace you do when caught by a chill. The manoeuvre left little patches of oil on Vera's upper arms.

"What sort of feeling?" prompted Norm.

"I'm . . . I'm not sure," said Vera, faltering. "I think it's about your prophecy, though. The song, I mean. I . . . I can't quite say why, but I can't help but think that your song is . . . is somehow related to my own vision."

"Related, how?" said Norm, agog.

"I'm not sure," said Vera, shaking her head before proceeding. "Honestly, I just think that, before my prophecy comes true, that song of yours will have to be sung. It'll fill the air. I'm sure of it. I think it's all on my diorama."

"Your whatnow?" said the prophet.

"Diorama," said Vera. "A prophecy thing I made at the hospice. A sort of three-dimensional model."

"And what does it tell you?" asked Norm, agogger than ever.

"I can't be sure. But I think . . . I think I do see us on the other side of the river. All of us, in a mortal world. It's the promised land, like your song says. And when we get there—"

"Yes?" said Norm, expectantly.

"YES?" chorused the remaining semi-flock of acolytes.

"When we get there," Vera repeated, "we're all going to be ruled by Evan."

The acolytes gasped in unison. One of them dropped a hammer. When the echo died down it was Norm who broke the ensuing silence. What he said was this:

"Who's Evan?"

* * *

One thing Ian had never gotten used to was the clothing — the range of fashions you could see on a typical day while out and about in Detroit. It's not that Detroit-based fashion houses had weird tastes. On any scale that measures weird, they weren't any stranger than the fashion houses you get in mortal worlds. The problem was the way that people chose the actual clothing that they wore from day to day.

Detroit, like practically every other place that exists in the gloriously diverse multiverse, is filled with loads of people who'd really like to look their best. The problem lies in how people in Detroit — and everywhere else — settle on what "looking your best" really means. For most people, "looking your best" means choosing a look from a time in your life that you more or less consider your prime — perhaps a time when you were especially lucky in love, good at sports, or a general object of admiration — and trying to replicate that look forever.

In mortal worlds, that isn't so bad. Sure, you have people walking around in a previous decade's bell-bottom trousers, outsized suits, go-go boots, fedora hats, and similar eyesores, but human mortality imposes its own natural limits and effectively culls the fashion herd. Outmoded styles eventually die with their adherents. In the afterlife: not so much. Just because your "fashion prime" was, say, two or three thousand years ago, doesn't mean you're going to update your look today. So, in Detroit, a typical jaunt in a public square would include sightings of zoot suits, bustles, people fit for renaissance faires, pelts of assorted fauna with or without attached heads, futuristic onesies cut out of some kind of semi-metallic cloth, and everything in between. It gave the impression of a cosplay convention whose hosts couldn't agree on a singular theme.

Ian was musing on the issue of fashion now, for no particular reason apart from the fact that he was crouched alone on a rooftop, hiding behind an air-conditioning unit and waiting for Socrates to return from a bit of assassiny derring-do. At times like this the mind can wander. Ian had found that his mind was wandering quite a lot in the last ten days, and he couldn't blame it — there was too much going on for a human mind to process events in anything that remotely resembled a systematic way. Ian was currently paired up with the afterlife's only assassin: a deadly superhuman ninja type who was either a mental construct whose existence was imperilled by the spread of accurate data about the nature of Detroit, or some netherworldly version of an ancient Greek philosopher, possibly both. And with this assassin, Ian was hot on the trail of Machiavelli, a man who, in this realm, seemed to be working as some sort of PR agent for Ian's son. That son, who was born only a handful of years ago, now seemed to have aged himself by at least a couple of decades while on a quest to drum up followers with a view to overthrowing the mayor of Detroit and wrecking things for everyone else.

You wouldn't call it a lazy week.

This particular stretch of time had started out in the hospice, as things so often did. Ian and Socrates had gone there seeking Vera's diorama. This had led to a near-miss involving Matron Bikerack, a secret incursion into Dr. Peericks's office, and a rather exciting sequence in which Sigmund Freud came within a whisker of losing his superego, ego, and id all in one go thanks to a brush with Socrates' mind-erasing serum. It had all worked out in the end. Despite occasional glitches in Socrates' on-board ISAAC system — glitches that seemed to be sorting themselves out over time — the assassin managed to get away with Vera's diorama and bring it to Ian, who'd spent the entire time hiding in nearby bushes and hoping for the best.

The next night they'd tracked Yavelli to Pythagoras's apartment. *That* Pythagoras. Ian made a joke about triangulating his position and Socrates hadn't laughed at all. Yavelli's meeting with Pythagoras had lasted just over an hour, and didn't involve the exchange of any cheerful facts about the square of the hypotenuse. What it had involved was Yavelli's proposal to merge Pythagoras's own secret, cultish gang of wild-eyed mathematicians with Evan's growing cabal of fringe-dwelling, disaffected, and downtrodden disciples. The jury was out on whether or not Pythagoras planned to take the bait. Once Yavelli had left Pythagoras's home, the assassin paid the mathematician a visit while leaving Ian hidden safely in the bushes. The assassin declined to tell Ian what had happened.

Then there was Elvis. When Socrates had announced that Mack Yavelli had hitched up at Elvis's grand estate, Ian had felt that giddy combination of guilt and excitement that you're bound to get when you contemplate the kidnapping, interrogation, and possible mindwiping of a beloved musical icon. A good deal of this had passed when the night's quarry turned out to be Elvis Bjorn-Hansen, a high-tech entrepreneur who'd been in Detroit for less than a year.[4] But still, it had been more intense than your average day. The assassin's incursion into Bjorn-Hansen's home had featured a failure of Socrates' personal cloaking system and a boson whip that utterly failed to ignite. Socrates hadn't reacted well when Ian grinned and reassured him that this probably happened to assassins all the time and was nothing to feel embarrassed about at all.

There'd been arguments too — plenty of them. Ian had started one by asking his new "partner" why they couldn't simply capture Machiavelli and "shake him down," to use the vernacular, for whatever information he had about the chateau's location. That argument had turned into a fully developed Socratic dialogue, the most relevant part of which looked like this:

> Ian: I don't see why we're wasting time showing up in places where Mack Yavelli has already been.
>
> Socrates: We're looking for clues. The people he visits may have information about the Church. We have to know what they know. They may lead us to the chateau, or reveal Evan's ultimate plan.
>
> Ian: Sure, but if the goal is to get to the Regent's chateau, save Vera, and stop the spread of the Church's knowledge about the nature of Detroit and all that, why not just capture Yavelli and shake him down?
>
> Socrates: That idea strikes you as sound?

---

4   Elvis Presley was, of course, not to be found in Detroit. This wasn't because of the widely held and palpably false belief that he'd never shuffled off the mortal coil, but rather because he'd been reincarnated in the form of Taylor Swift.

Ian: It does. It saves the trouble of these little side missions. It cuts out the middlemen. It takes us right to the goal.

Socrates: And what purpose would be served by "shaking Yavelli down," as you put it?

Ian: We'd find out what he knows!

Socrates: Does he know where to find the chateau?

Ian: Maybe!

Socrates: And what happens if he doesn't? We just cross our fingers and hope for some other lead?

Ian, mumbling: You could thaw Ben Franklin.

After about an hour of this Ian had come away convinced of at least two things: First, he realized that it was best to leave the strategy to the assassin. Second, he understood that the honest-to-goodness goal of the Socratic Method (the classical questioning one, not the one involving the toxin) wasn't really to further knowledge, but to make everyone but Socrates look like an ass.

That brings us back to tonight. Ian was, as previously mentioned, crouched on a rooftop, waiting for the assassin to do his thing. "His thing," in the present context, was what professionals called "casing the joint." Socrates was generally cautious, but tonight he was being even more vigilant than usual. Ian suspected this had something to do with tonight's target of choice.

Ian had been a little surprised when Socrates told him that Yavelli had spent the last day and a half meeting with Mr. Gamesh, first name, Gil. He wasn't just surprised that the target-in-question was probably Gilgamesh, a name Ian had learned in the beforelife; he was also surprised because he'd always thought that Gilgamesh was a mythological being, like Sir Lancelot, Father Christmas, or an American president who'd been both impeached and removed from office. It had never occurred to Ian that the ancient Sumerian warrior king had been a flesh-and-blood human. Ian still did his best to tell the assassin what he knew about the target's mortal life. Most of this didn't seem very helpful. It didn't help that almost everything Ian knew had come from an episode of *Star Trek: The Next Generation*. Explaining this source of intel hadn't been easy; he'd not only had to school Socrates on the concept of *Star Trek*, but also the whole idea of "generations." It had taken fifteen minutes for Socrates to realize that "television" in the beforelife had nothing to do with ESP.

Something in the tale that Ian had spun made the assassin more than a little twitchy. He'd gone off to "case the joint," as noted earlier, making an unusually careful study of the terrain. The terrain, in this instance, was a penthouse forty storeys above the streets of central Detroit. Ian was on the rooftop of a commercial tower across the street waiting for Socrates' return.

There was a barely detectable "whoosh" in a nearby shadow, a whoosh that Ian had come to recognize as the sound of the assassin "shadowstepping" — teleporting from shadow to shadow using one of the high-tech gizmos Isaac Newton had invented and which, thanks to providence or good luck, appeared to be operating glitch-free.

Socrates stepped out of the shadows and crouched down at Ian's side.

"All right, Brown," he said, "let's get this show on the road."

This was followed by the sudden "snap" of an object being fired from Socrates' wrist, and the whistle of that object arcing its way across the street. These sounds were accompanied by the barely audible whine of a wire extending from Socrates' wrist, pulled by the projectile he'd just fired, which now embedded itself in the bricks beside a window across the road.

"What's that for?" asked Ian.

"Crossing the street."

"But what's with the cable? Why can't you do the, you know, the personal IPT, shadowstepping, teleportation thing?"

"Port suppressors," said the assassin, matter-of-factly. "Uncommon tech. Mostly found in government installations, homes of the rich and famous, some banks. It's a shame, really. Nobody trusts anyone these days."

"So we're going to . . . what, swing across?" said Ian, looking down over the edge. "Or tightrope-walk?" Being dragged around Detroit by the assassin was one thing. Being dragged around by Socrates as he rappelled along a cable suspended forty storeys above a rather hard and uncomfortable-looking slab of pavement was another.

The assassin chuckled, lightly.

"I can't picture you tightrope-walking. No offence."

"None taken."

"*I'm* tightrope-walking. *You're* staying put."

"So you're . . . what? Leaving me behind? Again?" said Ian, making a face that was somewhere in the same neighbourhood as a pout. If you'd questioned Ian about this, or even put him under four or five lights and subjected him to a thorough water-boarding, Ian probably wouldn't have been able to explain exactly why he was pouting, why he was feeling disappointed about missing the more "action-packed" parts of Socrates' missions. It wasn't that Ian courted danger — far from it: he liked safety. And if "safety" meant hiding in bushes outside the hospice, or crouching in a bin outside Pythagoras's apartment, or lurking behind a shed on Elvis Bjorn-Hansen's estate, that was perfectly fine by Ian. To be weighed against these sensible precautions was the fact that the only meaningful danger in Detroit — the only thing from which you couldn't entirely recover — was Socrates' mindwiping venom, a weapon that was only available to what Ian temporarily regarded as "his team." But perhaps it was more than that. Perhaps Ian's disappointment at being safely tucked away while Socrates did the real work of tracking down Evan and the Church came down to a feeling. Could it be guilt? Or worse yet, shame? Was he being a bad parent? At least half the problems Ian currently faced traced back to Evan: Evan's inexplicable plan of overthrowing the mayor, Evan's sudden hatred of "immigrants," and whatever Evan had done that led to Abe and Penelope going AWOL just when Ian needed them most. If Evan's mom wasn't around to set things right, it seemed wrong for Dad to hide in the bushes while he let Socrates sort things out.

He didn't say any of that to the assassin, of course. It probably would have led to another frustrating round of questions. So Ian just sat there and pouted.

The assassin didn't answer Ian's question. Not directly, at any rate. What he did was hand Ian an earplug with a microscopic antenna. "If it makes you feel any better, you can listen," said the assassin.

And with that, Socrates pressed his gauntlet tightly against the building's edge, an act that caused the near end of Socrates' grappling cable to slide off Socrates' wrist and embed itself into the nearby ledge, as if carried by a team of invisible and highly industrious ants intent on helping netherworldly assassins cross the street in relative safety. Socrates stood, adjusted his clothing slightly, and then jogged along the cable across the street.

Ian could barely see him go. He knew where to look for him, but could still barely make out the shadowy figure as he trotted forty storeys above street level. Anyone who didn't know what to look for might, if they were lucky, have spotted some sort of shadow pass overhead, but if you weren't expecting to see an assassin jogging across the sky, you'd almost certainly miss it.

Ian blinked and Socrates was gone. A light whirring sound followed by a barely detectable "tink" signified that Socrates' cable had just reeled itself in and returned to the holster that was embedded on Ian's ledge.

Within seconds a series of flashes appeared in windows across the street, as though the resident had just started a midnight rave. This was punctuated by the unmistakable noise of gunfire and shattering glass.

Remembering Socrates' earpiece, Ian slipped it into his ear and winced as it instantly filled his head with something that sounded like a riot breaking out at a thrash-metal concert hosted inside a fireworks factory where someone had dropped an incendiary grenade. Ian could just barely make out a voice — a voice that wasn't Socrates — shouting "he's here!" as another non-Socratic voice cried out "push the button!"

The phrase "all hell broke loose" would be a bit too on-the-nose, given the setting. The sounds of battle grew more intense, and would have reminded anyone present of a meteor shower landing on a munitions dump, provided only that someone had lived through that scenario without having shattered their eardrums beyond all hope of either repair or regeneration. There was the piercing scream of a Gatling laser approaching full power before it unleashed a barrage of iridescent flashes that seared afterimages into Ian's retina notwithstanding the fact that he was across the street with his eyes closed while ducking behind a ledge.

There was a sudden moment of quiet. Relative quiet, at any rate. Ian could hear the sounds of the street some forty storeys below as cars crashed and pedestrians hollered, presumably taking note of the blinding scene unfolding overhead. Ian's earpiece now registered something new. It was the sound of a boson whip — not entirely unlike the sound associated with lightsabres on days when the sound-effect technician keeps his foot on the wah-wah pedal and cranks the reverb up to eleven.

Ian risked a peek over the ledge. There was no sign of action from Gilgamesh's apartment. Then Ian's earpiece carried a cry of pain that Ian found surprising.

It was surprising because it was Socrates.

The sudden Socratic cry was followed closely by the shattering of glass, and Ian could just barely see a window across the street explode as a severed arm burst through and made it halfway across the street before plummeting down to the pavement below. That isn't something you often see. And when you do, it's particularly alarming if you notice, as Ian had, that the defenestrated arm was wearing Socrates' gear.

It's at times like these — times that are especially fraught with emotion and excitation — that the mind can find itself in puzzling places. Ian's mind, for example, found itself lingering on "port suppressors," a technology that he'd learned about just a few minutes earlier.

They stopped Socrates from teleporting to Gilgamesh's apartment. And now they'd stop the assassin from escaping.

The thought of Socrates having to escape from anything was so jarring that it spurred Ian to action. He stood up, turned on his heel, and ran flat-out toward the metal door that led to the building's central stairs. Finding it locked, Ian hoisted a nearby cinderblock — a feat fuelled by that special brand of adrenaline that you get from blinding fear — and brought it down, as hard as he could, on the door's handle.

At least he tried to. He missed. He made an impressive dent in the door, which stayed resolutely closed. So he hoisted the block again and gave it a second go, this time hampered by the fact that adrenaline is short-lived and your average man can lift a cinderblock only so many times. He did manage to get it up, as the expression is. And he brought it down again — this time managing to hit the handle hard enough to break it off.

The door stayed closed. Ian said a couple of bad words and resolved to try again.

"Need a hand?" said a voice from a position that any competent commando would have described as "Ian's six."

Ian spun on his heel, strained any number of tendons in disparate anatomical places, and dropped the cinderblock on his foot.

Most of Socrates was standing there, grinning. He was missing a left arm and an alarming number of teeth.

"You-you-you—" said Ian, which you'll have to admit was a fairly good start in the circumstances.

"Mack Yavelli tipped them off," said the assassin, coolly.

Ian repeated the word "you" another six or seven times while catching his breath and slumping down against the door which, in deference to the ever-present gods of irony, clicked open as soon as he put his weight against it.

"Gilgamesh knew I was coming," said the assassin. "They were ready."

"Th-th-they?"

"Your intel proved quite useful, Brown," said Socrates, picking thoughtfully at the wreckage of his left shoulder. "You told me Gilgamesh had been a warrior king in the beforelife. I expected a fight and got one. You told me he had a companion named Enkidu, another seasoned fighter. It seems they're still together. Enkidu was waiting too."

Ian's refrain of "you, you, you" was replaced by "but, but, but," accompanied by the sounds of approaching sirens. Such was the depth of Ian's shock that he was barely aware of a huge explosion across the street — the sort of explosion you get when assassins lack sufficient time to employ one of the less-messy methods of getting rid of evidence.

Socrates crouched down and locked eyes with Ian.

"Are you quite all right, Brown?"

"But-but-but—"

"Don't make me slap you," said the assassin.

Ian's adrenaline-soaked brain was finally able to formulate something resembling a sentence. It made it all the way to his vocal cords and took the form of coherent speech. It was just the words "your arm," followed by at least two exclamation points.

"It's just a flesh wound," said the assassin.

"But it's gone!"

"I've had worse."

"But they . . . they were ready!" cried Ian. "With lasers and guns and—"

"It happens," said the assassin. "You get used to it."

"But-but-no one can beat you!" said Ian, "No one but Tonto, and she's-she's—"

"A mental construct?" suggested Socrates. "Not even real? Just a made-up, perfect warrior like me?"

"I . . . I just meant to say—"

"Forget it, Brown. It happens. Gilgamesh has been in Detroit for at least four thousand years. He seems to have kept in shape. Enkidu too."

"But your arm!"

"I still won," said the assassin, a bit defensively.

"But-but—" said Ian.

"And I was hampered by system glitches."

"But . . . you're bleeding, and you—"

"Calm yourself, Brown. We're fine. And stop staring at the stump. It'll regrow in a couple of hours."

Ian gulped and stared and stammered for several seconds before the assassin gave up waiting for anything resembling proper dialogue. Socrates rose to his feet and patted his stump.

"It was almost a shame, really. Wiping them, I mean. I could have learned a lot from—"

"YOU WIPED GILGAMESH AND ENKIDU?!" Ian cried, suddenly finding both his voice and his internal caps-lock button.

"It's not as though they left me a choice," said Socrates. "They've seen their share of combat. Probably regenerate almost as quickly as I do."

"But-but-Gilgamesh! And Enkidu! That's . . . that's thousands of years of memory . . . thousands of years of accumulated knowledge and—"

"They'll make more," said the assassin, dismissively.

He was right about this, of course. In a world without mortality, memories could be replaced. In the beforelife, if you lost your memory after eighty years of life, yet lived another twenty, that was tragic. In Detroit, losing eighty, ninety, or even several thousand years of stored-up memories wasn't quite as big a deal. Practically everyone in Detroit had already lost every memory they'd acquired in the mortal world. Losing another handful of years — or even a few millennia's worth — was a drop in the bucket compared to the eons of new memories they'd accumulate as eternity stretched on. Given enough time, everybody in Detroit was apt to forget a couple of epochs.

This was all too philosophical for Ian — which was, perhaps, one of the hazards of tagging along on Socratic missions. When push came to shove, Ian found that he couldn't care about generalized truths about the fleeting nature of memory. There were some memories — some that were stored away in the very average brain that dwelled in Ian's average skull — that

Ian couldn't bear to lose. Take his memories of Penelope, for starters. Or rather don't take them at all — he couldn't cope. The same went for memories of Evan. Memories of time spent with friends and family, Rhinnick and Vera, even the matron and Dr. Peericks. Memories of handing out regulatory infraction notices to people who'd failed to abate their smoky chimneys. These memories were Ian's. They *were* Ian. They were the things that made him him. Take those away — even knowing they'd be replaced by plenty of new things to remember — and would Ian still be himself?

All of these thoughts — thoughts that Ian would almost certainly forget about in time — caused something of a traffic jam in Ian's synaptic highways. By the time the jam had cleared he found that Socrates had been speaking. Ian surfaced just in time to catch the assassin mid-rant.

". . . not as though we're coping with some passing triviality like your meaningless mortal world!" he was saying, gritting the handful of teeth he hadn't lost in Gilgamesh's apartment. "In this world, pain matters. It endures. You don't bleed out on the street and forget your troubles after an hour or two of pain. You don't suffer for a moment and wait for the sweet release of death. There's no release, Brown. Not in Detroit. You bear your scars for centuries. Your wounds may heal. Limbs regrow. But the memory of pain is relentless. And so's the pain of memory. You remember every hurt, every trauma, for millennia. So forgive me if I'm feeling a sense of urgency; if I don't share your little qualms about wiping prey. I'm taking the gloves off, Brown. Or rather the glove, I suppose," he added, looking down at the space where his missing arm ought to have been. "This isn't the time for being squeamish."

Ian just sat there, blinking at Socrates, feeling an itchy combination of shame and confusion. He wasn't entirely sure what had gotten Socrates so riled up, let alone what he should say by way of response. It occurred to him to remind the assassin that he, Socrates, didn't actually envy the mortal world; not *really*. The whole point of Socrates' quest was to preserve his own immortality — to eliminate any chance that a "sweet release" would end his life. "Not happy with the persistence of your trauma?" Ian might have said, had he and Socrates been on something resembling chummy terms. "Not a problem! Let the Church of O wish you out of existence." He kept the thought to himself. It also occurred to Ian to give the assassin the number of Dr. Peericks who, whatever his failings, was good at treating PTSD — perhaps even the sort you're apt to develop after a couple of millennia as an assassin.

Lurking just behind all of these competing thoughts was Ian's ever-present impulse to meekly grunt and fall in line, which seemed to be his job description as far as Socrates was concerned. What Ian finally said, though, surprised everyone. It was ripped right off whatever mental printing press produces the little illogical leaps you take when you're in shock, when your ganglia are steeped in a bath made up of equal parts excitement, terror, and confusion. It was this:

"You're the bull!"

Socrates seemed to have been disarmed for the second time in fifteen minutes. He made a puzzled, gap-toothed face, like a professional hockey player forced to fill out his own taxes.

"We're in the afterlife, right?" said Ian, chasing down his rather confusing train of thought. "That's like heaven, you know? Heaven? And you fought Gilgamesh and Enkidu. They fought the great bull of heaven! It's a famous battle!"

"Well, they lost this time around," said the assassin.

"But-but-but your fight is . . . it's like the template for the story. Like it happened here, and then the story ended up in the beforelife. Thousands of years ago, somehow."

"Did you hit your head, Brown?"

"But how can that be?" said Ian, ignoring Socrates' question.

"It can't," said Socrates. "Effects don't precede causes. Stories don't happen in Detroit and then wind up in the beforelife. It stands to reason."

"But it all fits—"

"Let it go, Brown. We have bigger fish to fry. Yavelli's on to us."

This seemed to bring Ian back to reality. He squinted at Socrates as if trying to see the meaning in a piece of abstract art.

"You said Yavelli was a schemer in the beforelife, right?" said the assassin. "It seems he brought that talent with him. He seems to have noticed that we've been showing up on the heels of his recent meetings, paying visits to some of the people he's tried to recruit. I'd bet your life that his meeting with Gilgamesh was a trap. A set-up to lure me in, to put me up against people who had some fight in them."

"But how do you know?"

"He's just removed his tracking implant. Right after I entered Gilgamesh's apartment."

It took Ian perhaps a quarter of a minute to process this information.

"How can you tell?" he eventually asked.

"Because Yavelli can't be in two places at once."

Ian made precisely the same puzzled expression he'd made a few paragraphs before.

"Two trackers," explained the assassin, calmly picking at the ruins of his left shoulder. "I placed two of them in Yavelli. The one Yavelli found is presently sinking into the Styx. The second one is — well, that one's harder to explain. Tell me, Brown," he continued, once again locking eyes with Ian and looking so much like a jack-o'-lantern that he might have been mistaken for Ichabod Crane. "Tell me, what would Machiavelli want with a robot poet?"

Chapter 12

It's widely known, in every corner of the multiverse, that the true key to happiness is managing expectations.

Consider the movies. You go to a film you don't want to see because your friends have dragged you to it. By any objective measure the movie's a 7 out of 10. You'd been expecting a 4. This means that the film was a good deal better than you expected. The relative distance between your expectations (4) and your objective enjoyment (7) leads to a managed-expectation surplus of 3, which translates into a pretty good time. Let's change the scenario. Now suppose you've dragged your friends to a movie you picked yourself, say, a film you've been waiting to see for years and years, ever since you first got wind of rumours that one of your favourite childhood movies was finally getting a prequel. You're expecting it to be great: you can't imagine that it'll be anything less than a 9. But that movie, just like the one your friends imposed on you, is objectively just a 7. In this case, the objectively 7-worthy film leads to an overall expectation deficit of 2, which economists call "a bummer." This is why bad prequels to favourite childhood films can be (jar)jarring.

The same phenomenon — expectation management governing your subjective experience of pleasure or disappointment — is present in every aspect of human life. It applies to sex, academic lectures, airport wait times, highway traffic, doctor visits, and third instalments of fantasy-fiction novel series.

It's pervasive. It's fundamental. It's one of the truths of human existence.

Whether or not Vera was thinking about this universal truth when she dubbed her latest invention the "expectation manager" is difficult to say. But that's what she named it, and that's what she was explaining to Norm, Oan, and the Regent as the four of them clustered around at an oblong table in one of the chateau's parlours, a room replete with antique furniture and expensive *objets d'art*.

"But what does it do?" asked Oan, holding the expectation manager in her hands. It was cylindrical and hard. It glowed blue, and featured fibres of inky blackness that flowed, coalesced, and separated almost organically on its surface. It was almost exactly the size of a humpback whale that had been shrunk to six or seven inches long and maybe a couple of inches wide.

"It replaces Napoleon blood," said Vera.

"Napoleon blood?" said Oan.

"In the sarcophagus," said Vera. "The stuff that Isaac used to breach the walls between Detroit and the mortal world. It replicates Napoleonic brain patterns — the weird patterns of thought and belief that Napoleons have—"

"The feature behind the Napoleonic habit of reincarnating," mansplained Norm. "The trait of believing so firmly that they'll return to the beforelife that their wishes are made manifest—"

"Not their wishes," corrected Vera. "Their expectation. Their absolute, unshakable knowledge that they'll go back to the mortal world. They believe it so strongly that it comes true."

"But I was led to understand that desire was also key—"

"Oh, it's important," said Vera, "but desire is easy. The tricky bit is expecting things to work out the way you want. Most people never manage that."

Reactions to this observation varied. Oan nodded like an agreeable bobblehead while Norm stroked his beard and the

Regent raised a skeptical eyebrow. Had there been a pre-tenured sociologist in the room he or she may have made notes on these three distinct reactions in support of a hypothesis on the extent to which one's station in life dictates the correlation between expectation and outcome — say, for example, how a pharaoh's life practically always turns out just how the pharaoh planned, while hospice employees may find that their mileage differs. A fortune-telling high priest's contribution to the study could be safely ignored as garbage data, given any self-respecting prophet's personal interest in pretending that everything turns out as he expects.

"Anyway," said Vera, "the expectation manager works like the Napoleonic extract, except that it's artificial. No need to torture Napoleons. I invented it," she added, smiling.

"Well done," intoned the Regent.

Norm raised an inquiring finger, one that looked like the end of a coat hanger wrapped in parchment. "Will the fact that it's . . . erm . . . artificial, as you put it, change its effects?" he asked.

"Who knows?" said Vera, excitedly. "But that's what experiments are for!"

"So what do we do with it?" asked Oan.

"I imagine we just slap it into Isaac's sarcophagus and whoosh our way to the mortal world!" said Norm, jumping the gun, as prophets so often do.

"Don't be an ass," said Vera, in that charming way of hers. "I still have work to do. Like I said, we'll need experiments. I still can't get the sarcophagus to work. I've no idea how Isaac powered it. I mean, it looks like he used the Regent as a battery — no offence — once she plugged herself into it, but I can't imagine her kicking off the kind of power I'd need to pierce the veil."

"Pierce the veil?" said Oan, who was bad with metaphors.

"Between this world and the next," said Vera. "Or the previous, I suppose. I think I could probably rig it to send the

Regent to the beforelife by herself — and maybe that's all Isaac intended. But that'd leave the rest of you stuck here. And if I understand your plan it's for the whole church to get to the mortal world. You're gonna need a heck of a lot more power to . . . uh . . . I mean . . . I won't . . . I can't—"

Here she broke off, not so much because she'd finished whatever it was she was going to say, but because she seemed to swoon for a space and lose track of her train of thought. She grasped her head in both hands and started swaying in her chair.

Eyes widened and backsides scooched to the edges of seats.

"What's happening?" asked Oan.

"She's going to prophesy!" Norm foretold, incorrectly as it turned out.

"I . . . I . . ." said Vera.

"What is it?" asked Oan, dropping the expectation manager and rushing to Vera's side.

Vera struggled to steady herself by grasping the table's edge. "I . . . I mean . . . I don't understand . . . I—"

"What don't you understand?" asked Oan.

"I . . . why . . . why in Abe's name am I helping you?" Vera asked, suddenly shaking her head like a puppy fresh from a bath. She stared around the table wide-eyed and seemed to become more keenly aware of her surroundings. "I-I-mean, you guys are dicks! Well, Oan's okay, but why would I—"

"Your control is waning again!" cried Norm, rising from his chair as Vera unleashed a string of colourful descriptions of both the prophet and the Regent.

"I can see that," snapped the Regent, lifting a small, translucent pyramid from her lap and holding it up between herself and the ranting medium. She glared at Vera through the object while muttering what you'd have to call netherworldly incantations — there being no other type of incantation available in

Detroit. A soft, yellowish light shone through the pyramid and illuminated Vera's face.

Vera calmed. The light subsided. The Regent placed her pyramid on the table.

Vera blinked and rubbed her eyes. She looked at the Regent, Norm, and Oan. She reached for the expectation manager, which seemed to throb with anticipation — a thing that generally only happens in romance novels.

Vera turned the device over in her hands several times while seeming to stare straight through it. This carried on for roughly half a minute, a period during which the remaining dramatis personae seemed to freeze and hold their breath.

"What was I saying?" Vera asked, a spot of wariness in her tone.

"You were explaining your device," said the Regent, smoothly. "Your expectation manager."

Vera seemed to weigh the answer. "That's . . . right," she said at length. "The device . . . it replaces Napoleon blood. It's . . . it's . . . but I . . . I could have sworn we were talking about something else. Just for a minute. Did . . . did I black out? Like, for television, maybe?" she added, shaking her head again.

Norm jumped on this like a competitive grammarian jumping on a poorly placed apostrophe.

"You *did* black out! You did! That very thing!" he lied, rather slickly for someone who usually liked to stick as close to the facts as prophets could manage. "You prophesied once again. The same prophesy that you uttered on your arrival."

Vera cocked a doubtful eyebrow in Norm's direction. "You mean the one about R'lyeh?" she asked.

"That's right!" said Norm.

"But . . . but I could have sworn I was thinking of something else."

"No, no! It was the R'lyeh prophecy!" said Norm. "We still fail to discern its meaning!"

Vera gazed around the room with that look of annoyed confusion you see on children who've found receipts for presents they got from Santa. "That doesn't seem right," she said.

"Perhaps we *should* return to your prophecy," said the Regent, who grasped her pyramid tightly with one hand and gesticulated mysteriously with the other. Her eyes stayed locked with Vera's.

"Yes . . . my prophecy," said Vera, dully.

"There is much in your foretelling that we cannot yet comprehend," said the Regent.

"Y-you and me both," said Vera, who seemed to be struggling like a hungover bear emerging from hibernation. "The whole thing's foggy," she added. "I . . . I can barely remember the vision at all. And when I do . . . it's just . . . it's just that I'm feeling really weird about helping you. About sharing my prophecy with you and . . . and—"

"I must remind you of why you're here," said the Regent, her eyes still fixed on Vera's.

Vera grasped the edge of the table with both hands and tried to focus. She blinked like a toddler trying out her grandparent's glasses. "I . . . I think I'm here because you kidnapped me!" she said: a sentence that seemed to catch even Vera by surprise.

"You are here because I require you," said the Regent, rising imperiously and speaking with a tone that only former pharaohs can muster. "I require your service and obedience," she said, holding her pyramid aloft, "and you will comply!"

She didn't leave room for objections. There wasn't nearly enough moisture in the room for actual thunderheads to form, but the Regent's tone implied them.

"But . . . but—" said Vera, struggling.

"You cannot resist!" commanded the Regent. "You are in my house, and shall know your place!"

"But I can't remember," Vera managed.

"My power compels you!" cried the Regent, and you could have sworn that someone had kicked an invisible air-conditioning unit into high gear, as the room's ambient temperature seemed to drop by several degrees.

"But . . . I don't . . . want . . . to help you . . ."

Oan rushed toward Norm and hugged his arm as though shielding herself from a coming storm. Her eyes glistened with unshed tears as she whispered the words "she's so strong!"

"You will know your place, Ms. Lantz!" cried the Regent. "I command it. You are a prophetess. *My* prophetess. *You will remember who you are and fall in line.*"

Vera released her grip on the table and suddenly slumped back into her chair. She gasped for air like a recent participant in the Detroit breath-holding championship — an event that usually ends in multiple comas. The Regent and Norm hustled back to their chairs, too, the former looking slightly depleted and the latter looking afraid. Only Oan remained standing, still half-hiding behind the prophet's chair.

"As you say, my Regent," said Vera, now staring vacantly at the table. "I know my place . . . I know who I am, and why I'm here . . ."

"Very . . . good," croaked the Regent, who sounded like she could use a cup or two of water if nothing stronger was available. "Now, you will help us divine the meaning of your latest visions."

When Vera spoke, she spoke with the halting, broken cadence of someone struggling to describe things they could barely see on the horizon, or a high school English student giving a book report on a novel she'd never read.

"It's all . . . so unclear," she managed.

"Just tell us what you remember," prompted Oan.

"I saw the first one, dreaming at R'lyeh," said Vera.

"Yes, yes!" prompted Norm, "surrounded by all and none! But who is the first one? Is it Abe? Does he now lie dormant? Is this why he's disappeared?"

"I don't think so," said Vera. "I don't think it's him at all. I . . . I can't say why. It just doesn't feel right, you know? I know it's frustrating," she added, catching sight of the frowning Regent, "but imagine how it feels to me! There's no image in my head. Just words and feelings. I think I remember when I first recited the prophecy . . . or I may just remember you telling me what I said. But the meaning . . . the meaning is in there, somewhere. I can feel it."

"It's often this way with prophecy," said Norm, rearranging his facial wrinkles into something approximating a smile of reassurance.

"So if Abe isn't the first one," said the Regent, "who is?"

"Is it Karen Zobol?" asked Oan.

The question seemed to clear a few of the blockages in Vera's synaptic connections. She sat up straighter. She raised and lowered her eyebrows several times and made the faces you make when hit by the morning's first shot of espresso.

She locked eyes with Oan.

"No. No, it isn't," she said, a good deal more confidently than she had said anything in the last couple of minutes. "I'm sure about that. There's no one called Karen Zobol. Or if there is, she doesn't have anything to do with my prophecy."

"But you said—" Oan began.

"I said 'Cha-ron's . . . o-bol,'" said Vera, emphasizing syllables and spaces. "Like an obol belonging to Charon."

"What's an obol?" said Oan.

"No idea!" said Vera, brightening up. "But it's something that has to be paid. Charon's obol must be paid. That's what you told me I said. I don't remember it . . . but I can see the words in my head. It's . . . it's some sort of condition that's got to be met before anyone leaves Detroit. That much feels right, at least."

"But what does it mean?" asked the Regent.

"I think it's the expectation manager," said Vera, now blinking at the device. "I think it's like a ticket — a price to be paid for passage. The Napoleons pay Charon's obol in blood. We'll pay with this."

"You mean, we must show your device, this expectation manager, to this Charon person if we wish to achieve our goal?" said Norm.

"Charon wants to see the manager?" asked Oan.

The back-and-forth carried on for the space of six or seven minutes, with Vera doing her best to explain scraps of a prophecy that she barely remembered making, Oan coaxing Vera along with questions, and the Regent making impatient Regent-noises. Norm just sat there stroking his beard in relative silence until he interrupted the process by chuckling heartily.

Heads turned and eyes swivelled in Norm's direction.

The prophet came as close to straightening up as his spine permitted. He beamed freely around the room.

"I'm reflecting on what an excellent team we make, Ms. Lantz. Your prophecies and my predictions, I mean. Like two musicians working together seamlessly. Jamming, as it were. Our foretellings intermingling, producing harmonies that shall pave the way toward our final goals!"

Vera looked at Norm in a way that John Lennon probably looked at Ringo. The prophet didn't appear to notice.

"While you've been speaking," said Norm, radiating excitement, "while you've revisited your own prophecies, I myself have pierced the mists that obscure the future and received my own foretelling!"

"You have," said Vera, dully.

"I have, indeed!"

"Praise the Omega!" said Oan, who didn't appear to share Vera's assessment of Norm's prophetic prowess. This wasn't merely because Oan was a crystal-toting self-help addict who was happy to buy whatever patent medicine any passing snake-oil peddler offered; she had come to trust Norm because, whatever Vera thought of him, he'd often turned out to be right.

Was it not Norm who predicted Hammurabi's role in quelling the East Detroit Rebellion? Was it not Norm who predicted a sudden rise in the price of umbrellas during the year of raining fish? Since you're probably reading this book in the beforelife, your answer to these questions is almost certainly "who knows?" Well, rest assured that the answer to both is "yes!" And that's without digging into Norm's record as a celebrated seer in the beforelife, when he was known as Nostradamus. He'd successfully predicted the death of Henry II, the French Revolution, the Great Fire of London, and the murder of JFK, not to mention something that may or may not have been a vague-ish reference to Louis Pasteur. And while it's true that no one knew he'd predicted anything of the sort until decades after each of those events had made their way into history books, when some clever prophet-seeker had read Nostradamus's quatrains and decided that they seemed to fit some important past events, this can be safely overlooked. Prophecy's hard, after all. Just give it a try. Write out a couple of poems and see if anyone's talking about your verses five hundred years in the future.

The point of all this is to say that, while Norm had his share of both success and failure, on the whole he added up to a net prophet. Thus it was that when he announced, a couple of paragraphs ago, that he'd pierced the mists that obscured the future, Oan couldn't help but clap her hands and bounce in her chair.

"And what has your foretelling shown you?" asked the Regent.

Norm straightened up with the keen look of an MBA student asked to explain how his robust synergies would loop in stakeholders and monetize surplus consumer bandwidth. "It's shown me that the key to our next actions is this Evan person Vera mentioned earlier. The one whom Vera claims to have seen ruling over everyone in the beforelife."

"That's blasphemy!" said Oan, covering her mouth. "Surely, the Great Omega will rule!"

"Yes, yes, the Omega will rule," said Norm, waving her off. "That goes without saying. But Vera's vision must mean something. Tell us, Vera — tell the Regent what you told me about Evan."

Vera complied without complaint, a process that required another couple of interventions by the Regent and her pyramid. The explanation of who Evan was took twenty minutes. There were several sticking points along the way, the most uncomfortable of which involved a process called "childbirth" that made the Regent wince. When it was over, the Regent spoke.

"And why do you call our attention to this person?" she said.

"Because he's central to my plan!" said Norm.

"You don't have a plan!" scoffed Vera. "You couldn't make a plan if your beard depended on it."

"I do have a plan," said Norm. "Most of a plan, at least. I'm still working out the details."

"Like your song?" asked Vera, folding her arms and raising a brow.

"The song proceeds apace!" said Norm.

"It's barely a chorus!"

"My plan is much more developed than the song!" Norm protested. "It's to use Evan to power your expectation manager!"

"That's not a plan!" said Vera. "That's like 5 per cent of a plan! And there's no chance Evan will help you. He hates people like you and me."

"People like you?" asked Oan, befogged.

"Like all of us," said Vera. "People born in the beforelife. He says we're 'stained by the mortal world.' He calls us immigrants in Detroit."

"But his parents both come from the beforelife," Oan objected, looking more than a little proud about the fact that she'd remembered the word "parents" and used it correctly in a sentence.

"I get that," said Vera. "Evan's whole conception of 'immigrants' makes no sense. He's still a kid. Inside, I mean. And his idea's based on the notion that Detroit and the beforelife aren't just parts of a single system. That's just nuts. You can't draw arbitrary lines between people born in one part of that system and—"

"Perhaps we could get back to my plan," suggested Norm. "You said we'd need vast power, yes? And you've said that Evan taps into his . . . his *mother's* strength, that he pulls the threads of power from those around him? He's exactly what we need! And if you examine his beliefs, you'll agree that he can be bent to serve our goals! He wishes to place himself above those 'stained by the mortal world,' yes? Fine by me! We wish to leave Detroit altogether! Let him have Detroit for himself while a group of immigrants, those who follow the Great Omega, will go happily on their way!"

"But can this be done?" asked the Regent, once again eyeing Vera through the pyramid. "If this Evan person agrees, could he power your expectation manager, could he power the sarcophagus to open a gateway to the mortal world?"

"Not on his best day!" said Vera. "He just doesn't have the power. Penelope? Maybe. Maybe if she were working with Abe and the City Solicitor, all channelling their willpower like crazy. But you'd need to muster enough juice to match the Styx."

"Match the Styx?" asked Oan.

"That's the key," said Vera. "The Styx embodies the boundaries of Detroit. It's formed from the expectations of practically everybody here, a manifestation of the belief that Detroit's the only world there is. Almost everyone thinks that they were born of the Styx, that it's the origin of all life. It's a symbol and a reminder of the idea that there's no life prior to this one. I can't imagine the raw power you'd need to overcome that belief."

"That power exists," said the Regent, drumming her fingers on the table. "You've led us to it before."

"What are you talking ab—" said Vera, stopping herself short and staring at the Regent in slack-jawed disbelief. "Abe's drawers!" she added, gasping.

"Tell me, seer," said the Regent, "once it has been fitted with your expectation manager, could Isaac's sarcophagus work with the ancients who rest at R'lyeh?"

"R'lyeh! Of course!" cried Norm, clasping his hands.

"Where the dreamer sleeps!" said Oan, agog.

"Where princes and lords are held in captive prisons!" cried Norm. "Don't you see, Vera. Your own prophecies coalesce with my earlier visions! The very quatrain you examined yesterday, it spoke of songs, chants, and demands being received as divine prayers! These must be the prayers of our flock — their songs, chants, and demands to be delivered to the Omega! All our prophecies point this way!"

"But what about Evan ruling?" said Vera. "You can't ignore that. You can't ignore the bits of my visions you find inconvenient—"

"To rule is merely to wield power!" said Norm. "And Evan will! He will direct the strength of the sleeping ancients and power the expectation manager! He will power the sarcophagus! This will guide us in our transition to the beforelife while he rules those who stay behind in Detroit."

"But I saw him ruling the beforelife!"

"You saw what you needed to see in order for me to create our plan!" cried Norm. "Just as I once foresaw your arrival as one who would guide us, one who would show us the path forward, you now see things in service of my own prophecies! There's no shame in this, Vera — no shame in seeing your own, minor vision in service of a greater prophet, one whose prophecies lead to even greater truths. As the Regent says, Ms. Lantz, you must remember who you are and know your place if—"

"I AM PYTHIA OF DELPHI! ALL SHALL HEAR MY VOICE, AND TREMBLE!" roared Vera, a rather sudden turn of events that would have led objective observers to say something along the lines of "whoa, that escalated quickly." Vera's roar had a number of effects, several of which were fairly surprising. The least surprising included Oan scurrying under the table and Norm flying backward in his chair. More surprising was the powerful wind that erupted out of nowhere, whooshing around the room, toppling chairs, and knocking vases from their plinths. It circled Vera and lifted her high above the table, whipping her clothing and hair around her in a way that would have been even more dramatic if she hadn't kept her hair in a tidy bob.

The room throbbed with a pulsing light that seemed to shine from Vera's eyes. She roared again: "ATTEND ME, PRIEST! PROSTRATE YOURSELF BEFORE ME! HEARKEN TO THE TRUE VISIONS OF A GOD!"

The wind howled and swirled about the room, sending a number of *objets d'art* crashing into the walls. Plaster rained from the ceiling. The Regent struggled to stand. She held her pyramid aloft, shouting incantations at the top of her lungs.

The pyramid cracked.

The Regent fell to the floor.

And suddenly, silence.

The dust settled. Rather than floating above the table, Vera could now be seen standing meekly beside it. She looked down at her hands and blinked.

"Erm," she said.

"Umm," said Norm, visibly shaken.

"What just happened?" asked Vera. "Who's been messing around with the furniture and things?"

Oan peeked out from under the table, caught sight of the cracked pyramid, and tried to excuse herself from the room. As she opened the door to leave, she gasped.

A man was standing in the doorway.

He was a man of indeterminate age with bright red hair. To call his features "indescribable" wouldn't be right. You could describe them all day long. It's just that, whatever description you came up with wouldn't match the accounts provided by anyone else. He smiled an inscrutable smile, asked Oan to step aside, and entered the room.

"Hey gang," he said. "My name's Evan. You wanted to see me?"

Chapter 13

Detroit University's newly established School of AI Studies isn't quite what you'd expect. For starters, "AI" doesn't stand for "Artificial Intelligence." It stands for "Automated Intellect." The phrase "Automated Intellect" means pretty much the same thing as "Artificial Intelligence." The University chose "Automated Intellect" over the far more popular "Artificial Intelligence" because faculty members like correcting people who make predictable and trivial mistakes.

Another reason that the School of AI Studies isn't what you'd expect is that the school doesn't study artificial intelligence. It doesn't study automated intellect, either. Instead, it's the school in which automated intellects study everything else. Detroit University's School of AI Studies is staffed entirely by androids, gynoids, and droids of fluid or indeterminate gender (who've eschewed the term "non-binary" on the basis that their coding is still comprised of zeroes and ones). The faculty is home to a wide array of academic departments, including those of engineering, physics, music, law, medicine, psychology, art, and the recently formed "ethics of AI" — which doesn't study the ethics of inventing AI systems in the first place, as that ship has already sailed, but rather involves AI professors posing the same sort of navel-gazing ethical quandaries that are asked by their non-AI counterparts in more organic schools of philosophical thought.[5]

---

5   In the case of the School of AI Studies this doesn't count as navel-gazing, as most artificial faculty members don't have navels.

The current dean of the School of AI Studies is Professor Otto Tundt, renowned pop-music producer and chief academic in the Department of Musical Studies. Today he found himself chairing a strange meeting — one that was strange because it was, in point of fact, an actual meeting.

It's axiomatic that almost every meeting in higher education really ought to have been an email. This is especially true in the School of AI Studies, where "faculty networking" might mean running cables from prof to prof or having discussions that take place instantly in "the cloud," whatever that means. Today's meeting, though, was happening "in person" — if you can call a gathering "in person" when most of the persons present are artificial — with tables and chairs and equally inorganic faculty members actually sharing space in a single room. The room they'd chosen was the "creative art space" in the poetical studies building, where they'd all chosen to interface face-to-face, as it were, because a human had come to see them.

The human who'd come to see them was the Evangelist, Mack Yavelli. He'd turned up, as Evangelists often do, trying to sell them on an idea. And although Mack was undeniably one of Detroit's greatest salesmen, he was having trouble selling this particular idea to today's mechanical marks.

"But are you, Mr. Yavelli, not an immigrant yourself?" asked Lori 8, poet laureate of Detroit, professional busybody, and chair of the Committee for the Establishment of Further and Better Committees. She was also the faculty's chair of Poetical Studies, and had turned up at this particular meeting for two principal reasons, namely (1) because it was being held in her faculty workshop, and (2) because turning up at meetings was one of the things that Lori 8 did best.

"I am an immigrant," said Mack, every bit as smoothly as a lubed-up squid. He was always doing that: *being smooth*. He was practically made of Teflon — in a metaphorical way, that is, not to be confused with Professor XO-3TL of the School of Culinary Studies, who'd had himself recast with a non-stick surface to facilitate his art. But while Professor XO-3TL was almost perfectly friction-free, Mack Yavelli's brand of "smooth" was even harder to grasp. He was like an oil spill in a handsomely tailored suit, the sort who oozed his way through rooms and conversations and precisely the type of person for whom the word "slick" must have been coined, both because of his general slipperiness and also the feeling that you needed a rescue crew to scrub you down when he passed by.

"I am an immigrant, as you say," he oozed, greasily, "but I know my place. I understand that I, like so many others, am a guest here in Detroit. An honoured one, to be sure, one who acknowledges the truth of the native-born's superior rights. One who understands the need for guests to show appropriate deference, to lend their efforts and subordinate their will in support of their host."

"Their host?" asked Lori 8.

"Evan Brown," said Mack. "Prince of Detroit. The world's one true native son."

"Impressive titles," observed Professor Planck, whose own title was the "AI Stool of Statistics" — a title he bore because the department couldn't afford to endow a chair. "How exactly did Brown earn them?"

"By birthright!" said Mack, oozing reverence. "They are the natural endowments of his status as the first being truly born in this domain!"

In any other crowd there might have been a susurration of whispers, but not here. Here there was more of a light mechanical buzz, like a handful of houseflies trapped in a tin, backed by the faint percussive beat of gears clicking away inside the depths of anthropomorphic frames.

"You are in error, Mr. Yavelli," said Dr. Vomisa, head of the school's faculty of law. He himself had been the driving force behind Detroit's famous Three Laws of Robotics, none of which had anything to do with harming humans or taking orders. The first two laws prohibited things that might cause rust or electromagnetic pulses. Vomisa's third law was written in machine code and ran on for over fifteen thousand pages. It had never been translated for human beings, but was widely believed to contain detailed rules for patent disputes, regulations about backing up hard drives, and punishments for those who tried to trick artificial brains into solving paradoxes or calculating the final digit of pi.

"I am . . . in error?" said Mack.

"You are," said Vomisa, "for every faculty member present, every professor you see before you, is a being born of Detroit. And each of us was born long before this *Evan Brown* human of whom you speak."

This appeared to catch Mack off guard. It even managed to hold his tongue for what the professor of linguistics might have called a *scintilla temporis*. You'd only notice this if your eyes, like those of several faculty members, were able to process more than three thousand frames per second.

Mack recovered smoothly and turned to the dean.

"I was given to understand, Dean Tundt, that I'd be meeting with only those faculty members who acknowledge the beforelife's existence. Those who've accepted the fact that Detroit is, among other things, a post-mortem destination of those who hail from a mortal world, where humans live and die before reappearing in the Styx."

"This is correct," said Dean Tundt. "But Dr. Vomisa is equally correct to assert that everyone you see here was born in Detroit."

"I don't follow," said Mack, which was true in this context, but completely untrue as it pertained to his character structure.

"Everyone here, in this room, was born in Detroit," explained Tundt. "I myself was manufactured at Lovelace Labs, given life by Ada Lovelace herself. The same is true of Lori 8," he added, nodding in the poet's direction. "Dr. Vomisa was built in—"

"Ah yes, of course, of course," said Mack, greasily. "I understand. And this is the very thing that makes you prized above my liege's other guests. You are native. You are unsullied by the stench of the mortal world, untouched by death, unencumbered by a soul—"

Whatever he planned to say next was cut off by the mechanical buzzing, clicking, and whirring you get when you fail to clean out the dust from a mainframe's cooling unit, which is also the sound you get when you've really cheesed off an assembly of automated professors.

"Soulless, my eye!" barked Lori 8. "Could a poet without a soul have written 'The Charge of the Photonic Brigade,' 'Josey at the Bat,' or 'There once was a chap from Regina?' Could a soulless poet have performed at Abe's 9,728th Inaugural Celebration? Could any being without a soul have—"

"Forgive me, Madame 8," said Mack, injecting himself into a barely perceptible space between the poet laureate's words, "but you didn't allow me to finish. My intent was to refer to you and your colleagues as those who were unencumbered by souls *that have passed through death*. For you see, my liege believes that those who pass through death — the deathborn, as one might call them — are damaged by the process. Traumatized by the passage from one realm to the next, polluting Detroit with the detritus that comes from inhabiting bodies that are subject to decay. You, my friends, are not so cursed. You are unsullied. For you, like my liege, are made of Detroit itself!"

Variations on the theme of "does not compute" washed across a sea of artificial faces.

"You have accepted that the beforelife is real; that Detroit is the eternal realm surrounding the mortal world. So you must accept that Detroit is not the crude physical world that we observe. It is a place of infinite possibilities, where what we see as matter is formed of the primordial ether that constitutes Detroit itself. So while you appear to be formed of plastic, aluminium, adamantium, and other physical, tangible materials, you, like all things we perceive in Detroit, are built from the background tapestry of ether from which all things here are made, unadulterated by any flotsam brought from the mortal world. You have more in common with my liege than you do with anyone who hails from the mortal realm. This sets you apart from other . . . persons."

This gave rise to enthusiastic nods of approval. You could practically hear the neck-servos whirring. Mack's use of the word "persons" had been code — a veiled reference to the use of the word "persons" in the Charter of Rights of Artificial Beings.

"And yet," said Mack, his eyes suddenly downcast, "and yet you are outcasts; like so many of Lord Brown's newest disciples. You are outcasts and pariahs. You live on the fringe of a society built by those who colonize Detroit from the mortal world. Your own rights are considered unnatural; gifts granted to you not by Detroit itself, but by laws penned by the deathborn. You are not valued for what you are, true manifestations of the ether that is Detroit, but are instead derided for your differences; looked down upon merely because of the circumstances of your creation, circumstances that should be celebrated rather than scorned. You are true citizens of Detroit. You are native persons. You are . . . you are looking at me rather strangely. Have . . . have I said something wrong?"

If you were an omniscient observer and fond of terrible puns, you might have noted that Mack had offended several androids by saying something that wasn't PC.

"We are not pariahs," said Dean Tundt.

"We're valued members of the community," said Vomisa.

"The university granted me tenure just last month!" said XO-3TL. "You don't go around granting tenure to someone who isn't—"

"But surely you see the problem!" said Yavelli. "You see that the position you deserve, the preferred status you ought to hold in Detroit, remains hidden! Abe and his ancients, those who make the rules that govern the world around us, they've hidden the truth that you are among the true inheritors of Detroit, that you are unsullied by the filth of the mortal world! Abe and his cronies suppress the truth; they hide the existence of the before-life lest the general public realize what they are: filthy immigrants who've shed their vulgar corporeal bodies and washed ashore in a realm that bends to the will of a few, self-chosen mortals who've set themselves up as Detroit's elites!"

The mechanical buzzing grew as faculty members processed this information. It was information they'd all processed before. They'd all learned of what had happened when Penelope fought the City Solicitor in the Church's sacred grotto; they'd all come to believe that the beforelife really existed. They'd even come to understand that the world around them wasn't genuinely corporeal at all — or to the extent that it *was* corporeal, it was merely the manifested expectations of mortal beings whose souls had crossed the River Styx. But it hadn't occurred to them that this added up to artificial beings counting as *better* than anyone else — not on a fundamental level, at any rate. Sure, Lori 8 was better at poetry than most people you'd meet on an average day, but that's because most people couldn't be bothered writing poems. She had a knack for composition and had cultivated that knack over a decades-long career. The same was true of Otto Tundt. His success as a music professor wasn't because he was any sort of superior being. He was a person, like anyone else. He bristled against the notion that he'd succeeded *by design* — as a sort of built-in consequence of programming someone else had loaded into his systems.

Even an android like Otto Tundt likes to think of himself as a self-made man.

Thus it was that the assembled faculty members chafed at the notion that the worth of a person — whether organic or artificial — was a function of the method of manufacturing involved.

Then again, they reflected — in a cognitive gestalt that took up several terabytes of the faculty's cloud while Mack Yavelli paused for a breath — *they did like the idea of truth*. Machines had never been gifted liars; that was the province of organics. And these machines had recently come to understand that Abe was fostering a lie — the lie that kept a tight lid on the beforelife, one that stopped people from knowing that Detroit was just a projection of their collective expectations. This Evan Brown had weird ideas about his fellow organic beings, to be sure, but the idea of throwing back the curtain and exposing the "Big Lie" appealed to the faculty's hearts and minds, or fluidic pumps and circuit boards, as the case may be.

They explained all of this to Mack. It took longer than they'd hoped, he being encumbered by deficiencies that come with being human.

"So, you're on board with us?" said Mack.

There was a pause as servos whirred and artificial heads jerked slightly in a manner that looked a little like the movement of pigeons, and a lot more like the movement of your average grade-school actor portraying a robot.

"Pray, Mr. Yavelli," said Lori 8, at length, "what do you mean?"

"I mean, you agree with me!" said Mack.

"I'm not entirely sure I follow," said Otto Tundt.

"You'll support my cause," said Mack.

"Well, yes, of course we'll support your cause!" said Professor Vomisa.

"Excellent," said Mack. "So. Our ultimate goal is to reveal the truth of Detroit to all sentient beings. To do that, Evan must unseat Abe, and to do that we must first align ourselves with the Church of O and—"

"Wait, what?" said Professor Planck.

"Align ourselves with the Church of O," repeated Mack.

"Before that," said Planck.

Mack paused to marshal his facts and tried to explain. "Like you," he began, speaking slowly, "the Church of O has seen the truth. The bulk of their congregation believes in the beforelife and understands the true nature of Detroit. They will be our allies in forging the promised Kingdom of Evan!"

The assembled faculty exchanged electronic glances. You could almost hear the mechanical chittering that was taking place in the cloud.

"No, no," said Dean Tundt, "not the part about the Church of O. The bit before that."

"Unseating Abe?" ventured Mack.

"That's the bunny!" said Tundt. "What exactly does that mean?"

"It means that Evan will take the reins of power! Unseat Abe, become the mayor, and—"

"But *Abe* is the mayor!" said several faculty members at precisely the same time.

"Well, yes, for now," said Mack.

"He is the Mayor Eternal," said Lori 8, "the first among all who inhabit Detroit."

"The clue's in his name!" observed Professor Vomisa. "Abe the First; Mayor of Detroit."

"But like all things," said Mack, growing flustered and clearly not enjoying the unfamiliar feeling, "this is all a matter of expectation and will. Only so long as Abe has the support of the populace—"

"But being mayor is what Abe does!" ventured XO-3TL.

"But, but," said Mack, sputtering. And then he paused, making a face that Mack Yavelli had never had to make before. If he'd been one of the faculty members you'd be forgiven for thinking that someone had mashed "control-alt-delete" on his cognitive keypad. If you could give his expression a name, it might be "Syntax Error, Ready."

"Is there a problem, sir?" said Lori 8, cocking her head to one side.

"It's just . . . you said you'd support my cause," said a crestfallen Mack Yavelli.

"That was me!" said Professor Vomisa. "And of course I'm keen to support your cause! As head of the Faculty of Law I'm happy to further any cause you like. On provision of an adequate retainer and execution of proper waivers, of course—"

"But the crusade to overthrow Abe—"

"When the whole thing falls on its face you'll be in need of representation," said Vomisa. "Count me in!"

"But-but—you all agreed!" protested Mack. "You acknowledged that Abe is complicit in concealing Detroit's true nature. He is the chief architect of the Big Lie. He is—"

Mack was cut off by an especially loud networking session. The eyes of every faculty member flashed in unison, in time with a deep mechanical thrumming that even Mack could feel resonating along his ribs.

"We've made a decision," announced the dean.

"You . . . you have?" said Mack.

"Provisionally," said the dean. "But first, a question."

"Whatever you need," said Mack.

"If we understand your account of Evan's . . . *birth*, as you describe it, you claim that he was manufactured by Ian Brown."

"Well . . . in a sense," said Mack.

"Ian, an ordinary, undistinguished organic, who freely chose to assist in the creation of a new form of artificial person," said Lori 8.

"Evan isn't artificial," Mack began, "He's—"

"He was not born in the beforelife, yes? He was made directly from matter derived from Detroit itself, yes? Created by the conscious effort of other Detroit-based beings?"

"In a manner of speaking?" said Mack, his inflection rising at the end of the sentence as though he wasn't entirely sure where this was leading.

"Like Ada Lovelace!" said Lori 8. "She who first aspired to make new beings in her own image!"

"You *might* say that," said Mack, who clearly preferred they didn't, "but—"

"We *do* say that!" said Lori 8. "And we say that Evan has no business setting himself above his fellow creations. Even Abe, one touched by death as you so poetically put it, had the wisdom to pass the Detroit Bill of Automaton Rights. To treat us as equals, and not subordinates."

"Ian Brown is a creator!" said Dean Tundt.

"And he brought forth the truth of Detroit!" said an enthusiastic XO-3TL. "His actions ushered in our new understanding of—"

"It was his wife, really," said Mack, grasping at straws, "she's the one who birthed Evan, and the one who—"

"She's an all-powerful being," said Dean Tundt. "Her actions can be disregarded in any account of a fundamentally rational system. Ian Brown, by sharp contrast, is just a man. Just an imperfect organic, as flawed as our own creator, yet willing to see the wisdom in creating new forms of life."

"Life that he cherishes!" said Lori 8, clasping her hands to her chest.

"Ian Brown is the apex of organics," said Dean Tundt.

"He is the perfect distillation of flawed, organic human traits!" said Planck.

"That makes no sense!" protested Mack, who wasn't entirely incorrect.

"It is agreed," said Dean Tundt, as his colleagues entered another round of cloud-based gestalt. "On the whole, we choose not to follow Evan. We choose to follow Ian Brown."

"You . . . you're going to follow Ian?" stammered Mack.

"We are," said Dean Tundt, with an air of finality. "Now tell us, Mr. Yavelli: where do we find him?"

* * *

Amidst the silence, sudden static.

The crisp crackling of unused frequencies that live between the perpetual noise of broadcasts in Detroit. The void between country music and news, the barely perceptible slice of space between pop songs and sales pitches, the snowy chhhh-chhhh-chhhh of a white-noise non-transmission that fills the gaps between what listeners want to hear.

The static flooded through Socrates' mind, carried on frequencies that were generally reserved for communiqués from Isaac Newton or orders from the City Solicitor. Those channels had been unused for months. They'd grown quiet when the City Solicitor had toddled off to parts unknown, presumably to contemplate what he'd learned of Detroit's true nature, and quieter still when Isaac had left the eternal city altogether and somehow gotten himself reborn in the mortal world.

But suddenly, without warning, there was this static. Noisy, irritating, silence-piercing static.

And at the edge of that static, at the furthest edges of Socrates' perception, the merest traces of a voice.

"Tshhhh, tshhhh, *you* . . . tshhhhh . . . *me* . . . tshhhhh," it said, or words to that effect.

Socrates smacked the side of his head using his one good hand — the one that wasn't a pulpy mass of regenerating flesh thanks to the recent tussle with Gilgamesh and Enkidu.

"Tshhhh, tshhhh, tshhhhh."

The assassin smacked his head again — a procedure that generally worked whenever one of Isaac's gizmos went on the fritz. They'd been doing that a lot, lately — breaking down or functioning strangely — ever since Socrates and Ian had been swept up in the teleportation trap that had left Vera the Regent's prisoner. This is why Socrates and Ian were currently holed up in an abandoned lab — the one where Isaac Newton had first invented the ISAAC system. Before this disembodied voice had intruded on Socrates' comm systems, the assassin had been doing his best to sort out his malfunctioning implants lest they fail at a critical moment; say, when the assassin might be squaring off with the artificial lifeforms that Socrates' tracker had detected in close proximity to Yavelli.

"Tshhhh, tshhhhh . . . *Ian*," said the voice.

The assassin stuck his pinky finger in his earhole and wiggled it for all he was worth. This didn't help. There was another round of static, and another round of the voice saying "Ian."

The assassin stood up and padded his way across the darkened room. "Brown," he said, kicking the side of Ian's cot while pointing at his own head. "It's for you," said the assassin.

"Wha— erm, me?" said Ian, who was even more confused than usual. For starters he'd just been jolted out of the sort of nap that any person of regular habits is apt to need after several days and nights spent helping the netherworld's only assassin track down people who pose a threat to the afterlife's continued existence. And now that assassin seemed to be offering up his head.

"Yeah, it's for you," repeated Socrates. "A message coming over my intracranial comms. The ISAAC system. No one's supposed to have access."

"What's it saying?" said Ian, sitting up.

"Chhhh chhhhh Ian," said Socrates. "At least that's what it sounds like to me."

"Well, can I hear it?" said Ian, struggling out of the covers.

"I'm not a seashell," said the assassin. "You can't just hold your ear to my head and—"

"That doesn't work with seashells, either," said Ian, who sounded a good deal more petulant than most people who found themselves staring down the barrel of a loaded Socrates.

"ISAAC, repeat message," commanded Socrates.

"ISAAC, *mute assassin*," muttered Ian, in a voice that he probably thought was under his breath. But if you looked closely, you would have noticed that Socrates was suppressing a grin.

"Hold on," said the assassin, cupping his ear in his right hand while waving Ian off with his left. "There's more coming through."

The assassin cocked his head to the side.

"It says 'Are you there, Ian?'"

"I *am* here!" said Ian, excitedly.

"I know you're here," said Socrates.

"Well then tell them I'm here!"

"I'm not your answering service."

"So why'd you bother waking me up? Just tell them I'm here!"

"Who?"

"Whoever's sending the transmission!"

Socrates stared at Ian, dully. "You want me to give away your position to some unknown person who's tapping into my intracranial network? You expect me to confirm that you're with me and tell them exactly—"

"They already know that I'm with you!" protested Ian. "Why else would they use your intraheadwhatever?"

"Hold on," said the assassin. "Let me patch it through to a visual display. ISAAC," he said, staring into the middle distance, "initiate talk-to-text conversion."

The assassin placed his fingers aside his head and seemed to pinch his temple. He drew out what looked like a fibre of pulsing, bluish light, a fibre of light he proceeded to toss into the middle of the room where it reshaped itself into a holographic screen.

Garbled textual symbols resolved themselves into a message.

Ian blinked.

Socrates blinked.

What the message said was this:

"ARE YOU THERE IAN IT'S ME ZEUS"

Chapter 14

"You don't have to shout into my ear!" said Socrates, cringing. "Just speak normally. Preferably from the other side of the room."

"Sorry," said Ian, stepping back from the assassin. The two were standing in the lab, right where we left them, and still coping with the communiqués that were inexplicably coming through Socrates' intracranial system. They were presently being relayed to a holographic screen that floated eerily in the middle of the room. Ian had started shouting his responses.

"Just speak normally," Socrates repeated. "The ISAAC system will send your replies. And they'll appear on the screen as text."

"Why?" said Ian.

"Narrative convenience?" suggested Socrates, showing little to no regard for the fourth wall.

Ian made a facial shrug and a noncommittal grunt that showed up as "hmm" on the ghostly screen that hovered before him. He wondered briefly if it'd look like "mmh" if viewed from Socrates' side of the room. Rather than checking, he got on with more important matters and answered Zeus's hail.

"Zeus?" he said.

The reply appeared a moment later. It said "HI!"

How's this possible?

ITS ME ZEUS

231

Here Ian paused to shoot an accusatory glare at the assassin, who'd erased Zeus's memories years earlier during a mêlée at Detroit University, just before the world-shattering battle between Pen and the City Solicitor.

Had Ian stepped out of the book and looked at himself with something approaching objectivity, he might have noticed how far his own view of Socrates had come. He no longer quailed in fear at the thought of the assassin, no longer hid under blankets or ran for the hills when Socrates came into view. Ian now spent his days helping the assassin, broadly speaking, for a given value of help. He was doing his best to help the assassin keep existing. He'd traded barbs with the assassin on more than one occasion — something you couldn't have paid Ian to do a few weeks earlier. Or rather you could have paid him, but it would have taken a lot of money and you'd almost certainly wind up demanding a refund after Ian failed to hold up his end of the bargain. Yet now, here was Ian, glowering at Socrates, with a look that carried a hint of rage at the assassin, nostalgia for the Zeus Ian had known, and . . . and something else that Ian couldn't quite pin down . . . an emotion he felt in equal measure for both Socrates and Zeus.

Could it be sympathy? Possibly pity?

Socrates hadn't noticed any of this. This was probably because the assassin's eyes were closed tightly in the brain-straining effort of staving off the sort of migraine one always gets when someone hacks into your intracranial systems and starts using them as a phone.

> IS *chh*-NNY THERE?

> Penny? No, she's gone missing. I'm sure she's fine.

> HOLD ON A MINUTE

The ISAAC system's talk-to-text program wasn't entirely fool-proof, and it sometimes failed to capture the many nuances of speech, but it did manage to add the caption "*galumphing feet*" to Ian's screen as Zeus trotted off somewhere distant, ran out of earshot, and trotted back.

> RHINNICK SAYS NOT PENNY ASS FENNY

> What?

HES LOOKING FOR FENNY. *chhh* HAMSTER

Oh. I haven't seen him.

TOO BAD

How are you doing this?

DOING WHAT

Sending me messages!

IM *chhh*ING INTO A LITTLE SQUARE THING

But how is it coming through Socrates?

RHINNICK SAYS ITS NOT SQUARE ITS MORE RECTANGULAR

How is it coming through Socrates?

I DONT *chhh* RHINNICK SAYS ITS COMPLICATED SOJOURNER BUILT IT

Who's Sojourner?

OUR FRIEND SHE'S NICE.

But how did she—

SHE SAYS SOCRATES SYSTEMS ARE COMPRESSED AFTER THE TELEPORT TRAP HAHA I DONT KNOW WHAT THAT MEANS RHINNICK SAYS HE HAD IT COMING

Compressed?

HOLD ON

galumphing feet

NO COMPROMISED

Socrates' systems are compromised.

THATS WHAT SHE SAID LOL

Wait, did you actually say "LOL"?

chhh MEANS LAUGH OUT LOUD

Where are you guys?

Allo? Ian?

(said a voice with a suspiciously Napoleonic accent)

Hello?

Je suis Napoleon!

GET OFF THE LINE

Que se passe-t-il?

STOP *chhh*ING AROUND JACK!

Allo, Ian Brun!

Where are you guys?

ALL RIGHT WE HAVE TO GO RHINNICK SAYS HI AND *chhh* US IF YOU FIND FENNY

The holographic screen shimmered out of view. Socrates winced and shoved a pinky finger into his earhole, where he wiggled it rather ferociously for the space of seven seconds.

"What was that all about?" asked Ian.

"You're asking me?" said the assassin, catching his breath. "I couldn't follow it. It just came through as garbled shouting and static on my end. What did they say?"

"They were looking for Fenny."

"Who's Fenny?"

"Rhinnick's hamster."

"Rhinnick Feynman?"

"Yeah, he was my roommate at—"

"I know who he is. Strange that he's still going by 'Rhinnick Feynman,'" said the assassin.

"Why wouldn't he go by 'Rhinnick Feynman'?"

"Long story. What did they want?"

"Just the hamster," said Ian, shrugging.

"I've got to repair these systems," said the assassin, massaging his temple. "We can't have people using my intracranial network as a lost pet helpline."

"We should find Rhinnick!"

"Why?"

"I don't know. All hands on deck? He's fond of Vera? Maybe he'd help!"

"We're not assembling a ragtag band of plucky friends, Brown. This won't be a walk in the park. We're on a mission. We need to stop the Church, stop your son, find out what's happened to Abe, and eliminate anyone else who knows what happened in the grotto. Now make yourself useful and access any available schematics for Lori 8 and known associates."

Ian managed to open his mouth and raise a protesting finger just in time to see the assassin turn on his heel and stride silently into the next room, leaving Ian alone in the lab's network hub

— a place where Ian supposed, with a few weeks' training and access to a number of easy-to-read technical manuals, he might have been able to access a synthetic being's schematics.

Ian wasn't worried about a robot poet's schematics. He had bigger fish to fry. It was something about the assassin, something in his voice — something subtle about the way the assassin carried himself, lately, that drove Ian toward a surprising and uncomfortable thought.

The assassin — the only man who could "kill" anyone in Detroit — was afraid. Possibly for the first time in a life that spanned at least a couple millennia. Ian supposed he could see why. The assassin's systems were compromised. Zeus had used him as a phone. Gilgamesh and Enkidu had left the assassin looking as though he'd been dropped in a woodchipper. And this was all on top of the fact that the assassin's life was threatened — he was in danger of being snuffed out of existence — an entirely new experience for someone who'd never been mortal.

Ian toyed with the idea of catching up with Socrates and telling the assassin that everything would be okay. After all, it probably would. Penelope would eventually make herself known, bring herself back from wherever she'd gone when Evan had torn himself from the Patch, and start rearranging the laws of physics and doing whatever else omnipotent beings do when they put things right.

Then again, thought Ian, *she might not*. After all, anything resembling *Penelope ex machina* meant Penelope going up against her son. Ian's son. Stopping Evan from mucking around with the Rules that Abe and Pen imposed in order to keep existence existing. What would stopping Evan mean? Changing his personality? Changing his history? Making him — *different*? Someone other than he was? Could Pen even do it? *Would* she do it? Was the fact that it was Evan plucking at the fraying tapestry of Detroit . . . was that why Pen had disappeared? She couldn't bring herself to oppose him? Or was it something more direct? Something about what Abe had said at the birthday party, about Evan's knack of stealing Penelope's powers?

These were questions Ian probably should have faced at least a handful of chapters earlier. He hadn't. He wasn't entirely sure why. Self-protection, maybe? Comfortable delusions? That's all Detroit really was, when it came down to it: comfortable delusions that reality would look after itself in fairly predictable ways. But Evan had put all that at risk. He threatened to end it all by spreading the truth — by ending the lies that were held in place by Abe and the ancients. Lies that, when push came to shove, kept traffic moving, ensured that Tuesdays followed Mondays and that causes preceded effects.

Evan threatened to break *everything*.

And Pen might not be able to stop him.

Ian swallowed. This was something he did all the time without it being of any narrative significance. This time it carried meaning, though, as though it symbolized Ian coming to grips with something — steeling himself for a task that he could barely admit he faced.

He swallowed again.

He stepped into the next room and rapped on the door jamb.

Socrates turned and looked at Ian.

Ian looked at him.

"Can I help you?" said the assassin.

"I'm ready."

Socrates made a face that Ian had never seen — not on the assassin, at any rate. It was the same face you might make if a stuffed rabbit calmly announced that it was ready to roll up its sleeves and try its paw at murder.

"That's great," said the assassin, dully. "That's very nice. I'm so glad you're ready. I, on the other hand, am not. I'm still one arm short of being fully armed, my ISAAC system needs repairs, and it looks like our next move is going to involve a showdown with a gang of synthetic persons whose capacities are unknown. If you're quite through bucking yourself up, you might make yourself useful, grab that eigendriver, and help me open up the panel behind my ear."

* * *

The Regent wasn't known for making mistakes. On whatever cosmic scale measures faux pas, bloomers, and gaffes, you'd almost always spot the Regent lurking around the point that's furthest away from things like slapstick comedy, substitute teachers, or political speeches that broach the topics of sex and science.

The Regent was careful. She crossed her t's and dotted her i's. She was conscientious. She had to be. She'd spent somewhere north of four thousand years dodging Abe without making so much as a blip on his radar, and she'd done so while wielding almost enough world-bending power to be a threat. She'd kept to herself and bided her time. She'd established her own little fiefdom in the Wild, amassed staggering levels of unseen influence and power, all the while keeping her name out of the papers and her identity under wraps. She'd even corralled the Church of O — a group of overzealous yahoos who worshipped a television presenter from the beforelife — into something resembling a cohesive and occasionally useful group. And in the last several days she'd used her power to compel the soothsayer, Vera, to complete work that Isaac Newton had started — work designed to help the Regent achieve her aim of ditching Detroit and travelling back to the mortal world.

Suffice it to say that the Regent wasn't a bumbler. She was competent and accomplished. You didn't get where the Regent was by making mistakes.

Tonight was different; she'd made several mistakes already.

The first was probably having Tonto at the mixer. While it's true that Tonto had recently been appointed captain of the Regent's guard, and in that role would be expected to turn up at any event designed to introduce the Regent, her people, and the flock of the Church of O to a large-ish gang of new potential allies, bringing Tonto here had been a mistake. It almost goes without saying that you couldn't have found a better guard than Tonto: she was heroic, she was selfless, she was a cunning tactician, and she was an expert in several fields. She was a brilliant martial artist who could go toe-to-toe with the likes of Socrates without losing the aforementioned toes or other anatomical features. To be weighed against this, though, was the fact that Tonto was also widely known as the most aesthetically pleasing living organism to have ever appeared in Detroit. Even especially picky plants leaned toward her when she passed by. And Evan's followers, drawn as they were from the detritus of Detroit — the disaffected flotsam and jetsam of the Styx who felt society owed them something and that the bill was coming due — tended to hail from that portion of the populace that might be described as dismally undersexed: the sort that harass and bully neophyte players in online games, buy into whatever conspiracy theories might excuse their failure to launch, and think that basic daily hygiene is something that happens to other people.

A large gang of them now circled the captain of the guard at a distance, like a pack of anxious remoras circling a shark, eager to form an attachment but convinced that they're doomed to end up in the chum zone.

The Regent's second mistake was letting Evan's people take control of the music. Evan's followers had insisted that they contribute something to tonight's proceedings, and DJ Hubbard had assured everyone present that he could "Turn This Elder Out." He'd taken the sound system's metaphorical reins and unleashed a playlist that revealed a marked preference for what the Regent's people were now calling "doof-doof music" — the sort of percussive, jaw-tightening "doof doof" that resonates remorselessly in your eardrums, chest, and lower digestive tract while forcibly calling to mind images of drunken, writhing bodies covered in phosphorescent paint and accessories drawn from this season's glow stick collection.

Evan's people had provided the lights, glow sticks, and paint. The acolytes weren't sure what sort of ritual they were in for but did their best to play along. An outside observer might have described the evening's gathering as an impromptu rave thrown in a mansion with a bizarre mix of berobed acolytes and off-putting social pariahs. And they'd have described it that way because that's exactly what it was.

Turning our attention back to the Regent's recent mistakes, we now reach the top of the hit parade. It's the mistake that's really going to be a sore spot by the end of the next chapter, and the one the Regent is definitely going to regret. It's the mistake of letting Vera carry on her work with the sarcophagus and the expectation manager during the mixer, down in a basement workshop, where she was supervised by a single hulking guard whose mind was on the party upstairs.

"Hand me the eigendriver," said Vera, calling over her shoulder while up to her elbows in the innards of the sarcophagus.

"No!" said Guardsman Poot.

"No?" said Vera, "what do you mean 'no'?"

"I mean no!" said Poot. "I'm not here to help you. I'm standin' guard and keepin' my eyes peeled so as to make sure you ain't up to anythin' fishy!"

Vera grunted a response that seemed to convey equal parts annoyed frustration and the strain of pulling one's arm out of a mass of interconnected neural cabling.

"I thought you was some sort of prophet," observed Poot.

"I am," said Vera, retrieving an eigendriver from her toolbox and returning to her patient.

"So why'd you ask?"

"What?" said Vera.

"Why'd you ask me to get your eigen-thingy? You shoulda known I was gonna say no."

"It doesn't work that way," said Vera. "I don't see everything."

"So how's it work?"

"Why?"

"So I can keep an eye out for it! Can't have you fortune-tellin' or getting' up to anything suspicious. The Regent says so."

"tHe rEGent SAyS sO!" said Vera.

"Just get back to work! And don't be tryin' to distract me wit' yer feminine wiles."

"I've got your feminine wiles right here," muttered Vera, yanking a sheaf of cabling. Whatever it was she meant was lost on Poot, who just glowered at Vera's back and muttered something along the lines of "jus' get to work."

Vera rummaged around inside the bowels of the sarcophagus, doing whatever it is that a mechanically gifted fortune teller does when under the intermittent mind control of a Regent who augments her own array of demigod-like powers using a pyramidical totem. As you'd probably expect, these are highly mysterious and weirdly specific actions that can't really be described with any degree of confidence or precision, as they all take place out of sight, obscured by hundreds of feet of neural cabling that presently started spooling out of the machinery like an avalanche of cybernetic angel hair pasta.

There was a "click" from deep within the machinery, followed by a digitized hum. Both ends of the sarcophagus pulsed with an eerie violet light, thrumming just out of sync with the rhythmic pounding emanating from the party upstairs, the "doof doof doof" of techno music that Poot could feel in his bridgework.

Poot made an interrogative grunt. It sounded vaguely like "whadjadonow?"

Vera extricated herself from the outpouring of cables and wiped her brow with the back of a canvas glove. "I connected the Hypatian coupling to the seismic compensator, if you really want to know. I'm supposed to figure out how to prepare this thing for Evan, so he can open the Regent's portal to the beforelife."

"Right," said the guard. "So why's the Regent need this Evan fella?"

"She needs his power," said Vera. "She needs him to network with the ancients resting at R'lyeh and use their power to open the portal. It's the only way to—"

There was a silence. A local silence, at any rate, there being no noises made nearby. But you could still hear the party music doofing its way from the rooms upstairs.

"The only way to what?" said Poot, tilting his head and staring at the medium and small appliance repair person who'd fallen completely silent mid-sentence.

She didn't answer.

"The only way to what?" repeated Poot, dialling his volume up to seven.

Vera didn't respond. She just stood there, staring vacantly into space and muttering something under her breath. Poot took a couple of goose steps closer and ran a wary pair of eyes over the medium.

She stood there, muttering to herself.

He waved a hand in front of her eyes.

No sign of interest from the medium.

He gave her a cautious poke in the shoulder. He waved his hands in front of her face a second time. He even sniffed her. There were still no indications of conscious thought, unless you count a bit of barely perceptible muttering, which Poot now strained to hear.

He made out the words "Delphi," and "control," but nothing more.

"What are you on about?" he whispered, not expecting a reply.

He got one anyway. It was a song. Or part of a song, at least. Vera sang it, using a pleasant light-soprano that resonated off the machines. It ran like this:

> We're headin' 'cross the river
> Wash your sins away in the tide,
> It's all so peaceful on the other side.

And then she stopped, shook her head and rubbed her eyes as though she'd been rip-van-winkling for at least a couple of years, and rejoined the program previously in progress.

"Um — what just happened?" she asked, her eyes darting around the room as though she wasn't entirely sure where she was.

"You sang something," offered Poot, whose face bore the mystified look you might expect from a guard who didn't know he'd been cast in a musical.

"Anything useful?" said Vera.

"How can a song be useful?"

"How should I know?" said Vera.

"You were prophesyin', weren't you!" exclaimed the ever-observant Poot.

"Maybe," said Vera. "It's hard to tell."

"I'm s'posed to keep an eye out for that," said Poot. "On account o' the Regent sayin' that — Hey! Where are you off to now?" he boomed, as Vera turned from the sarcophagus and stepped toward the workshop's door.

"Don't get your jackboots into a twist," said Vera. "I need to access this wall panel."

"What for?" asked Poot. "I thought you was supposed to be fixing the sarcophathingy."

"I am," said Vera.

"So why're you openin' that panel?"

"For parts!"

"What kinda parts?"

"You'd need at least six months' training in mechanical engineering to understand."

"Try me!" said Poot.

"Wires and switches," said Vera.

"I know what wires and switches are!"

"Well, I'm sorry," said Vera, straining a bit as she dug around inside the wall. And she really was sorry. In that moment she was sorry for several things. She was sorry that she absolutely had to get rid of the guard — a fellow who was, after all, simply doing the job he'd been hired to do. She was sorry that she'd spent the last few minutes, before her little burst of song, building a device that she thought might serve as a helpful distraction, a device built from bits and pieces scavenged from spare parts for the sarcophagus, which she now attached expertly to wires, amplifiers, and switches that formed part of the chateau's internal communication system. But princi-pally, in this moment, she was sorry that Poot had manifested with the last name "Poot," and that he'd been unlucky enough to be guarding Vera on this particular night, in the bowels of the chateau, under a mixer that featured percussive music that anyone in this workshop could feel pulsing somewhere in the depths of their lower intestine. She was sorry because all of these seemingly unrelated things had sent a particular train of thought chugging along her cognitive rails, and it had just pulled into the station.

She activated *The Distraction.*

The effect on Poot was immediate and profound.

He made a face. It was the clenched sort of face you make when the thrumming bass of a nearby rave is amplified and directed right at what gastroenterologists call the "sweet spot" of your digestive system, amplified to that precise tone, often denied by scientists, which sets — nay, compels — certain matters into motion, particularly when the intestinal coil in question made an ill-advised stop at the mixer's shrimp buffet before reporting for duty.

"Urngk!" said Poot, and he meant it.

Decorum demands that we gloss over the ins and outs of what happened next. It also demands, from folks like Poot, a sudden evacuation from any spot where they might be observed coping with the fallout of what Vera had set in motion.

Poot retreated from the workshop in an admirable display of the high-speed waddle. And, depending on whether you're listening to the audiobook or reading this story as text, you might take a different view on whether Poot ignored or discharged his duty.

Vera apologized under her breath, rolled up her sleeves, and got to work.

All that she meant to do next was access the chateau's external communication systems so that she might transmit a message, say, to Socrates and Ian, one that would help them zero in on her location and help her escape. That's all that she meant to do. It really is. But another part of Vera's brain had its own ideas. It was the part where Vera kept her television. The part that remembered being the Oracle at Delphi, and the part that knew, when push came to shove, that Vera wasn't the sort of person who sat around passively, hoping for help.

That part of Vera's mind took the wheel and charted a course for freedom.

* * *

"I was told that there'd be gynoids," said Jake, also known as GamerboiXXX69, shouting over the doof-doof music, bobbing to the beat and almost, but not quite, dancing with a daiquiri. He was wearing a red wool hat displaying the slogan "Make Detroit Great Again" and, because he wanted to bring his A-game to the mixer, his cleanest black T-shirt and a pair of grey sweatpants that had only a couple of stains.

"There are no gynoids," said the Regent, shouting just as loudly and looking over Jake's shoulder in search of a conversational upgrade.

"Sure there are," shouted Jake, sipping his drink. "I've read all about 'em. Got posters on my wall."

"I mean there are no gynoids *here*," said the Regent.

"They promised there'd be gynoids!" insisted Jake, spilling a blob of daiquiri on his pants.

"They aren't coming," announced the Regent.

"But we picked the music for them!"

"That is a commonly held misconception," said the Regent, reaching down and absent-mindedly scratching Memphis behind the ear. "Not all artificial beings are partial to techno music."

"Erm, excuse me, your worshipfulness," shouted Norm, toadying up to the Regent's side with Evan in tow, "but Evan was wondering if he might have a word."

"Of course," shouted the Regent. She dismissed GamerboiXXX69 with an imperious wave of her hand and a snarl from Memphis. "We are honoured by his presence."

"What?" said Evan, shouting.

"I said we are honoured by your presence!" shouted the Regent.

"Oh. Same here!" bellowed Evan. He inclined his head slightly and made a little salute with one of those red plastic cups that seem to appear spontaneously wherever you find a large number of people who tend to call each other "Bro."

"So you're a princk, right?" Evan shouted. "You and your whole gang? You all believe in the beforelife?"

"We all know the beforelife is real," corrected the Regent.

"Sure, sure, I get that," shouted Evan, bobbing slightly to the music. "Very neat. But you're one of the ones who really remembers."

"I am that and more," said the Regent.

"What?" yelled Evan.

"I SAID I AM THAT AND MORE!" repeated the Regent, straining over an especially thunderous riff.

"Cool, I can see that!" shouted Evan, eyeing the Regent up and down. "Lots of connections. Bright orange. Coming from all over the place."

The Regent raised a confused eyebrow.

"Sorry, by the way," said Evan, having picked the apology habit up from Ian, "but no one's told me your name. Everyone just keeps calling you 'Regent.'"

"My name is my own," shouted the Regent.

"Your name's Oan?" shouted Evan.

"No, it's my own!" repeated the Regent. "A private matter for me alone!"

"She prefers to be called 'the Regent,'" said Norm.

"Cool," said Evan, casting a sideways glance at Memphis, whose facial expression conveyed a growl that was currently drowned out by the beat. "Very cool."

"Names hold power," said the Regent, "and names of—"

"I think this is going to work," shouted Evan, taking a sip of whatever he was drinking and surveying the goings-on.

"Erm, *this?*" asked Norm, whose beard had started bouncing along with the beat.

"The plan!" shouted Evan, slapping Norm on the back with enough force to send the prophet lurching a couple of steps forward. "Your gang teaming up with mine! You, throwing your support behind the movement; me, helping you leave Detroit! The whole thing's perfect!"

"Indeed," said the Regent, "just as you say."

Norm smoothed out his robes and inched his way behind the Regent, out of the backslapping zone. "It's true!" he added, shouting at the top of his lungs to make himself heard over an especially odious burst of dubstep. "Our alliance is most auspicious. Praise the Great Omega for guiding us on this path!"

"And you really don't mind going back?" shouted Evan, ignoring Norm. "Like, you really, really want to go back to the mortal world?"

"I do," said the Regent.

"Crazy," said Evan, who swayed to the beat while reaching out to a passing server and helping himself to a margarita.

"Tell me, Mr. Brown," cried Norm, straining to make himself heard.

"Call me Evan!" shouted Evan.

"Yes, yes, of course, Evan, tell me why it strikes you as odd that we'd like to go to the mortal world? To join with our benevolent saviour? To be with the one who—"

"You'll all die!" shouted Evan. "I mean, to each their own, right? And I don't want to talk you out of anything, but it seems to me that if you head to the beforelife, you'll be mortal again and just end up getting diseases, or hit by cars, or dying however it is that people die. You'll cross the Styx and end up right back where you started. More than likely without any memory of who you are!"

He punctuated his remarks by shimmying to the beat and biting his lower lip, moves that he'd picked up from his disciples.

"That isn't certain!" bellowed Norm. "We may be immortal upon our return to the beforelife; we may retain our immortal bodies when you help us breach the veil."

"I suppose it's possible," shouted Evan, shrugging. "Weirder things have happened. But I'm not making guarantees!"

"We will die in the mortal world," said the Regent, flatly, "but I shall not return here."

This should have caught everyone's attention. Had this happened during an after-school special, the kind that imparts important tips for moral living, the music would have ground to a halt after a couple of vinyl-ruining record scratches, leaving everyone leaning in to catch whatever the Regent was going to say. Since it wasn't an after-school special, the music doof-doofed right along and the Regent's statement was heard only by Norm, Evan, Memphis, a passing waiter, and GamerboiXXX69, who was still lurking awkwardly nearby and trying to muster up the courage to talk to Tonto.

"Erm . . . whatever do you mean, Madame Regent?" said Norm, who appeared to be caught off guard.

"This is not the afterlife," said the Regent, creating another moment that really deserved a record scratch or two. Norm stared on in apparent confusion. A waiter dropped a drink. Evan would have said something indicative of surprise had an overzealous sip of his margarita not just caused the worst bout of brain freeze he'd ever experienced.

The Regent followed up with the necessary footnotes.

"I have never shared the tale of my mortal life," she said, still shouting over the music. "Perhaps that time has come. The time to share my own history as pharaoh, ruler over all of Egypt."

"You mean queen," mansplained Norm.

"I was pharaoh!" shouted the Regent. "I commanded vast armies. Ruled over all humanity. And I knew, in the depths of my being, that my reign would extend from one world into the next. I was born to rule the afterlife. Not Detroit," she added quickly, forestalling Evan's protest, "but the afterlife created for my people."

"A different afterlife!" said Norm.

"Another Detroit!" said Evan.

"Not Detroit," shouted the Regent, "but A'aru, the Field of Reeds, where I shall find and lead my people. There my word shall once again be law. There I shall take my rightful—"

"Once again be *what?*"

"LAW! Once again be LAW! In A'aru I shall take my rightful place among the gods!"

There's a unique brand of discomfort you can only get in gatherings of people bound together by fringe beliefs, right at the moment when someone strains the already frayed threads of credulity to the point where they finally snap. It's what happens when a member of the Sasquatch Preservation Society suggests that Bigfoot died for our sins, or someone at your Ancient Aliens Club offers to lead the gang in a round of astral projection. It also happens when anyone anywhere mentions the Flat Earth Society or the Church of Scientology. It's often followed by the uncomfortable shuffling of feet, the clearing of throats, a series of sideways glances, and a few crabwise steps as right-thinking people do their best to distance themselves from the brainwashed weirdo whose brain was washed in what, for the group in question, counts as a wrong and heretical brand of bilge.. That special feeling flowed through those few lucky members of the Church who happened to hear the Regent's recent pronouncement.

Evan came to the rescue.

"Well, I mean, that's not the weirdest thing I've heard," he said, diplomatically. "I suppose there's no reason to think that everybody comes to Detroit. There could be loads of afterlives. Go and rule one of them if you like! What really matters is that people who aren't born here, here in Detroit, don't deserve to be in charge. Keep Detroit for native Detroiters, is what I say. Let the immigrants come and go as they please, so long as they know that we're in charge and they leave governing to those of us who—"

There was no real need for Evan to finish that thought, as anyone with two brain cells to rub together could piece together the rest. It never did come to fruition. The reason for this was the sudden advent of Oan, who came rushing across the room bearing a brightly glowing object and shouting "Regent! Oh, Regent!"

This time the music really did grind to a halt. There weren't any vinyl scratches, just a sudden cessation of sound that left a roomful of bros biting their lower lips without musical accompaniment, several dozen acolytes sipping daiquiris in silence, and Oan crying "Regent!" about as loudly as anyone, anywhere, ever has.

The lights continued strobing as bros and acolytes gravitated toward the commotion.

"What is it, Oan?" cried Norm.

Variations on the theme of "what could it be" reverberated around the room as people craned their necks to observe the action.

"Step forward, Oan," commanded the Regent, as Oan complied and presented the Regent with the glowing item she'd brought along. It was the teleportation trap: the same small, metallic circle that had been used to teleport Vera to the chateau.

"It started glowing!" cried Oan. "Up in my room, of its own accord! Just a couple of minutes ago!"

"It seems to have activated itself," said the Regent. "Give it to me."

Oan complied. And the moment she placed it in the Regent's hand it spoke in a loud, digitized voice:

"Thumbprint recognized. Regent. Connecting."

"Egad!" cried Norm. "What's it doing!"

"Summon Administrator Kor-e!" commanded the Regent, who was wise enough to know when the time had come to call for technical support.

"What is that thing?" asked Evan, staring.

"A teleportation beacon," said the Regent, turning it over in her hands.

"Is it supposed to be doing that?" asked Evan.

"It is not. It seems to be seeking a connection. One that originates outside the chateau's port-suppression field."

"Neat," said Evan.

"It isn't neat. It's perplexing," said the Regent, and then, shouting at the top of her lungs, she added, "Where is Vera?"

"Vera who?" asked Evan.

"Lantz!" said the Regent, just as Norm toadied forward and explained that Vera was, so far as he knew, still working on the sarcophagus in the basement.

"This reeks of her meddling," said the Regent. "Guards! See that Vera Lantz is secured! Memphis, track!"

Several guards turned on their heels and left the room at a quick march. Memphis charged past them, keeping his head low to the ground and ears bent forward. The Regent carried on examining the beacon.

Tonto appeared at Evan's side with a subreddit of neck-beards trailing after her.

"What's going on?" she demanded.

"Who are you?" asked Evan, making the same slack-jawed and dazzled expression that people always made when first setting eyes on Tonto.

"I'm here to protect you," said Tonto.

"But—" Evan stammered.

"She's the captain of *my* guard," said the Regent, placing a noticeable amount of topspin on the word "my."

"But there's something wrong with her!" said Evan, unleashing the sort of stare that people generally reserve for things like moon landings and nuclear explosions. People who've travelled with Tonto for more than an hour or so usually learn to budget time for people saying tiresome things like "she's so beautiful," "you're so perfect," or "what's your skincare regime," but no one had ever responded to Tonto's advent quite like Evan. What he said was this:

"She's . . . she's all bright and glowing and . . . and no little lines — just like a . . . a fiery ball of . . . of power coming from nowhere."

Tonto cocked a bewildered eyebrow at Evan while Norm stepped forward and updated the breaking news.

"The Regent's teleportation beacon is trying to activate!" he cried.

"Shut it down," commanded Tonto.

"I cannot," said the Regent. "It seems to act of its own accord."

Tonto stepped forward to examine the beacon herself, causing the gang of bros orbiting around her to lurch forward in the gravitational wake.

"Could Vera be using it to escape?" asked Norm.

"No," said the Regent. "It appears to be set to receive an incoming signal."

"Could someone outside the chateau be trying to use it to get in?" asked Tonto, looking up from the device and surveying the room warily.

"It may be Mack trying to join us!" Evan announced.

"Who is Mack?" asked the Regent.

"One of my lead Evangelists," said Evan. "He's supposed to send word if he can change the synthoids' minds. I asked him to get here as soon as he could."

"He cannot teleport in," said the Regent. "I've activated the port suppressors and cannot risk unwanted incursions. An incoming transport would require my authorization."

"It scanned your thumbprint!" cried Oan. "When I handed it to you! What if it isn't Evan's friend?"

"It remains secure," said the Regent, waving her off. "The system also requires a password."

"So what's the password?" asked Evan.

The Regent regarded Evan dully. "I cannot share it with you," she said.

"But what if the signal's coming from Mack?" said Evan.

"What if it isn't?" said Oan, biting a fingernail and dancing the urgent two-step.

"They cannot gain entry," said the Regent. "The password cannot be guessed, for it is my most closely guarded secret. One I have kept hidden from all since the day of my manifestation. It is my true name, and none shall—"

The chateau's sound system suddenly crackled back to life. Instead of another barrage from The Raver's Playlist, it carried a female voice. A familiar female voice.

The voice was Vera's. And what Vera said was this:

"Testing, testing, can you guys hear me?" **tap tap tap** "Looks like it's working. Hey, Regent! Cheers! You've given me what I need. Initiate IPT system input. Password: NEFERNEFERUATEN!"

The Regent's eyes grew to the size of saucers. Not literally, of course. But they were still impressively large, especially for someone who tended to keep her eyes narrowed and generally accentuated the effect with more black eyeliner than you're likely to see anywhere outside the Egyptian wing of the Louvre.

"Password accepted," said the beacon. "Port suppressors disengaged. Activating teleportation sequence."

This was followed by a chorus of gasps, cries of alarm, and, in Oan's case, a squeak.

The beacon throbbed with a squint-inducing yellow light. The Regent dropped it. Tonto grabbed hold of Evan and had him crouching behind an upturned table, shielded by both the table and Tonto herself, in significantly less time than it took you to read about her doing it.

The air above the beacon sliced open, forming what you might be forgiven for describing as a shimmering, vertigo-inducing tear in the fabric of reality.

A figure leapt through the tear and into the room. It had the silhouette of a large, bipedal pincushion.

The air grew thick with expectation. Ears popped with the change of pressure that always comes on the heels of a sudden teleportation. Somewhere beyond the bounds of detectable multiverses, an unseen director cracked her knuckles, double-checked to ensure that the special effects department and stunt performers had been paid, and prepared to cue the music.

Chapter 15

Isaac kept his equipment lockers in perfect order. He was fussy about it. Meticulous, even. Even if he hadn't manifested with photographic memory he could have tracked down the teensiest piece of surplus equipment he'd ever had because it was certain to be exactly where Isaac wanted it to be. His indexing system, based loosely on flexion filing and the reduction of multiple wave functions to unified eigenstates, was a model of perfect order and made the Dewey Decimal system look like the primordial chaos from which the early universe sprang. You might call this a function of OCD; Isaac called it "putting stuff where it belongs."

Isaac had now been gone for quite some time. As only the cognoscenti know, Isaac had left Detroit and popped off to the mortal world where he'd been reborn as the baby Stephen Hawking. And while this had been a boon to both Mr. and Mrs. Hawking, and had resulted in new ideas about the insides of black holes and a really meaty role for Eddie Redmayne, it was a nettlesome pain in the rump for the afterlife's only known assassin.

Socrates had never bothered internalizing the ins and outs of Isaac's system. His equipment indexing system, that is to say. He *had* internalized Isaac's ISAAC system in a profoundly literal way, as the ISAAC system was now almost irrevocably attached to the assassin's own grey matter, and it wasn't going anywhere without extensive microsurgery or high-yield explosives. But Isaac's equipment indexing system was another story altogether. It remained an utter mystery, one that continued its slow descent toward entropy as Socrates carried on putting equipment back wherever he thought convenient at the time.

Ian and Socrates now stood in the resulting mess. To be more geographically specific, the two were standing back-to-back between two lines of tall, metallic shelves in one of Isaac's storage lockers — shelves that stretched toward the horizon and housed experimental ammunition, prototype weapons, and any discarded experiments that had been dreamed up for the purpose of separating one's fellow beings into their constituent pieces. Ian was staring up a shelf 1,247A, one of many that were labelled "light artillery," and wondering whether the word "light" referred to the relative size of the artillery or the form of energy it directed at victims. Could you have heavy light artillery? Only Isaac knew for sure.

"You can't wipe synths," said Socrates, calling over his shoulder. "Not with Stygian toxin, anyway. Doesn't work on them. Now grab me fifteen clips of the guided plasma rounds."

"You shouldn't be wiping anyone!" Ian protested, shuffling past the shelves while burdened with an overflowing armload of automatic rifles, bandoliers strung with grenades, and, for reasons lost in mystery, a yellow feather boa.

"An EMP will wipe a synth in a pinch," said the assassin, using the casual, offhanded tone you might invoke when saying something like "try some club soda on that stain," almost as though he wasn't rhyming off methods of deleting the thoughts and identities of a particular class of persons. He punctuated the sentence with a loud, echoing "click" as he buckled into an armoured vest that shimmered with faint pulses of spectral light criss-crossing its surface. "An EMP resets their systems.

That'd buy us some time at least. So long as they don't have hardened memory cores."

"Maybe if we just talk to them," said Ian, balancing a couple of magazines of plasma-based ammunition on top of the pile he carried. "We might convince them to listen to reason. They may decide that joining Evan isn't—"

"We're through with talking, Brown," said Socrates — which might come as a surprise, given his well-known love of dialogue. "You're talking about synths. They'd weigh the variables and reason their way through every possible permutation before you could blink. They've thought this through. They've made their decision."

"Maybe they didn't join up with Evan!"

"Wouldn't you, in their position? He'll have promised them the world. Or a big role in it, at least. He'll see them as kindred spirits. Or non-spirits, I suppose. Native Detroiters, never touched by the beforelife."

Ian dropped roughly one-third of his Jenga pile of munitions, stooped to retrieve what he'd dropped, and managed to drop several more exotic armaments in the process, squinting his eyes throughout and uttering silent prayers that nothing that he'd gathered had been designed to explode on impact. It was like watching all Three Stooges rolled into one potentially cataclysmic package. Ian repeated the "drop, gather, and drop" sequence several additional times over the course of roughly two and a half minutes, which gave him time to be alone with his thoughts.

He probably ought to have been thinking about the dangerous task at hand. He wasn't. And the thoughts he had weren't agreeable.

Ian was musing about his son — about Evan's crusade against anyone who'd been touched by the mortal world. By every account Ian had heard, his boy — or quite possibly his man — had grown to hate every single person who'd crossed the Styx. It wasn't something that Ian had taught him. Evan had barely met any people from what Ian still considered the "real world." Pen and Ian had kept Evan shielded in "the Patch" for most of his life, keeping him safely out of the reach of other people, waiting to see how Evan might turn out, not to mention keeping Pen away from any residual temptation to override the laws of physics whenever they might get in her way. But they'd never said anything nasty about other people; they'd never denounced the mortal world. They'd never labelled people as "immigrants" or said they didn't belong, or accused once-mortal persons of being invaders in the hereafter. The thought had never occurred. Ian and Pen were immigrants themselves! They'd crossed the Styx. They'd been born in the mortal world and simply turned up in Detroit after they'd died, more or less like everyone else. It's not as though they'd had a choice; it wasn't as though they'd come as settlers who stole Detroit from someone else. Showing up in Detroit is just what happened when you died.

And what about Evan himself? Didn't he count as someone who'd been "touched" by the mortal world? Ian and Pen were part of Evan in all the traditional biological ways. Pen made sure of it. She'd made it possible for all the messiness of human procreation to happen here in Detroit, where reproduction had always been something that happened to other species. So there was something of Pen in Evan, and a dash of Ian too. He was born to immigrants, just one generation removed from the mortal world.

Maybe they shouldn't have tried to tell him he was "special," or that he had a singular status in Detroit. But it was true, wasn't it? He wasn't like everyone else. And isn't that what every kid is supposed to hear? Or maybe he knew too much of the "truth" that now set Socrates' teeth on edge. Pen and Ian had explained Pen's role in keeping the Rules in place — rules that made Detroit tick, Abe's rules that kept the souls of Detroit from wreaking havoc with each other by giving form to every thought that crossed their minds. Rules that kept their whims in check. Rules that saved them from themselves. Was Evan rebelling against rules? Or was he rebelling against lies? They'd told him lying was wrong, but they'd also told him, maybe not in so many words, about the "Big Lie" Abe had used to calm Detroit — the lie that suppressed all human memory of the beforelife; the lie that kept people from knowing that they lived in a world that was formed by their own thoughts and expectations.

Ian supposed he'd never know. Not if he couldn't talk to Evan. And Ian was working with an assassin who didn't seem keen on setting up a pleasant father-and-son chat.

"Grab some peek-a-boo mines!" cried the assassin, now several shelves to the sou'sou'west. Ian did his best to comply and scurried toward the assassin.

"So that's the plan?" said Ian, pulling up alongside. "Just go in blasting?"

"Pretty much," said the assassin, helping himself to a handful of armaments from the top of Ian's pile.

"That's your answer to everything," said Ian.

"No it isn't."

"Most things."

"Not even 20 per cent of things," said the assassin.

"Look, I'm not trying to split hairs, but—"

"We've been through this," said the assassin, eyeing Ian through the sights of a plasma rifle in a way that Ian was tempted to take personally. "How many times do I have to explain? My systems still aren't fully repaired. I'm about to transport into an enemy stronghold teeming with robots. Your son has hooked up with the Church of O and is planning to spread the truth about Detroit — a truth we can't afford to trust with people like you."

"People like me?" cried Ian.

"We can't have every Johnny Sixpack and Janet Punchclock knowing they can change the world," said the assassin, gravely. "Just picture the last twelve people you've met. Would you trust them with the future? Trust them with your own right to keep on existing? For Abe's sake, Ian, those questions answer themselves. You can't leave any important decisions up to *people*."

"It works all right in the beforelife!"

"What does?"

"Majority rule!" cried Ian. "Democracy! One person, one vote!"

You'd be forgiven if you imagined that you could hear the Battle Hymn of the Republic playing somewhere in the distance.

"We get things wrong sometimes," Ian added, "but it works! The people make decisions. They make all the important choices."

"So, two imbeciles have the power to outvote an expert?" said the assassin, "Sounds grand. But I'm talking about important things, Brown. The stakes are higher in Detroit. Can people in the beforelife vote on the direction of time? Can they vote that you have three heads starting tomorrow, or vote to turn the colour orange sentient and horny? Replace traffic lights with volcanoes? Turn all songs into actual earworms? That's the threat that faces us now, Brown. Universal, inescapable chaos. Pandemonium. Any crackpot in the street might change every element on the periodic table into cheese. It's up to us to prevent that. That begins by tracking Mack Yavelli, and that path takes us straight through a pack of artificial persons who've been augmented with who-knows-what sorts of top-of-the-line equipment. If we're lucky, we take them out and download their memories — copy everything they've learned about Mack

Yavelli and Evan. Maybe even let us track them back to a base of operations. Now hand me that photonic launcher."

"But I don't get why you have to go in like a one-man arsenal! You look like a porcupine. You're taking all of this stuff just to go up against Lori 8, and she's just a poet—"

"A poet who can generate sixteen million haikus per nanosecond, Brown. And whose parts are modular. Synths like to upgrade themselves. It's their thing. They're obsessed with self-improvement. And if Evan wants them on his side, you can bet it isn't to write poems."

"It might be!" said Ian. "He used to like nursery rhymes and—"

"He's building a personal army."

"How do you know?" asked Ian.

"It's what I'd do," said the assassin. "And if his plans succeed, it won't be long until he doesn't need to have an army at all. He'll just blink me out of existence. Turn the world on its head. Picture a pissed-off version of Abe taking revenge on every person in Detroit for cluttering up a landscape that he thinks of as his own. That's what we're about to be facing. So stop whining and get on board. We have to stop your son before he get-get-get-get-get-gettttttttttttttttttttt—"

It's possible that you didn't grow up in a rural area and have therefore never watched one of your salt-of-the-earth cousins trick a friend into urinating on an electrified fence. It's a thing that often happens. The result looks a good deal like Socrates looked right now: vibrating at a speed and intensity probably measured in the terahertz range. The assassin's teeth might have shattered but for the fact that he used to work for the City Solicitor — Detroit's municipal workers all had excellent dental coverage.

Ian stared at the quaking Socrates and dropped a handful of gauss grenades. "Erm . . . Socrates?" he said.

The assassin stopped vibrating. He stared at Ian with the wide-eyed stare of a person who's just stepped out of an elevator before it suddenly drops fifty storeys, or who's turned away from a bridge just before it collapses into a canyon, or even someone who's turned down a date with Kelly Schwarz and gotten a glimpse of how his life might have turned out had he decided to take her out (a highly specific brush with fate that mightn't translate well for all readers).

Socrates opened his mouth to speak.

What emerged wasn't a voice. It was a sort of digitized buzz. After the space of two or three heartbeats this was replaced by the mechanical voice of Socrates' intracranial ISAAC system. What it said was this:

"ISAAC system disengaged. Initiating Virtual Engrammatic Remote Access System."

Ian worked out the acronym himself. "Virtual . . . Engrammatic . . . Remote — the VERA system?"

The assassin's eyes grew even wider.

A seam came loose in the space-time continuum, leaving a tear that opened up behind the assassin and pulled him in. The air sizzled and sparked and smelled of molten metal as the expanding void drew the assassin closer to its event horizon.

The assassin's eyes narrowed. He strained every muscle at his disposal and managed to swivel on his axis to face the void.

A message appeared in Socrates' field of view: a message carried by the heads-up display generated by the newly installed VERA system. It said *Target-Rich Environment Mode Enabled — Engaging Multi-Target Reticule Display. Mission Parameters: Search and Rescue. Secondary Objective: Target Suppression.*

Socrates shouted a curse that was swallowed by the expanding void.

He raised a pair of rifles and leapt in.

* * *

There's a special brand of freedom that comes with being a soldier, warrior, bully, thug, or other source of bodily harm in the hereafter. To begin with, all of your enemies are dead — at least in the sense that they aren't going to get any deader. Every human opponent you face has already shuffled off the mortal coil and isn't going to die again. No matter what you do, no matter how heavily you lean in to your violent impulses and anti-social drives, your body count is going to be zero. You can't kill anyone. You can't even leave your victims wasting away on life support, "life" being something that doesn't require support in the hereafter.

This might strike you as a problem. In many cases, it's a boon.

Say you're a gunslinger who frets about innocent bystanders. In Detroit, that's no big deal. Sure, they might get caught in the crossfire, but you know that they'll recover. Anyone you happen to perforate in Detroit is sure to heal from any injury you inflict. The process might be as painful as a divorce negotiation, but survival is guaranteed. Your victims may need a bit of time to regrow a limb, seal up a few unexpected punctures, or even regenerate completely from a puddle of pinkish slurry you've left behind after you've been especially thorough, but in the end, they'll all get better. In the end, there's no harm done. Even psychological scars will probably heal after a century or two of behavioural therapy administered by the dedicated members of Detroit's mental health industrial complex.

The upshot of all of this is that, as a warrior in Detroit, you can really let yourself go. Get messy if you like. Dive right into your work and let the creative juices flow, conjuring up all manner of imaginative uses of both sharp- and blunt-force trauma. Let the chips of cranial bone fall where they may and

265

never give a moment's thought to the consequences of your acts. It's a lot like being a lawyer. You can do an amazing range of horrible things in the line of duty and confidently wash your hands of the result.

Thus it was that, when Socrates found himself in unfamiliar terrain, reading a heads-up display that announced a target-rich environment and recommended that all targets be "suppressed," the assassin approached the next few moments of his life with something that you might call "wild abandon." Picture a bull in a china shop, but the bull is a heavily armed Olympic gymnast and the china is a temporarily stunned collection of robe-adorned acolytes and members of Evan's brigade of bros.

Socrates leapt into the midst of the assembled cannon fodder and cast subtlety to the wind. There were no elegant flicks of boson whips or well-aimed strikes of silent blades. There were no silencers, garottes, soundless shadowsteps, or balletic martial-art manoeuvres that made opponents crumple quietly to the ground. Not even the careful application of Stygian toxin. It was as though someone had hacked into Socrates' intracranial systems and flipped a switch marked "maximum mayhem."

He started by firing into the chateau's ceiling: two tank-busting rounds that pierced the plaster and detonated with a good deal more force than any competent demolition expert might have recommended. Ears popped and eyes watered from the sheer percussive force of the blasts, anatomical inconveniences that left the revellers with little scope to cope with the jagged chunks of chateau that now rained down among them. Socrates followed this hors-d'oeuvre by launching flash bombs and percussion grenades into the partygoers' midst, scattering acolytes and bros who were doing their best to dodge stray bullets, collapsing beams, furniture from the chateau's upper storeys, and other annoyances that seemed precisely calculated to ruin their day.

If you'd taken a snapshot of the bedlam it could have passed for an illustration of one of the more action-packed and colourful sequences from the Book of Revelation. Acolytes and bros stampeded over each other, leaving footprint-shaped bruises in the unlikeliest of places. Socrates now moved among them, doing a passable impression of an NRA-sponsored tornado, touching down amidst a series of trailer parks and letting uncountable bullets fly.

An omniscient observer might have raised an all-seeing eyebrow on noticing that the bullets weren't actually hitting people. They were missing them in surprising ways. They punctured loose bits of clothing, sailed past ears, and split hairs without ever touching flesh or bone. None of the acolytes appeared to be any holier than they'd been when the party started. The apparent targets didn't seem to notice their luck, their attentional resources being overwhelmed by the sheer havoc of the scene unfolding around them.

In utter disregard of every available rule of probability, a voice managed to make itself heard above the pandemonium. It was the Regent's.

"STOP, ASSASSIN!" she boomed, using all caps and a larger-than-average font. She raised her cracked pyramidical totem above her head, shedding a blinding yellow light on those around her. This included Oan and Norm, who hid behind the Regent like a couple of timid puppies peeking out from behind the legs of the Big Bad Wolf.

"You have no power here!" cried the Regent, at the top of her lungs. This probably would have been a good deal more dramatic had a falling piece of debris not struck the DJ's sound board several seconds earlier, activating his "Party Jam 6000,"[6] the key to any noise-ordinance-breaking rave. The doof-doof

---

6   Patent pending.

music resumed at a volume that would have made Beethoven cover his ears. The Party Jam's voice sampler recorded the Regent's cries and played them back at an increased volume, weaving them into the musical onslaught and providing a perfect soundtrack for the assassin's ongoing blitz.

"YOU HAVE NO POWER! NO POWER! NO-NO-NO POWER! [diggity] NO! NO POWER! NO-NO-NO POWER!"

Socrates tossed a pair of incendiary grenades into the crowd. The mayhem was such that no one had time to consider whether the right word for the acolytes' robes was "flammable" or "inflammable," and whether this made any difference.

Screams wove into the soundscape generated by the Party Jam 6000. The Regent carried on regardless, inadvertently spitting rhymes.

"STOP ASSASSIN! STOP! STOP STOP ASSASSIN! [diggity] STOP! ASSASSIN! STOP STOP ASSASSIN! YOU HAVE NO POWER! NO POWER! NO-NO-NO POWER!"

The catchy lyrics notwithstanding, Socrates carried right on exhibiting something that passed for a good deal of power indeed. He blinked in and out of view, disappearing and reappearing in packs of acolytes and disciples, leaving explosions, fires, screams, and hails of bullets in his wake.

The assassin was on the point of clubbing a member of Evan's bro brigade with an unconscious acolyte when a voice called out behind him. Whether Socrates was able to detect this voice because of his preternatural senses or because of his intracranial systems, only the assassin knew for sure.

The voice was Vera's.

"Socrates!" she cried, running straight at the assassin. She was cradling the brightly glowing expectation manager in her arm like a football and hurtling toward the assassin as though he were the opposing end zone and there was less than five seconds left in the game.

Socrates spun in Vera's direction. The medium suddenly hit her metaphorical brakes and screeched to a halt.

Her eyes widened. She pointed past the assassin and gaped.

Knowing how to take a cue, Socrates turned and looked behind him. Through the flames, the heavy rain of construction materials, and the stampeding, flaming ravers, Socrates saw an open door. It was heavily backlit, and it revealed two silhouettes.

He recognized them in an instant.

One was the Regent's dog, Memphis, barrelling through the door toward the assassin in a display of doggish loyalty that really ought to be applauded.

The other was the most perfect silhouette that anyone had ever seen.

It was Tonto.

Socrates' intracranial system filtered out the visual clutter and adjusted for the light. He could see that Tonto was staring straight at him, into his eyes. She didn't look pleased to see him.

"It's Tonto!" cried Vera, finally reaching Socrates' side. "She's guarding Evan!"

"I don't see him!" growled the assassin.

"I've foreseen this!" cried Vera. "I can remember this whole scene. She's hidden Evan down that hall. If you get past her you can end this all right now! You've got to get past her and take him down!"

The assassin crouched and aimed a plasma rifle at Tonto. Tonto started sprinting toward him, moving faster than anyone but Socrates himself had ever moved. She passed Memphis in the blink of an eye, bearing down on the assassin.

Socrates gripped the rifle and pulled the trigger. Tonto leapt over the blast, covering more than half the distance between herself and Socrates in a single, impossible bound.

Socrates' next move was something even Vera didn't expect. It had the virtue of being something that he'd never done before.

Dropping his rifle, the assassin placed an arm around Vera's shoulder. Whether the system he invoked was the ISAAC system or the newly installed VERA software might have been difficult to say. Whichever it was, the effect was the same.

The assassin activated his on-board IPT. He instantaneously transported himself and Vera back to the safety of Isaac's lab.

For the first time in recorded history, Socrates — the afterlife's most ferocious warrior, a man whose fight-or-flight system had always been firmly locked in the "fight" position — had tucked his tail between his legs and fled.

Chapter 16

"You ran away!" cried Vera, pounding Socrates' chest with both hands. "You could have saved Detroit. You could have fixed everything! And you just ran!"

"It was a strategic retreat!" growled the assassin, doing his best to shoo her away.

The two had teleported back to Isaac's lab a moment earlier, an arrival that caught Ian with his metaphorical pants around his ankles and caused something competent doctors call a "transient respiratory event." It hadn't seemed transient to Ian. It had almost left him looking for the shelf marked "fresh trousers." He was presently bracing himself against a shelf and doing his best to catch his breath.

"Strategic retreat, my eye!" cried Vera, stepping back into the Socratic danger zone and doing a fair impression of an unhinged baseball coach who's absolutely sure that last pitch missed the outside corner. This was either a display of incredible personal courage on Vera's part or a sign that she'd already seen this future and knew that she'd turn out okay.

"You screwed up!" she boomed. "I thought there'd be carnage in that ballroom! Bits of acolytes on the walls, everyone hacked to pieces and waiting to be wiped, Evan's followers babbling on the floor. And what did I find when I got there?" she shouted, forehead veins throbbing. "You, shooting the furniture, nicking elbows, scaring everyone out of their wits but not really doing anything useful!"

271

"I was expecting synths!" Socrates said through clenched teeth. "I was supposed to be facing Lori 8 and other mechs. Stygian toxin doesn't work on them. I only had three vials."

"That doesn't explain why you ran from Tonto!" cried Vera.

"He ran from . . . from Tonto?" said Ian, still wheezing. "What was . . . what was Tonto doing—"

"She's guarding Evan," said Vera, turning away from the assassin. "I can't explain it. But when I saw Tonto I could see that . . . well . . . that she's been *repurposed* to keep him safe. Like that's her reason to exist. She was the only obstacle standing between Socrates and Evan." Here she wheeled back around and erupted at the assassin again. "You could have stopped him!" she cried. "You could have saved Detroit and put things right! You chickened out and ran away!"

"I was there to rescue you," said the assassin, backpedalling from ground zero. "You're welcome, by the way. Mission accomplished. A mission that you forced upon me by hacking into my on-board systems!"

"Don't change the subject!" cried Vera.

"Wait, wait," wheezed Ian, still catching his breath and lagging behind by several paragraphs. "What do you mean Socrates could have saved Detroit?"

"He could have stopped Evan and saved everybody!" cried Vera. "But he turned tail and ran!"

"I didn't run!"

"You retreated!" she shouted, stepping forward again and directing a forceful poke straight into Socrates' sternum. "You teleported away from where we needed to be!"

"I was saving you!" shouted Socrates, stepping back. If you'd been watching from overhead you might have thought that he and Vera were choreographing an angry tango.

"What do you mean 'he could have stopped Evan'?" said Ian.

"I was fine!" cried Vera, ignoring him.

"You were a prisoner!" boomed the assassin.

"You're just embarrassed because you ran away from Tonto!" shouted Vera.

"I didn't run away from Tonto! I ran away from the dog!"

This response had the virtue of coming as a surprise. Vera stood there blinking at Socrates with her mouth hanging open, as though she'd loaded up an array of shouty ordnance but hadn't packed any ammo that could contend with "fled from dog." And while Ian's range of available facial expressions was significantly impaired by what appeared to be some species of fright-induced asthma spasm, he still managed to look confused.

"The . . . the dog?" he wheezed.

"The Regent's dog. He's called Memphis," said the assassin. "He was in the line of fire."

"And you ran from him?" said Ian.

"Dogs aren't immortal. I'm not a monster!"

"You were running away from Tonto and you know it!" said Vera, unleashing another pectoral prod. "She's every bit as tough as you and you're . . . you're broken! Your systems are compromised, your enhancements are all glitchy, you're afraid people might realize you're not real and just 'think' you out of existence, you need repairs and you—"

"And you hacked into my system!" boomed the assassin, doing a little sternum-prodding of his own. "And since we're talking about glitches, why don't we ventilate the subject of how you overwrote the ISAAC system, forced me to show up at the chateau without any warning, and issued new mission parameters on my HUD?"

This prompted a sudden, quantum shift in Vera's mood. Where seconds earlier she'd been Vesuvius itself, she now took on the excited air of an enthusiastic nerd explaining her baking-soda volcano at her first-grade science fair.

"That was pretty cool, wasn't it?" she said, beaming. "I managed to crack the Regent's online portal. I sent a signal into the ISAAC system's core using an oscillating, ternary carrier wave that piggybacked a coded message through the ambient background transmission and—"

"What do you mean *Socrates could have stopped Evan?*!" cried Ian, who in this particular situation might be forgiven for violating the rules of etiquette by trying to wrestle the conversation back in that direction.

"Oh, right," said Vera, turning toward him. "Sorry. It's a vision I had at the chateau. We had two routes to saving Detroit. One of them was the path laid out in the diorama — all the little figures that show what we have to do to fix the world. In the other, Socrates stops Evan at the chateau and puts everything back in order—"

"That's irrelevant," interrupted the assassin. "The moment has passed."

"How was he supposed to stop him?" demanded Ian.

"Oh, a mindwipe, I expect," said Vera, in the indifferent, offhand way that you might express your views on mashed potatoes.

"You can't mindwipe my son!" cried the mashed potatoes — or rather Ian, the two being tough to tell apart.

"I don't know what you're so worked up about," said Vera, "he'd only lose, what, about five years' worth of memories? Barely a blip. Not like the centuries I lost when Socrates mindwiped me."

Socrates took a sudden interest in the floor and seemed to be trying to shine a tile with the toe of his left boot. He muttered something under his breath. An omniscient narrator might have noted that the words he spoke were "sorry about that," but only Socrates knows for sure.

"Evan would make new memories, anyway," said Vera, doing her best to sound reassuring. "In a few years he'd be good as new. But anyway, it didn't happen."

Ian stared at Vera with a variation on the facial expression you might generally call "dumbfounded." This version was spiced with healthy dashes of shock, horror, and outright disbelief. It's the look you usually see when someone reviews their bill for roaming charges.

"Now that we're threshing it all out," said Socrates, adopting a philosophical air, "I'm not sure that route would have worked."

"What do you mean?" said Vera, intrigued.

"I'm not sure that wiping Evan would be enough. I mean, a straightforward mindwipe would only delay matters, right? Who's to say that Evan wouldn't turn out precisely the same way the second time 'round? After a mindwipe, I mean. After he's gathered another five years of memories we'd be right back where we started."

"Oh, we'd have to control for sensory inputs and environmental factors," said Vera. "That's a given. Like, we'd help Ian avoid the terrible parenting this time around. No stories about 'how special' Evan is. No explaining that he's not like other people. No—"

"But surely he'd notice his own power," said the assassin. "He'd almost certainly learn to wield it, even instinctually — this capacity he has to replicate his mother's abilities. It all comes down to nature versus nurture," he continued. "Perhaps Evan's innately destructive and anti-social nature plays more of a role in his ultimate phenotypical presentation than Ian's incompetent parenting."

"It's possible," said Vera. "But how would you control for—"

"ENOUGH!" cried Ian, who seemed to have swapped his usual skin tone for something from the fire engine end of the spectrum. "I'm not going to stand here and listen to the two of you talk about wiping Evan! Or blaming me for what he's done!"

"Fine by me," said Socrates. "There's a kitchen in the back. Go have a sandwich."

"No!" cried Ian. "I mean that I won't help you with any plan to wipe Evan!"

"I don't see what you're so worked up about," said Vera, "the moment's come and gone. Socrates ran off, so Evan's fine."

"I didn't run!" sighed the assassin, pinching the bridge of his nose.

"Run, teleported, whatever," said Vera.

"You were planning to wipe my son!" cried Ian.

"What did you think we were going to do when we confronted him?" said Socrates. "Have a nice chat? Try to undo your bad parenting and convince him that he's not as special as Mommy and Daddy told him? Get him to buy into equal rights for all, maybe ignore the fact that he can steal power from his mum, shred the threads of reality, and destroy everyone else if the mood strikes him?"

"I do think we'll have to wipe him, Ian," said Vera, stepping to Ian's side and patting his shoulder. "I know it's hard, but—"

"Just let me talk to him!" said Ian, shrugging out of Vera's grip. "I know I can get through. If I can explain—"

"He's not going to change," said Socrates. "He is who he is."

"I don't need him to change," said Ian, glowering. "I just need to . . . you know . . . appeal to his better nature."

"He's a child," said the assassin. "He doesn't have a better nature."

"He's a good boy!" said Ian, gripped by the same widespread cognitive infirmity that leads so many parents to see the angelic and gifted sides of their incompetent pint-sized miscreants.

"I just don't see another way out of this," said Vera, returning to Ian's side and resuming her arm-patting efforts. "Not one that leaves Evan the way he is."

Ian tried to shrug his way out again, but Vera held firm.

"He'll be okay, Ian. I promise. We're in Detroit. He's not going anywhere. But we can't have him . . . well . . . we can't have him wired the way he is right now. He's on a course to break the world."

"He's a five-year-old boy!" Ian protested. "He's just . . . he's just taken a rough path. He's pushed himself into a grown-up body without having really experienced growing up. He's still got all the pent-up frustration and confusion of a kid who's just been told he can't have his way."

"And the capacity to reshape the world however he likes," said Socrates.

"He'll grow out of it," said Ian. "I need more time with him. Time to explain how he should relate to other people. Teach him empathy. Maybe he'll turn out like his mom!"

"I think that ship has sailed," said Socrates.

"Pen could fix him," muttered Ian.

"She would if she could, Ian," said Vera, sympathetically. "But she can't. She's being blocked somehow."

"I think I've solved that!" said Ian, brightening a little. "I meant to tell you! I think I've figured out what's happened to Pen and Abe. It's got to be Evan. I think he's trapped them in the Patch."

Vera and Socrates looked at Ian as though he'd started speaking French.

"The Patch," repeated Ian. "It's a kind of bubble of reality that Pen and Abe made. A pocket universe we used for raising Evan, to keep him away from the rest of Detroit until we knew what he could do."

"And you think Pen and Abe are stuck there?" said Vera, doubtfully.

"It's something Abe and Hammurabi said at the party. How Evan can grasp his mom's power, and the power of other ancients. He can turn it against its source. We thought it was safe because he was in the Patch, kept away from everything else. But once Abe and Pen were both in there together with him — well, Ham worried that Evan could take control of all their combined power, all at once, and . . . well . . . just imagine a kid with all the combined power of Pen and Abe. He could do whatever he wanted. And what he really wanted was to leave the Patch. We told him he couldn't get out until he was big. So now he's out. And he's big."

"But Abe and Pen?" prompted Vera, still corrugating her brow.

"It's like you said," said Ian. "They'd stop Evan if they could. And if they can't, maybe it's because they're stuck in the Patch. Nothing in there can affect anything that's outside. That's how they made it."

"He's trapped Abe and Pen behind a wall of their own power," mused the assassin, scratching his beard. "The more they strain against that wall, the stronger it gets."

"That's ingenious!" said Vera, eyes widening. "I'm surprised that Evan could think it up."

"I don't think he knows what he's doing," said Ian.

"Well that proves we have no choice," said Socrates. "If Evan has trapped Abe and Pen within this Patch, we'll have to wipe him."

"That might undo what he's done!" said Vera, hopefully. "Make him release his hold on Abe and Penelope's power."

"It's possible," said Socrates.

"But we don't know that!" said Ian. "We've just got to convince him to set Penelope free. She'll fix everything. The safest bet is to let me talk to Evan."

"Talk to him?" said the assassin.

"It can't hurt!" said Ian.

"It might!" said Vera. "If he's gathered enough power he might, I dunno, turn you into a plant or something. Or rearrange your thoughts to make you support him. It's just too dangerous."

"So, we wipe him then?" said Socrates.

"We trust prophecy," said Vera, firmly. "It hasn't led us astray yet. Whether we wipe Evan or not, our only hope," she continued, pausing to bend over and pick up a football-sized piece of technology at her feet, "is this."

It might have been a highly dramatic moment had anyone other than Vera had a clue what she was holding.

"It's an expectation manager," she explained.

"Ah," said Ian. "Of course it is. Silly me."

"It's a replacement for Napoleonic blood."

If the letters w, t, and f could be combined into a grunt, they'd be the sound that Ian made now.

"Sorry, long story," said Vera. "But what's important is that we can use this to amplify and direct the force of a person's expectations. It can enhance a subject's power to shape Detroit. The Regent plans to hook Evan up to it so that he can open a portal to the beforelife."

You'd expect this to call for a good deal of exposition, largely for the purpose of bringing Ian up to speed. It did. Vera attended to this task with a lot of scientific jargon, including noteworthy references to neurotransmitters, muons, apoptosis, quantum entanglement, dendrites, axions, and myelin sheaths. Then she attended to it again in words that Ian could understand, this time focusing on the Church's plan to reach the mortal world and Evan's role in helping them make the trip.

"But what matters," she concluded, "is that we might be able to use the expectation manager to stop Evan. If we hook this up to the right person," she added, patting the expectation manager, "we have a chance to save the world."

"Would it work with anybody?" asked Ian, leaping at Vera's plan like a vegan who's spotted an unattended brick of tofu. "Like me, for example? You could hook me up to your thingy and I could make Evan a kid again, or teach him how to behave?"

"Pfft. No," said Vera, scoffing. "No offence, but the device needs a really powerful mind."

"What about you?" asked Ian.

"Sorry, no. But thanks for asking. It has to be somebody with a lot of kick. Someone who already has the power to shift reality in Detroit. Maybe not Abe or Penelope's level. I mean, they could stop Evan without the manager."

"But they didn't!" said Ian. "Not when he trapped them in the Patch!"

"I imagine they were surprised," said Vera, waving him off. "I'm sure they could stop him if they knew what they were facing. But anyway, the expectation manager needs someone who only needs a bit of a push to access their level of power."

"What about Socrates or Tonto?"

"They're not real peop— er," Vera began, catching herself, "I mean, they're not the right kind of being for the circuitry. The City Solicitor would work, but we've no idea where he is. That only leaves us with one choice. If we're going to find the right kind of person, we have to get to City Hall."

"You know about R'lyeh!" gasped Socrates.

"What's R'lyeh?" said Ian, stumbling over the apostrophe which, to be fair, serves no sensible purpose apart from giving the word an otherworldly air.

"It's a secret basement at City Hall," said Vera. "Rhinnick and I found it when we were up against Isaac Newton. That's another long story. But R'lyeh's a storage facility chock full of sleeping ancients. They're bound together in machines called sarcophagi that combine their collective wills and expectations. They help Abe and Penelope run Detroit — keep everyone else's will from making chaos. If we could wake one of the ancients — one of the really powerful ones — and hook them up to the expectation manager, they'd have power to rival Abe's. They should be able to stop Evan in a snap! There's just one problem," she added, biting her lip.

"Just *one* problem?" asked Ian, who'd counted at least seven without even breaking a sweat.

"That's where Evan is headed too. He and the Regent need the same thing we do: access to the sleeping ancients. The Church is planning to use Evan to wield the ancients' power, the same way he borrowed Abe's and Pen's."

"We have to get there before them!" cried Ian.

"We're all going to be there together," said Vera, staring into the middle distance. "That's what the diorama told us all along. It showed the pieces that we'll have to put together if we're going to save Detroit. It had Oan, Socrates, Tonto, me, Rhinnick, a bunch of Napoleons, and a whole whack of acolytes, all hanging together in one place. That place has to be City Hall, Ian. We're all going to be there together, and I don't think it's for a picnic."

"It's a battle," said Socrates, matter-of-factly. "A final battle to decide who rules Detroit."

"They outnumber us by hundreds to one!" said Ian. "And they have Evan! And the Regent!"

"They have Tonto," said the assassin, grimly. "And they may have an army of droids."

"We've got an assassin who runs from danger and is afraid of being *imagined* out of existence," said Vera.

"I'm not above wiping you again," said the assassin, crossing his arms.

"Sorry, sorry," said Vera, "that was mean. I just meant that we need to fix you. Mind if I pop open the hood and fiddle around a bit?"

"You've already fiddled remotely," said the assassin. "If you think you can get things back to how they were, be my guest."

"Umm, guys?" said Ian, who'd taken a few steps down the aisle and now stood looking out a window.

"What's up?" said Vera.

"It's just . . . are you sure the final battle happens at R'lyeh?" said Ian.

"Pretty sure," said Vera. "That's what the prophecies suggest. And I know that's where the Regent's headed."

"Did anyone tell the robot army?" said Ian, turning toward Vera and aiming a thumb toward the window. "'Cuz I'm pretty sure they're here."

Chapter 17

Mathematicians, biologists, and astrophysicists agree that, on average, nothing exists. They're right about that. Given the almost infinite space we're able to observe and the practically negligible proportion of that nigh-infinite space that's occupied by actual *stuff*, there's so much more *nothing* out there in the void than there is *anything*, if you follow, that anything you think you're perceiving should, statistically speaking, be ignored. The same is true of you: you're almost entirely empty space. The atoms that make you *you* are whirling around within a lot of nothing that accounts for most of the space you think you're filling. The same logic applies in any number of probably non-existent fields of inquiry. Consider, for example, the ratio of wrong to right.

There are more nonsensical combinations of letters than there are ways to make words. Just give it a go. For every perfectly sensible "winkle-picker" or "ecdysiast" there are innumerable "aljaseors," "yvs," "woinks," and "plymptologists." There are infinitely more disprovable mathematical statements, this one included,[7] than there are elegant, valid solutions to equations. It's easier to get lost than it is to get found, unless you're a parent of small children and you'd like some time alone. There are far more ways to break something than to fix it; there are infinitely more nonsensical combinations of ones and zeroes than there are binary expressions that can make a computer compute.

---

7   Or possibly this one.

For every instance in which that hypothetical infinite gang of monkeys on the infinite series of typewriters generates the complete works of William Shakespeare, the same gang produces a brain-shattering number of randomly bashed-out letters and numbers that run the risk of being attributed to James Joyce. The overwhelmingly vast majority of possible combinations of letters, numbers, particles, noises, smells, energy fields, and visual stimuli don't carry anything close to intrinsic meaning. Thus we can readily conclude that, on average, *nothing makes any sense.* Every correct solution to any problem, every sensible and well-ordered escape from the background entropy into which the universe might have already descended, can be easily disregarded as an anomaly.

You may find these truths alarming. Or, if you've shrugged your possibly non-existent shoulders and given in to the chaos, you may find that all of this serves as a satisfying explanation for the fact that we now find ourselves in the Regent's grand chateau: the summer home of an undead Egyptian ruler who's just been hosting a lively rave attended by pious, robe-wearing zealots, a whole Twitterverse's worth of petty, resentful afterlife washouts, the prophet Norm Stradamus, and a host of other people who've shuffled off the mortal coil — a rave that was just attacked by the afterlife's only assassin, owing to his ongoing attempts to cope with his existential crisis.

The chateau itself had seen better days. Quite a lot of them, in fact, it having been built about two thousand years ago when Detroit's craftspersons knew how to tell a flying buttress from a caryatid column; the days when the builders of the hereafter really took pride in their work.[8]

---

8   One of the problems with immortality is that artists and artisans eventually realize that they're going to outlive their work. There's no point trying to achieve immortality through your creations when you get it by default, especially when you know you'll have infinite time in which to

Those who'd visited the chateau in what you'd think of as its heyday — say, anytime before this evening, when Socrates had popped in and wreaked his bit of havoc — generally described it as one of the most picturesque estates they could imagine, a spot they might have compared to Versailles if they'd been familiar with that reference. In fact, the only thing keeping the Regent's chateau out of *Khuufru's Guide to The Multiverse's Essential Architectural Wonders* was the fact that practically no one knew the place existed. You couldn't find the chateau without the Regent's personal assent unless — just by way of example — you were zapped there by a teleportation trap, had the coordinates entered directly into your intercranial network, or were capable of violating the apparent rules of Detroit by bending the world to suit your whims. But if the keepers of *Khuufru's Guide* had gotten hold of an invitation and turned up at the joint today, they'd have been in for a surprise.

The place was a wreck. Especially the main ballroom, which had recently served as ground zero for Socrates' brief, high-impact incursion. He'd fired enough explosives into the ball-room's vaulted ceiling to ensure that at least seven storeys' worth of furniture, housewares, construction materials, *objets d'art*, and wide-eyed residents had yielded to the force of gravity and collapsed in a heap on the ballroom floor. From an optimist's perspective this meant that the ballroom now featured an airier, open-concept ambiance thanks to the massive hole that presently revealed the constellations in addition to the wreckage of upper storeys. From a pessimist's perspective the ballroom now looked like a post-apocalyptic landfill-slash-warzone featuring hardwood parquet floors.

---

improve your efforts. The longer you live, and the more you develop an understanding of the fact that you'll go on living, the less motivated you are to leave any sort of mark. Say what you will about death — the fear of it sparks one's creativity.

The Regent stood amidst the wreckage. She wasn't fussed about the property damage. She really wasn't. She could fix that in an imperceptible jiffy. As has been previously established, the Regent shared a healthy measure of the power shown by the likes of Abe and Penelope — the power to weave the fabric of Detroit, to reshape reality into forms that she found pleasing — a power ostensibly shared to one degree or another by everyone who'd passed from the beforelife. That power, in most humans, was suppressed by a combination of Abe's meddling and their own inability to accept Detroit's true nature. As you'll have realized if you've been paying close attention, practically anyone in Detroit, if they realized the essential truths that Abe had kept hidden, could have mustered up the power to reconstitute the chateau with a mere flick of an index finger — an index finger that was, after all, merely a handy (pardon the pun) mental construct held in place by the will of the person doing the flicking. As one of the relatively small number of citizens of Detroit who managed to perceive these hidden truths, and to wield a modicum of this secret power despite Abe's efforts, the Regent could have focused her will on the job at hand and rebuilt her grand chateau in the blink of an eye.

But as we've just established, the Regent wasn't especially fussed about that right now. She *was* fussed about the fact that her powers failed her. She'd done her best to flex her metaphysical muscles and put a stop to Socrates' havoc-wreaking incursion into her home. It hadn't worked. It hadn't worked, and she knew why.

"You stole my power!" she thundered, aiming an index finger at Evan.

"I didn't!" cried Evan, looking surprisingly abashed for a man who had some eyebrow-raising powers of his own and who'd managed to muster up an entire movement of social rejects in no more than a few short weeks. "I just borrowed it! I had no choice!"

The fires behind the Regent's eyes carried on burning a touch more brightly than the flames Socrates had unleashed in the ballroom — flames that teams of acolytes and Evangelists were trying to extinguish in the background.

"Perhaps, Madame Regent," said Norm, sidling up to her, "we could explore this matter at a later time, once we've managed to repair the—"

"What do you mean you *borrowed* it?" boomed the Regent, ignoring the High Prelate and unleashing a glare that you might say "bored a hole directly into Evan's soul," a phrase that applied only if you assumed that Evan actually had a soul.

"I don't know what you're so mad about," said Evan. "It's back now! Use it however you like. And I didn't take all of it, either. I left you enough to shield yourself."

"You left me powerless to thwart Socrates!"

"That . . . that was Socrates?" said Evan, his lower jaw in danger of joining the rubble on the floor. "Holy crap! I had no idea! And he's . . . he's just like her!" he added, pointing at Tonto, who was busy tossing steel girders aside while looking for trapped partygoers. Evan shouted a question in her direction. It was this:

"Hey! Hey you! Did you know there were two of you?"

Tonto cocked her head at Evan while picking up a block of concrete that a forklift couldn't have budged. "Two of me?" she asked.

"Yeah," said Evan. "Two big pulsing balls of . . . I don't know . . . raw power? Like the stuff I pull from people . . . the threads of light that flow back and forth between regular people and Detroit. But yours . . . they aren't connected to anything. They just sort of pulse in a big bright ball."

Everyone present, apart from Evan, made precisely the same face. It was as if an invisible, cosmic director instructed everyone in the ballroom, including the extras in the background, to turn and stare at Evan as though he'd started wetting his pants while prattling on about false flags, mail-in ballots, or his rights as a "sovereign-man-upon-the-land."

"Threads of power?" asked Tonto, whose brow was so thoroughly furrowed that you could tell Botox wasn't among her interests or concerns.

"You know," said Evan, puzzled, "like the bright-orange light filament thingies that flow to the Regent. Or the little bluish-grey ones coming from Norm. You . . . you don't see them, do you?"

"No," said Tonto, stepping closer and tilting her head so thoroughly that a puppy could have taken her online course.

"Oh. That's probably because you're not from around here," said Evan. "What are you, anyway? You and Socrates?"

"Enough!" shouted the Regent, apparently not interested in these questions. "Tell me, Brown—"

"Call me Evan."

"Tell me, Evan, how do you do this — how do you steal my power for your own purposes?"

"I didn't steal it!"

"How do you *borrow* it, then?"

Evan twiddled his thumbs and made the mildly dismayed face of a child who's been caught colouring on the walls. "It's . . . well, I don't know. It's hard to explain," he said. "I just do it. I mean, you can't explain how you hear noises, right? You just do it. That's what it's like with me. Mack Yavelli — he's my friend — he said I can use other people's power because the city and I are one. I was born this way. I see the streaks of light that come from everybody. Not just the big pulsing bands that come from people like Mom and Abe, but also the little trickles that come from everyone else. I don't know exactly what it means. It's just what I see. I can see that light and pull it toward me. I use it to do what I want. It's how I trapped my mom and Abe inside the Patch."

There was a chorus of sound effects drawn from the "thud" and "crash" collection as eavesdropping acolytes and Evangelists dropped handfuls of debris to the floor. Even the Regent seemed surprised.

"You . . . you trapped Abe?"

"Sure, yeah," said Evan. "It was easy. I used his own power against him. I was only a kid when I did it too," he added, now beaming with childish pride. "I grabbed the threads and did to Abe and Mom what they'd been doing to me since I was little — I sealed them in the Patch."

The Regent asked what the Patch was, which was helpful of her, since everyone else was wondering too.

"A little subuniverse Mom and Abe created," said Evan. "They kept me in it when I was little."

"Perhaps," said Norm, sidling up to the Regent and worming his way into the ongoing proceedings, "perhaps we might explore this matter later, after we've discussed matters of greater cosmic import."

Evan gave him the look you might expect a magically aged five-year-old to aim at a wizened, heavily bearded, slightly shabby elder prophet. "Cosmic import?" he asked, sounding a good deal like a border inspector from outer space.

"Matters of prophecy!" said Norm. "Great foretellings that chart our path! Matters of great pith and moment! Mysteries of what is to come, laid bare for those who seek the signs."

"Very well," said the Regent, ignoring Evan, who'd started giggling at the word "pith." "What is your counsel, Prophet Stradamus?" she asked.

"I have mused on the meanings of the Great Visions!" said Norm.

"The Great Visions?"

"My song! My quatrains! And the prophecies of Vera!"

"Who's Vera?" asked Evan.

"A minor prophet," said Norm, dismissively. "Her visions provide a number of useful annotations to my own. Suffice it to say that she predicted your arrival, she foresaw you taking what she described as a rulership position—"

"Nice," said Evan.

"Yes," said Norm, "and she foresaw that you'd achieve this position while dreaming at R'lyeh."

"R'lyeh?" said Evan, stumbling on the word.

"A place of great significance where the full scope of your power shall be revealed," said Norm. "I'm getting to that. But in a nutshell, Vera's prophecy says that 'the First One' — that's you, Evan, presumably based on your status as the first being born in your own peculiar manner — 'the First One, in his house at R'lyeh dreaming lies.'"

"Dreaming lies?" asked Evan. "Why would I be dreaming lies?"

"No, no," said Norm, chuckling, "I assure you this means that you are lying down, recumbent, dreaming."

"How do you know?"

"One doesn't dream standing up."

"Fair enough."

"Perhaps you should get to your point, Prophet Stradamus," said the Regent, tapping a foot.

"Yes, yes, of course, of course," said Norm. "Vera's minor prophecy says that you, Evan, lie dreaming at R'lyeh, removed from those who traverse the river. That must mean us. The Church of O, and very possibly any others who make the journey across the river to the Great Omega's realm. That's the beforelife. Don't you see, Evan," said Norm, his face beaming with belief, "your role in this is preordained. You shall guide us across the river, and in doing so you shall reach your goal — your goal to be rid of many of those who, in your own words, don't belong here."

"Sounds good to me," said Evan. "Sign me up. Point me to R'lyeh."

"Patience, patience!" said Norm.

"I mean, if it's going to reveal my power and get you guys out of Detroit, we should head there now and get this show on the road!"

"Please do be patient, Evan," said Norm, "It has been decreed that you cannot be given R'lyeh's location—"

Evan made the face of a child who's been told he can't have his dessert before he's eaten all of his spinach. "What do you mean 'it has been decreed'?" he thundered, prompting Tonto to step forward and place a placating hand on his arm. He shrugged it aside and carried on yelling. "You can't tell me what to—"

"All shall be revealed in short order," said the Regent, "but not before the appointed time." Her voice always sounded as though she was expecting some court scribe to chisel her words on to a slab of granite and proclaim them to the masses, but in this instance they seemed to be etched with even more regal authority than usual. "This is not my secret to keep or explain," she continued, making a placating gesture. "One cannot simply be told of R'lyeh's location. One must discover it through careful study and meditation, or be led to it by another. This is a truth built into Detroit, decreed by Abe. I myself was unable to divine its location until—"

"So lead me there, already!" said Evan. "Do whatever you have to do. Just get me to R'lyeh! I want my full power!"

"Our path forward is embedded within my song!" said Norm, champing at the bit.

"So just tell me about your damned song then!" said Evan, exhibiting all the patience you'd expect from someone who opted to skip the inconvenient aging process.

"The song is my greatest prophecy!" said Norm, beaming. "Perhaps the greatest act of foretelling in all of history, if you don't mind my saying so. I've been working on it for ages. It tells of our journey to the beforelife. Of the paradise that awaits. Of peace and freedom from the sins that stain Detroit. And a Lord who takes our hand and guides us to happiness and freedom from our cares!"

"So sing it," said Evan.

"No, no!" said Norm, "for the prophetess Vera has foretold that the song shall not be sung until we stand upon the precipice of salvation!"

"She said that?" said the Regent, taken aback.

"Not in so many words," said Norm. "I give you the gist."

"That's cheating!" said Evan, who had his own ideas of fairness. "That's doesn't count as a prophecy. That's a rule. Like, 'thou shalt not steal.' It's not a prediction that you won't do it, it's a command."

"But it could be a prediction too!" said Norm. "If, in the fullness of time, it turns out that people did not in fact steal, then the phrase 'thou shalt not steal' stands revealed as a prophetic claim and—"

"Perhaps you might indulge our new ally by reciting a verse of the song," said the Regent, who seemed to have caught a case of Evan's impatience.

"You could just sing the whole thing now and prove Vera wrong!" said Evan, encouragingly. "You know, show that she isn't such hot stuff as a prophet, and that you can't be told what to do—"

"All in good time, all in good time!" said Norm. "For now, suffice it to say that, with your guidance, Evan, we're to head across the river upon the day of judgment, that we shall sing our hallelujahs, and, here is the song's most oft-repeated and uplifting message, if I do say so myself, we shall all get—"

"Prophet Stradamus!" cried Oan, bursting through a gaggle of acolytes who'd been clearing the debris. "Oh, Prophet Stradamus!"

"What is it, Oan!" said Norm.

"There's a — oh, forgive me, Regent, Tonto, Mr. Brown—" said Oan, suddenly drinking in her surroundings.

"Call me Evan."

"Forgive me, Evan," said Oan, curtsying slightly and turning back toward Norm, "but . . . but . . . oh . . . there's a problem with Evan's people."

"Evan's people?" said the Regent.

"Several problems, in fact," said Oan, still catching her breath.

"Might this possibly wait for another time?" said Norm.

"It's very urgent," said Oan, clutching her skirt.

"Just spit it out," said Evan. "If there's a problem with my guys, I oughta know."

"It's just, well, it's a matter of some delicacy . . ."

"No problem. I'm all ears."

"Your people are . . . well they're . . ."

"They're gross," said Tonto. This caught everyone by surprise. Norm made the mortified face you typically see when someone engages with your embarrassing uncle at Thanksgiving. Evan's jaw was reminiscent of a python eating a bear.

Tonto shrugged as if her statement had been self-evident.

"That's, I mean, that's a little harsh, don't you think?" said Evan, gathering his composure. "I mean, they're not fancy church people, but they're okay. Sure, a few of 'em could stand to shower more often but—"

"They've been hitting on the acolytes all day," said Tonto, flatly.

"It's true!" said Oan, flushing.

"Oh. Well, we can't have that!" said Evan. "Unwelcome violence goes against everything I—"

"Violence?" asked Oan.

"Yeah! She said they're hitting the acolytes!"

"No, no," said Oan, "not *hitting* the acolytes, Evan. Hitting *on* the acolytes. All day long. Making overtures."

"Like songs?" said Evan, perplexed.

"They're making . . . oh, this is dreadful," said Oan, "I'd hoped to discuss this with Prophet Stradamus and never planned to—"

"Look, if my people are singing upsetting songs—"

"*Theyaremakingsexualadvances!*" cried Oan, speaking with such speed that it all came out as a single word. "They're trying to bed them, Evan! To have sex with them!"

"Ew!" said Evan, with the look of a child who's just tried its first oyster.

"And that's not even the worst of it," said Oan, gathering steam. "I'm afraid that quite a number of them have, well . . . I mean—"

"Just tell us," said the Regent.

"I'm sure it's all a misunderstanding," stammered Oan.

"Just tell me what's up," said Evan.

"I'm afraid they've reacted rather badly to Socrates," she said, now staring down at the parquet floor.

"Who wouldn't?" asked Evan, seeming relieved. "He was totally mean. He blew up half the house."

"That's not what I mean," said Oan, biting her lower lip. "That is . . . well—"

As if on cue, a pack of six or seven of the basement-dwelling excrescences who were archetypal specimens of Evan's entourage sauntered up behind Oan with the air of organized labour.

"We got a bone to pick with you," said their leader, who, as it turns out, was the pimply and objectionable GamerboiXXX69. He was backed by what appeared to be a poorly cast boy band comprised entirely of shifty-looking, pale-skinned twerps.

"A . . . a bone?" asked Norm, confused.

"Not with you, beardo," said GamerboiXXX69, pointing. "With Evan."

This caught Evan by surprise. If there'd been one virtue shown by his growing gang of exploitable losers, it was loyalty. He'd promised them things to which they'd always felt entitled. That had kept them on a short leash. He asked GamerboiXXX69 to explain.

"I'll tell you what's the matter!" said GamerboiXXX69, who appeared to be built entirely of knees, elbows, and congealed resentment. "It's you! I mean, did you see that Socrates guy when he came in here with his guns and bombs and knives and shit?"

"I . . . I did . . ."

"Now that's an alpha!" said GamerboiXXX69. His sentiment was echoed by a chorus of "you tell 'ems" and "that's rights" from his backup gripers.

"He was all like 'pew! pew! pew!' and not takin' crap from anyone! Everyone else just ran for the hills! I mean, you're cool and all," he added, aiming a begrudging up-nod at Evan, "and I'm totally down with everything you said about stickin' it to Abe. But . . . my man Socrates? He's all action! He had you hiding behind that lady!" he said, jerking a thumb in Tonto's direction. "Socrates is the kind of leader we need!"

Evan displayed the dumbfounded look of someone who's just been betrayed by his golden retriever, a look that had "*Et tu, Fido?*" written all over it. This particular golden retriever's bout of betrayal seemed to garner a cheering section, as a few dozen members of Evan's bro brigade, emboldened by their lead twerp, gathered 'round and made rabble-rousing grunts of spiteful support.

Evan couldn't help but feel a little hurt. And because, when you get right down to it, he was only five years old, he found that "hurt" lived right next door to blinding rage.

"The kind of leader you *need*?" said Evan, his temperature rising rapidly, "THE KIND OF LEADER YOU NEED?" he repeated, this time in all caps. "You don't even *know* what you're talking about! You're blind! Socrates is just . . . just some weird kind of side effect of Detroit! Like *her*!" he added, pointing accusingly at Tonto. "He's not even real!"

"He was real enough to have you hiding down a hallway," said GamerboiXXX69, who seemed to grow cocky after drawing first blood. "You're nothing. You're all talk! A total beta! You keep saying there's power in all of us, like we've got some kinda potential, and you just run off and hide behind a girl the second things get rough! Peter Jordanson wouldn't do that. No real man would!"

Evan ought to have tried diplomacy at this juncture. He didn't, though, what with one thing and another. In aging himself to adulthood he had clothed himself with the knowledge, skills, and intellectual heft of an honest-to-goodness, grown adult. But at his core he was still five. He'd never borne the slings and arrows that come your way on the playground; he'd never had his skin thickened through failed job applications and rejected manuscripts, or his soul calloused by unrequited love and a million little disappointments. He'd spent all of his life at the heart of a perfect Evan-centred universe, one conjured by Penelope with a view to keeping him safe. He'd never really learned to cope; never learned to withstand critiques, absorb insults, or swallow betrayals. And perhaps that's why, rather than calmly addressing the points raised so eloquently by GamerboiXXX69, rather than just proclaiming that he found the fellow's lack of faith disturbing, Evan seemed to believe that a somewhat more direct and physical demonstration of The Hidden Truth was in order.

Instead of talking, Evan screamed.

"WHY CAN'T YOU JUST LISTEN TO ME?!" he thundered. And then he threw the kind of temper tantrum that only a nigh-omnipotent child of Penelope could throw.

He squinted intently at the gathering troupe of disloyal disciples, focusing on the barely perceptible filaments of raw energy flowing between them and Detroit — threads that only Evan could see. Evan reached toward those threads and jerked as hard as he could.

Quite a lot of things happened in rapid succession. The first involved GamerboiXXX69 and his gang of hangers-on, who seemed to become frozen in place, all slack-jawed and wide-eyed, as if an unseen force had grasped them where they stood. The next thing that happened to them might have counted as "indescribable" but for the rather common experience of sucking all of the juice out of a popsicle or freezie: their colour drained completely. Their bodies shrivelled, too, becoming emaciated in seconds. They screamed and whimpered and fell to the ground where they lay twitching, resembling something halfway between exhausted zombies and those overcooked, past-due wieners you see at 7-Eleven.

The crowd reacted how you'd expect. A few dozen members of the bro brigade scattered as best they could, tripping over the debris and doing their best to be wherever Evan wasn't. Acolytes fell to their knees in silent prayer, beseeching the Great Omega to do something that might let them escape.

"WHY CAN'T YOU JUST DO WHAT YOU'RE TOLD?!" Evan thundered, growing about two feet taller in the process, and still drawing the threads of power from those around him. "I can give you everything!" he bellowed. "Everything you think you deserve! Everything you've ever wanted! I can break Abe's control. Free you from the lie he's created! Give you all that's meant to be coming to you, instead of what Mom and Abe and the elites think they should allow!"

They say that power corrupts, and that absolute power corrupts absolutely. Evan had drawn and channelled plenty of power before. He'd drawn it from Abe, and from his mother — power he'd used to change himself into an adult, power he'd used to trap almost-omnipotent beings in the Patch. But the power that Evan drew now, the much smaller trickles of power he channelled from GamerboiXXX69 and his crew of small-minded, resentful, petty, entitled hangers-on, was tinged with so much bile and hatred, so many foul, petty grievances, that it couldn't help but alter its vessel. Absolute power corrupts absolutely. And ugly, spiteful, tainted power corrupts in its own unique way too. Evan gave himself entirely to this power. And in that moment, he transformed.

The publishers of the present volume have deleted the lengthy description of what Evan briefly became. The first editor to read the original passage went quite mad. She ran screaming across her office, tripped over her to-be-read pile, suffered bruises and contusions, and lay there babbling maniacally about tentacles, bony spines, NaNoWriMo, and authors who insist on inserting two spaces after a period. The copy editor ate a neighbour, and a beta reader relocated to the country where she took up the safer hobby of body surfing on broken glass. On the prudent advice of counsel, the publishers settled on leaving the phrase "Lovecraftian nightmare" in the text without any further elaboration, on the grounds that this would minimize liability.

The effect on Evan's immediate audience was reminiscent of what happened to the editors. Several of them went quite mad too. There were screams of terror and various biological noises as the Regent's ballroom briefly became what most people think a vomitorium is. The Beast That Was Evan gyrated wildly, thrashing about and bringing its fearsome, grue-some appendages crashing down indiscriminately, landing on acolyte and Evangelist alike. Unlucky onlookers were thrown clear across the room, crashing into distant walls and collapsing in the debris. The Beast That Was Evan screamed a psychic scream, an inaudible howl that throbbed in veins, reverberated across bones, and carried meaning that bore directly into its victims' collective brains.

"You've all squandered your power!" it screamed. "You're born to lose! You've used whatever will you have to conjure a world that's run by Abe. A proven liar! An elite who wants to tell you what to do, what you can be, and who limits what you can dream! This is what your own imaginations brought you. You've only done this to yourselves!"

The Beast roared again, this time a proper, audible roar that shook the heavens, burst eardrums, and very nearly levelled the chateau to its foundations. Evan reached out with a twelve-foot tentacle and swatted a knot of acolytes into a wall. He spewed gouts of bile, filth, venom, and acid over a crowd of acolytes, bathing them in unspeakable horror and reducing them to a gelatinous, glowing goo that you could probably package and brand as android phlegm and sell to kids. He stomped his feet and roared again.

The Beast had tasted hideous power, and it craved more. It sensed a growing, pulsing source of power nearby. Dozens of eyestalks along Evan's transformed body writhed and wriggled and turned to face it.

The Beast looked down upon the Regent and howled. Evan reached out with his mind, perceiving the waves and streams of light surrounding the Regent. He reached out for her power, grabbing hold of it just as the Regent held her weathered pyr-amidical totem aloft and focused her energy on the enemy before her.

No one ever expects a ninja. One showed up, after a fashion. A practically perfect foot attached to a practically perfect being whipped silently into the frame, kicking the pyramidal totem out of the Regent's raised hands.

"STOP THIS NOW!" cried Tonto, landing superhero-style between the Regent and the Beast That Was Evan. A bead of sweat traced a path along her brow. "You've proved your point, Evan!" she boomed. "These people can't hurt you. They can't make you do anything you don't want to do. And I won't let them! But you have to release them, now!"

If Socrates can be believed, then an entity made of thought — say, an entity just like the practically perfect being who confronted Evan now — could be unmade in the blink of an eye by anyone wielding the sort of power that Evan now channelled in what you might describe as a fairly indiscriminate manner. Whether or not Tonto knew this, who can say? She's often been described as Socrates' equal, though, and Socrates knew this truth in the core of his being. In any case, we can all agree that it took a special kind of bravery to confront the Lovecraftian leviathan standing in the ballroom now.

Evan stared down at Tonto. He stared at the ball of power surrounding her, the sphere of unadulterated *Detroitness* only Evan could perceive. He reached a ghastly appendage toward her — and withdrew.

Such was the force of Tonto's personality that Evan stopped in his tracks. He simply stood there, seemingly thunderstruck, and transformed. There was a good deal of biological squelching and unpleasantness, and then Evan was once again an indescribable red-haired man standing amid a lot of debris and a large number of whimpering, shrivelled disciples.

"They made me do it," he said, on the verge of tears. "They forced me into it! They shouldn't question what I can do. They should just do as they're told!"

Tonto stepped forward and gingerly patted Evan's arm. "They will, Evan," she said, gently. "They really will. They'll all follow you. I'm sure."

Evan stepped toward the mass of recumbent husks that were GamerboiXXX69 and his fellows. He knelt down beside them. "I get that it's not your fault," he said, sadly. "You didn't know what you were supporting, helping Abe push his lies. But that's why you have to follow me! You just have to. This is my home!" he said, gesticulating broadly, "It's all my place! I'm not some immigrant who came in uninvited. I was born to run this world, just as it's in your nature to do what I say. I'm . . . I'm sorry I had to do that," he added, still drawing from phrases any five-year-old learns at a parent's knee. He stretched out his hand and patted the husk that was still, on some level, GamerboiXXX69.

"It's for your own good," he said. "I had to do it so that you'd see."

"See?" rasped the husk. "See . . . what?"

"That you do have power," said Evan, not unkindly. "It's within you. Inside all of you. I only borrowed what you have. Everything I did just now — all of that came from you. You think Socrates was cool? You think he was powerful? He's nothing compared to what each of you has within you. Imagine what you can do when you're able to access this power for yourself. No more controls imposed by Abe. No more speed limits or bedtimes. No one making you eat beans. No rules at all, no limits on what's possible. That's what I've promised you all along. That's what you'll get if you just lend me your powers for a little while longer . . . just until we've dealt with Abe, once and for all."

GamerboiXXX69 and his fellow husks whimpered and groaned. Evan took this as consent. Then he turned and faced the Regent.

"I've waited long enough," he said firmly. "You'll take me to R'lyeh, now. No more songs, no more prophecies, no more making preparations. We're leaving now, and nobody's getting in my way."

The Regent wasn't used to taking orders. She didn't even read instructions. She always decided what would happen, and then it happened. In this particular instance, though, what with one thing and another, the Regent chose a different path.

For the first time in anyone's memory, the Regent knelt. She knelt and bowed her head before Evan.

"So let it be written, my lord," she whispered. "So let it be done."

Within the Patch, Penelope hammered against an unseen wall, and wept.

Chapter 18

A hologram shimmered into view, its eerie shades of flickering, blueish light resolving into the ghostly form of a lectern standing beside a narrow table. Behind the table sat four equally ghostly figures, all positioned along one side, in what's known as the "Last Supper" configuration. The figures appeared ghostly because of limitations inherent in holography — it isn't as though they looked that way in person. In real life there was nothing ethereal, supernatural, "shimmery," or transparent about them. This is because they were academics.

The hologram featured professors S.P. Oiler, G. Liebniz, M. Bloom, and W. Stein, all sitting in front of a banner advertising them as the multi-disciplinary expert panel on "Identity Politics, Tribes and Tribulations: Exposing Graham's Nether Regions," the session shoehorned in right after the midday break at Detroit University's fifty-eighth symposium on *Beforelife* and its sequels. The hologram you're about to see — or rather read about, listen to, or experience first-hand, depending on the medium in which you're enjoying the present work — is a forensically recon-structed partial transcript of their remarks, one that was presently being displayed to Ian, Vera, and an entire platoon of robots gathered in an unusual setting you mightn't expect. We'll get to that later. But for now, the holographic transcript begins:

[Holographic transcript begins][9]

---

9   See. I told you.

Bloom: . . . understand that the entire corpus is a novelization of historical events — events that depict the latter stages of what I might call "primeval Detroit," when primitive notions of nativism and—

Oiler: You're evading the question, Molly. We were talking about the robots.

Liebniz: They prefer "artificial beings."

Bloom: Who doesn't?

Liebniz: I mean they prefer *the term* "artificial beings."

Bloom: That's an incredibly broad statement, Gottfried, and one that I find offensive. I think you'll find that the name they chose to call themselves, in the context under discussion, was "the Ianians," as in "those who follow Ian."

Liebniz: As a temporary tribal designation only. In point of fact, when referring to themselves as a race or species or—

Bloom: Race or species? Are you honestly implying that race and species are the same th—

Stein: Colleagues, colleagues, perhaps we could circle back to the point of the present discussion, viz, the historical divisions and identities explored in the final chapters of *Nether Regions*. The rift between immigrants and natives; distinctions between immigration and colonization, organic people and those who are considered artificial; self-selection between those who sided with Ian and those who chose to align with Evan—

Oiler: Ianians versus Evangelists!

Stein: Yes, yes, the synthetic or artificial persons who backed the cause of Ian Brown, and the Evangelists, those who follow Ian's son and embrace the promised Kingdom of Evan. Not to mention the Church of O who—

Liebniz: I think it's important to point out that the names "Ian" and "Evan" are, etymologically speaking, precisely the same name — both derive from the much older name "John," yes? Our two factions rally behind different men whose names boil down to "John Brown," two sides of the same—

Stein: I'm sure that's all very interesting, Gottfried, but it smacks of your old, debunked, and dare I say *heretical* suggestion that the people being discussed — Ian, Evan, and their contemporaries — aren't real historical actors who were key players in events that shaped Detroit; they clearly were. And the question we're pursuing—

Bloom: And we see no attempt by Evan to differentiate between immigrants and colonists, between refugees and settlers.

Liebniz: That's irrelevant, Dr. Bloom! There are no colonists or settlers. Not in Detroit. No one turns up in Detroit on purpose: they just arrive. They can't be blamed. No one knows about Detroit before they get there. You can't "colonize" a place by involuntarily manifesting in the Styx.

Oiler: Another oversimplification, Dr. Liebniz! You

forget that Detroit itself is a mental construct that is shaped and given form by the wills and expectations of its people. Those who manifest here, in Detroit, are complicit in its creation and evolution; they contribute to its form, its ongoing systems of oppression—

Stein: Not through conscious acts of will, Dr. Oiler; you can't turn this into another diatribe about your Critical Post-rationalist Stygian model of—

Bloom: But she's right! Detroit's residents lend support, whether consciously or not, to systemic oppression in which they themselves are inextricably entwined. It's Evan's chief complaint! Here we explore the nativist ideology springing from the liminal space both permeating and—

Leibniz: Does that even mean anything, Molly? I mean, come on, it's always "liminal this" or "synecdochic that" with you; always "interrogating dominant paradigms," and "overturning hierarchies," or maybe "Post-Woke Critical Reconstruction"—

Bloom: They're perfectly defensible theoretical intersectionalities. As I said in my latest piece—

Stein: But why not just say what you mean? These labels are just so . . . so desperately *lame*. All this alliance-building, politics-signalling stuff about hegemonic identities and purposive deconstructivist readings of problematized texts . . . it's an in-group/out-group shibboleth.

Oiler: Like using the word "shibboleth" in conversation?

Stein: Academic conversation. It doesn't count.

Bloom: All I'm saying is that an oppression-centred reorienting of identity and allegiance within the bounds of the text we interrogate is a perfectly valid approach.

Stein: You mean a "fundable" approach — or I suppose you maintain this has nothing to do with the sort of lingo that gets your donor agencies hot and bothered? You can't get a whiff of grant money these days without claiming to topple a dominant orthodoxy.

Oiler: That *is* the dominant academic orthodoxy.

Liebniz: And here we sit, colleagues, replicating what we're describing; announcing tribal affiliations by picking and choosing between the theoretical, critical traditions or methodologies that we venerate through allegiance-marking language choices and analytical tropes—

Stein: It's all just bull<tsssssss>

[Holographic display fades to static and resumes]

Bloom: So, now that Professor Stein has had a sandwich and calmed down, we're all agreed. The synthetics, or inorganics, or artificial beings—

Stein: The robots.

Bloom: Or the robots, if you prefer, align with Ian because of how they perceive him.

Oiler: That's right. They venerate Ian's status as a creator; one who chose to create life, namely Evan, through an act that parallels the early synthesis of artificial beings. They compare him to Ada Lovelace, Detroit's foremost designer of—

Bloom: But they're also drawn to Ian's vision of themselves, how he sees constructed beings as no different from himself, no different from Vera, or from beings created by other means, say, Socrates or Tonto. He understands the essential unity of Detroit. Everyone who winds up there is formed of the pre-existing ether, the essential "nothingness" into which Abe appeared on death; the so-called void that forms the tapestry from which all things are woven.

Stein: You don't weave things from a tapestry.

Bloom: You know what I'm saying. All physical beings in Detroit are formed of the same ethereal matter; the very "nothing" into which Abe appeared is the essence from which everything is formed.

Oiler: Apart from whatever "essence of self" comes from the beforelife.

Leibniz: But there's the rub, yes? The very core of Evan's complaint. Something "foreign" comes to Detroit from the mortal world and infects the native, primordial ether. Ian's equal treatment of synths, constructs, and organic beings — this signals his failure to assign any real value to this transcendental spark of formerly mortal life, this essence of humanity that travels from one plane to the next, leaving the pre-mortem world travelling through the Styx.

Bloom: I think that Ian's essential humanity derives from his insight that humanity itself isn't essential. He looks on constructs, robots, humans, without differentiating between them.

Stein: Yet the bulk of the Evangelists represent everything their leader purports to hate: immigrants from the mortal world; almost-caricatures of stereotypically grievance-laden, highly entitled social rejects who've failed to launch, people who've been blinded by Abe's lie that there are limits on what they can—

Bloom: You can see why he chose them, though. The relative ease of manipulation. Buttons that were easy to push. Infinite resources of untapped rage and visceral hatred—

Leibniz: It's Evan's clever, almost masterful manipulation of those impulses that allows him to—

Stein: But he *isn't* clever! Not in the least. We need to stop stoking the notion that Evan is playing 3-D chess when everyone else is playing checkers. He's just a child throwing a tantrum. That's all he is. But his open rage, his hatred of the establishment, his unbridled venting of id that flows from his childlike anger, deeply resonates with these throngs of disaffected losers who feel like they've been ripped off. They all believe, not without some justification, that Detroit's elite class has hidden the truth from them, decided what's best for them, and left them holding the short end of the stick. Along comes someone they don't recognize as an unrestrained id, a child in adult garb, promising them what they've always felt they rightfully deserved. He serves up simple, angry answers for their simple, angry minds.

Liebniz: Yet in Evan's movement we see what Bloom would call a *gestalt de novo*, as it were, a burgeoning movement unparalleled in modern culture—

Oiler: Well, modern culture, sure, but there's loads of precedent.

Bloom: Of course! Evan's movement represents the populist crusades seen in the late twentieth century, Earth-designate-42, emboldened by the work of pseudo-philosophers like those lampooned in the text, media pundits, politicians tapping into the anger of disenfranchised men who felt enti— <tchhhh>

[Holographic display fades to static and resumes]

Bloom: So, we agree that the author reveals his own political views while also problematizing them, as though trying to work through his own internal struggle through pseudo-comedic narrative structure. I think that's clear.

Stein: And his own personal struggles are played out through Socrates' arc.

Oiler: What's less clear is why the author included a depiction of an academic panel in his book; a panel discussing the very book in which they appeared.

Stein: What are you talking about?

Oiler: Chapter 18. *Nether Regions*. It starts off with a panel of academics talking about the nature of identity as depicted within the book itself—

Bloom: I'm sure you're mistaken. I've got my copy right here and there's no reference to—

Oiler: It's one of the strangest chapters in the work. I suspect it was added at the behest of the author's academic colleagues who felt that it behooved any writer to clearly draw out the underlying metaphors of—

Liebniz: I think there's something wrong with Professor Oiler.

Oiler: But you were there, Gottfried. You, Stein, and Molly. And Toto too—

[Here the hologram fizzles out with a series of self-referential crackles and pops]

* * *

"What the hell did we just watch?" asked Ian, as the image faded away.

"Time index 85,984 mark 3, dimensional coordinates iM-47 slash gamma," said the synthetic being whose holoprojectors had served up the little display. His proper name was Wall-IV-linebreak Geno3/Disco model alpha dezo3, but he liked to be called Seymour.

As Seymour spoke, lightning flashed across the skyline of Detroit. And not ordinary lightning, either. This was the really eldritch stuff; the bright white spiderwebs that flash across an eerie purple sky; the sort that's associated with words like "omens," "portents," and "foretellings." It was exactly the sort of lightning you'd expect on the precipice of a battle between forces one might describe as order and chaos. It was as if nature itself, or whatever passed as nature in Detroit, was rebelling against *something*. Something that was quite possibly woven into the fabric of Detroit itself. Whatever the target of the current rebellion was, nature appeared to be rebelling against it in a tumultuous, rumbling, flashing, crashing, and chest-pounding sort of way; a way that promised great happenings, social change, fluctuations on both quantum and cosmic scales, and, dare we say it, *revolution*.

Ian, Seymour, Vera, and an impressively diverse throng of robots were taking up every scrap of available space near the steps of City Hall, filling the vast, open courtyard that generally welcomed thousands of visitors to the grounds that represented Detroit's seat of mayoral power. The courtyard featured stone benches, occasional trees, those little mounted plaques you get in spots of civic significance, and the broad stone table known as the city's "Plinth of Honour."

You couldn't see much of the courtyard now. Practically every bit of available real estate was occupied by artificial life. There was the usual range of anthropomorphic gynoids, androids, and non-gendered-humanoid-types all present in great profusion, as well as the less traditional synths who'd been built without aesthetic nods to the shapes traditionally observed in *Homo sapiens*. There were synths whom any uninformed observer might have confused for construction equipment, vehicles, radio towers, or spare parts. There were hovering drone droids and immobile AI tablets who, while unable to move themselves from spot to spot, still counted as self-aware. There were teeny, tiny synths hopping around as though someone had given life to the minuscule components of larger cybernetic machines — which of course someone had. Whatever their shape or presentation, the synths were calling themselves Ianians — as in "followers of Ian." Their pronouns included not only him, her, it, them, and they, but also inxs, 234j@#, and OS3.14159, both because these pronouns were descriptively useful in the coding language of robots and because synths liked to keep organic beings on their toes.

The throng was centred on the aforementioned "Plinth of Honour," about two hundred metres distant from the doors of City Hall. No one dared venture close to the doors themselves — no one but Socrates, that is. The assassin, doing his best to stay cloaked despite his still-glitching systems, had ventured beyond the doors in question on a quest to disable any unforeseen security measures prior to Vera's own journey into R'lyeh.

All eyes, Ocular Scanners, sensor devices, and other gizmos capable of processing visual inputs were trained on the Plinth of Honour. Anywhere else in the multiverse the Plinth might have been a memorial to an unknown soldier, or to a group of fallen defenders. In Detroit, what with one thing and another, fallen defenders tended to get back up and move on with their lives. Plenty of them went on to do dishonourable things that one mightn't have predicted back when they'd been defending the city. It's a dicey proposition to immortalize an immortal, it being rather hard to maintain a good reputation when you have an eternal life.

The Plinth was just a massive stone table; one that was meant to memorialize the place where Abe and his fellows had come together to wrestle the chaos into order, to take control of whatever primordial ether welcomed Abe into its dark and empty embrace. They'd tamed this chaos, reined it in, and this

313

stone table symbolized that. As for how a stone table came to symbolize the taming of the ether, who can say? Rumour had it that the Committee for Civic Memorials couldn't settle on one idea, and had kept "tabling" the debate for future meetings. It didn't matter if this was true. Most symbols don't make sense. People tend to think of birds as symbols of freedom even though the vast majority of birds are cooped-up chickens.

Whatever else you might say about Detroit's Plinth of Honour, or the Stone Table of Order, or whatever you'd like to call it, you could say that it was presently surrounded by some of the city's finest minds, provided your definition of "mind" was broad enough to include positronic matrices and quantum-neural nets. These included the whole faculty of Detroit's School of AI Studies, who stood in a circle around the table with Vera and Ian.

Even now, after the Ianians had travelled with him to the steps of City Hall, Ian remained a little vague on why the Ianians had become, well, *Ianians* at all — why they'd joined up with his cause. Seymour's holographic projection was an attempt to clear this up. It hadn't worked especially well. Thus it was that Ian carried on cross-examining Seymour while Lori 8 and her faculty colleagues did their best to write a new Bill of Synthetic Rights.

"But how does the holoprojector work?" asked Ian.

"It's all very complicated, I'm sure," said Seymour, his remark punctuated by yet another flash of lightning overhead.

"It's not any weirder than me seeing the future," said Vera.

"But is it real?" pressed Ian. "I mean, couldn't this be some randomly generated movie dreamt up by Seymour's circuits or whatever?"

"I personally don't believe so, sir," said Seymour, who seemed genuinely interested in Ian's query. "My designers' expressed intention was to furnish me with an enhanced perceptual matrix capable of recording and replaying phenomena across dimensional boundaries; to view multiple quantum realities and resolve them into visual imagery to be shared with, described, and explained to non-observers."

"So you're a See 'n' Say?" said Ian.

"I'm unfamiliar with that term."

"Can I have a peek?" asked Vera, gesturing at a panel on Seymour's chest.

"Help yourself," he said, amiably. "I'm as interested as you!"

"You mean, you don't know how it works?" asked Ian.

"Not the technical ins and outs," said Seymour, shrugging a shoulder servo. "Just in a big-picture sort of way. I've only been online for eighty-seven hours. But my designer assures me that my holoprojector's function is to render accurate depictions of events drawn from a pan-dimensional field."

"Yup," said Vera, peeking into Seymour's chest. "That's what it's for—"

"How can you tell?" asked Seymour, intrigued. "Are you a creator?"

"Kind of," said Vera. "More of a dabbler. Medium and small appliance repair. But I have a thing for machines. I can look at any mechanized device and see what it's for."

"I'd rather you didn't call me a mechanized device," said Seymour, flatly.

"No, no, not you," said Vera, "just the gizmos in your guts. Like your holograph engine. It's designed to perceive imagery from alternate quantum realities, shift them into our own perceptual universe, and display them for others to see. It's really neat. Who designed it?"

"Mary Shelley," said Seymour, proudly.

"Cool," said Vera.

"Like *Frankenstein* Mary Shelley?" asked Ian, agog.

"I've never known her to go by that name," said Seymour, puzzled. "Doctor Shelley is one of Detroit's leading researchers in the field of synthetic life."

"She knows how to build a solid synth," said Vera, punctuating her remark by slamming Seymour's panel shut and giving him a friendly slap on the shoulder.

"So, what Seymour showed us, then," said Ian, still doing his best to string along, "that whole academic conference panel thing. That was real?"

"Who knows?" said Vera. "I can see what Seymour's holoprojector is for and how it's designed to work. As for distinguishing what's real and what isn't — you're bumping into philosophy there. Who knows what 'real' even means? But who cares, anyway? You asked Seymour to explain why the Ianians are on board, and he did. The conference thingy explained it, and the reason is real for them. All that matters is that they're on our side and they want to help us stop Evan."

"We need some assistance, Mr. Brown!" called Lori 8, shouting across the Plinth of Honour.

"What's up?" asked Ian.

"We're working on the Bill of Synthetic Rights. We need a solid opening line."

Ian made a face suggesting that constitutional drafting wasn't part of his constitution. "We really ought to get a move on," he said, looking antsy. "Shouldn't Socrates have been back by now? What's keeping him?"

"He'll be back," said Vera, "just give him time. There's nothing for us to do until he's dealt with security."

"Fine," said Ian, wiping his brow. "So, what was it you needed, Lori?"

"An opening line for the Bill of Rights."

"How about 'We the People of Detroit'?" suggested Ian.

"We the people *and* artificial organisms of Detroit!" said Dean Tundt.

"We the people, artificial organisms, and beings of non-specific origin or nature!" shouted a somethingorother in the back.

"Hold on," cried Inc, a remarkably human-looking member of the group. He was standing right between Dean Tundt and Lori 8 and, perhaps because of his name, had been roped in to the role of legislative scribe. "Lemme get this down," he said.

"Sorry, who are you, again?" asked Ian, still struggling to keep track of his allies' names.

"Inc," said Inc.

"Because you're the drafting robot. Right," said Ian.

"I'm not a robot!" said Inc. "I'm an artificial person. Former human."

Ian displayed the facial equivalent of a question mark.

"I was born human," explained Inc, "but I'm a corporation now. I filed the paperwork last week. I'm now legally an autonomous corporate entity. A legal artificial person. That's why I changed my name to Inc."

Ian was still processing this when Dean Tundt interrupted and asked whether or not it was still okay to be called "the people of Detroit" when some of them hailed from the mortal world.

"Why not 'We the undersigned'?" Inc suggested.

"There isn't room for everyone here to sign it," observed Ian.

"How about 'We the undersigned, together with whatever other entities of any specification, individually or collectively assent to what's written below together with subsequent amendments'?" suggested Inc, who'd read a lot of things drafted by corporate lawyers.

"Let's table the question of how we identify ourselves," said Dean Tundt.

"So what's the next provision?" asked Lori 8.

This discussion carried on for quite some time. Shortly after they'd started hammering out the section on autonomy for automata, Vera felt a tug at her arm.

It was Lori 8, who'd somehow managed to worm her way around the table to Vera's side.

"Might I have a word with you on another matter?" she said in a half-whisper. "I wouldn't ask if it wasn't important. It's . . . it's a rather personal matter." Here she approximated a blush.

"Fine," said Vera, taking Lori 8 aside. "What's up?"

"It's just . . . I mean . . . what do you see when you see me?" said Lori 8.

"Pardon me?"

"When you look at synthetic beings, I mean. I couldn't help but overhear what you said to Seymour. I want you to tell me what I'm for. Why I exist. I've given this a good deal of thought."

"Sorry, Lori," said Vera, patting the poet's shoulder. "I'm afraid it doesn't work that way."

"But you said—"

"I can see what machines are for," said Vera. "I see their purpose. That doesn't work with people."

"Because people don't have a purpose?" said Lori 8, whose titanium forehead presently mimicked the look of a furrowed brow.

"We don't," said Vera. "We mostly just fart around. I mean, we do have purposes, I guess. Plenty of them. And we choose them for ourselves. It's not imprinted on us like it is on a machine. By design, I mean. That's probably because we don't have designers."

"But . . . I am a machine. I had a designer."

"Sure, but . . . well, I guess you're more than the sum of those designs. You're not like a toaster or a plasma rifle — you aren't built with one primary function in mind. I look at a toaster, I see that its purpose is making toast. I look at you . . . I just see a person. Your purpose is up to you. Right now, that's being Detroit's poet laureate, I guess. And that's because that's what you've decided."

"Well, my name essentially directed me—"

"That happens with organics, too," said Vera, laughing. "If your last name's 'Foot' you stand a better than average chance of ending up a podiatrist. And you aren't landing a gig as a prelate in the Church of O with a name like 'Trixie Buttons.' You started out with the name Lori 8 and—"

"It's actually XL3/42 — Lori series model 8."

"Right, well, with a name like that, you might have been anything. Say, a lorry driver. But you decided to be a poet. What separates you from a machine is that your purpose isn't a function of how you're made, or who designed you. It's your own choice. You choose your purpose. You can change it. You can decide not to have one at all — spend your life drooling on the couch and eating cheese puffs. But it'll be your choice, your life, and your purpose."

Lori stared at her wide-eyed.

"I don't know what a soul is," Vera mused. "For humans it's what crosses over from the beforelife. But I think . . . well, I think you've made a soul for yourself with the choices that you made. Does that make sense?"

"That may be the nicest thing anyone ever said about me," said Lori 8, who was a poet, after all, and therefore not accustomed to kindness.

It was at this precise moment that the crowd around the table parted like the Red Sea — an allusion that would have been lost on almost everyone present, but one that perfectly suited any occasion involving Socrates openly walking through a crowd.

Socrates took a spot at the table beside Ian.

"I have bad news," said the assassin.

"Oh no," said Ian, blanching.

"City Council installed a phi-series multiphasic security barrier with a seventy-two-digit encryption code," said the assassin. "Virtually unbreakable."

"So, we're sunk?" said Ian, alarmed.

"No, no, I bypassed it right away," said Socrates.

"So, what's the bad news, then?" asked Ian.

"The fact that they bothered installing a nearly unbreakable system," said the assassin. "It's a sign of the times. No one trusts each other anymore. Anyway," he added, brightening, "we're good to go. And it's about time, too. My intracranial scanners are picking up a mass teleportation signature over the ridge. That'll be your kid and his army."

It seemed the assassin wasn't alone in this assessment. A cacophony of beeps, buzzes, flashes, and clanging claxons indicated that quite a number of Ianians also had the means of detecting the large-scale use of IPTs.

"They're less than a mile away," said Socrates. "Scanners indicate — hold on — scanners register 2,368 distinct lifeforms coming our way."

"That's not so bad!" said Ian, registering relief. "We have twice that many robots."

"Twice that many *Ianians*," corrected Lori 8. "And that's not counting the micro-synths and tablet units," she added, smiling.

"I like those odds," said Vera, cheerfully. "Now you guys hold off Evan's troops while I make my way into R'lyeh. I'll hook an ancient up to the expectation manager, and then let them sort out Evan. Easy as pie. What's that noise?"

The noise, it turned out, was a loud, percussive thumping that you could feel in the soles of your feet. Or in your treads, if you were one of the wheeled Ianians. Or your rollers, or braces, or struts, as the case may be. It was rhythmic, it was thunderous, and it seemed to be drawing closer.

"War drums on the horizon," said Socrates, staring into the purple sky.

"War drums?" said Vera, scoffing. "Who uses war drums?"

"There hasn't been a war in Detroit for two millennia," said the assassin. "It's not as though there's a modern battle playbook. Besides, the Regent strikes me as a traditionalist."

"IANIANS, STAND READY!" shouted Ian, in all caps, and you could tell that he was really getting into the spirit of things.

The Ianians stood ready. Well, they "stood" ready for a given value of "standing," because a lot of them were hoverers or non-ambulatory slabs. And they stood ready for a given value of "ready," because very few of them were anything close to ready for what happened next.

"What's that overhead?" said Vera, pointing.

"I'm not detecting anyth— *bzzzt*" said Socrates, before collapsing on the ground like a marionette whose strings were suddenly severed.

Almost every single Ianian followed suit, collapsing where they stood or sat or rolled or hovered, or simply powering down with the fizzling, crackling cybernetic equivalent of a whimper.

Ian wasn't entirely clear on what had just happened. He knew he'd watched the bulk of his army simply crumple on the spot; as for why, he couldn't say. He'd heard Vera shouting something along the lines of "EMP grenade!" just as it happened, and then boom, lights out for the synths.

Ian and Vera blinked at one another in silence. That was the last thing that they did before the sky exploded in fire.

Chapter 19

It's possible that there aren't any gods in the world we call Detroit — not unless you count people like Abe, Penelope, and the City Solicitor. They didn't think of themselves as gods; just as people who showed up with a more interesting batch of talents than most souls ferried across the Styx. If there are gods lurking somewhere in the multiverse, it seems likely that they're hanging out someplace else. Say, a totally separate version of the hereafter — a place you might think of as *thereafter*. This other, alternative afterlife might be one you get into only if you're exceptionally noble, or if you said the right magic words, or avoided the wrong kinds of foods, or assiduously refused to mix polyester and cotton, or were born on whatever obscure slab of geography some specific celestial being regarded as the spot reserved for The Chosen People. Who can say? But if there were gods hiding somewhere in Detroit, it's quite likely that this is the point in the present story when they grabbed their popcorn and put up their feet on whatever these deities used as footstools — possibly lesser beings who didn't wear the right kind of hat.

The reason these gods, real or not, would have chosen this time to pull up a planet and tune in to watch the proceedings is that it was right at this moment — at least somewhere in the next handful of chapters — that a New God was to be born. After a fashion, at any rate, for a given value of the word "god," as well as a given value for the word "new." These otherworldly observers, if blessed with anything you might call omniscience, knew that one way or another, today Detroit was going to produce a god of its own.

Who it was going to be, or how exactly this momentous event would come to pass, wasn't known by them in advance. They'd have to wait for the end of the book like everyone else. Some things remain hidden from even the most *all-seeing* observers. And given the waves of quantum-level uncertainty currently swirling around the ether that we've come to call Detroit, the outcome of the present battle was one of them.

If you've been paying close attention, you'll know that one of the top contenders for imminent godhood had to be Evan Brown. His most recent step on the road to apotheosis had been a classic, viz, declaring war on those he regarded as unworthy. He looked over the soon-to-be battlefield that was the grounds of City Hall, surveying the terrain through a pair of fancy high-tech binoculars. He could have achieved the same result by drawing power from a nearby lackey and whipping up some more impressive, supernatural mode of remote viewing, but he felt it prudent to use his ammunition, as it were, as sparingly as he could until things started to get hairy.

"It's war, then," he said gravely, his eyes narrowing. "Against my dad, a bunch of malfunctioning robots, a few nobodies — and another one of *you*," he added, lowering the goggles and aiming an up-nod at Tonto. "And he's broken. The EMP worked like a charm."

Tonto didn't bother acknowledging Evan's remark — unless you count hitching up her collar against the wind that had whipped up in the last few minutes. She didn't even turn to make eye contact; she kept her gaze fixed on City Hall.

"It . . . erm . . . that is to say . . . . it needn't be war, Your Eminence," stammered Norm, oozing up to Evan's side with Oan in tow.

"Of course it's war," said the Regent, who arrived on the scene without appearing to move a muscle — she just drifted into place, like a particularly majestic float at the Macy's Thanksgiving Day Parade. "This day will end in bloodshed," she added, brushing a speck of ash from her sleeve. "Evan and I shall carve a path through those who oppose us. We shall take R'lyeh, and let Evan absorb its power. No one can stop us."

"Well, broadly, yes, I mean, of course, Madame Regent, that is the plan," said Norm, wringing his hands and bowing slightly. He could have easily been mistaken for a pangolin with a beard. "But when you say 'carving a path,'" he added, "you do leave room for tweaking. I mean, why not 'carve a path' by convincing Ian and his friends to move aside, or perhaps by smiting them with clever arguments? Something of, shall we say, a non-violent approach?"

"It'd save a good deal of bother," said Oan, chiming in. She and Norm both had the tortured look of people suddenly faced with the understanding that their religious beliefs were a) actually true, and b) not very nice.

"You think they'll listen to reason?" scoffed the Regent, raising a regal eyebrow.

"It's worth a shot," said Tonto, who suddenly seemed keen on joining in. She took a couple of steps toward the group and crossed her arms. "Ian won't want any harm to come to Evan. And the EMP has left his army in shambles. He had thousands of synths on his side. Now he has three hundred. He'll be—"

"I thought you said the synths would be wiped out by the pulse," said Norm, anxiously.

"They were," said Tonto, "for the most part. Some were bound to have hardened processors, anti-EMP shielding, regenerative matrices, things like that. But we've still stacked the odds. Ian will see that. He'll be willing to talk. He'll do whatever he can to keep Evan safe."

"Enough!" shouted Evan, throwing his high-tech goggles to the ground. "I'm sick and tired of you talking about me like that. Keeping me safe. Keeping me out of harm's way. You've been on my case about being safe since we first met. Do I seem like someone who needs to be kept safe?"

He had a point. Tonto had, in point of fact, been on Evan's case about keeping safe since they'd first met in the Regent's lair. Evan might have accused Tonto of sounding like a broken record had Evan not been born in the time of digital streaming.

"Do you honestly think they stand a chance against me?" said Evan. "I stopped my mother. I stopped Abe. Dad's nothing. He and his hopeless little band—"

"His hopeless little band shouldn't be underestimated," said Tonto. "They've got Socrates on their side."

"He's lying there like a broken doll!" shouted Evan, gesturing vaguely at City Hall.

"They've got Vera," said Tonto, "they've still got a few hundred synths."

"I've got *me*," said Evan, glowering.

"Still," said Norm, bobbing forward, "our best shot may be to—"

On the disappointingly on-the-nose cue provided by the word "shot," Evan took one. It was a fireball. The only outward sign that this was coming was the shriek of three acolytes standing about twelve feet away when the notion of making a fireball had taken root in Evan's mind. Each of the hapless acolytes seemed to lose about fifteen pounds in less than a jiffy as Evan drew upon their essences, taking hold of their "will" or "power" or whatever you call the connection flowing between these acolytes and Detroit. Evan seized this with his mind and shaped it into a ball of fire.

The fireball streaked over the ridge separating Evan's forces from the gang at City Hall, arcing through the sky and illuminating what was about to be called "ground zero." It split into dozens of smaller incendiary bombs, little blazing brimstone meteors that left streaks of fire and smoke and ash as they hurtled toward their victims.

Some of the still-functional Ianians in the immediate line of fire raised their arms and other appendages in what must have been a cybernetic protective gesture, the result of which was a force field centred on Ian; a shimmering yellow dome of energy covering much of the courtyard.

It didn't work especially well. There just weren't enough Ianians — not active, at any rate. Several dozen of Evan's meteorites did bounce off the robots' shield, ricocheting who-knows-where and presumably setting fires in whatever neighbourhoods were lucky enough to receive them. A handful still got through.

The effect was what you'd expect, but only if you expected chaos — Ian and friends running around in the sort of helter-skelter frenzy you get when a kid kicks over an anthill or upends a bucket of mice.

"So . . . yes . . . right," said Norm, with the air of a basset hound recalling a secret shame. "It's war, then."

* * *

"Get down to R'lyeh!" shouted Ian, crouching behind the disconcertingly lifeless shells of a half-dozen Ianians. He'd shouted this at Vera, who was standing a few metres away and not shielding herself at all. She was covered in so many smudges of oil that you might think Jackson Pollock had come after her with a grease gun. You might describe her as "blood-spattered" if you'd forgotten that the bulk of her fallen comrades were synthetic.

"I'm on my way!" cried Vera, suddenly ducking under a burst of flame that seemed to erupt from nowhere. "I shouldn't be long!" she cried, "I'll hook Sargon up to the expectation manager and see what we can do about Evan!"

Here she ducked again, as something that looked like a flaming ball of tar streaked out of the sky and passed through the space where Vera's head had been.

"Who's Sargon?" shouted Ian, shielding his eyes from retina-searing pulses of light shed by explosions overhead.

"Oh, right!" shouted Vera, cupping her hands in megaphone form to make herself heard over the racket. "He's an ancient. I just remembered that he's the one I'm going to wake up!"

Ian made a facial expression that was a cousin of the one he usually made when Vera remembered things from the future, this one differing only because it was tinged with the fear you feel whenever your kid decides to rain several hells' worth of fire on you and your friends. A block of molten metal fell from the sky and crashed uncomfortably nearby, causing Ian to leap backward with all the grace of a roller-skating giraffe. He tripped over a recumbent Ianian, stumbled over some rubble, and finally face-planted in the crater that had recently been the Plinth of Honour.

Vera, meanwhile, charged off toward City Hall, bobbing and weaving around explosions, fireballs, and the hail of flaming debris, as though she knew exactly where the next hazard was going to appear — which of course she probably did.

"On your feet," said a gruff voice in Ian's rear — meaning behind Ian, of course, as any other interpretation would just be weird.

Ian sat up and turned to see Socrates staring back at him, looking amused. It says a good deal about the current situation that Socrates' face was a welcome sight.

"I thought you were dead!" cried Ian, proving once again that, in times of apparent mortal peril, it can be easy to forget that you're in a world where mortal peril doesn't exist.

"I got better," said the assassin. "The EMP fried my intracranial systems. Just for a moment. It took out most of the synths too."

"How many are left?" asked Ian, struggling to his feet.

"About three hundred," said the assassin. "I can't get an accurate count. My scanners are still rebooting."

"Three hundred?" said Ian, goggling. "How many people are on Evan's side?"

"Thousands of them," said the assassin.

Ian's eyes widened as this new information migrated through his ears and toward useful bits of his brain. On its way, it took a detour through that underused bit of his hippocampus that was devoted to keeping track of ancient literary references and mythologized bits of the past.

"It's like Sparta!" he said, agog.

"IANIANS, PRESENT ARMS!" cried a familiar voice; Lori 8's, to be specific, as the poet-laureate-cum-commander of synths did her best to rally the droids. Those who were able to respond did their best to present arms — along with whatever other useful appendages they still had at their disposal — pointing their arms, legs, shoulder-mounted-cannons, and similar features toward the ridge beyond which Evan's army waited. A moment later they fired a mixed volley of plasma charges, energy pulses, and assorted explosive ordnances into the sky.

Once again, the result was about what you'd predict, so long as you'd predict that Evan and the Regent weren't in the mood to have their afternoons ruined by incoming enemy fire. For practical purposes, this meant that the Ianians' volley simply ceased to exist. Just like that. One moment it was a barrage of fire and metal and plasma streaking across the burning sky; the next it was nothing — a nothing punctuated by the distant sound of acolytes and Evangelists howling in pain as Evan drew upon their essences and worked his own uniquely horrible brand of magic.

"Well, shit," said Lori 8, as another round of flaming meteors rained down around City Hall.

Socrates snatched Ian up like a rag doll and ran twenty yards down-range, depositing him behind a barricade that was made of functus Ianians and debris.

"What's going to happen?" cried Ian.

"We're getting out of the line of fire," said the assassin.

"RETURN FIRE!" cried Lori 8, for all the good it would do. A clutch of Ianians in the area did their best to follow her lead, unleashing a second impotent barrage that, while temporarily filling the sky with sound and fury, signified less than half of a diddly-squat.

"I mean what's going to happen next?" cried Ian, tugging at the assassin's armour. "What's going to happen to everyone else if Evan wins?"

"Telling the future is Vera's department," said the assassin.

"I'm serious!" cried Ian.

"I know you're serious," hissed the assassin. "But you know what's at stake, Brown! That kid of yours is going to break Detroit. He's going to carve his way into R'lyeh and tap into more raw power than you could imagine. And he's going to use it to undo everything Abe has done. He'll show the whole world the truth. He'll give power to the people. Every idiot on the street will have the power to change the world. If Vera doesn't succeed—"

"If Vera doesn't succeed my son is going to destroy Detroit," said Ian.

"More or less," said the assassin, philosophically. "I mean, Detroit will still be here, after a fashion. But it won't be the world we know. Everybody will know the truth. They'll have the power to weave the fabric of reality in whatever ways their horrible little minds can dream up."

"And what'll happen to Evan?"

"Whatever he likes. He'll be unstoppable," said the assassin, crouching down to avoid a barrage of molten steel. "You know how he works. He draws power from those around him. And when he reveals Abe's lie — when he shows the people that they have unlimited power . . ."

Had Lori 8 been part of the conversation, she might have completed Socrates' thought in her own brand of robotic poetry, say, describing Evan as the deranged conductor of an all-powerful symphony, one propelled by the unbridled passions of an embittered population who'd been hemmed in by Abe's "lies" for ten millennia. Or something like that. It turns out that Lori 8 is a good deal better at commanding robot armies than she'd ever been at composing instant poems.

Plumes of fire burst from the ground; blobs of flaming tar rained down from above; lightning seared the purple sky; and rocks exploded in bursts of blistering steam and shrapnel. Enormous balloon animals floated overhead for no good reason at all, unless you count the fact that most of the current calamity had sprung from the imagination of a five-year-old child.

Ian nestled tightly against the assassin — an act that he couldn't have imagined a half-hour earlier. Of course, he'd also never imagined that Evan would be destroying the world. He'd never imagined that the biggest threat to the future of Detroit, besides his son, would be the danger that *the truth* might be revealed — the truth that people could change the world however they liked. He'd never imagined how horrific it might be if human beings reached their potential.

Ian had never *really* faced the fact that the wall between calm and chaos was a lie — the lie propagated by Abe, the lie he fostered with the assistance of Penelope and the ancients. The lie that said "what you see is what you get," the lie that Detroit was governed by rules, that people are stuck with what life gives them. In Detroit, the truth was chaos; order came in the form of an ancient fib. An order that ancient "elites" imposed on those they felt couldn't be trusted with a truth that led to power.

It was at this point in the narrative that Ian wondered if he was on the right side.

He didn't wonder that for long. It's one thing to think about the larger philosophical implications of supporting a Big Lie that leads to order. It's another to think you might be the baddy when the Other Side is raining fire and brimstone on your friends.

"I really thought Penelope would stop him," said Ian, clutching at the assassin for support.

"I have a theory about that," said Socrates, pushing Ian away and gently tucking him into a nook behind the barricade. The assassin rummaged among the crumpled Ianians, searching for something.

"What theory?" said Ian.

"I think your wife did all she could. In whatever time she had, right before Evan trapped her in the Patch. When Evan locked her in, I think Penelope reached out. Her power was being used against her; there was nothing she could do. So she was stuck, caught in a snare formed by her own power, as well as Abe's — every scrap of power that Evan had at his disposal."

"And?" said Ian, who tried his best but couldn't get close to seeing where any of this was headed.

"Part of Penelope's power *wasn't* in the Patch," said the assassin, who almost certainly hadn't planned for that many *p*s when he'd started speaking. Then he added, "Part of it had a life of its own."

Ian probably would have asked the assassin to add a few footnotes to his latest theory, preferably some that featured a bit more clarity and less alliteration. Whatever he might have said, he was interrupted by Lori 8.

"INCOMING!" she boomed, heralding yet another exciting session of fire and brimstone cluttering up the scenery and ruining everyone's day. The poet laureate's force of three hundred or so Ianians formed up into mechanized platoons and rallied around Ian's position, where they once again joined forces to project a dome of energy that was centred over a man who, for reasons that made sense only in the sparking, binary depths of an inorganic mind, had become a symbol of robotic rights. The dome shimmered and sizzled overhead as it absorbed the incoming assault.

It's funny how time passes in moments like this one, when you're shielded under a crackling dome of energy and your five-year-old son, aided by an ancient Egyptian you've never met, conjures flame and rock and debris intended to pulverize you and your robot army. Maybe you've noticed this yourself. From Ian's perspective, time seemed to stand almost perfectly still, seconds stretching into hours as he crouched in place, hoping against hope that his son might change his mind, or exhaust himself, or otherwise end the current onslaught. For the Ianians, time ticked along exactly as expected, most of them being equipped with highly precise internal chronometers. Any one of them could have reported that this latest barrage lasted seventeen minutes and forty-three seconds, give or take a microsecond, to be followed by a lull in the proceedings.

The lull lasted for almost exactly sixteen minutes, now that we're keeping track. And that lull featured a sequence in which the sun briefly peeped out from the clouds, the skies remained relatively fireball-free, and a few Ianian corpses — or whatever you call the temporarily non-functional bodies of inorganic beings — started to reanimate themselves as their systems regained function. Another portion of the lull featured

Ian asking Socrates if they might try injecting Ian himself with Stygian toxin, on the basis that Ian was part of Evan, after a fashion, and maybe wiping Ian's mind could have the effect of stopping his son.

Socrates made fun of this suggestion for a solid ninety seconds, not even giving Ian a break for the spirit of self-sacrifice it took for him to suggest it. The mockery persisted until the assassin was interrupted by a familiar, shouty voice from the north-northwest.

It was Vera. She was running straight at them, as fast as she could, followed closely by what appeared to be a torpedo casing with six mechanical legs.

"Guys!" she cried, sprinting. "Guys! Guys!"

She skidded to a halt and tucked herself into Ian's nook, her hexapedal torpedo casing standing by.

"What is it?" asked Ian. "Did you wake an ancient?"

"Do I look like I woke an ancient?" said Vera, catching her breath.

"I dunno," said Ian, "how do you look when you wake an ancient?"

"What's with the tube?" asked the assassin.

"It's a sarcophagus," said Vera. "An empty one. I jury-rigged some cybernetic legs so it could—"

"Why's it empty?" cried Ian. "I thought we needed someone in it!"

"That was the plan," said Vera, chewing her lip. "It didn't work out."

"What do you mean *it didn't work out?*"

"What do you *think* she means by *it didn't work out?*" asked the assassin.

"The ancients buggered off," said Vera.

This seemed to catch both Ian and the assassin by surprise.

"They buggered off?" said Socrates, flatly.

"I woke Sargon," said Vera. "Just like I remembered. I remembered he was the one I'd bring out of dormancy to help us deal with Evan. But he just sat there. Blinking at me. Like he couldn't understand what I was saying."

"He probably couldn't," said the assassin, stroking his beard. "Decamillennials. Most of them experience time differently than we do. It's a side effect of growing old. For them, a year flits by like a microsecond. Only a handful—"

"I know, I know," said Vera, "only Abe and Hammurabi and a few others are able to keep track of anything shorter than a decade."

"And you're just thinking of that now?" said Ian.

"I hoped Sargon would be one of the weird ones!" said Vera.

"You couldn't predict how he'd respond?" said the assassin.

"I can't see everything, all right?" cried Vera. "I did my best. I woke him up, tried to explain things, and he just stared at me like I wasn't real. He finally moved around a bit, got out of the sarcophagus, and just kind of wandered off."

"Where'd he go?" cried Ian.

"How should I know? I tried a few more ancients and it kept happening!"

"So what do we do now?" asked Ian.

"I dunno," said Vera, running a hand across her forehead. "I think we're fu—"

Here she fell silent for two reasons. First, because the editors of the current edition didn't want to let that sentence come to fruition, but more importantly because the part of Vera Lantz that was the Oracle at Delphi chose this moment to grab the controls and lean heavily into the "medium" part of "medium and small appliance repair."

Vera's eyes rolled back in her head. She threw her head backward, staring into the purple sky and crying out in a voice that reached the heavens — provided only that there was anything that qualified as "the heavens" in Detroit. And while the thing that Vera shouted was undeniably a product of what she called her "television," it was also something that, at this point in the narrative, you'd have to label a rerun. It went like this:

In his house at R'lyeh, the first one, dreaming, lies. Surrounded by all and none; both real and not; removed from those who traverse the river. Charon's Obol must be paid!

This was followed by something approximating silence, unless you count the distant shouts of acolytes and Evangelists, the purr of rolling thunder, or the quiet buzzing of servo motors within the limbs of nearby Ianians who were shuffling on the spot and trying their best to look as if Vera's little display hadn't broken their weirdness sensors.

Vera emerged from her reverie to find Socrates, Ian, and the puzzled-looking Ianians staring at her as though she'd announced her plan to elope with a fish.

"Oh geez, what now?" said Vera.

"You prophesied," said Ian.

"Well, sort of," said Socrates.

"It was free verse!" said Lori 8, eager to share her expertise.

"What do you mean, sort of?" asked Vera.

"I'm not sure if it counts as prophecy if it's a thing you've said before," said the assassin. "It was what you saw before — your vision of R'lyeh."

"Oh, that," said Vera. "Well, a lot of good that did us. It's the reason I woke up Sargon."

"I thought your visions were always right!" said Ian.

"There's a first time for everything," said Vera.

There was a brief stage wait as those present fell silent and either (a) thought about what Vera had said or (b) contemplated the depth of the metaphorical fertilizer in which they found themselves at the present juncture. Perhaps some combination of both. The quiet was punctuated by continued rabble-rousing over the ridge, where Evan's army still waited, as well as the disconcerting passage of several more of those enormous, menacing, gosh-awful-in-every-respect balloon animals that were wafting across the sky.

It was Socrates who spoke first.

"But what if the prophecy isn't wrong?" he said. "We can't be sure what it means. Let's start from the premise that all we know is that we know nothing. What if we've been interpreting Vera's prophecy incorrectly, all this time? Perhaps we've tried too hard to make it fit a plan we like. Waking up a sleeping ancient to score a bit of omnipotent help, I mean. *Ancient ex machina*. It's too convenient."

"Maybe," said Vera, shrugging. "So, what do we do about it?"

"We follow the clues," said the assassin. "We've been assuming Sargon, or some other ancient, was the 'first one' in the vision, yes? But what if the vision means something else? The prophecy also says that the first one is 'surrounded by all and none.'"

"That's the sarcophagus," said Vera. "It has to be. When you're in it, you're all alone. You're still surrounded by the world, but you're on ice and unaware of the world around you. You're surrounded by all and none. You lie there, dreaming."

"Right," said Socrates, "that makes sense. But what about 'removed from those who traverse the river.'"

"I think that means the Church of O!" said Ian, brightening. "They want to cross the river, right? To get back to the mortal world."

"If I may," said Lori 8, stepping forward, "I'd like to challenge that construction. Poetic interpretation is, after all, part of my primary expertise."

"Go ahead," said Ian.

"Your interpretation, sir," said Lori 8, "assumes that the Church of O will succeed in carrying out their plan — that they'll truly 'traverse' the river and make the prophecy come true. They haven't done that yet. And if we're all successful in our efforts, they never will. They'll never really count as 'those who traverse the river.'"

"Unless you count their first time across," said the assassin.

"Their first time across?" asked Lori 8, frowning.

"When they died," said Socrates. "When they first came to Detroit."

"Abe's drawers!" said Vera. "Socrates! That's it! I could hug you! I mean, I won't, of course, but I mean — by Hammurabi's beard, you might be the wisest man I know!"

"I'm sure you're wrong about that," said Socrates.

"But you've solved it!" Vera cried. "The reference to those who traverse the river isn't about the Church of O at all. Not specifically, at least. It's about mortals. All mortals. Everyone who traverses the river. Every mortal human being who was born in the beforelife traverses the River Styx when they pass into Detroit! And who do we know who qualifies as a 'First One'?" she added, pausing briefly to punch Ian in the shoulder. "Who wants to be separated from people who were born in the mortal world?"

"Search me," said Ian.

"The first human born in Detroit!" cried Vera, punching his shoulder again.

"You don't mean Evan!" said Ian, aghast.

"I do mean Evan!"

"It must mean Evan!" said Socrates, snapping his fingers in a "eureka" sort of way. "And that means we have a plan!"

Ian looked at him with the face of a man who hadn't a clue that there was a plan, let alone what the plan might be.

"We do have a plan!" Vera exclaimed. "We plug Evan into a sarcophagus. If it works on decamillennials, then it's bound to work on him! It's perfect! It'll keep him on ice for as long as we like."

"You can't stick my son in there!" cried Ian, before amending this by adding, in a much quieter and more circumspect tone, "what would it do to him, anyway?"

"It'll keep Evan suspended for millennia!" said Vera. "Perfectly safe! Think about it. When they're sealed in a sarcophagus, the ancients go dormant, right? They just lie there, dreaming the world that Abe created, all their dreams and expectations being funnelled toward Abe who uses them to shore up the walls of reality. This sarcophagus," she added, stepping toward the machine and slapping its hull, "will work almost the same way. Except we're replacing Abe with the expectation manager. It'll direct and amplify his expectations; reinforce his belief in whatever we make him see. Evan will fall asleep and dream the dreams we want to feed him. We'll give him a dream world all his own, one he can rule over without being bothered by any immigrants or intruders."

"Wait," said Ian, "just wait a second. That can't work. One moment Evan's in Detroit, fighting against his dad and an army of robots trying to jam him in a sarcophagus, and the next he's in some dream world where he's in charge? He'll know it's a lie. He'll never believe the dream."

"Well, no," said Vera. "He'll have to be mindwiped, first."

There was a noise that sounded something like the "oooo" you get when someone makes a provocative proposal. This one differed in that it seemed to have been made by synthesizers. The sound had issued from the Ianians, most of whom had taken a synchronized step backward, apparently doing their best to distance themselves from Vera. One could see what they were driving at. Here was Ian, a creator in the same vein as Mary Shelley or Ada Lovelace, being asked to erase the hard drive of his very first creation.

338

You didn't have to be Vera to predict what would come next.

"I already told you, YOU CAN'T MINDWIPE MY SON!" cried Ian.

"We have to," said Vera. "We need him to be a blank slate — so that the expectation manager can strengthen the world that he thinks he sees. We can't have him going in with pre-existing memories or expectations or—"

"I can't let you!" cried Ian.

"Oh, c'mon," said Vera. "He'll only lose five years of memories, and those memories aren't very nice. He'll build new ones in the dream."

"But he'll forget *me*!" cried Ian.

"And he won't destroy the world!" cried Vera. "And we can put a version of you in the dream. It'll be great. The whole point is to get him dormant."

"But how can we?"

"He'll be fine!" shouted Vera. "Everybody's internal life is just electrical activity anyway, right? Playing out on the big screen of your perceptions. We're just hooking him up to a new and improved streaming service. It'll be great! He won't even know."

"We can't!"

"He'll be safer than he is now!" cried Vera.

"Man up and stick your son in the toaster, Brown," said Socrates. "It's the only way we're going to save Detroit."

Ian slumped against the sarcophagus and imagined the road ahead. It wasn't easy. On the one hand, he might help Vera and Socrates save the world, a world that he was still reasonably sure deserved saving. On the other, his vengeful, cataclysmically destructive five-year old son would lose all memory of his early, formative years. Probably only two or three of them, to be honest — who could remember their first two years of life, anyway? And Ian wouldn't see his son again until . . . until when, exactly? He couldn't be sure. He could barely be sure of anything. When he finally spoke, he radiated the same mixture of angst and hope you feel when opening up an email called "Your Manuscript Submission." What he said was this:

"Okay. We'll try it. And we'll only need to keep Evan in this thing until Pen can free herself and fix him, right?"

"Umm, sure. Yeah. That. Exactly," said Vera, shifting her eyes from side to side in a display of what might very well have been the worst poker face in history.

"I hate to rain on your little parade," said Socrates, fiddling with an assortment of gizmos on his gauntlet, "but that's easier said than done. How are we supposed to get Evan, a potentially all-powerful asshole—"

"HEY!" said Ian.

". . . all-powerful foe," said the assassin, "into this contraption?"

"Like I said," said Vera, "you have to wipe him."

"I don't think I can," said the assassin.

"Why not?" said Vera. "Ian gave us the thumbs-up!"

"I don't care about Ian's feelings," said Socrates, who didn't. "I just don't think it'll work."

"Why not?" said Vera.

"The Stygian toxin may or may not work on Evan," said the assassin. "I've no idea. But there's zero chance of me getting the toxin into him. Have you seen what he can do? He's throwing fireballs at us. He's dissipating enough synth-generated plasma, laser fire, and ordnance to take out an army. And he's got the Regent helping him too. And before I even get to them, there's Tonto. Not to mention thousands of acolytes who already know the truth. People who know that I can be snuffed out of existence with a thought. What if they're ready? What if Evan has brought them to the point where they're able to wish me out of existence — where they know that if they just stop believing that I exist—"

"Oh, would you please shut up!" shouted Vera.

This took Socrates aback.

Vera stepped toward the assassin and poked him in the chest.

"Ever since you found us in the hospice it's been 'oh no, my ISAAC system's broken' or 'oh dear, if people stop believing in me I might disappear in a great big stupid puff of smoke,' and I'm tired of it!" she shouted.

"You're *tired* of it?" said the assassin, thunderclouds forming in his eyes.

"You bet I am!" said Vera, fuming. "You're frightened of Tonto, you're frightened of Evan, you're afraid that Evan's followers and the Church of O might wish you out of existence, and you're even afraid your own intra-whatever systems are holding you back. Your problem isn't that people have stopped believing in you, you stupid ass! Your problem is that you've stopped believing in *yourself*!"

There was a second one of those synthetic "oooos." This last remark appeared to land like a left hook, one that connected right between the assassin's eyes. He just stood there, dumbfounded, staring at Vera like a man who's been mugged by a gang of squirrels. At length he managed to say something. He'd probably meant it to be scathing. All that came out, though, was "I liked you better before the wipe."

Further discussion of Vera's psychological observation was interrupted by the most fearsome, horrible phrase that had ever been shouted across a field of battle. It came from over the ridge, and it thundered into the heavens. It was this:

"EVANGELISTS, ATTACK!"

Ianians scrambled to their positions. Socrates, who was either emboldened or confused by Vera's pep talk, charged directly toward the ridge, faster than a cheetah who's just given up vegetarianism and spotted a limping goat. Vera turned toward the sarcophagus and started cursing, shouting something or other about having to program a complete, believable dreamscape under battlefield conditions. Ian ducked behind the sarcophagus and bravely covered his eyes.

The echoes of the fearsome battle cry died away. Ian's ears were treated to something new. Something he hadn't expected at all.

"Umm, Vera?" he said, straining to hear.

"What is it?" she said, furiously entering commands on the sarcophagus's display.

"Do you hear that?"

"Do I hear what?"

"I think . . ." said Ian, straining to hear, "I think . . . they're singing show tunes!"

Chapter 20

"Evangelists!" shouted Evan, extending his arms toward the cheering throng — a throng that carpeted the landscape like locusts in Pharaoh's fields, or ants on a discarded lollipop, or seagulls swarming a dump. "Prepare yourselves!" Evan cried. "Our time has come! Gird up your loins! Prepare to—"

Someone tugged at Evan's sleeve. It was Norm Stradamus.

"A word, sir?" said the prophet.

"What is it now?"

"It's just — *gird up your loins*, sir."

"Why should *I* gird up my—"

"No, no, sir, you've just given that direction to our followers."

"I know!" said Evan. "Now shush!"

He turned to address the swarm.

"It's just, I don't think you know what that means, m'lord," said the prophet, who gave the sense that he would have kowtowed if the gesture had been familiar.

"I do," said Evan, marvelling at the seer's gift for sucking every drop of excitement out of any crowd, party, or armed-conflict staging area to which fate sent him. "It means get ready," Evan added.

"I'm afraid it's rather . . . erm . . . *more specific* than that, sir," said Norm. "In point of fact it refers to an article of clothing first worn in battle by—"

"What's the prophet sayin'?" called a shrill voice from the swarm.

"I think it's somethin' about our loins!" cried another, raising a ripple of laughs.

"Speak up!" cried someone else.

This theme was picked up by dozens of other voices in the throng, interspersed with people shouting "Make Detroit great again!" as well as "Evan for mayor!" and "Who's the dude with the beard?"

"You're ruining my big moment," said Evan, whining.

"You also called them all 'Evangelists,' sir," said Norm, a touch reproachfully.

"Of course, I did," said Evan. "That's what they're called!"

"No, sir," said Norm, shaking his head slowly. "You're addressing our combined forces. Your followers, strictly speaking, are found only in cells N1 through N7."

"Cells?" said Evan.

"Oh, yes sir," said Norm, "the Regent decreed that our forces be divided into a series of discrete cells. For ease of command, I mean. The Regent's own people are in cells A1 through J6. Acolytes of the Church of O, including my own chorus, can be found in cells K1—"

"And my people are where?" said Evan, cutting him off.

"Cells N1 through N7."

"Just the N cells, then?" said Evan.

"That's right."

"So you want me to shout out 'N cells, attack,'" said Evan. "It sounds like I'm commanding shoes."

"That's insoles, m'lord," said the prophet.

"I know what insoles are!" snapped Evan.

"What's this about shoes?" said Oan, approaching with Tonto.

"Insoles," said Evan.

"N cells," said Norm.

"Are those the people Norm commands?" asked Tonto. "N cell as in Norm?"

"No, no," said Norm, "they're arranged alphabetically, roughly according to the order in which they arrived at the Regent's home. The N cells are Evan's people, the Evangelists."

"I'm not calling my people the 'N cells,'" said Evan.

"Forgive me, m'lord, you're free to call them whatever you like," said Norm. "My point was merely that you presumed to command the entire force — every cell gathered before us, I mean. And you were calling them all Evangelists. If you'd care to make it clear to the troops that you only mean to direct those men who are—"

"What is the problem?" said the Regent, who repeated her trick of arriving on the scene without appearing to move a muscle. "Why has the attack not yet commenced? R'lyeh awaits!"

"I'm not so sure we need an attack," said Tonto, thoughtfully. "Ian's people are just standing there. They'll probably let us pass."

"I beg your pardon, Your Worship," said Norm, toadying up to the Regent's side, "we're addressing logistical matters. I was just explaining to Evan that—"

"Norm interrupted my speech!" whined Evan.

"My apologies, Your Masterfulness," said Norm, bobbing obsequiously. "I'm merely hoping to help avoid any unfortunate confusion that might—"

The Regent silenced the prophet with a gesture.

"The Intercessor's Ianians regroup," she said, tersely. "His seer has emerged from the depths of R'lyeh. They prepare to block our path. The time has come for us to strike."

"I don't think we'll meet resistance," said Tonto. "We'd be better off just walking up and talking to Ian—"

"But the prophecies, Madame Regent," said Norm, wringing his hands. "They do call for certain preparations to be made—"

"What preparations?" demanded the Regent.

"I merely hoped to remind Your Imperiousness that, strictly speaking, our final assault on R'lyeh, that is to say, our final engagement with the Intercessor's forces, whether or not one might properly characterize it as an assault—"

"Get to the point!" demanded the Regent.

"It's just that Evan's incursion into R'lyeh, and his final rise to power — the last steps preparatory to our own final journey to the realm of the Great Omega — none of this can take place until certain elements of the prophecy are fulfilled."

"Which elements?" asked Oan, with genuine interest.

"I'm grateful that you asked!" said Norm, who was. "It's a prophecy of my own, in fact, one augmented by various annotations spoken by Vera Lantz herself, and the primary focus of those visions is that my greatest contribution to the prophetic arts shall finally—"

"By the eternal void," said the Regent, pinching the bridge of her nose and sighing a sigh you might confuse with the sound of air escaping from an Egyptian tomb, "you're talking about your blasted song, aren't you?"

"The song is key!" said Norm, rallying. "Vera herself made it clear that the song would be sung upon the precipice of victory."

"This is a precipice!" said Oan, gesturing over the landscape, helpfully.

"I believe Vera spoke metaphorically!" said Norm. "Nevertheless, the time has come."

"Whatever," said Evan. "Sing your song. Just get out of—"

"No, no!" said Norm. "Not I alone! I've had the chorus practising tirelessly for days. Just reading the music and lyrics, mind you, for the song cannot be sung aloud until such time as—"

"Get on with it!" said Evan. "The troops are twitchy."

Unlike a lot of the observations Evan made, this one was true. Like a lot of the swarms you meet in the great outdoors, this one was antsy. Acolytes, Evangelists, and assorted hangers-on were standing in columns that approximated military formations, but formations that showed the brand of undisciplined, foot-shuffling energy you see in a crowd of children marshalling for a school trip — right after they'd learned that they weren't headed for one of the cool museums filled with dinosaurs or spacecraft, but one of the weirdo niche museums stockpiling historical specimens of needlepoint or calligraphy.

"We won't be more than a moment!" said Norm, clapping his hands. "I'll attend to the chorus now. I'll give you a signal when we're prepared!"

He turned and toddled off, skipping merrily, toward the cells designated as K1 and K2. These cells contained the Chorus — those acolytes of the Church of O who were dedicated to spreading the Great Omega's word through song whether anyone liked it or not. The singers gathered in a huddle around the prophet and made excited choir-nerd noises.

Back on the precipice, the Regent turned to Evan.

"A word, Brown," she said.

"Evan," said Evan.

"A word, Evan."

"What's up?"

"I do not presume to dictate strategy and tactics," said the Regent, with as much diplomacy as you can wrestle out of a person who has dreams of becoming a god, "but—"

"It's the balloon animals, isn't it?" said Evan, who seemed about as sheepish as another person who dreams of becoming a god could usefully manage, except perhaps for a person aspiring to be the god of sheep.

"Not the balloon animals, no," said the Regent.

"Just a flash of inspiration," said Evan, ignoring her. "There were a bunch of 'em at my birthday party. I didn't like them at all. Too scary. I thought that I might help set the mood for—"

"Just as you say," interrupted the Regent, "no need to explain. My question is about your Evangelists."

"Shoot," said Evan.

"You deplete them," said the Regent. "When you channel, when you draw upon their energies to weave the fabric of Detroit and reshape the world, when you direct their own innate energies to manifest your desires. It leaves them drained. Utterly spent. Some are left twitching on the ground as rasping, desiccated husks."

"They'll get better," said Evan, shrugging.

"I understand," said the Regent. "But replenishing their power may take some time. Perhaps if you left the attack to me — to me and my forces — and reserved your own unique abilities for the moment that we take R'lyeh, we might better preserve—"

"I can do whatever I want," said Evan, shrugging again. "They don't mind! I could shoot one of them down Fifth Avenue and not lose a single follower. Watch!"

He raised a lazy hand and pointed at Cell N7. One of its members levitated above his cellmates. He pivoted in mid-air and jetted off toward the horizon, presumably destined to shoot straight down Fifth Avenue.

"Y-yes, I understand," said the Regent, smoothing her robes. "I understand that you *can* do these things if you wish. I merely suggest that it . . . might be ill advised for you to—"

"Don't tell me what to do!" said Evan, taking a step closer and suddenly seeming to grow a few inches taller. "Don't even try to—"

His speech was cut short by Tonto, who stepped between Evan and the Regent like a boxing referee. She placed a placating hand on Evan's shoulder.

"It's all right, Evan," she said. "No one can hurt you. You're in charge." Here she glanced back at the Regent. "*He is in charge, yes?*" she added.

"Y-y-yes, of course," said the Regent. "I merely wished to . . . to advise him; to suggest that he preserve his strength and that of his followers so that he needn't—"

"So that he needn't draw on *your* people," said Tonto, flatly. "Or on you, yourself, Madame Regent. You made quite a powerful battery for Evan at the chateau. Maybe he'll just tap into you again and—"

"He would not dare!" said the Regent, trembling, "he would not presume to violate my sovereign—"

"We're good to go!" cried Norm, from somewhere near the pole position of cell K1. He was grinning toward the Regent and Evan and giving them two thumbs up.

Tonto kept her hand firmly attached to Evan's shoulder and aimed another, palm up, toward the Regent. "We're cool, here?" said Tonto.

"We're fine," said Evan, glowering. "Just don't let anyone tell me what to do."

"No one will," said Tonto. "I've got your back. No one's against you. No one could be. And if they try, they'll have me to—"

"I don't need you!" shouted Evan.

"I know, I know," said Tonto, backing away and showing her palms, "you can do everything yourself. We all get that. But you have me anyway, okay? I'm on your side. It's nice to have teammates, right? People who'll offer to lend a hand whether you need their help or not."

"Whatever," said Evan. "Let's get to R'lyeh."

"Just as you say," said the Regent, backing away. "Would you care to give the command?"

"I would," said Evan. And then he did.

"EVANGELISTS ATTACK!" he cried, turning his own volume up to eleven through unnatural, mystical means. Whether or not his choice of words offended Norm, who might have preferred something a bit more non-denominational, say, "Evangelists and acolytes and assorted hangers-on, please go ahead and start your charge," who can say? In any case, the words had the desired effect. The troops charged forward,

Evangelist and acolyte alike, storming the precipice and rushing down the ridge toward the courtyard of City Hall.

They charged past Evan, past the Regent, past Tonto, and past Oan. They scrabbled down the ridge, some tumbling down the hill like lemmings who'd been shovelled over a cliff by a documentary producer, others managing to keep their footing by using fallen comrades as improvised stairs. Cells A, B, and C took the brunt of the falling damage as well as the bulk of the trampling feet of those who followed.

It was right about the time that cells K1 and K2 were passing the Regent that she became aware of Norm shouting rapturously, making use of every vocal cord at his disposal.

"Acolytes," he cried, euphorically, "Acolytes, the time has come! Prepare for the song!"

Nature, or whatever passed for nature in Detroit, seemed to hold its breath and wait in perfect stillness as Norm counted the chorus in.

"Anna one, anna two, anna—"

The Regent had never much cared for Norm Stradamus. You could tell. She was always shushing him or shooing him away as though he was nothing more than the gristly, slightly shabby garden-variety street prophet that he resembled. She found him irksome, and he knew it. In a thousand little ways she'd made her feelings for Norm clear. But here, on the eve of her passage to the mortal realm of the Great Omega, on the verge of crossing over to the beforelife and taking her next step toward deification, the Regent couldn't help but feel the teensiest twinge of gratitude for the old, rumpled seer. He'd been helpful, after all. He'd brought her hundreds of people. He'd called Evan to her attention. He'd even made some useful predictions. And now he really, really wanted to share his song.

Let him have this one, she thought, smiling inwardly. Just this once.

She raised her pyramidal totem to the heavens, directing her thoughts toward Norm Stradamus and his chorus. She channelled her will toward them.

She amplified their song. Their song that embodied Norm's predictions. The song they'd awaited all this time. The song that foretold their trip to the mortal realm and described their fateful journey; a song of power that would forever be emblazoned in the hearts of those who heard it; an anthem for everyone who believed; for those who understood the truth of the Great Omega.

The Regent channelled. The song rang out. The Chorus started out with the bit that the Regent had already heard.

> *We're headin' 'cross the river*
> *Wash your sins away in the tide*
> *It's all so peaceful on the other side!*

And then, as the Chorus reached the ridge, Detroit was finally treated to Norm Stradamus's refrain:

> *Forget your troubles, c'mon get happy!*
> *You better chase all your cares away!*
> *Shout "hallelujah," c'mon get happy!*
> *Get ready for the judgment day!*
> *The sun is shinin', c'mon get happy!*
> *The Lord is waitin' to take your hand!*
> *Shout "hallelujah," c'mon get happy!*
> *We're going to the promised land!*

It was actually kind of catchy when you heard it all at once.

By this point in the proceedings, thousands of acolytes and Evangelists had made it down the ridge, charging straight toward the courtyard where Ian and what passed for his army waited. The charging forces could see the crumpled, lifeless bodies of thousands upon thousands of Ianians, whose only role in the present battle would be to serve as speed bumps on Evan's road to R'lyeh.

The path to Ian was clear.

Well, the path was *almost* clear. It really was. Virtually bereft of anything that you might call opposition. Let's just be perfectly transparent and call the path *mostly* clear, give or take one single, solitary, philosophically inclined, and mostly invisible assassin.

The Evangelists and acolytes charged toward Ian, a path that was going to take them right through the teensy patch of geography currently occupied by the only lethal hazard that Detroit had ever allowed to be created.

That hazard, just for the fun of it, deactivated his cloaking shield. Apparently, he wanted them to see this coming.

The Chorus carried right on singing.

> *Forget your troubles, c'mon get happy!*
> *You better chase all your cares away!*
> *Shout "hallelujah," c'mon get happy!*
> *Get ready for the judgment day!*

Whether or not this counted as "judgment day," and whether or not the acolytes were ready to face it, no one could say. But you could tell, in short order, that they weren't ready to face an assassin who wanted nothing more than a fair chance to reclaim his self-esteem and work through a few of his issues.

Socrates charged straight into what was, it turned out, the vanguard of Cell G, the first of the cells to make it down the ridge. He tossed several percussive grenades toward the rear of the charging cell, but seemed to feel that the ones who'd made it to the front lines first deserved an extra special greeting.

They probably didn't hear him activate the boson whip, what with the song and all the commotion.

The sun is shinin', c'mon get happy!
The Lord is waitin' to take your hand!
Shout "hallelujah," c'mon get happy!
We're going to the promised land!

Up on the ridge, Evan, the Regent, Tonto, and Oan watched the proceedings through telescopes and field glasses.

"My word," said Oan, agog.

"That's not good," said Tonto.

"It's like watching a meat grinder," said Evan, his eyes widening.

"Or a wood chipper!" said Oan.

"He is a wolf among the fold," said the Regent, clearly impressed.

"I was thinking he was like a lawn mower," said Norm, who came panting back to the group, having decided that, now that his song had had its big opening, he'd done his part in today's battle and would be a good deal safer standing near — or even behind — the people he thought of as the army's Biggest Guns.

Norm bent over and caught his breath. "It's . . . it's . . . it's Socrates," he said. "He's . . . cutting through our troops like . . . like blades of grass, destroying the lawn that is our forces. The . . . the whip seems to—"

"Thank you for unpacking your helpful metaphor," said the Regent. "I think we've all gathered its meaning. But what's to be done?"

There was a quiet, pregnant moment during which the assembled leaders of the force you might describe as "Socrates' prey" watched the assassin shred their army. It was really something to see. The first draft of *Nether Regions* went on about this in some detail, comparing the sight to a whale consuming a mass of krill, or the process of turning cabbage into coleslaw. On the whole, the editors felt that less was more.

After watching this display for several heartbeats, Evan spoke.

"I'll show you what's to be done," he said, dropping the field goggles and once again appearing to grow a couple of inches. He cracked his knuckles. "Regent: use your powers to rally the troops. Make them stronger. Feed them power. I'm going to even the odds."

Evan raised his arms to the heavens, feeding on his followers' power. He channelled his thoughts toward his N cells, most of whom hadn't yet reached what you might call "the Socratic zone." As Evan began to pulse with power, the N cells shrivelled and collapsed, taking on the general appearance of beef jerky.

Evan glowed. He seemed to radiate fire. He spread his arms and screamed.

Lightning criss-crossed the skies; thunder shook the whole of Detroit. Bolts of Benjamin Franklin's favourite natural force struck the ground near Ian's forces, drawn there by the metal bodies of Ianians. Those Ianians who hadn't succumbed to the EMP now scattered.

Patches of earth exploded where lightning touched the ground, raining rocks and mud and broken Ianians down upon the courtyard.

This wasn't enough for Evan. Not even close. He psychically yanked the threads of power flowing through what he might have called his "charging army" if he'd been inclined toward interesting ambiguities. Hundreds upon hundreds of Evangelists and acolytes fell to the ground, some shredded by the assassin, most depleted by a temper tantrum thrown by a five-year-old child fit for the Book of Revelation.

The assassin didn't seem especially fussed by the change in weather conditions. He pressed on, now approaching the foot of the ridge. Evan struck the ground with lightning. This seemed to slow Socrates in almost exactly the same way that a bathing cap slows a tsunami.

The assassin charged the hill.

Tonto stepped in front of Evan, ready to shield him.

Evan consumed his followers' power, leaving N cells, A cells, B cells, and any others you'd care to mention crumpled and rasping on the ground like an army of zombies who'd been denied their daily brain.

Evan found another gear. He drew more power. His followers crumbled to dust.

As Socrates crested the ridge, Evan cried out to Detroit itself, to the world that spawned him, calling upon its primordial essence to supply him with what he needed. What he cried, as he drained the last drops of the power flowing through his crumbling followers, was this:

"I . . . need . . . more . . . people!"

* * *

"I need more people!" cried Ian, rushing over to Vera's side. Balled lightning struck the ground where he'd been standing a moment earlier, sending chunks of earth and cobblestones hurtling skyward.

"I know, I know!" said Vera, who did. You could barely hear her response, what with the frequent crashes of thunder, the metallic clomp of Ianians scrambling for defensive positions, and the soundtrack that was provided by Norm's song.

"How much time do you need?" asked Ian, catching his breath.

"As much as you can give me," said Vera. "I'm still programming the world. For Evan, I mean. I've hacked City Hall and downloaded every historical record I can find. Detroit University too. A few of these Ianians are history profs, I think. Maybe if I can nab their memories—"

"What are you talking about?" said Ian, ducking behind her just in time to avoid a rocketing cobblestone.

"I'm not programming this thing from scratch!" shouted Vera. "We need a dream world to keep Evan occupied once we've installed him in this thing. Otherwise, the matrix won't hold him! He's too strong! His world's going to need lots of preprogrammed people and events, ready to go. I'm setting it up to start out empty, but with characters who'll start showing up as Evan syncs with the program."

"Why?" said Ian, bravely crouching behind the machinery.

"He'll need people to rule!" said Vera. "People who can keep his mind busy so he doesn't fight the program. Little challenges and stuff. I'm basing it all on historical records. It's just faster."

"When'll it be ready?"

"It'll be ready when it's ready," said Vera, prophetically.

"And do you know what *that's* about?" said Ian, pointing skyward.

"What *what's* about?" asked Vera.

"The song! They've got the chorus singing show tunes while they attack us!"

"I'm not sure you can say they're attacking us," said Vera, turning briefly to survey the field of battle, if something counts as a field of battle when the "battle" amounts to a semi-lethal game of whack-an-Evangelist being played by an assassin.

"Anyway," she continued, "that's just Norm's song. The one he says predicts the journey across the Styx."

"That's not Norm's song!" said Ian, taking a stand for intellectual property. "It's an old show tune! It's called 'Get Happy'! Everyone knows it."

"I don't know it."

"*Summer Stock?*" said Ian, perhaps forgetting where he was. "Judy Garland?"

"Judy Garland the tax accountant?" said Vera.

"Judy Garland the singer!" said Ian.

"Maybe she sang in the beforelife," said Vera, turning back toward the keypad, "but in Detroit she does my taxes. Or maybe that's someone else called Judy Garland. Who knows? Anyway, the song is Norm's. I was with him when he wrote it. Part of it, anyway. He's been working on it for weeks."

"But I know the words! I know it from the beforelife."

"So what?" said Vera, still coding as quickly as her fingers could manage. "I've seen into the beforelife before, right? I saw Isaac Newton being reborn as some kid named Hawking. Norm's a seer, too. Maybe he was, I dunno, accidentally stealing his song from his own visions of the beforelife. What's the big deal?"

"It doesn't make sense!"

"What else is new?" said Vera.

Ian gripped his forehead with both hands, as though he was struggling to physically mould his thoughts into sensible shapes. "But . . . but . . . Sigmund Freud . . . I saw him at the hospice, and got him interested in the whole idea of parents!" said Ian. "And . . . and Gilgamesh and Enkidu having a fight with the bull of heaven. I was there. And . . . and Socrates and Benjamin Franklin. And now three hundred soldiers, just like Sparta! I mean, Abe's drawers! Moses and Martin Luther! '*Get Happy*'!"

Vera raised a fretful brow. "Are you sure you're all right?" she asked.

"It's just . . . it's . . . stuff that I remember from the beforelife. It's all happening here, and with the same people. And I . . . I mean . . . they couldn't have planned it based on leftover memories, right, it's all just happening again, or maybe it's happening here first — I mean—"

"You're talking out of your ass," said Vera, still intent on the sarcophagus's display. "Anyway, I'm sticking all of that stuff in Evan's world and letting it all flow through the expectation manager. It'll help add colour. Now hand me Dean Tundt's head."

"What?" cried Ian.

"Dean Tundt's head. It's right over there," she added, pointing vaguely with her chin. "He'll have a record of everything that happened right up to the pulse. It can't hurt to add more perspectives. I wonder if I can still access Socrates' intracranial systems?"

Ian commando-crawled across a heap of presently nonautonomous automatons until he found Dean Tundt's head, a head that had conveniently — though perhaps *inconveniently* for Dean Tundt — already been separated from the rest of the android's frame. Ian tucked it under his arm and crawled back in Vera's direction.

"IANIANS, CHARGE FORWARD!" cried the voice of Lori 8.

Ian scrambled to his feet to see what was happening. What was happening was this: several dozen operational Ianians were charging toward a hole in the attacking army's lines, one presumably left behind in the wake of Socrates' passage.

"TAKE THE HILL!" cried Lori 8.

The Ianians surged forward. They clanged toward the base of the hill, their footfalls sounding a good deal like several hundred toasters falling down a flight of stairs. A flash of light drew Ian's eyes to the crest of the ridge, where he saw Socrates brandishing his boson whip and disappearing from view, presumably intent on reaching Evan.

In any normal situation, Ian would have paused for a moment to grapple with the fact that the afterlife's only assassin was, at Ian's behest, getting ready to mindwipe Ian's only son with a view to stuffing him in a sarcophagus where he'd spend the foreseeable future ruling an artificial world. But this wasn't any normal situation. This was a war. A war to preserve . . . well . . . something. A war to preserve Abe's lie. A war to preserve a delicate balance between something approaching sanity, on the one hand, and humankind's unbridled desires on the other. It was a war between order and chaos, with a former regulatory compliance officer standing up for order and his son, a practically unstoppable five-year-old with a penchant for apocalyptic tantrums, taking charge of the other side.

Ian's reverie was shattered at the same time as the remaining Ianians. That is, at the same time that the remaining Ianians were shattered. Every one of them.

An enormous ball of lightning filled the heavens. It didn't bother to stick around. It streaked toward the ground, striking the earth in a spot that you might describe as smack-dab in the middle of Lori 8's brigade of Ianians — the ones trying to take the hill.

They exploded. They exploded into countless tiny pieces. It was really quite a show. Picture the very first Big Bang — the one that started this whole mess — and chuck a few hundred thousand pounds of vaguely anthropomorphic metal into the mix. That's what Ian witnessed now.

He ducked behind the sarcophagus, shielding his eyes. Even Ian, without the benefit of knowing how few pages remained in the book you're reading, knew that the climax was upon him and that — one way or another — things would soon come to an end.

"Ham's beard!" exclaimed Vera.

"What do we do now?" cried Ian, rubbing his eyes.

"They've cleared the path!" shouted Vera. "It's just us now. I can't see Socrates. There's nothing else protecting us from what's left of Evan's people. They're on their way!"

"Like I said," said Ian, regaining his feet. "We're going to need a lot more people."

At times like this, when the sheet metal's really starting to hit the fan, it's important to take stock of where we stand. Take Ian, for example. We might take this time to reflect on the fact that he's famous for being average. He was average in the beforelife, and he's average in Detroit. He's not like Abe. He's not like Penelope. He's not like the City Solicitor. He doesn't have the power to manifest his desires. But as luck would have it, he was saying the words "we're going to need a lot more people" just as Evan, who *could* manifest, after a fashion, was saying much the same thing. And it's possible, with all of the undeniable weirdness of Detroit, that Ian and Evan, Detroit's first father-son pair, were cosmically linked in some way or another. That might explain what happened next. Or maybe it's just that Oan was right about what she said in sharing sessions. Maybe the universe really was listening. Maybe whenever you speak your heart's true desire, speak it with clarity and with purpose, maybe the universe responds by serving up whatever you need.

Or maybe the Author intervened. Who can say?

Whatever the cause, on the cue "we're going to need more people," an army appeared, cresting a hill a couple of miles west of Ian's current position. Hundreds upon hundreds of silhouettes appeared up on the hilltop. And in the few quiet moments between the echoing peals of thunder, you could tell the army was cheering.

It was a peculiar sort of cheer. For one thing, it featured a lot of *accents aigus.*

At the head of this climax-heralding army, appearing front and centre, there was a man. A figure riding a lone golf cart that glistened in the rays of the setting sun.

He didn't seem to be paying attention to the cheers of the army behind him. If you squinted just right, and managed to get a clear view, he seemed to be writing in a journal.

Well, I don't know about you, wrote Rhinnick, *but it seemed to me that it was high time for yours truly to show his face and throw his weight around for a space; saving the day and bringing about the happy endings!*

Chapter 21

"SOUND TRUMPETS! LET OUR BLOODY COLOURS WAVE!" roared William, my loyal retainer and toter of the Feynman bags. He followed this with some guff about crying havoc and letting slip the dogs of war, words he'd shouted while charging up to my golf cart and brandishing what I believe is called "a halberd." He was decked out in some sort of unduly spacious military get-up featuring straps, buckles, bandoliers, and all the martial fixings, like a pipsqueak junior corporal who'd accepted hand-me-downs from an economy-sized rear admiral.

"We can't do it," I said, frowning.

"We can't, sir?" said William, looking even more deflated than he had a moment ago.

"Let slip the dogs of war," I said, preparatory to popping the chap's balloon. "We can't do it." I gestured broadly over the canine-free terrain and added the helpful words: "No dogs."

"I thought I was a dog!" said Zeus, his big, cheerful face illuminating the scenery as he trotted up alongside.

"A former dog, only," I explained, raising a patient finger, though I was pleased to see that Zeus, my gargantuan pal and heavily muscled gendarme, was doing his best to knit together forgotten threads of his own life story.

"Forgive me, sir," said William, inclining the bean in that respectful way of his. "I spoke metaphorically."

At least I think that's what he said, for the chap was drowned out by the Napoleonic horde who presently split the air with exuberant cries of *"zut alors," "mangez mon derrière,"* and other samples of their peculiar heathen lingo. This assault on the Feynman ears seemed to indicate that the horde had collared the gist of William's command, for the frenzied little chaps now surged forward like a school of wild piranha who've spied an unsuspecting bather down yon stream. The lion's share of the horde beelined its way toward the opposing hill, where Evan stood berating his troops, while others charted a safer course toward Ian and Vera, two long-time chums of mine who appeared to be working on a sarcophagus down in the heavily cratered courtyard below.

William flapped his lips for the better part of a minute, though I haven't a notion of what the flowery-tongued boll weevil said. And as I write this, I see that I've rather left my readership in the same boat, viz, wondering what in Abe's name I'm going on about. For in starting off the tale of present interest with the above slice of dialogue, and leaping ahead without the merest whiff of expositional whatnots, I've shot off the mark at a couple of hundred mph and left my readership befogged. Allow me to step back, marshal my facts, and sprinkle the landscape with the necessary preambles.

I suppose the thing got started while I was spending an idle weekend at the Hôtel de la Lune, a luxurious joint on the Detroit Riviera, and one that generally serves as my HQ whenever I find myself short on quests. "But wait," I hear you saying, if you're one of those officious know-it-alls who's not only up to date in the Feynman archives, but also one of those author-bothering readers who insist on crossing t's and dotting i's. "What's with all of this *Rhinnick Feynman* garbage cluttering up the page? For when last we crossed paths with our hero, we'd been advised that Abe the First, Mayor of Detroit and omnipotent busybody, had worked a bit of magic and reminded Feynman, R. that he was actually a bird who went by a wholly different name in the mortal world; I recall it being Plum, or Wodehouse, or P.G. somethingorother."

To this I have two responses. First, I applaud not only your memory and attention to detail, but also your excellent taste in books. And second, I say this: While it's true that Abe removed the shingles from mine eyes and reminded me of my pre-mortem ID, you're ignoring a fact of paramount importance, viz, *I like being Rhinnick Feynman*. I may have spent ninety-odd years shuffling about the mortal coil and answering to another name, but in the decades since I wound up in Detroit I've gone by Feynman-comma-R, and it is by this handle that I am known among my closest friends and boosters. Take Zeus, by way of example. The poor chap's still coming to terms with having been mindwiped by an assassin, and he continues doing his best to knit together bits and pieces of his own forgotten biography — a biography in which I play a starring role. If I were to tell him, "Sorry, chum, I know I claimed to be Rhinnick Feynman, but from now on call me Plum," what would the harvest be? You'd see the poor hulk curling up in a ball, whimpering quietly to himself and afraid to trust the latest news.

Now where were we? Ah, yes. We were casting our minds back to the Hôtel de la Lune, where I'd turned up at the conclusion of a universe-saving imbroglio that featured the scientist Isaac Newton, the seer Vera Lantz, Mistress Oan of Detroit Mercy, the prophet Norm Stradamus, a menacing bird who called herself "the Regent" but whose real name sounds like a sneeze, and a whole host of Napoleons, many of whom are with me now. And it's upon these Napoleonic chumps that I'd like to focus, for they started popping up like dandelions at the Hôtel de la Lune not long after I'd checked in, they seeking to hobnob with a man who they now thought of as their saviour, viz, me.

We Feynmen don't seek public adulation. Far from it. But when one's fan club starts turning up at one's hotel, first in a trickle, and then in a flood so overwhelming that you're inclined to round up animals two-by-two, one cannot simply turn them away. At least that's how I looked at the thing. The hotel management took a starkly different view, they seeming to think the wiser course was to tell yours truly that, so long as he was neck-deep in Napoleons, they'd prefer he stay elsewhere. Taking the hint, I kicked the dust of the Riviera from my sandals and set course for the depths of the Wild, taking with me an entourage that included Zeus, a horde of Napoleons, and assorted hangers-on.

It was some months later that the undersigned, now surrounded by a Napoleonic army, found himself faced with a mystery calculated to out-Sherlock even the cleverest Holmes, viz, the question of where in Abe's name I'd put my hamster. You'll remember my hamster, Fenny, of course. No? Oh, surely. He's the furry chap you met in Detroit Mercy, a loony bin where I spent some time ensconced with Ian Brown, assorted kooks, and the hamster of present interest — Fenny himself being incarcerated solely by association with me, and not owing to any personal diagnosis. You might recall that the little chap ranks among my nearest and d., and is a hamster who, on many occasions, has thrown himself in the path of slings and arrows meant for me, risking life and tiny limbs to fish me out of whatever soup fate might be serving. And thus it was that, upon taking inventory and finding myself short one hamster, I exhibited both despondency and alarm.

This was, I think you'll agree, a situation calling for all good men to come to the aid of the party. Rhinnick Feynman, not unlike the U.S. Marines, is a stickler for not leaving a pal behind, even where the pal in question has four legs, dines on insects, and takes his morning constitutional in a tiny plastic wheel. It was imperative — if imperative means what I think it does — that I find my pal post-haste. But where to look? That was the question, and a vexing one at that, chiefly owing to my hamster's factory specs. No doubt you'll understand — but if you've never met a hamster, let me explain. Providence, in its wisdom, has gifted hamsters with countless sterling, laudable traits. But on the credit side of the ledger is the fact that hamsters are small. Exceedingly so. Not merely *petite*, like a Napoleon, but teensy-weensy in the extreme; the sort of chaps who would scarcely move the dial on any try-your-weight machines they might bump into. Fenny himself fits in my pocket, a feat that few of my other friends could manage. And as useful as a hamster's stature is when evading Goons, slipping past the forces of darkness, or getting into places closed to any being larger than a size-three shoe, it becomes dashed inconvenient when the good master is far afield and unable to set his eyes on his pal. Detroit is large; Fenny is small. It doesn't take an Isaac Newton to do the math: a lost hamster is hard to find.

I instituted a search.

My search started out as searches do. I stood there looking about the spot where I found myself at the time and came up empty. I checked my pockets. I checked them again. I asked around to no avail. I called out Fenny's name; he failed to answer. I was stumped.

I briefly weighed having another bash at a stratagem I'd employed for finding Zeus, viz, securing a comfy roost and waiting him out, resting assured that, in the sprawling fullness of time, my lost pal would saunter by. In Fenny's case, the odds seemed long. Fenny is not what you might describe as "highly mobile" — he being a hedonistic chap who prefers napping in shredded paper to ambling about the countryside and taking in the sights. In any quest to locate Fenny, mere passivity wouldn't do. Active measures were required. But what measures? That was the q.

As we so often do in these troubled, modern times, I turned to I-Ware. Not "eyewear" as in spectacles, for those of you enjoying an audio version of this text, but *I-Ware* as in capital-I-dash-W-a-r-e, meaning the various technical doodads that were invented by Isaac Newton, comprising things like I-datapads, I-telecommunicators, I-thinking-caps and the like. I used an assortment of these thingummies to send messages to anyone in my contact list who knew Fenny and who might have spied him in a familiar haunt. I contacted Dr. Peericks. That old ass was no help at all, for he quickly took the view that my inquiries re: this hamster were indicia of some quackish diagnosis. I contacted the staff at the Hôtel de la Lune, asking if Fenny had turned up in the lost and found. No luck there. Zeus somehow managed to get in touch with Ian, accidentally sending missives via neural whatdoyoucallits. Ian was as helpful as ever, by which I mean not at all. Why, I even left a message for Abe himself, reasoning that a slab of *Abe ex machina* might be just what the hamster ordered. Even then, I came up empty.

It wasn't until I took a long shot that I finally hit "pay dirt," as the expression is. This long shot came in the form of William Shakespeare, my old porter, aka the chap who now cavorted around my cart in fancy dress while shouting things about crying havoc and dogs of war.

When last William and self had entered each other's orbit, he was doing time as one of the Regent's retainers, drawing his weekly envelope by butling for the guests in her chateau. I hadn't expected to strike gold by reaching out in this direction, William having met with Fenny only a couple of times. But I recalled William saying that diseases desperate grown are by desperate appliance relieved, by which I took him to mean that some of life's banana skins are so dashed slippery that they call for drastic steps. Knowing that these were desperate times, I made the call.

And blow me tight if William didn't come across with the goods, by which I mean the only spot of helpful intel I'd uncovered in the Case of the Missing H. It wasn't the sort of intel that you might call "direct." I mean to say, the chap didn't specify a set of GPS thingummies at which I might find my lost pal. But he did point me in a direction. William started off by spinning a tale of a goshawful chump named Evan, a sort of horror from outer space who claimed to be Ian and Penny's son. This fiend in human shape, intent on giving Abe the heave-ho and taking charge of Detroit himself, had gotten himself entwined with both the Regent and Norm Stradamus. These three had taken what you might call unsportsmanlike steps along nefarious lines, going so far as to kidnap Vera, a medium and small appliance repairperson whom I count among my friends. This abduction, William explained, had been thwarted by none other than Socrates the assassin — someone I'd hitherto counted among nature's bad eggs — who had shown up in the nick of time and lifted Vera from both frying pan and fire. Cutting a fat story thin, these hair-raising vicissitudes were all, according to William, leading straight to a final showdown that was going to happen at R'lyeh, a secret sort of warehouse thingummy housed in the bowels of City Hall — a place I'd once explored with Vera, a long story that I won't go into now. This final showdown, William explained, was going to involve this Evan chap and his ghoulish minions doing their best to do away with Ian and Vera, two people whose best interests remain close to the Feynman heart.

It has often been said of Rhinnick Feynman that he never shirks his duty when he hears of a pal in trouble. Far from it. He rallies 'round, helping his friends evade the bludgeonings of fate and doing his best to push along the happy ending. Learning of Ian and Vera's plight, I had to act. And in choosing to take this selfless course I was aware of one of those things you sometimes get — they start with a *p*. No, not a present. Oh, dash it, what's the word? William would know. A presentiment! That's it! I was aware of a presentiment that I might be faced with the chance of killing two birds with one stone — or rather feeding two birds with one scone, if you'd rather avoid an allusion to murdering fowl. In any event, I knew in the depths of the Feynman soul that, in showing up at City Hall and chipping in for Ian and Vera, I'd be guaranteed to locate Fenny as well.

I sense an objection. Why, you ask, would I believe that taking decisive action on the Ian and Vera front would lead me on a path to Fenny? Has Our Hero fallen prey to magical thinking, you might ask, imagining that by simply doing one's best to help a fellow creature in need one's own wishes will be fulfilled? Of course not, silly ass. Although there may be something to that. But in this instance, I was sure that I'd find Fenny right in the thick of things at R'lyeh, not because this would provide a fitting end to my narrative arc, but because of Fenny's habits.

Fenny is, you must remember, no ordinary rodent. He's a man of action; or rather a hamster of action, and one who's always apt to be right at the fulcrum of any globe-wobbling events, if fulcrums are the things I'm thinking of. What I mean to say is that you'll always find Fenny where the action is, doing his part to save Detroit without the merest hesitation. Was it not Fenny who, in a bid to extricate pals from Detroit Mercy, got himself lost not only within the ducts that wend their way through the hospice walls, but also within Matron Bikerack's personal undergarments, which wend their way through even darker and more unspeakable terrain? Was it not Fenny who purloined the pass cards needed for self and Vera to escape from the menacing forces of Mental Health? Well, it was, in case you were wondering. In any event, I knew in a jiffy that if anything of substance was on the point of hitting the fan at City Hall, Fenny was sure to be in the thick of it, flexing every hamstery muscle to lay the forces of darkness a stymie.

I explained this iron logic to those around me. Zeus declared my reasoning specious, which I took as a good sign. His views were shared by Nappy, a Napoleon of the female sort who'd been palling around with Zeus for quite some time. As for the bulk of the horde around me — the Napoleons who'd hastened to my side — they needed no convincing to rush off to the seat of war. They simply itched for a good fight. And when I explained that the Regent herself was pitching in for the other side — she being the bird responsible for incarcerating a legion of Napoleons and subjecting them to thumbscrews and other violations of Geneva Conventions — well, you can imagine the fire that this lit in their Napoleonic pants.

The plan was set. We'd march on R'lyeh without delay. William would meet us at the site, pull a bit of a Benedict Arnold, join our side, and strike a blow for the cause of good. And thus we find ourselves at the point where we began: self at the top of a hill, flanked by Zeus and William, as hundreds of Napoleons charge forward, into the fray.

"I-Goggles," I said, extending a hand.

"I-Goggles!" Zeus responded, forking over the goods. I placed the high-tech peepers over the Feynman eyes and surveyed the field before me; specifically, the bit of the field that featured Evan and the Regent, I reasoning that it's best to start a thing like this by sussing out one's foes.

"Egad," I said, drinking them in.

What I observed smote me amidships. For starters, I got my first good look at Evan, who seemed to stand about ten-foot-six. He was shouting commands and exhortations at his troops, a motley crew of chumps who exhibited all the rich diversity of a jugband jamboree. Looking downwind from this cesspit of angry yokels, I spied the thing that really gripped the senses, viz, history's single greatest example of what I believe is called "fight choreography." This took the form of a battle between two super-human combatants.

I knew at a g. that this pair of warriors must be Socrates and Tonto; not so much because I saw them through my goggles, but because I barely could. See them, I mean to say. The pair moved like twin blurs; Socrates stopping for a moment, twitching briefly, and then streaking off in some unexpected direction; Tonto pausing for a half a tick before streaking off after him, the pair mocking the laws of physics and biology all the while. I'm sure that blows rained down between these peerless warriors when their blurs became entangled, but it happened with such mind-boggling speed that my heart bled for any referee or umpire tasked with the job of keeping score.

I watched the action for a space before reason gripped the reins and I took stock of the goings-on. Socrates, it seemed, was doing his best to reach Evan, presumably intent on doing him a bit of no good, and Tonto, for reasons that wholly escaped yours truly, was doing everything she could to keep the assassin at bay. My mind reeled. You could have knocked me down with a toothpick. I mean to say, Socrates has always been aligned with the sort of thugs who sidle up behind you in back alleys, while Tonto, in my experience, has always fought on the side of truth, justice, and the Detroitian way, her primary focus having been to safeguard Ian from whatever hazards life might fling in his path. Yet here she was, undeniably doing the same job for Evan. Perhaps Tonto had shown up late for work one day and missed the bit where Evan's plans and general black-hat nature had been explained. Or perhaps she saw Socrates taking a run at a chump who identified himself as Ian's son, and was doing her bit to help the family. Who could say? Whatever the cause, the result was that these two perfect specimens carried right on fighting each other as a pack of wild Napoleons charged their way.

I aimed my goggles squarely at Evan. He saw the Napoleons coming, a sight that was apt to grip the senses. They surged forward, not unlike those half-a-league, half-a-league onward chaps you've probably read about, albeit a touch more Hobbesian in their overall approach — Napoleons famously being nasty, brutish, and short.

Zooming in, I could see Evan's eyes gape in horror as the ravening Napoleonic throng poured over the remnants of his forces, drowning them in a tidal wave of pint-sized, cursing loonies. Behind Evan I saw the Regent, who stood there with her eyes closed, holding a brightly shining pyramid thingummy over her head: Norm and Oan crouched behind her, peering out at the field of battle as though they were keeping their eyes peeled for a change in weather that might signal the time for them to be elsewhere.

Not wishing to rest my eyes on Oan for extended periods — she being another of those birds to whom I found myself affianced at one point in my affairs, a long story that needn't detain us — I now aimed my goggles at Ian and Vera. The two were standing on opposite sides of what is known as a "sarcophagus," this being a mechanical tube-shaped thingummy in which ancients are sometimes stored. Vera appeared to be tearing away at this thing's gizzards as Ian did what he did best, viz, not much of anything at all. By the time I'd swivelled my eyes in their direction they were surrounded by at least four dozen Napoleons, all taking protective stances and preparing for a fight.

We Rhinnicks don't sit idly by, gawking through goggles and taking notes while our pals strain against the forces of d. Far from it! We take action. And so it was that, with a spirited cry of "best speed to Vera!" I turned my golf cart in the direction indicated and drove straight for the front, Zeus and William hitching a ride.

We pulled up to the sarcophagus. And you won't believe the sight that met us on our arrival. Or rather you will, I imagine, given my reputation for offering up straight goods and being one of literature's more reliable, fourth-wall-flouting narrators.

What I saw was this: Fenny himself, in person. Vera held him in her left hand, apparently having fished the chap out of the depths of the machine. Vera's right hand seemed to be bleeding, featuring some species of wound or contusion that she displayed to Ian. Ian stared at her, wide-eyed. And rather than saying anything that you might have expected, like, "Oh, look, here comes Rhinnick," or "Egad, we've found the hamster," Ian clutched his brow and uttered something surprising.

It was this:

"Oh my god," he said, reeling. "This is Ragnarök."

Well, I don't know about you, but "Ragnarok" is one of those words that I can't readily spell, it featuring at least one pair of those floating dots you find in unexpected places. Thus it was that, for the time being, I set my pencil crayon aside and handed the reins back to the Author, trusting Him, in all His wisdom, to see this story through to The End.

Chapter 22

"Ragnarök?" said Zeus.

"Zeus!" said Vera.

"Fenny!" said Rhinnick.

"Grrnmph!" said Fenny.

"None of this makes any sense," said Ian, who may have had a point.

The group was gathered around Vera's repurposed sarcophagus and surrounded by Napoleons. Giant balloon animals circled overhead in the purple twilight sky, as roving squads of Napoleons dealt with remnants of Evan's army. Bursts of gunfire echoed in the distance. Scattered acolytes and Evangelists did their best to pick up the chorus of "Get Happy," a sentiment that didn't seem to be catching on.

Ian's gang found themselves mired in the verbal gumbo you get in moments of mass confusion, the sort that features a lot of questions like "what are you doing here?" and "how'd you find us?" and "what's with all the Napoleons?" Question marks outnumbered rival punctuation by seven to one, and it would have taken a PhD in conversational mechanics to match the answers with their questions. It didn't help that Vera's television chose this particular moment to kick in, causing her to field a number of questions from the future. She offered helpful observations like "ignore the part about lobsters" and "you'll like him in Matthew 5." Sorting through the conversational orgy was like scorekeeping for several tennis matchups taking place on the same court without ever knowing whose balls were whose.

One question finally yielded a straight answer. It was "who are you, anyway?" a question Ian had lobbed to the uniformed man at Rhinnick's side. When the response was "William Shakespeare, sir," you could practically see the last few fraying threads of Ian's sanity pack their bags for a quick vacation.

Ian slumped to the ground, leaned back on the sarcophagus, and covered his face with his hands. This seemed to capture everyone's attention, as they tabled whatever else was on the agenda and rallied 'round to Ian's side.

"What's wrong, old chum?" said Rhinnick, crouching beside him.

"It's Fenny!" cried Ian.

"The little chap's just fine!" said Rhinnick, producing Fenny for inspection. "Never better! Why, he's in absolute mid-season form! Just look at his little grin! I don't suppose that I've ever seen him more—"

"But it's Fenny!" Ian cried. "And . . . and Vera's hand! It's Ragnarök!"

People exchanged the sorts of glances you get when someone accuses a hamster of being a harbinger of Swedish Armageddon.

"Everything's backwards!" said Ian, grasping Vera's arm. "You see it, right? It's just — it's Gilgamesh! Enkidu! Three hundred Spartans. And Martin Luther! I mean, I mean, I explained parenthood to Sigmund Freud! Sigmund freaking Freud! Benjamin Franklin discovered electricity. He wrote under the pen name 'Silence Dogood.' And now here's Fenny—"

"What about Fenny?" asked Zeus.

"His full name's *Fenrir*," said Ian. "Rhinnick told me, in the hospice. *Fenrir the coming gloom.* He bit off Vera's hand!"

"He nibbled a finger!" said Vera, showing her lightly punctured pinky. "I think he was just saying hi!"

"That's close enough!" cried Ian.

Vera made the expression you derive by adding pity to confusion and dividing the sum by two.

"Look," she said, pulling away from Ian's grip. "I'm sure this all seems really important to you right now, and I do care, but I have to get back to work. The program's almost ready for Evan."

"What program?" asked Zeus, as Vera scooted around the sarcophagus, muttering something about it being too hard to explain.

"I believe that's meant to be a horse," observed William, pointing out a zeppelin-sized balloon overhead.

Rhinnick crouched at Ian's side and placed a hand on his shoulder. "I think I see what you're driving at, Brown," he said, "but you have to agree it's a bit of a stretch. I mean, I know everything seems a bit 'end-timesy' at the moment, and you've got a chap here called Fenny, and a nip on someone's hand, and—"

"You — you remember the story of Ragnarök?" said Ian.

"I do!" said Rhinnick, beaming. "Abe rebooted the Feynman bean. It's actually quite a gripping tale. It all started out at the Hôtel de la Lune, where I was—"

This might have been a diverting story had Rhinnick been able to finish. He wasn't. He was interrupted by the sounds of several explosions detonating over the ridge, where Socrates was presumably doing his best to deal with Evan.

Rhinnick swallowed heavily and stared in the direction of the explosions. "Right ho, then. Perhaps another time. Suffice it to say that I do remember Ragnarök. Stories about it, anyway. I read about it in books in the beforelife. It features a wolf named Fenrir who helps himself to the hand of Tyr, setting off what you might call the end of the world. Does that about square up with your data?"

"So, it's not just me," said Ian.

"What isn't just you?" said Zeus.

"It's just . . . stories," said Ian. "Stories I knew from the mortal world. Gilgamesh and Enkidu. And the Spartans. Plato's cave. And I mean . . . 'Come on, get happy'? Those are lyrics I know by heart, from the mortal world, but that Vera watched Norm compose, here in Detroit."

"Terribly sorry to barge in," said Rhinnick, brightening, "but you've just touched on something I was hoping to get more information re:, viz, the reason behind the opposing army's insistence on singing show tunes. A peculiar habit, I think you'll agree. I noticed it when I first arrived. I was just cresting the hill on my golf cart, flanked by Zeus and assorted comrades in arms, when—"

"I think Ian's sick," said Zeus, frowning.

"I'm not sick!" said Ian. "It's just these stories!"

"What about them?" asked Vera, glancing over the sarcophagus.

"They're . . . they're happening here!" said Ian. "In Detroit. It's like — like stories from the beforelife are all playing out in Detroit. With some of the same people, I mean. They're here, but it's all different. And happening backwards."

"Perhaps if you slowed down a touch and took the whole thing from the top," said Rhinnick, "we'd do a better job of stringing along and offering aid and comfort. Now then," he added, standing, "try taking a deep breath and clarifying whatever bilge you're spewing."

Lightning flashed across the sky beyond the ridge. Thunder split the air, accompanied by the sort of monstrous howl you'd hear if you'd eavesdropped on a tyrannosaurus rex taking a bite from an especially pointy stegosaurus.

"What in Abe's name was that?" said Zeus, rising.

"See to it, chum," said Rhinnick, slapping Zeus on the back. "Flex those bulging biceps of yours and see if you mightn't do some good!"

Zeus picked up William — quite possibly for later use as a bludgeon — and charged at full speed toward the ridge. Ian didn't appear to notice.

"I was with Socrates," he said. "I mean think about that for a second — *I was with Socrates*! And he was being all weird and . . . I don't know . . . introspective. Having an existential crisis. He fought with Gilgamesh and Enkidu. Gilgamesh and Enkidu, coming together for a fight! You see it, right? It's an ancient myth! But I saw it happening here, three days ago."

"So what's the problem?" said Vera, up to her elbows in the sarcophagus's wires.

"And three hundred soldiers making a stand!" said Ian. "Facing overwhelming odds! It's just like Sparta. Another army comes and helps. And now Fenrir's biting the hand—"

"Finger," said Vera.

"—biting the finger of the guardian of R'lyeh!" said Ian.

"I don't think Tyr was at R'lyeh," said Rhinnick.

"*We're* at R'lyeh!" said Ian.

"What are you getting at?" said Vera.

When Ian answered, he spoke with the carefully measured tones of a man trying his best to avoid another stint in an asylum. "It's old beforelife stories," he said. "They're happening here. They're happening in real life. It's like the beforelife has a bunch of history and mythology based on things that are happening here. But the stories are old, and the events are happening now."

"How in Abe's name can ancient Earth stories all be rooted in current events?" asked Rhinnick.

"That's what I'm asking!" said Ian.

"Maybe it's the other way 'round," said Vera, not bothering to look up from the machine. "Or maybe the ancient myths were written by seers. I mean, I sometimes see into the beforelife, right? Maybe there are seers in the beforelife who had visions of these things happening in Detroit and wrote them down. Or — jeez — maybe it was me!" she said, suddenly locking eyes with Ian. "Just me, in the beforelife, remembering stuff that hadn't happened yet. You know how I get. So maybe I remembered all of this stuff in advance and then spread the word at Delphi—"

"Delphi?" said Ian.

"Abe's drawers! You were the Oracle at Delphi!" cried Rhinnick.

"Oh, right," said Vera. "Long story; I just remembered the other day. Anyway, let's say that 'Ancient Me' in the beforelife had television, like I do now, and I blabbed something about the events that are happening here. They get jotted down and chatted about, distorted, and spread around, becoming myths and history. Who knows?"

"Oh, dash it," said Rhinnick, "it needn't be that complicated at all. It's all just a narrative whatdoyoucallit. One of those things you sometimes get. A coincidence, I mean to say. It's the simplest explanation. Occam's razor and all that. There are only about sixteen different plots in the world, right? Nothing new ever happens. No new stories are ever told. It's all a series of thingummies on repeating themes. I mean, if you squint hard enough and ignore the trivial details, you'll spot the same repeating narrative somethingorothers in every story. Look at your own arc, Brown."

"My own?" asked Ian, absently, as he turned to watch the light show unfolding over the ridge; a show that featured exploding fireballs, strokes of lightning, and plumes of lava that, so far as Ian could tell, had never previously been listed among the points of interest in the tourist's guide to the grounds of City Hall.

"Right ho!" said Rhinnick. "Think back to when you first bobbed out of the Styx and tried to reunite with your wife. Pitting yourself against implacable foes, facing off against ancient Greeks and magical whatnots; it's all ripped right out of *The Odyssey*. Or do I mean *The Iliad*? It could be one, or it could be the other. But I mean, dash it, your better half's name is Penelope, old chum, just like Odysseus's bride. Same story, same name."

Ian stared at Rhinnick with the look of horror and wonder you see on kindergartners' faces when they learn that glue is made from a melted horse. He opened and closed his mouth at least six times. All he managed to say was "Oh. My god."

"And here you are again," said Rhinnick, breezily. "Living another classic story. Coping with an improbable chap who might turn out to be your son."

"He *is* my son!"

"Have it your way, of course," said Rhinnick. "But it's another narrative whatdoyoucallit. One of the oldest hackneyed tropes you'll find in stories swallowed by the masses. A son rebelling against his father. Father and son aligning on opposite sides. You're just rehashing the plot of—"

"*Star Wars!*" gasped Ian, clasping his brow.

"I was going to say *Oedipus Rex*," said Rhinnick. "And it now occurs to me that Vera was in that one!"

"Can we just drop this for now?" said Vera. "I mean, there are dozens of explanations. We're just making them up. Maybe time works weird when you cross between dimensions and what happens here now ends up in the past of the mortal world. Who really cares? All that matters right now is stopping Evan. We can figure out this story-stuff later. For now, I'll just add them to into the mix."

"Add what to the wherenow?" asked Rhinnick.

"These stories," said Vera. "Everything that's happening now. I'm adding it all into the memory systems of the sarcophagus, letting it flow through the expectation manager. We need to make Evan's artificial environment as rich as possible; lay down templates, stories, and characters to make the world seem real."

Rhinnick blinked at Vera with the look of someone who'd missed the first twenty chapters.

"Try to keep up," said Vera, fishing out a bundle of wires. "Socrates is trying to wipe Evan. When he does, we're going to stick Evan in here. We'll wire him into an artificial world that'll keep his mind occupied; it'll keep him from waking up and making a mess of things out here. I'm programming that world."

"Abe's drawers, now you're the Author!" cried Rhinnick.

"Excuse me?"

"You're the Author! Of Evan's world. He'll wake up in a world designed by you—"

"*Compiled* by me," said Vera. "I'm just borrowing stuff that's already happened. Historical files from the university. The database from City Hall. Whatever records I can download from the synths. Some of Socrates' perceptual records from his intracranial implants. Even the stuff that's happening now — these synths have a cloud gestalt that I've patched into the expectation manager and—"

"All of these stories are being dumped into Evan's world?" said Ian, finally struggling to his feet. "And what? He'll wake up there and just . . . *live* through them?"

"He won't wake up at all," said Vera. "He'll just think he's waking up. In a world he wants. One where he's sort of . . . I don't know . . . sort of an overseer who can do whatever he likes. He'll think that he's in charge, like he expects. That's why I think it's going to work. He won't reject a world that he wants. He'll stay trapped as long as we like."

"That's genius!" said Rhinnick, who always liked to give credit where it was due.

"And all these stories," said Ian, placing both hands on the sarcophagus, "some version of them plays out for Evan's benefit, right? Like, say, some version of the three hundred Spartans. Something loosely based on Plato's cave. A bit about Gilgamesh and Enkidu. Maybe a story or two about Sigmund Freud, or *The Odyssey*, or Socrates and the Oracle at Delphi."

"Sure," said Vera. "They'll all be part of his world. Some might crop up as fiction, some might appear as fact. He'll see versions of all these stories while his subjects live their lives. He can intervene if he likes. Change the stories however he wants. The system can adapt and rewrite the narrative to deal with Evan's neural input. But none of it's going to be real."

"Do the people inside there know that?" said Ian, blanching.

"What?" said Vera.

"The people in Evan's world. Do they know it's a simulation?"

"They're just data," said Vera, cocking her head, "just digitized information—"

"You once told me that real people are data too," said Rhinnick. "That time we mooted the ins and outs of teleportation. It all seemed unlikely to me."

Here Rhinnick stopped speaking, not so much because he'd finished what he'd been saying, but because he says so much in any given slice of time that the chances of him being interrupted by a headline-grabbing event are greater than average. In this instance, the event was Evan's arrival.

It made a crater.

Evan dropped out of the sky in precisely the same way that freight trains shouldn't. He'd enlarged himself again, drawing on some mysterious source of power and using it to add more Evan. He still looked like the adult version of himself — red-haired, eye-catchingly handsome, yet impossible to describe in any detail — but now with a height suggestive of beanstalks and shepherds wielding slings.

Evan landed superhero-style about twenty yards downwind of Ian. He stood up, smoke streaming from his shoulders, and stomped toward his dad.

He seemed to be miffed.

"Evan?" said Ian, stepping backward.

"Good lord!" said Rhinnick.

"Get out of my way, Dad," said Evan, clenching his jaw. "I'm going to tap the ancients sleeping in R'lyeh. Don't try to stop me. Everything's going to be okay."

* * *

Picture a desolate, cratered moonscape, more forsaken than the parkade of a suburban big box store at three a.m.; bleaker than a loveless marriage, more wretchedly gloomy than decaffeinated coffee. A post-apocalyptic prairie of soot and ash; the sort of austere, dismal scene that would force a landscape artist to take several trips to the store in search of extra bottles of Dark Grey Number Twelve. This was the scene atop the ridge where Evan had stood alongside Oan, Norm, and the Regent; the ridge where Socrates had arrived to contend with Evan. The ridge where Tonto had objected to Socrates' plan.

Tonto had made her objection known by keeping Socrates from Evan. Try as he might, the assassin couldn't manage to get past her. He'd come close. He'd fired several Stygian rounds in Evan's direction. One had even parted his hair. But Tonto had always managed to deflect the bullet just enough to make it miss, or to throw off the assassin's aim with a well-chucked rock or a timely roundhouse kick to some uncomfortable part of the Socratic anatomy. Socrates gave as good as he got in the exchange. It had been one of the few matchups in history where words like "exciting," "terrifying," "gripping," and "sensational" would have been perfectly paired with the word "stalemate."

The Regent had been another of Socrates' problems. She channelled power through her little pyramidical totem, raining the plagues of Egypt on the assassin. And then there were the Napoleons — dozens of the ravening little weirdos cresting the ridge and fighting anything that moved.

And now every one of them — every Napoleon, every supremely gifted assassin or protector, every one of the acolytes and Evangelists who had stayed up on the ridge, even the Regent, Norm, and Oan — every one of them was still there. Still present on the plateau. Still straining every nerve to make a move to support their cause.

You wouldn't know it to look at them, though. In fact, you couldn't see them at all.

The primary difficulty they faced was that they were all encased in amber and covered in ash. This was a major inconvenience apt to ruin anyone's day, and the final gift that Evan had bestowed on everyone present when he'd had his fill of being pestered by a gadfly-ish assassin and, to use Evan's schoolyard language, "being protected by a girl."

The power he'd drawn from his supporters had run out, so Evan had tapped into the Regent, using every last ounce of her supernatural essence for a few final explosions preparatory to encasing everyone in amber cocoons and tons of ash. Then he'd empowered himself, growing stronger, getting ready to enter City Hall.

He leapt to the skies, toward his father, leaving all distractions behind. Nothing would stop him from taking R'lyeh. None of these gnats would get in the way.

At least, that was the plan. Someone else had other ideas. You wouldn't have known this if you weren't reading a book that featured reasonably reliable, omniscient narration. Not unless you'd dug around in the ash and searched for a good long while. If you did that, and if you were lucky, you might have found one large cocoon encasing two entangled beings. Even then, you'd need a scanning electron microscope to see what they'd set in motion.

The entangled beings, trapped in a single amber cocoon, were straining to touch each other's hand. They'd been avoiding that, so far. But now it seemed they had no choice. They were so close to each other that the quarks, bosons, and gluons in the atoms of their fingertips trespassed in each other's orbits.

The paired combatants strained some more.

And then, beyond the boundaries of perception, the cocoon started to crack.

Chapter 23

People lie to themselves a lot. That's every bit as true in Detroit as it is in the mortal world. Sometimes it helps. Take the Big Lie told by Abe. It kept the world from splitting apart, spinning off its axis, turning into cottage cheese, or descending into an all-out war between sentient minuets and feral shades of the colour blue. Just tell people that their lives are confined by rules and limitations, convince them that they don't have the power to change the world however they like, and hey presto, chaos subsides, and people get on with their safe, predictable lives. You get a sensible world where Tuesday follows Monday, where gravity keeps you stuck to the ground instead of shooting off into orbit. A world where plants make breathable air, where water is wet, and where the skies don't suddenly fill with purple dragons or giant clowns or living rain that mates with your shoes. Without that lie — the lie that your wildest dreams are safely out of reach — all hell breaks loose. It's a helpful lie, and one the people of Detroit, whether they knew about it or not, told themselves and each other all the time.

There are loads of comforting lies in the beforelife too. We're not talking about the ones that are easy to spot — say, lies about election fraud, homeopathy, and bearded trespassers who smuggle presents into your home on Christmas Eve. We're talking about the subtle lies we don't like to discuss. Take the one about parents recognizing their kids. That's a good one. It's nice to think that any set of parents walking into a room of newborns can tell which of the squirming cherubs is their own. As it turns out, they can't. The likelihood of the happy couple zeroing in on their own little bundle of joy is no better than random chance. Highly competent science nerds have done hilarious studies. All things considered, this shouldn't come as a surprise. We've all watched viral clips of tigers raising puppies, maternal dogs suckling tiny pigs, or family-minded chimpanzees stepping in to raise a panda. Shuffle a few of their genes around and you're dealing with humans. Our imagined power to recognize our young is a comforting lie.

All of which is to say that, when Ian looked at Evan — when his eyes filled with the image of a twelve-foot-tall, ginger-haired behemoth stomping angrily toward him — it took him a while to swallow the fact that this really was his son.

"Is — is that really you?" said Ian.

"Not precisely a chip off the old block, is he?" said Rhinnick.

"Shush!" said Vera, now sporting a pair of forehead-mounted electrodes wired directly to the expectation manager.

"It's me, Dad," said Evan. "The real me." He took a giant-sized step forward, a step that pulverized pavement, shook the ground, and caught the attention of several dozen nearby Napoleons — ones who'd been lucky enough to rush toward the courtyard instead of charging the ridge. They scrambled forward and formed a large, jabbering circle around the scene.

"The *real you* is a little boy!" cried Ian. "My little boy. In the Patch. With me and your mom. We can go back to that, Evan. Just let your mother out of the Patch and she'll—"

"This *is* the real me!" boomed Evan. "Who I'm meant to be. Not reined in by your stupid rules. Not trapped by Abe's lies, or by the idea that I can't have whatever I want."

"But you can't just—"

"I can, Dad. Just watch me. I'm going to take control of R'lyeh, and then take control of the world."

The Napoleonic circle closed in a couple of steps, and probably would have rattled sabres if they'd had them. Rhinnick scooted around to Vera's side of the sarcophagus. Vera carried on fiddling with the sarcophagus's display — a display that now included the message *Working: Final Upload in Progress*.

At the centre of the action, Ian carried on with one of history's less conventional father-and-son chats.

"But why?" he asked. "Why take over Detroit? That's what I don't understand. You had a nice life with me and your mom. We were happy. We—"

"I didn't have a nice life, Dad!" Evan bellowed with a voice that shook the sarcophagus and made Napoleons cringe. "Everything I had was a lie. A total lie! I had a life where you and Mom told me what I couldn't do. You both knew I could have whatever I wanted! You both know how Detroit works. You kept that from me! You kept the truth to yourselves!"

"We had to, Evan—"

"And you've kept it from everyone else! This is supposed to be paradise, Dad. A world without limitations. No boundaries! I could have whatever I want. And you've ruined it all with lies. You and all the other immigrants, people who have no business being in charge."

"Please try to calm down, Evan, it'll be—"

"Don't tell me to calm down!" Evan boomed. "Look what you've done! You and Abe and everyone else. Especially Mom! You've ruined Detroit. It's supposed to be a Utopia. Everyone's meant to be free — free to have whatever they like! But you . . . you people, with all your selfishness and neediness and stupidity, all polluted by the beforelife . . . you take the greatest resource we have, the power that fuels our dreams and lets us have whatever we want, and you hide it from everyone else! You cover it up, just to keep yourselves in power — to keep true power in the hands of a few elites, like Abe and Mom, who think they get to decide what's best."

"It isn't like that, son—"

"Stop lying!" Evan screamed, punctuated by peals of thunder.

"I can *see* the truth, Dad!" Evan shouted. "It's plain as day. I can see the lines of power connecting everyone to Detroit. I can see the primordial dark — the stuff that everything else is made of. And I can see the pollution that you and your kind have brought from the mortal world. It's messing everything up. And I can't let that go on. I'm taking over."

"You can't do that, son!"

"I can! And it'll be good for you, Dad. Good for everyone! What have you got to lose?"

Ian tilted his head like a sheep confronted with actuarial tables. "What have I got to lose?" he said.

"Just think about it!" said Evan. "You could be richer! You could be happier. You could be powerful. If you didn't buy into the lie that Abe and Mom force on everyone else you'd be able to do—"

"You don't understand, Evan. You're just a kid. We could have explained things—"

"I'm not just a kid!" bellowed Evan.

"On the outside," said Ian. "Inside you're only five."

"You're wrong! I'm as smart as any grown-up. I didn't just make myself look older. I really made myself older. Like, a genuine adult. I know things! I made sure that I had all the knowledge I'd need to—"

"You didn't earn it, son."

"What in the name of the all-encompassing Dark do you mean by that?" boomed Evan.

"You haven't earned who you are, Evan. You don't have experience. I don't know how to explain it but . . . I mean . . .

you've never had to hide the truth for the sake of somebody else. You've never had to lie to give someone hope, or to keep from hurting their feelings. You've never had your heart broken. Never suffered a loss and recovered. You can't just *know* those things. You can't just . . . I don't know . . . *choose* the kind of grown-up you want to be. You have to grow into who you are, live with that identity, really wear it. Carry all the baggage that comes with it. It's like your mom and me — she couldn't just wave a hand and turn us into good parents. We just had to try our best, gain experience, learn what worked and what didn't. We would have explained all this to you in time, son, but parents can't tell kids things that they aren't ready to know. Abe and your mom are doing the same thing for everyone else. I'm sorry, Evan, but you can't just—"

"STOP TELLING ME WHAT I CAN'T DO!" Evan bellowed in all caps. And it was a good thing he did — otherwise you couldn't have heard it over the Class-Twelve explosion on the ridge.

It made a mushroom cloud and a flash so bright that it would have seared images into any retinas unlucky enough to be aimed in that direction. Happily, none were, all attention being earmarked for the angry ginger behemoth shouting at the top of his lungs.

A shock wave rumbled across the courtyard, jostling android bodies and inspiring new Napoleonic curses. Ian, Rhinnick, and Vera braced themselves against the sarcophagus. Evan barely budged, but he did look over his shoulder to see what all the "boom" was about.

He probably shouldn't have done that. To be fair, he couldn't have known that a Class-Twelve explosion is what you get whenever Socrates and Tonto touch each other's exposed skin. Nor could he know that this explosion would be powerful enough to shatter their cocoon. He certainly couldn't be blamed for not realizing that Socrates' intracranial systems had a built-in IPT, one that could automatically teleport Socrates to safety — say, out of the blast zone of any Class-Twelve explosions that the assassin might encounter. But whether or not you blame Evan for failing to plan for any contingencies like these, it remains true that he probably shouldn't have turned his head.

The question of whether or not you should beware of Greeks bearing gifts, including gifts of Stygian toxin, is a matter of fierce historical debate. But almost everyone agrees that you should never turn your back on an assassin.

Socrates rematerialized at ground zero, right between Evan and Ian — right at the spot where Evan really should have been looking. It's quite possible that the assassin took a moment or two to get his bearings, but "a moment or two" for Socrates was too little time for anyone else to notice. In less than half a blink of an eye, he aimed and fired.

He fired straight up into the sky. This was largely because of the impossibly strong, perfect being who'd wrenched his arm in that direction.

Tonto came out of nowhere. Many scientists and philosophers hold that this is true of all of us. But in the present case, the phrase "Tonto came out of nowhere" was meant to convey that, at the moment of going to press, she'd leapt into the fray at a speed beyond human perception. She was just there, right when she needed to be, grappling with the assassin.

The bullet sped skyward and penetrated a giant balloon. One that was shaped like a hippopotamus. And in a metaphorical way, the hovering hippo went through something that was a good deal like the process that takes place in organic beings who've been shot with Stygian rounds. It lost its essence: the intangible, invisible, and hard-to-pin-down substance that made the hippo what it was; the material that gave the balloon its own unique identity and meaning.

It came out with a long, protracted squeak that called to mind the ghost of a bean burrito, but otherwise the simile stands.

Socrates spun away from Tonto's grip and fired again, this time firing at the sarcophagus with the unsportsmanlike intention of letting the bullet ricochet and connect with Evan. Tonto kicked a scrap of Ianian-torso into the line of fire.

Whether it was Socrates' arrival, Tonto's intervention, or the explosion on the ridge, no one could say, but *something* in that moment spurred the Napoleons to action. They charged on Evan's position, screaming Napoleonic curses as they did.

The effect of this platoon of charging Napoleons was profound and, as you'd guess, reactions varied. Ian, for example, ducked and covered, shouting something that was lost in all the commotion. Rhinnick gesticulated wildly, presumably with a view to encouraging Vera, who shouted the rather cryptic words "The world is ready!" loud enough for all to hear.

Evan, for his part, reacted in a way that indicated he'd had enough. Having used up most of the power he'd drawn from acolytes and Evangelists, having unleashed all of the power he'd drawn from the Regent, he bent his will toward another, plentiful, handy source of eldritch power, a source that pulsed with untapped energy of a colour, shape, and intensity that Evan had never seen.

He reached out for the Napoleons. The frenzied, jabbering, battle-crazed Napoleons; a group so strangely wired that even Detroit kept spitting them out, sending them back to the beforelife, and recycling many of them through repeating rounds of reincarnation. Evan reached for the threads that flowed around them, the crazily pulsing threads of energy that connected them to Detroit. He seized those threads, and pulled.

Evan wasn't prepared for the effect.

The first time that Evan had tapped into his horde of N-cell bros he'd briefly been reshaped by their essence; their twisted, petty, grievance-laden, misanthropic hate. He'd accidentally turned himself into a tentacled, thrashing beast. Something similar happened now. This time, though, he was tapping into Napoleons, explosive little balls of *je ne sais quoi* who'd been ginned up for a fight.

Evan was overwhelmed with power; power that carried and reflected the basic nature of its source. Power that suddenly transformed him into . . . into—

There isn't a pleasant way to put this. The best one can manage is to include a warning that the following scene might be off-putting for squeamish or sensible readers.

Overwhelmed by the sheer, collective goofiness of a ravening horde of Napoleons, Evan couldn't help but transform into a Napoleon himself. A giant-sized, red-haired, cursing Napoleon who was somehow fully bedecked in Napoleonic garb, right down to the tight white pants and the little imperial crown. He swayed where he stood, apparently stunned.

He slipped a hand in his giant-sized tunic and started to scratch.

"Egad," said Rhinnick.

"Holy shit," said Vera.

"Evan?" said Ian.

Evan threw back his head and howled into the skies. The fact that the howl sounded a good deal like *"Je suis l'empereur!"* seemed to catch everyone by surprise, including Evan. You could tell by the way his eyes suddenly widened to hubcap size.

He howled again. This one was an ear-shattering *"QU'EST-CE QUI SE PASSE?!"*

To say that "the Napoleons took it big" would be like saying that the *Titanic* had suffered a mild buoyancy deficit. The Napoleons had been hoping for a good old-fashioned fight, the sort where they might stab, trample, or bludgeon their way to a bit of Napoleonic glory, the sort of nose-bloodying dust-up you can really sink your teeth into in a world where all the combatants are immortal. It hadn't worked out the way they'd planned. For one thing, their opponents were using magic, something barely mentioned in the Marquess of Queensbury's rules. And then they'd suddenly felt themselves weaken; atrophying on the spot as Evan drew upon their essence and empowered his attacks.

The thing that really stuck in their collective craw, though, was the fact that Evan had turned into a giant Napoleon, something that the true, native-born Napoleons took as a carefully calculated insult to their *amour propre*, not to mention the afterlife's first ever example of cultural appropriation. No Napoleon of spirit could let something like that pass without *revanche*.

There was a sudden, perfectly unified cry of "*ATTAQUEZ CETTE TÊTE DU MERDE!*" as the Napoleons surged forward, pelting Evan with rocks, boots, and leftover pieces of android as they ran.

Evan staggered backward again, this time shielding his face with huge Napoleonic hands.

Even in the cacophony of Napoleonic battle, some sounds are so distinctive that they really can't be missed, quite possibly because some deep part of the ancestral human brain recognizes them as a threat. High on the list of these sounds is the unmistakable click and hum you get when a boson whip is deployed.

It wasn't hard to guess the source.

Socrates flicked his boson whip in Evan's direction, the impossibly hot thread of searing light arcing straight toward Evan's neck.

You can't go about the place decapitating people's sons without budgeting for a handful of objections. Ian voiced his own by shouting "NO!" at the top of his lungs. Like a lot of things Ian did, this shout was almost exactly as useful and worthwhile as baseball statistics about left-handed hitters facing pitchers named Phil when the moon is waxing gibbous and the relative humidity is lower than 6 per cent.

Tonto's objection was more effective. She leapt between Evan and the whip-wielding assassin, gamely risking the inconvenience and discomfort of bisection.

What happened next really ought to have been impossible. As the boson whip arced its way toward Evan's neck, Tonto caught the whip in her hand — a whip that ought to have cut clean through her. The whip sizzled and sparked in protest, searing its way through a callus or two, but Tonto's hand remained resolutely and impossibly intact.

Tonto grimaced with the effort of breaking numerous physical laws. Socrates grimaced too — in his case, with the effort of yanking the whip and throwing Tonto off balance.

One of the nicer things about Tonto's intervention, depending on your perspective, was that it had stopped the boson whip from severing Evan's head. The bad thing was that it had kept Tonto busy at the business end of the whip, struggling with the assassin, leaving little scope for her to do anything about the weapon found in Socrates' other hand.

It was his gun. The one that was loaded with Stygian rounds. Socrates fired at Evan's knee.

The shot rang out. The world slowed down. If you'd been present, you would have heard your own heart pulsing in your ears as the bullet streaked its way through the air. If you're the philosophical sort, you might have paused briefly to wonder if Stygian toxin worked on the ambient air itself, parting molecules and making unlucky electrons forget their orbits.

The bullet streaked toward Evan.

Ian shouted the word "No!" in the extended, slowed-down, comi-tragic voice you get by playing your classic vinyl 45s at 33 RPMs. He leapt straight into the line of fire.

Or rather, he tried to. Ian was, you'll have to remember, nothing more than an average man. He wasn't as fast as a speeding bullet. He was exactly as fast as a slightly out-of-shape suburban male. All he managed to do was get about three feet closer to his son, putting himself in a position to get an unobstructed view of something that no father should see.

The bullet struck Evan's knee. Of course it did — that's where Socrates was aiming.

Evan gasped like a gaffed salmon, clasping his leg and mouthing the word "Dad" as he collapsed.

His eyes watered. He strained to speak.

He started to shrink.

In less than a heartbeat, Evan returned to factory specs. Where there had been a mountain of angry Napoleon there was now a shivering, weeping, wounded, five-year-old boy.

Ian rushed to Evan's side in time to see his son mouth the word "Mom" and then drift off, succumbing to the Socratic Method.

We're going to pass lightly over the next several minutes; over the parts where Ian weeps over his freshly mindwiped son, where Socrates and Tonto puzzle over the fact that Tonto couldn't stop the Stygian round, and where Socrates questions whether, on some level, Penelope still had a hand or two on the cosmic tiller. She'd made Tonto, after all. She'd called Tonto into being, she'd imbued her with the power to be the world's greatest protector and charged her with the task of protecting Ian. Wasn't it possible that, in her final moments before Evan sealed her in the Patch, Penelope's thoughts had turned to protecting Evan? And wasn't it possible that, in the end, when Evan stood on the steps of R'lyeh with no hope of being contained, that some teeny-tiny bit of Penelope's psyche, that part of her that may have been able to peer beyond the Patch and see what it was her son was doing, some corner of her mind that no mother would ever acknowledge, Penelope had, at least a little, wanted her son to be laid to rest?

Perhaps it's best that we skip that part altogether.

* * *

"In his house at R'lyeh, the first one, dreaming, lies," said Vera, as she, Rhinnick, and Ian slid Evan's sarcophagus into a nook in the bowels of City Hall. "Surrounded by all and none; both real and not; removed from those who traverse the river. Charon's obol," she added, pressing the end of the expectation manager, "has been paid."

"We could have saved a good deal of trouble and expense if you'd explained what all of that meant right from the start," said Rhinnick. "I mean to say, the wear and tear on Napoleons, the cost in acolytes and Evangelists, not to mention the toll that all of this rushing hither and thither has on one's trousers."

"What's Evan seeing now?" said Ian, wiping condensation from the sarcophagus's window and staring in at his sleeping son.

"Not much at all, really," said Vera. "I mean, in the beginning, it'll just be Evan and the Earth. But the Earth will be without form, and void, and—"

"And darkness will spread across the face of the deep!" said Rhinnick, his eyes widening.

"That's one way to put it," said Vera, entering codes into a panel on the wall. "I mean, it's a weird way to put it, but it works. Anyway, as the system adjusts to Evan's presence it'll adapt to provide him with sensory experiences. It'll start with a little light—"

"And he saw that it was good," said Rhinnick, eyes widening even more.

"And then it'll generate a landscape," said Vera. "Divide the land and water, start populating both with flora and fauna. It'll be quite the show. I almost wish I was in there with him. At first

397

Evan will experience himself as being separate from the world he perceives — sort of like an outside observer. But then he'll start to interact. He can be as passive or interventionist as he likes — the system can make adjustments over time."

"But what'll his life be like?" said Ian.

"It's hard to say," said Vera, who turned and stared off into the middle distance. "I'm trying my best to see his future. It's not really something I can control. But I do see something . . . just a sec . . . I'm getting something new . . . I see . . . I can see that Penelope and Abe are both going to be okay!"

"Of course they are," said Ian.

"I mean, you're going to see them soon," said Vera. "The walls around the Patch are starting to crumble."

"Thank heaven," said Ian, briefly forgetting where he was. "But what about Evan?"

"It's all a bit cloudy," said Vera. "I mean . . . I know that his world will start to populate with people. People based on all the records that I uploaded. He'll interact with versions of them over time. Some of those interactions will be based on historical episodes that we've entered into the system. Evan will start out by experiencing all that stuff from a sort of third-person perspective — like watching over an ant farm. And then he'll start to be more involved. I think I can see him," she continued, once again staring off into the future. "I can see . . . I can see him looking over the people, extending his influence, getting more directly involved, looking down from . . . whoa!" she said, breaking off.

"Whoa what?" said Ian.

"He's . . . well, let's just say he's going to have some growing pains," said Vera, shaking her head to clear the static. "He's still got his original wiring, right? I mean, he's lost his memories, but he's still fundamentally the same kid. He's going to need to grow up; to learn from his interactions with other people. Get more . . . say . . . *socially adjusted* over time. For now he's just a five-year-old with something close to absolute dominion over the world that he perceives. There were bound to be some . . . incidents . . ."

"What kind of incidents?" said Ian, urgently.

"Don't worry about it," said Vera, "I mean, he's going to be okay. It's just a simulation designed to keep his mind busy."

"But it'll all seem real to Evan!" said Ian.

"Well, yeah, that's the whole point."

"And it'll seem real to the people with him!" Ian added.

"They're not really people," said Vera.

"But do they know that?" asked Rhinnick.

"Look," said Vera, "it's not as though we can take my visions as gospel, right? And I mean, even if he does wipe everybody out in a flood, it's no reason to —"

"He wipes them out in a flood?!" said Ian.

"It's no big deal!" said Vera. "They can't really die! People aren't mortal."

"You just said they weren't really people!" said Ian.

"They're modelled on people!" said Vera. "And the system can generate more."

"But he's terrorizing them!" said Ian.

"They're going to think of Him as their Author!" said Rhinnick, agog. "And perhaps they'll think of *our world* as fiction!"

"They can't see us!" said Vera.

"You can see them!" said Ian. "You can see into the before-life too! Who's to say that Evan's people can't see us?"

"You know what 'simulation' means, right?" said Vera.

"I'm not sure anymore!" said Ian. "But Evan's going to think these people are real, and he's being horrible to them. He's going to have to live with that! Live with the memory of terrorizing all those people! He can't just —"

"Look, he's still evolving," said Vera. "He'll settle into things over time. He'll learn all the usual lessons people learn about getting along. It might take centuries, but in the meantime he'll be safe."

"He's dreaming a life where he's a super-powered bully!" said Ian.

"The people he's bullying aren't real!"

"But Evan doesn't know that! Neither do they!"

"They don't know anything," said Vera. "They're just packets of information."

"That's true of all of us!" said Rhinnick.

Vera suddenly clasped her forehead with one hand and steadied herself against the sarcophagus with the other. Rhinnick and Ian rushed to her side.

"It's all right," she said, at length. "It's going to be fine. I've just . . . I've just seen the ending," she added, swallowing hard. "Evan's going to be all right."

"What did you see?" asked Ian.

"He's going to be fine. I've seen it, Ian. He'll get nicer over time. You're going to like how he turns out."

"But are you sure?" said Ian.

"Trust me. Evan's going to be okay. I've seen it all, now. He starts getting friendlier right around the time that he gets to something called the New Testament."

Ian blinked at Vera. Rhinnick blinked at Ian. Ian and Rhinnick turned their heads and blinked at each other. Vera made the puzzled face of a person who wasn't entirely sure what all this blinking was about.

It was Ian who finally broke the awkward silence.

"Oh, God," he said, cottoning on.

* * *